KING OF THIEVES

DEMONS OF ELYSIUM

JANE KINDRED

RIPTIDE PUBLISHING

Riptide Publishing
PO Box 1537
Burnsville, NC 28714
www.riptidepublishing.com

King of Thieves
Copyright © 2014, 2022 by Jane Kindred

Cover art: L.C. Chase, lcchase.com
Editor: Grace Stack
Layout: L.C. Chase, lcchase.com

ISBN: 978-1-62649-960-7

Second edition
April, 2022

Also available in ebook:
ISBN: 978-1-62649-959-1

KING OF THIEVES

DEMONS OF ELYSIUM

JANE KINDRED

RIPTIDE PUBLISHING

For my faithful readers, without whom the copulating demons in my head would be far more worrisome.

TABLE OF CONTENTS

CHAPTER ONE

To call Vasily a submissive would be an abuse of the term. Belphagor's "boy" was about as submissive as a cat in a bathtub. You could hold him down long enough to accomplish the needful, but you'd damned near scald yourself when the contained outrage burst without warning from every limb, and you could count yourself lucky if all he did was draw blood. And yet Vasily insisted this relationship was what he wanted, to belong so thoroughly to Belphagor that his will was no longer his own.

Belphagor sucked on the end of his burnt thumb, shaking his head at the demon glaring fire at him from where he knelt on the floor of their rented room. Their quarters in the back of The Brimstone—the den of iniquity where Belphagor had earned his reputation as the Prince of Tricks—were beginning to feel like the flames of Hell with the furious heat the firespirit was giving off.

In a nod to his element, Vasily had recently had his matted red hair magically enhanced to a molten-lava shade. It gave his locks the appearance of being an extension of his radiance—if demonic radiance were visible in Heaven. Something about the aetheric content of the air here dampened it, at least for the lesser orders of angels and their mixed-blood Fallen cousins. It wasn't until one fell to the world of Man that the elemental radiance of the lesser Host could be seen, most notably in the pair of wings composed of one's dominant element.

The memory of Vasily stretching his magnificent wings of fire for the first time, bathed in ruby light and soaring ecstatically against the northern Russian sunrise, was enough to send Belphagor's airspirit blood rushing to his cock with urgent need. Not that it wasn't already.

Vasily's defiance this morning had him so riled he could barely see straight. And Vasily knew it. It was a matter of perspective who was dominating whom.

All he'd asked Vasily to do was drop to his knees and service him, something Vasily normally seemed quite happy to do—sometimes more often than Belphagor could accommodate. But the boy had some kind of bug up his ass and had taken the request poorly.

A chuckle rose in Belphagor's throat at the phrase he'd conjured. He had better uses for Vasily's ass than inserting bugs into it. At the little sound of mirth, Vasily's skin flushed red with fury. The smallest offense had seemed to spark it this morning.

He'd knelt at Belphagor's command but refused to open his mouth, and when Belphagor had tried to open it for him, he'd gotten burned by unrestrained firespirit spittle for his efforts. He didn't relish the idea of subjecting the sensitive skin of his cock to that. Vasily had excellent control of the level of heat he produced in his bodily fluids, and for the most part, he kept them at a tolerable level.

"Would you like to tell me what your problem is this morning, *mal'chik*?" The endearment, Russian for *boy* usually softened Vasily's demeanor. Today, it seemed to do the opposite. He let fly a string of obscenities in the language of Men so colorful that even Belphagor had seldom uttered them.

Where in Heaven did he learn these things? There seemed to be no coherent message to the barrage of profanity other than a general recommendation that Belphagor perform any number of violent acts upon himself, followed by heartily consuming his own waste. At least it was in Russian. That one tenet of Belphagor's rules Vasily had chosen to obey.

Belphagor waited for a lull in the verbal onslaught, noting with a rush of satisfaction that Vasily's cock was almost bursting from his pants. "Are you quite through?"

"*Poshël na khui!*"

Lovely and erect as Vasily's *khui* was, Belphagor was tempted, but Heaven knew what temperature *that* would be right now. Instead, he picked up a large thornfruit from the breakfast tray and shoved it into Vasily's mouth when it opened on another imprecation. Wine-red juice burst from the ends and dribbled from the corners of his mouth into his long muttonchops.

"I'm going to eat this breakfast now." Belphagor sat at the vanity. "Which I purchased this morning in the market for you while you were snoring away in *my* bed. When you've finished having your tantrum and are prepared to do as I've bidden you—without damaging me— you may take that out of your mouth and beseech me to let you. And then we'll see about your punishment."

He ate the curls of bacon as he spoke, pretending not to look at Vasily, though he watched him out of the corner of his eye. There was no sign of capitulation, but Vasily was clearly uncomfortable, shifting position with one hand at his crotch to try to relieve the pressure of his jeans.

"Go ahead and unbutton." Belphagor licked his fingers. "Give it some air."

Vasily's head shot up, his cheeks now pink. As if anyone could have failed to notice *that*. Belphagor chuckled to himself, starting on the buttered porridge, and was rewarded with a strangled sound behind the thornfruit that was no doubt a curse trapped on Vasily's tongue. But despite his state—or perhaps to spite Belphagor—Vasily moved his hand aside and stared straight ahead.

Belphagor finished the entire tray of food—well more than he'd have preferred, particularly with an untended hard-on, and still Vasily hadn't given in. He had to resist the urge to relent and take the fruit from his boy's mouth. Vasily knew it was within his power to end his suffering, and sucking cock wasn't exactly something he hated. Whatever his problem was, Belphagor was sure it had nothing to do with the actual request and everything to do with the delicate firespirit feelings he was forever wounding without meaning to.

But Vasily would have to tell Belphagor what he'd done if he expected to get an apology. And in the meantime, the hard, bare chest heaving with anger, the orange glow of fire in Vasily's hazel eyes, and the furious hard-on Vasily was now refusing to acknowledge were driving Belphagor delightfully mad. He could wait all day if he had to. And it seemed he would.

With a long sigh of disappointment, Belphagor got to his feet. "I have better things to do than wait for you to behave civilly."

He drew aside the curtain in front of the makeshift wardrobe, took Vasily's prized velvet frock coat from its hanger, and put it on, knowing it would infuriate him. It hung ridiculously long on Belphagor, and the shoulders were far too wide, but fashion wasn't the point.

"Stand up." He delivered the abrupt command in the hard tone that always prompted instant obedience.

Vasily rose, glaring a good approximation of actual hatred down at Belphagor from his superior height. Though it might have been more impressive without his gob stuffed with thornfruit.

Belphagor busied himself with yanking Vasily's belt from its buckle and zipping it out of the loops, pleased with the deep intake of breath this inspired.

"Hands."

There was a slight hesitation before Vasily extended both fists, held together at the wrists to make Belphagor's job easier. So obeying Belphagor wasn't the problem. He'd knelt, he'd risen, and he'd given his hands to be trussed without resistance. It was only sucking cock he was taking issue with.

Belphagor bound Vasily's wrists and tied a knot in the leather, yanking it tight and spinning Vasily about to face the wall, where he hung the buckle on a hook above Vasily's head. Having to climb onto the chair to accomplish it took some of the edge off the action, but he was gratified by a little tremor shunting along Vasily's spine. He kissed the center of Vasily's back, causing him to jump and then shiver as Belphagor's lips lingered there. It was good to keep the boy on his toes.

"I'm not going to punish you yet." He kept his lips against the warm skin. "You'll get that when you've decided to behave." Belphagor placed another kiss below the first as he reached around Vasily's waist and began to unbutton his pants. With another kiss to the small of Vasily's back, he tugged on the jeans so the top of Vasily's ass was exposed and his cock was free. A groan escaped Vasily as Belphagor closed his hand around the inflamed erection. He placed one last kiss just above the cleft of the firm ass.

"I could make you come." His lips brushed lightly against Vasily's skin. "And leave you here, spent and angry, to think about whether you want to do as I say." He gave Vasily's cock a firm stroke. Hot blood throbbed in the flesh against his palm. Vasily's stance widened, as if to brace himself to be tossed off.

Belphagor dropped his hand and straightened, adjusting the collar of the frock coat. "But I think I prefer to imagine you squirming against the wall trying to relieve the tension yourself while I'm out. If I'm to have no relief, neither will you."

Vasily moaned, trying to speak behind his gag.

"Too late for appeals, *mal'chik*. I expect I'll be gone awhile." Belphagor kicked the chamber pot between Vasily's legs. "I imagine this will come in handy at some point today. I don't need you pissing on my floor."

Vasily made a strangled roar and banged his head against the wall. He was in a serious state. But it would hardly take any effort on his part to pull the peg out of the wall and work his hands out of the belt, and he'd made no attempt so far. As enraged as he was about whatever Belphagor had done, he wanted this.

Without another word, Belphagor went out. The difficulty would be staying away long enough to convince Vasily he'd been forgotten. It was the state of despair he could reduce Vasily to, the feelings of abandonment he wrung from him, that ultimately led to his boy's surrender. And the sex afterward was mind-blowingly intense. Belphagor himself had such a deep-seated fear of abandonment he couldn't imagine how Vasily could stand being pushed to this edge again and again. But it seemed to be worth the joy and release of being reclaimed by Belphagor for him to experience it.

There was always someone about for a game of wingcasting at The Brimstone, no matter the hour. Taking some poor fellow for his last facet seemed like a pleasant enough distraction from the ache in his groin.

"Nice duds." The player at the first table appraised him as Belphagor approached.

"Armen." Belphagor grinned. "Haven't seen you in ages." They locked arms for a friendly but masculine greeting. Armen was always conscious of how he was seen, making sure no one mistook him for one of Belphagor's kind.

"So, Belphagor." Armen shuffled idly as Belphagor sat across from him. "Do you still cheat at cards?"

"Do you still use that cheap accusation in an attempt to throw your opponent off his game?" Belphagor took the cards from him and gave them an expert shuffle of his own. "And does anyone still fall for it?"

Armen laughed. "Only amateurs."

"You wound me. Lumping me in with amateurs." Belphagor began to deal. "As if you'd be able to tell if I cheated."

Belphagor left Vasily until well after noon, when he couldn't stand another minute of thinking about the way the tugged-down pants had exposed the cleavage of his finely sculpted ass. Vasily stood where he'd left him, his head hanging and his cock echoing it. Poor boy was getting nothing out of this but misery. When Vasily didn't lift his head at the opening of the door, Belphagor lost his own budding erection.

"*Mal'chik.*"

Vasily's shoulders rose with a deep breath, but he didn't turn. Belphagor slipped the belt from the hook and gave the hunched shoulders a firm but gentle push to prompt him onto his knees.

"Turn and face me."

Vasily walked himself about on his knees, gazing up at Belphagor with resignation. The thornfruit had bathed his chin in sticky juice, and the thorns had drawn little pinpricks of blood around his lips. Belphagor shook his head and held his hand out for Vasily to spit the fruit into it. Once he had, Vasily kept his mouth open, waiting for Belphagor to fill it, his eyes defeated.

"I don't want your mouth. I want you to tell me what made you so angry."

Vasily looked up at him warily, his chapped lips still parted. Belphagor poured a cup of water from the pitcher on the vanity and held it to Vasily's mouth, and Vasily drank it with obvious relief.

Belphagor put the cup aside. "Well?"

"What difference does it make?" The gravelly voice was rougher than usual. "You win."

"I don't want to *win*, you silly boy. I want to use you because you want me to. And you clearly didn't want me to this morning, so I'd like to know why."

The defiance kindled once more in the hazel eyes. "*Because*," he growled, "my mouth is only good for one thing as far as you're concerned. You didn't even kiss me good morning."

Belphagor nearly laughed at the simplicity of it, but he restrained himself, knowing how laughter would go over. "That's what made you so angry. That I didn't kiss you."

"If I'd known all you cared about was my 'talented tongue,' I'd have stayed on the streets, where at least I got facets for it."

Ah, there it was. Belphagor had touched a nerve. Vasily's self-worth before he'd come to Belphagor had been measured in the unique oral skills that had him in high demand among demonic and angelic patrons alike. Last night, Belphagor had inadvertently triggered Vasily's defenses by remarking after a particularly lovely fellating that he almost felt selfish for keeping that "talented tongue" to himself. Almost.

Belphagor crouched in front of him and released the belt from around Vasily's wrists. "You're right." The shocked look on Vasily's face was nearly comical. Belphagor cleared his throat. "I've been greatly remiss in failing to show my appreciation for what else your mouth is good for. And you gave an excellent demonstration of that with the invectives you hurled at me this morning. Perhaps I should keep you permanently gagged."

As furious heat rose in Vasily's skin, Belphagor hooked a fist in the red locks bound at the crown and held him still, silencing him with a rough kiss. He savored the smoldering heat and the smoky flavor of Vasily's tongue, slick and willing despite his anger. A slight whimper reminded Belphagor of the thornfruit, and he eased off, nipping gently before sucking the plump lower lip into his mouth just to hear Vasily whimper again.

When he let go, Belphagor pressed his forehead to Vasily's and held his gaze. "You have the right to take exception to perceived mistreatment—whether I perceive it as such or not and whether I choose to give you more of it, which is my privilege—and to tell me when I've hurt you in ways I don't intend. And even to refuse to comply with a request that upsets you. But you do not have the right to fail to use the word we agreed upon for such matters, allowing me to continue to wound you without knowing it, and then to blame me for it."

The angry red in Vasily's cheeks faded to an embarrassed pink.

"Do you remember your word?"

Vasily nodded, and when Belphagor yanked on the hair in his fist, Vasily burst out, "Seraphim!"

"*Khoroshiy mal'chik.*" Belphagor kissed him again on the whispered words. "My very good, very lovely boy." He traced his thumb along one cheekbone above the rough patch of a coppery sideburn, eliciting a moan. "Now, which shall I punish you for first? Your failure to use the safeword or my failure to recognize your distress?"

From the periphery of his vision, he noted with satisfaction that the invocation of their perverse arrangement—that Vasily should take the punishments for both their failings—had provoked the customary response. The magnificent erection had resumed its former vigor. Belphagor's had done so the moment he'd sparked Vasily's defiance and gotten the truth out of him.

He tapped his chin, as though contemplating. "I think the punishment for not using your safeword will be to deny you the privilege of cocksucking until such time as I deem you to have earned it back."

"*Nyet, pozhaluista.*" As the little gasp escaped Vasily, his eyes widened with dread. He'd spoken out of turn, but the use of the Russian *please* and the genuine dismay at being denied Belphagor's cock was so gratifying that Belphagor decided to let this one slide.

"And for my transgression . . ." Belphagor paused for a moment to think while he unlaced his pants and stroked himself to give Vasily a reminder of what he'd be missing. "You'll watch someone else provide that service for me when I require it."

Outrage and dismay warred on Vasily's face, but he managed to keep quiet. He'd assured Belphagor that he was all for playing with others—so long as both he and Belphagor were always included in the play. But the idea of having to watch another demon enjoy Vasily's favorite activity while he was denied the pleasure had to be galling.

Belphagor lifted Vasily's chin with a finger. "Need I remind you that you have the right—and the responsibility—to tell me if this punishment is too much for you to bear?"

Vasily's eyes were stony. "*Nyet, ser.*"

"And do you wish to do so?"

Fire kindled behind the stone. "*Nyet, ser.*"

"Good." Belphagor rose and went to the door. "Because I require it now." He opened it, noting with pleasure that Vasily remained where he was, exposed cock and all, despite the entrance of a stranger. "This fine fellow claims to be quite good at it."

He cupped the cheek of the pretty rentboy—a half-angel bastard about Vasily's age who called himself Mikhail after the founder of the supernal House of Arkhangel'sk. Though he had the fair hair of the Fourth Choir Host, the jade green of his eyes and the tawny hue of his skin, unusual for a waterspirit, made him quite striking and gave him character most angels lacked.

Mikhail smirked. "Hello, Vasily."

If Vasily were a cat, his ears would have flattened. As it was, a steamy hiss escaped between his teeth.

Belphagor's pierced eyebrow lifted with curiosity. "You've met my boy?"

"We've competed for business."

Belphagor turned to Vasily. "Is he as good as he claims?"

"How would I know?" Vasily growled and then added a grudging "*Ser.*"

"Well, then, let's give him a test run, shall we?" He nodded to Mikhail. "Start with him. Let's see what you've got."

Mikhail affected a sort of exaggerated aristocratic walk and approached Vasily, dropping smoothly to his knees.

Vasily gaped at Belphagor. "You want him to suck *me*?"

"How else am I supposed to evaluate his technique? Come on, now, straighten up."

"No touching." Mikhail was firm as Vasily reluctantly obeyed Belphagor's command. "I'll do the work."

Vasily let out a rough groan as Mikhail got on all fours and swallowed him.

"Impressive." Belphagor nodded his approval. "He doesn't seem at all uncomfortable with such a mouthful."

Vasily, glaring down at Mikhail's enthusiastic, bobbing head, was just the way Belphagor liked him—furious and helplessly aroused. His breath was tight and shallow as he struggled to keep silent, his hips pumping involuntarily.

Belphagor stepped behind him and crouched, wrapping his arms around Vasily's chest and resting his chin on the top of Vasily's head. "He looks quite lovely with his mouth full of your cock."

Mikhail glanced up at Belphagor with an approximation of a smile and hummed with appreciation at the compliment.

"How would you rate his technique, *mal'chik*? Adequate? Above average? Superior?"

Vasily made a noise that was more of a grunt than an answer.

"On a scale of one through five, one being subpar and five superior, what would you—"

"Four," Vasily burst out, his face flushed. Mikhail doubled his efforts, as if above average were a challenge to exceed.

Belphagor had palmed his vial of almond oil before coming up behind Vasily, and he slicked some over his cock and let it press against Vasily's bare back above his ass. Vasily gasped and clenched his fists at his sides, having been forbidden to touch the rentboy vigorously sucking him.

"Put your hands behind your head for balance." Belphagor slid Vasily's jeans down to his knees. "Then lean into me." He pressed his cock between Vasily's cheeks, and Vasily shuddered, hands clasped behind his head, as the slick head spread him open. "I've got you, *mal'chik*." With one arm around Vasily's waist and the other hand at a taut nipple, he bit lightly at Vasily's shoulder and drove himself in.

Vasily groaned, rocking between the two opposing pleasures, balanced on his knees with his elbows wide at the sides of his head like wings.

"That's it, sweet boy." Belphagor ran his tongue up the side of his neck to circle the spiked steel post he'd pierced him with when they were in the world of Man. Mikhail, stroking his own cock with his hand down his pants, was going at him with gusto. "Is he going to make you come?"

Vasily let out a reluctant moan. "*Da, ser.*"

"Mind your heat," Belphagor admonished and fucked him without mercy, sending him over the edge.

Vasily shuddered in his arms and arched back against him with a shout that had to have been heard in the gaming room. Mikhail sucked Vasily dry, neither of them letting up until Vasily went limp in Belphagor's arms.

Looking quite pleased with his own performance, Mikhail sat back and wiped his mouth with a flourish, unabashedly fondling himself.

Belphagor nibbled Vasily's ear. "Satisfactory, then, Vasya?"

Vasily made a sound that might have been an attempt at speech.

"I'll take that as a yes." Belphagor nodded to Mikhail. "All right, then, my fine friend. I'll have my turn."

He pulled out and stood to rinse himself off, and Vasily dropped forward onto all fours as if he couldn't hold himself up.

After finishing at the basin, Belphagor stroked himself and stood over the two demons, pondering his options. He addressed Mikhail, with a nod toward Vasily. "Can you suck me off while fucking him?"

Vasily tensed, and Belphagor put a hand on his back. "Use your word if you need to." But Vasily remained silent. "Well, Mikhail?"

Mikhail grinned. "With pleasure. Though it'll cost you another five facets."

"Make it six, and make it last." Belphagor turned Vasily toward the mirror on the vanity so he could watch himself being fucked. Behind him, Mikhail perched on his knees, freeing his cock and rubbing himself with the oil Belphagor provided.

"Use his hair for a handhold," Belphagor suggested.

Mikhail grasped the tied bunch of Vasily's locks and mounted him. While Vasily clutched at the carpet, groaning, Belphagor stepped over him and straddled his waist, facing Mikhail. He held the rentboy's head in both hands, pushing himself into his mouth, making sure Mikhail made plenty of noise. He wanted Vasily to envision what was happening behind him while he was being fucked.

The jealousy and anger in Vasily's ragged moans brought Belphagor swiftly to the verge of climax, but he held back until Mikhail let out a groan of pleasure around his mouthful and bucked into Vasily with his own. With a somewhat exaggerated shout, Belphagor let loose, and Mikhail swallowed him. The half-angel was certainly good at what he did, but it was nothing to the desperate, thrilling experience of being sucked by his boy.

When Mikhail had extricated himself and gotten himself together, Belphagor gave him his pouch of facets and dropped an extra into it. "For your discretion."

Mikhail looked mildly offended. "I am always discreet, sir."

Belphagor twisted his hand in Vasily's hair as Mikhail went to the door. "Thank him for the service, boy." Fury radiated from the set of Vasily's jaw as he clenched out his thank-you.

"Don't mention it." With a bow to Belphagor, Mikhail went out.

Vasily was still on his hands and knees. Belphagor relaxed his grip and smoothed his hands over the tight shoulders. "Are you angry, *mal'chik*?"

"*Da, ser.*"

"But you chose not to use your word."

Vasily shrugged.

"Stand and pull up your pants." As Vasily obeyed, eyes downcast in a manner that was more of a sulk than humility, Belphagor moved his hands aside and buttoned the jeans for him. "Do you love me, *mal'chik*?"

Vasily sucked in a sharp breath. "*Da, ser.*"

"No Russian." Belphagor tugged on the waistband. "No obedience. Just you and me. Just the truth."

"The truth?" Vasily searched his face with a look of confusion. "Of course I love you, Beli. Why are you asking? Did I do something wrong?"

Belphagor bent to pick up the discarded belt and slipped it through the loops of Vasily's jeans. "It scares me a bit how much I enjoy what I do to you. You have to promise to tell me if you don't want something I want."

"I do want it. I will. I promise."

Belphagor kept his eyes on the tattoos that ringed his fingers, marks earned in the world of Man. "If I were to spend the rest of my days in a Russian prison, the vision of you with your arms stretched out, hands behind your head, while you came in that demon's mouth with my cock up your ass—it would sustain me until I died."

Vasily grasped Belphagor's hands over the buckle. "Why are you talking about dying?"

"Because, *mal'chik*." Belphagor looked up. "I love you so much, sometimes I think it will kill me."

CHAPTER TWO

Vasily seemed content to spend the rest of the day in their room with a book. Belphagor had taught him to read Cyrillic script, and Vasily had started on a copy of Dostoevsky's *Demons*, thinking it might have something to do with their kind.

Belphagor supposed it might, though Dostoevsky would never have known the Fallen lived among them in the world of Man. But who was he to say the revolutionaries and malcontents upon whom the author had based his memorable characters weren't of Fallen stock?

Belphagor returned to the tables, amused to see Armen still at it. He lifted an eyebrow once they were paired together by Belphagor's quick advancement through the ranks of players on his way to the master table. "Don't you have mouths to feed at home?"

Armen laughed as Belphagor dealt the cards. "And how else do you think I feed them?" He continued to chat as the round commenced, a tactical error Belphagor took advantage of to relieve Armen of half his cards in the first three casts as he failed to call the die correctly, while Belphagor called all but one of his.

"A pristine Ebony Wing." Belphagor laid down a consecutive set of First Choir cards along with the first order of the remaining three choirs in the suit of spindles. "It's going to be a short game if you keep playing like this."

Armen shook his head and gathered the cards as Belphagor collected the pot of facets. "As it happens, I was hoping to run into you again. There was something I wanted to discuss with you." His tone was casual as he shuffled and dealt, but this was obviously anything but if he was willing to forfeit so much crystal to make it seem so.

Belphagor perused his cards. "Oh?"

"I suppose you've heard of the Fletchery?"

Belphagor scowled. The Fletchery was the nickname for a house of ill repute that specialized in providing "unspoiled" entertainment to an exclusive clientele. The term was also a play on words, implying that the client would be teaching a fledgling how to fly. *Fletching* was a euphemism for being the first to have a celestial virgin, most often applied to young males.

Belphagor had never found the idea of inexperience appealing. He much preferred a partner who had experimented enough to know exactly what he wanted. But the Fletchery's appeal was all the more dubious because of the way it was said to acquire its talent.

The Demon District had no lack of venues for those inclined to sell their pleasures. But as a general rule, the inexperienced didn't choose to enter the profession voluntarily with the intent of selling their own "virtue." They were much more likely to be sold into it by a family down on its luck.

"I've heard of it." He moved around a card or two. "I am not a fan."

"There's definitely something to be said for experience." Armen flashed him a fleeting smile before his expression grew serious. "But as it happens, a nephew of mine has gone missing, and his mother suspects he may have been snatched from the Demon Market by fletch-peddlers."

"I see."

"Pavel is just a boy. Barely thirteen. And rumor has it the Fletchery has a private enterprise that engages in the particularly unsavory practice of supplying entertainment for clients who prefer . . . rather tender flesh." Armen cast the die after uttering the phrase as if flinging the idea away with it.

Belphagor frowned as the die clattered across the table, letting it strike the edge without calling it. He wasn't surprised to hear it, though it was something he'd made a point of not knowing about. The less knowledge he had of practices he despised and those who practiced them, the fewer people he felt inclined to harm.

He swept his cards into a stack in his palm. "I'm very sorry to hear that. Though I'm not sure how you believe I can help."

"Well, it's not as if *I* could make inquiries at such a place."

Belphagor had tired of the game. He tossed the cards face-down on the table.

"I mean," Armen hastened on, "to inquire about renting a . . . er . . ." His face reddened as Belphagor's gaze skewered him.

"Let me make something perfectly clear to you, Armen. I do *not* rent *boys*."

"Well, not *boys*, of course. But . . . you know . . . 'boys.' Like your firespirit. He's what, seventeen?"

Belphagor steeled himself not to go for Armen's throat. "Vasily is twenty. And my relationship with him began when he was well over the age of consent. In any sphere."

"Oh, of course, of course. I didn't mean anything by it. The age of consent in this sphere, after all, is sixteen. No one is questioning the propriety of your relationship. I'm simply saying that no one would be surprised to see you at the Fletchery."

Belphagor shoved back his chair as he stood. "Take heed, Armen. I am very close to delivering a savage beating to you regardless of anyone's consent."

Armen held up his hand. "You misunderstand me. Please. Sit and hear me out."

Belphagor remained standing, arms folded as he glowered down at Armen's apparent discomfiture while the latter attempted to appease him.

"I only meant to say that as your tastes run toward your own kind, and mine do not . . ." He shrugged. "The thing is, Belphagor, I'm rather desperate. Pavel is my sister's only child. And you are the only demon I know who could get into such a place—and express interest in purchasing male companionship—without raising eyebrows. It's not as if they make public any impropriety. And your reputation, obviously, is unimpeachable." He gathered the cards as Belphagor continued to scowl. "Are you really willing to leave an innocent boy to such a fate because of your pride?"

That hit him where it hurt. Armen's nephew wasn't his problem, but if he ignored the boy's plight when he had it within his power to spare the child, he was no better than those who'd subjected him to abuse at a similar age.

Belphagor lowered himself into the chair with a sigh. "I suppose I could make some inquiries. But I will not put myself in a position that compromises my reputation. I'm not going to pretend to be trolling for minors."

Armen gave him a grateful smile. "Of course. And I'm not expecting you to undertake such an effort without compensation for your time. I believe I can make it worth your while. If, while you made your inquires, you were also to gather information on some of the Fletchery's more prestigious clientele—angelic, to be precise—we could find my sister's boy *and* turn a tidy profit."

So that was his game. "Do you even have a sister? Or a nephew?"

"Of course I do. On my honor, the boy is missing. But I don't see why some good can't come of the situation. If he's there, as she suspects, we can redeem him from them and send him home to his mother before any harm is done. But that redemption fee will no doubt be costly. I see no reason not to make those responsible repay that fee—with interest. All it will take is someone in a position to gather the necessary information. That is where you come in." Armen smoothed a hand over the rim of the table. "But I also need someone on the inside."

"The inside?" Belphagor's skin prickled with unease.

"A youth. Or at least someone with the appearance of a youth."

"And just where would you find someone who fits that bill?"

Armen rolled the die lightly against the marble. "I may have someone in mind."

"Why do I get the feeling that I'm not going to like where this is going?"

Armen's smile did little to dispel his unease. "I have, in fact, enlisted someone willing to pose as the object of your attentions, so there'll be no need for you to compromise your principles. Someone of age, with whom you are already acquainted." He crooked his finger toward the bar, and a slender demon stepped out of the shadows. "Meet my young friend Khai."

Belphagor sucked in a breath and clenched his teeth around the full version of the name. "Mikhail."

"Khai" gave him an exaggerated bow. "At your service, m'lord." He grinned as he straightened. "Literally." He licked his lips as if still savoring what he'd swallowed earlier.

Belphagor didn't return the grin. "I hardly think anyone will take your 'friend' here for a fledgling, Armen—and certainly not a youth. He's undoubtedly had his share of patrons who know better."

"Why, sir." Khai put a hand to his chest in mock dismay. "Are you impugning my virtue?"

Armen ignored Khai's theatrics. "No more than they'd take your boy for one." He gave Belphagor an unpleasant smile. "Which is why we will employ a simple glamour that some of your generation use as a youth tonic." There was an obvious dig in that, as if Belphagor were past his prime. "It only takes off a couple years. And that's all either of them need, isn't it?"

Belphagor clenched his fists beneath the table. "Either of whom?"

"Khai. And your boy."

Belphagor rose once more and gathered his crystal. "I've heard quite enough. You can find your nephew and redeem him on your own. I'm sure Mikhail can ferret out all the information you require to turn your profit."

Armen kept his seat and his calm. "Khai can't do it on his own, and as I've said, I simply can't risk my own reputation. Besides, it's the price of admission into the establishment. That's how they keep their patrons tight-lipped. It's not as if you could present Khai as your price. Courting the very boy who served as your entry fee would be a dead giveaway that your interest isn't on the level."

Armen still seemed far too sure of himself despite the fact that Belphagor had cinched up his purse. "I wouldn't be so hasty if I were you, Belphagor. In the course of his services to you, Khai was in a position to confirm a certain rumor."

Belphagor paused with his hands on the drawstring. He knew he shouldn't ask. He also knew he had to. "What rumor?"

"Those interesting markings on your skin. I understand you earned them while incarcerated in an earthly prison for breaking the laws of that world. The *zona*, I think they call it?"

"So? I have never claimed otherwise."

"The rumor is that among your collection of ink, you bear certain marks—in intimate areas—that brand you as— What was the term, Khai?"

Khai had the good sense to step beyond the range of Belphagor's fist before he said it. "A *suka*."

"That's it. *Suka*. I believe it's an even more disparaging term where you acquired the marks than it is here. Signifying your status as a 'downcast.' Someone subjected to the . . . whims, let us say . . . of other inmates."

Belphagor tied the purse to his belt as he took a deep breath and let out the exhalation slowly. "Listen to me carefully, Armen Nekirevich. Because I'm only going to warn you once. If I ever hear you say that word again—about me or mine or anywhere near me—I will beat you within an inch of your life." He fixed him with his gaze. "And then I will make you wish I had taken the inch."

Armen swallowed, and sweat broke out on his forehead, but remarkably, he continued on in his folly. "It isn't as if I care one way or the other. It's nothing to me how your time in the world of Man was spent. But your Vasily . . . I suspect that history isn't the sort of thing you've shared with him."

"Armen—"

"If it were to become common knowledge, your reputation at the tables would suffer, though I'm sure you'd manage to bounce back eventually. But your boy would no doubt hear of it."

"You despicable piece of shit."

"You've forced me to play this hand, Belphagor. I will do what I must to keep my sister's boy from falling into the kind of life you're no doubt quite familiar with. Surely, you understand that."

Belphagor didn't respond. Couldn't respond. The sound of a youth wailing in pain and fear in a darkened Russian prison cell was deafening him. The guards had heard it. There was no way they couldn't have. But then the youth had gone silent. He couldn't recall whether the silence had come because of the filthy pillow stuffed into the boy's mouth or because he'd ceased to believe it was happening at all. (It was never himself in the memory because his "self" had simply drifted away.)

"Belphagor." Armen's voice broke through the noise in his head. "It's not as if you don't stand to gain handsomely from this endeavor, even as you're helping to save a boy from that fate. I'm offering you a lucrative opportunity. You'll take forty percent of the payoff."

Armen smiled without warmth. "Or risk having your behind exposed— I mean, what you've *left* behind."

Belphagor's nails dug into the outer wooden rim of the table hard enough to leave marks. He let his fingers relax. "I'll take sixty if I'm the one doing all the work."

"Fifty-fifty split."

Khai turned to glare at Armen with a hand on his hip.

Armen sighed. "And each of us to divide our share with our apprentices as we see fit."

Something was wrong. There were no orders or commands this evening, no dark looks that sent Vasily's stomach plummeting into his feet and his blood surging into his cock. Belphagor was maudlin, with more talk of death, and told Vasily more than once how much he loved him. Not that Vasily could ever tire of hearing it, but Belphagor wasn't usually one to make such declarations of devotion.

He more than made up for the morning's lack of kisses, which distracted Vasily from his worry for a time. Belphagor undressed him, kissing his way down the flesh he bared but tormenting him by bypassing Vasily's eager erection, only letting his skin brush against it as he passed it over—just enough to make Vasily gasp at the fleeting touch and moan with disappointment.

Then Belphagor perched above Vasily on all fours on the cot, unfastened his pants, and released himself, driving Vasily out of his mind knowing he couldn't put the cock in his mouth. He suffered a brief surge of ire as he replayed the sound in his mind of Mikhail sucking it with loud enthusiasm, giving Belphagor the pleasure Vasily was being denied the right to provide.

"Something wrong, *mal'chik*?" Belphagor stared down at him. Vasily reached to stroke him, but Belphagor grabbed both his wrists and held them at his sides. "Speak up, Vasya. Tell me what you want."

The breath tightened in his chest, nearly smothering him. "I want to suck your cock."

Belphagor shook his head. "You haven't earned back the right to pleasure me yet." For a moment, there was a devilish twinkle in his eye.

"Believe me, *mal'chik*. This hurts me more than it does you." He lowered his head and offered his lips instead, kissing Vasily. Sensuous. Ardent. Making it last as if it were the act of sex itself.

Vasily closed his eyes, breathing him in, sucking his tongue as a substitute for what he longed for. Belphagor was a master at turning the tables on him, finding new ways to torment him. Damn, he loved this demon.

And then he felt Belphagor's cock beside his own as Belphagor lowered himself and let their erections rub against each other, creating delicious friction, though Belphagor had to take his mouth away to keep their bodies at the same level. Instead, he kissed Vasily's chest, teasing his hardened nipples with slick circles of his tongue but not closing his mouth over them. Vasily bucked his hips up against Belphagor in frustration, and Belphagor pushed back, thrusting as if he were inside him, and they began to rock against each other, hardness to hardness, though the tender skin pulled with enough resistance that it hurt wonderfully.

Belphagor remedied that after a moment with a palm full of oil, and Vasily groaned with delight at the slipping and sliding of their cocks together, the sweet oil running down between his thighs. He would always associate the smell of almonds with wild desire and the thrill of being in Belphagor's arms. It was Belphagor's favored lubricant, and Vasily had never encountered it before him.

Just when he thought he might come from rubbing against Belphagor's cock, it slid down between his legs and pushed him open. Vasily shivered as Belphagor drove inside him, his body tingling as if his radiance had been sparked. With his wrists still pinned at his sides, he could only lie still and take it, moaning as Belphagor thrust against that spot inside him that made him feel like he was going to explode.

And then he did, drawing back his firespirit heat in the nick of time as he ejaculated with a loud groan, Belphagor's body trapping the sticky fluid between them while he fucked him harder, intensifying the sensation until Vasily thought he might go blind.

Belphagor withdrew at last and crawled forward, bringing his cock so close Vasily thought he'd let him take it in his mouth after all but stopping short, his fist jerking hard under the engorged head until he shot and nearly missed Vasily's mouth altogether. With a groan of relief, he pressed himself to Vasily's lips and let him take the rest while he growled out his release.

Then his mouth was on Vasily's once more, licking it clean, sucking his lower lip and smothering him with kisses until Vasily thought he'd pass out from lack of oxygen and happiness.

"I love you," Belphagor whispered again when he came up for air. "Always remember that. No matter where we are or what I do to you, I love you."

Clearly, something terrible was about to happen.

Despite his anxiety, exhaustion took over. Vasily slept in Belphagor's arms, waking in the morning to find him up early and getting dressed. Vasily propped himself on one elbow, noting with disappointment that Belphagor's pants were already laced up.

Instead of his jeans, he wore the elkskin leathers—Supernal Army dress breeches dyed black—that hugged his ass. He paired them with a loose, flowing white shirt tucked in at the waist, its ruffled collar and cuffs covering most of the visible tattoos. Belphagor almost never let Vasily see him walking about completely naked. It was infuriating.

Tying his cravat in the mirror, Belphagor saw him watching and glanced over his shoulder. "Do you trust me, *mal'chik*?"

That didn't bode well. Vasily studied Belphagor's attitude, trying to determine whether the question was meant as part of his discipline. He decided it was safest to assume.

He sat up. "*Da, ser.*"

"Will you do anything I tell you, without question?"

Vasily's heart beat faster. "*Da, ser.*"

Belphagor nodded, observing him. "Come."

Vasily paused. Did he mean *come*, or …? The body language didn't suggest anything sexual. He rose and crossed the room.

Belphagor drew his head down for a kiss. Eyes closed, Vasily sighed into his lover's mouth, but Belphagor let him go abruptly.

"Drink this."

Vasily opened his eyes. Belphagor held up a vial of an almost silver liquid, like the surface of the Acheron at dawn. He certainly hoped it wasn't water from the Acheron. The river that separated the Demon District of Raqia from Elysium proper was an undrinkable waste receptacle.

He accepted the vial and removed the stopper. Belphagor wouldn't give him anything dangerous. This was a test to see if he could manage to obey a single command without pitching a fit. His attitude had been childish of late.

The liquid tasted foul as it slipped onto his tongue. Vasily swallowed quickly, not wanting to pause to identify it. It made his face tingle. He reached up to scratch his beard and found smooth skin.

"What the hell?" The exclamation wasn't exactly in keeping with obedience, but he was too surprised to hold it in.

Belphagor turned him toward the mirror, and Vasily gaped at the reflection staring back at him. He looked like himself—at sixteen. He still felt the same height, but in the mirror, he matched Belphagor's, and he was as thin and lithe—with less muscle.

He met Belphagor's eyes in the depths of the glass. This was going too far. "You want me to look like a boy?"

"No, as a matter of fact, I do not. I quite prefer you the way you are. But for the next little while, you will not be *my* boy. You will be *a* boy."

"I don't understand." Heat crackled in his pupils. He'd never looked in a mirror while his fire had risen with his temper. It was a little frightening. And kind of hot. Figuratively, as well as literally. If only he didn't look like a scrawny youth.

Belphagor drew back Vasily's hair, hanging long and straight as it had before he'd grown his locks, and in his natural red. "I'm going to give you to someone at the Fletchery."

"You're *what*?"

Belphagor stroked a thumb down his cheek where the trademark sideburns ought to be. "You don't have to participate in any act that makes you uncomfortable. This isn't for my benefit. In fact, the more you play coy, the better, since you'll be playing the part of a virgin, and I'd prefer you weren't used by someone desirous of remedying that."

"A *virgin*?" Vasily whirled on him. "This isn't funny, Bel. Give me the anti-glamour." He flinched as Belphagor pressed his thumb to the piercing at his neck.

"This is your reminder of who you are and to whom you belong. And you have your word. If anyone tries to force you to do anything you don't wish to do, if this gets too difficult, you come to me and say the word."

"*Belphagor—*"

"But you will play the part as well as you can manage." Belphagor's tone was firm. "I need this from you, Vasya. I don't want it. But my hand has been forced. And it will pay us well."

So that was how it was. Someone had offered him enough facets that he was willing to make a fool of Vasily, to sell him to some pervert.

"I hate you, Beli." The words hissed out of him, unable to be taken back, but they were contradictory. He hadn't meant to use the name that told Belphagor he loved him at the same time.

Belphagor's dark eyes seemed to flinch, though it was his only outward reaction. "As well you should. Bring me the frock coat."

Vasily's mouth dropped open, and then he snapped it shut and stalked to the wardrobe to fetch the beautiful black velvet that was his prized possession. He'd earned it, though the memory of how he'd done so and what a fool he'd been to trust an angel instead of trusting Belphagor made his cheeks burn in an unpleasant way.

Belphagor held out his arms, expecting Vasily to dress him.

"Am I your valet now?" His voice had lost its deep rumble, though as it had been all his life, it was still raspy and rough.

"You're whatever I say you are."

Blinking back angry tears, Vasily shoved the sleeves over Belphagor's arms and buttoned it for him with sharp jerks. "You look stupid." He hurled the words at him, stepping back. "It doesn't even fit you."

Belphagor turned before the mirror, tugging the cuffs of his shirt out from inside the sleeves. "Better than it fits you at the moment. I suppose I could have the seamstress at The Cat take it in for me."

Vasily held his breath. Belphagor wouldn't dare.

"But we have an appointment. Get dressed and fetch a cloak to cover yourself. We'll go out the back way."

Vasily sullenly obeyed, though his own clothes hung on him. When he'd dressed, he pulled on one of the ragged cloaks they kept— the one sized for Belphagor and not himself—and opened the door.

Unexpectedly, Belphagor yanked him back from the threshold with a hand around his upper arm, where he ought not to be able to encircle it but did. "Say the word now, and I'll forfeit."

The quiet entreaty seemed tinged with distress, echoing Vasily's own. Perhaps he *should* say the word.

Belphagor searched his face as Vasily hesitated. "Tell me, *mal'chik*. I'll find some other way if you can't do this."

If he couldn't do this . . . If Vasily couldn't handle a simple, foolish game meant to line Belphagor's pockets. *Screw Belphagor and his stupid word.*

His answer was clipped and hard, giving the impression of a certainty he didn't possess. "*Nyet, ser.*"

Belphagor let out a breath he'd been holding and released Vasily. "*Khorosho.*"

They slipped through the rear of the bar and through the exit to the alley, and Vasily started when a slight figure emerged from under the eaves.

"Hello, Vasily." The blond boy smiled, and Vasily narrowed his eyes, trying to place the face he felt he ought to know. "Don't tell me yesterday was so commonplace you don't remember me sucking your dick."

Vasily's eyes widened. "Khai?" And then he realized how he'd been played by both of them. Belphagor had set this up to humiliate him as punishment for his disrespect. And it was working like a charm.

When Belphagor explained on the way that Khai would play the part of the youth who'd catch his eye at the Fletchery, he thought Vasily would invoke the safeword then and there.

"And why not me?" he demanded. "Why do we need Khai at all?"

"Because my reputation precedes me," Belphagor explained patiently. "If I bring my own boy to the Fletchery with me to serve my needs, it will seem contrived. Khai will encounter me there as if we've never met, and I will deliver you as the necessary price for my entry."

"The price for your entry is a virgin you've agreed not to fuck."

"Precisely."

"This whole thing is disgusting."

"Without question."

"Then why are we doing it? Why are you giving me away?"

Belphagor glanced at Khai, sashaying beside them like a smug ingénue. "We should part here. You've already been introduced to the Fletchery, correct?"

Khai nodded. "A friend pretending to be a firedust addict introduced me for a finder's fee and said I was his recently orphaned cousin. Since he didn't own me outright, I was promised a roof over my head and food in my belly if I offered my services. They let me see how I liked it there for a few nights, and I told them I'd think about it." He beamed, demonstrating his innocent look once more. It was quite convincing. "So looking forward to assisting you in any way I can." Khai took off down a side alley, and Vasily fumed, watching him go.

"Listen to me, *mal'chik*." Belphagor spoke sharply, getting Vasily's full attention. "I am not giving you *away*. I am giving you up temporarily to play a part. I will play mine well, and I expect you to do the same. But you mustn't mistake my skill at the game for truth. Regardless of how I treat you once we're inside, you are my *mal'chik*. You're *mine*, do you understand me?"

Vasily gave him a sullen nod.

"If I promise to reward your good behavior, will you promise to deliver it?"

Vasily's smoldering hazel eyes were suspicious but interested. "What reward?"

"A very intimate, bare-handed thrashing your ass won't soon forget. For starters."

Vasily bit his lip.

"Yes, just like that." Belphagor nodded thoughtfully. "Play the coquette. Aloof and a little shy, but sensual." From his own experience as a youth, he knew it would appeal to the sort that patronized the Fletchery. "Are we agreed?"

Vasily let out an almost wistful sigh, as if thinking of the promised thrashing. "*Da, ser*."

Once they were inside, Raum, the demon who admitted Belphagor, looked Vasily over with skepticism. "You say he's a fledgling? Isn't this the boy who's been living with you at The Brimstone?" He gave Belphagor a knowing glance. "We're well aware you're the Prince of Tricks."

"My apprentice is an adult. As you'd know if you were indeed acquainted with me. This is a cousin of his, Rubiel. I won him in a wingcasting tournament."

"And you haven't sampled him for yourself?"

Belphagor laughed. "One firespirit is plenty. But I have trained him."

"Trained him?"

"Rubiel." Belphagor snapped his fingers and pointed to the floor.

Vasily stared at him for a split second longer than he ought to have before dropping to his knees and bowing his head.

"He'll follow any command and will only speak when spoken to." Belphagor wrapped his fist in Vasily's hair. "Isn't that right, boy?"

He could feel the heat radiating from Vasily's skin, but Vasily managed a respectful enough, "*Da, ser.*"

Belphagor gave the sleek fall of hair a sharp yank. "In angelic, boy. This isn't Russia."

"Yes, sir." Vasily let out a sharp gasp when Belphagor kept twisting. "I'm sorry, sir."

"Good boy." Belphagor relaxed the hold and stroked his hair. There would be a great deal to make up for after this adventure, but that had been particularly cruel, a violation of their contract with one another that Vasily would never be punished or humiliated for obedience. But it couldn't be helped. Belphagor couldn't afford to have anyone recognize their intimate connection with such a slip.

Luckily, Raum didn't seem to know Belphagor's reputation as well as he believed. "He isn't *human*, is he?" The word was delivered with a grimace of distaste.

Belphagor laughed. "No, indeed. Just a bit dim." At this, he pressed his hand to Vasily's shoulder as silent reassurance that he was only playing the part and these words weren't his true feelings, but he could sense the hurt through the warm skin. *Damn.* This game was going to be harder than he thought—and the stakes much higher than he'd intended.

"Well, isn't he lovely?" The familiar voice from the entrance to the salon made Belphagor's skin prickle with unease.

He met the other demon's nod with a frown. "Kezef."

He'd had dealings with Kezef before at the wingcasting table, but it was his reputation as a dominant that Belphagor didn't care for. From the stories he'd heard, Kezef didn't believe in a consensual exchange of power. He took advantage of a submissive's desire to please in order to reduce him to a state of acute distress, exploiting the submissive's fear and shame to keep him from reporting any abuses or seeking to flee them.

"I'm surprised to see you here, Belphagor. You're usually such a stick in the mud."

"Nonsense. Unlike some, I merely require a willing partner."

"And what about this little morsel?" Kezef approached and lifted Vasily's chin to look him over. "Is he willing?"

Belphagor resisted the impulse to strike the hand away. "His father was willing enough to offer him as collateral for his debts. I'm not sure the boy knows yet whether he's willing or not." He realized as soon as he'd said it that this was a mistake.

Kezef's eyes gleamed as he ran his thumb over Vasily's full lower lip. "Well, I hope to see more of him. Perhaps he and I can make that determination together." He gave Belphagor a gallant bow. "Your contribution to the Fletchery is most intriguing. I'll put in a good word for you with the charter members."

"The charter members reserve the right to vote on any new applicants," Raum explained at Belphagor's inquiring look. "It ensures that only the right sort are admitted into our exclusive membership. In the meantime, Kezef can show you around while I take Rubiel to be instructed on his role here."

Belphagor frowned, but he knew he couldn't object. Vasily wasn't supposed to be here for him. "Certainly. Though I'd like to check in on him later if you don't mind. I promised his father I'd keep an eye on him and see that he's well-treated."

Raum gave him a distracted nod. "Stand up, boy. I'm talking to you."

Kezef held out his arm toward the salon, and Belphagor had no choice but to leave Vasily and go with him. He glanced back at the door and saw Vasily's escort taking him by the arm and steering him toward another corridor leading away from the entryway. Vasily looked up and met his eyes, a blaze of pure hatred flashing at Belphagor for an instant before he lowered his head and followed.

CHAPTER THREE

A pair of dormitories lined either side of the corridor, girls in one and boys in the other. Though Vasily had known plenty of demons as young as these who'd worked the streets—and had done it himself—it unsettled him to see them corralled here like cattle to be bought and sold by others instead of choosing to sell what they had. Not that demons who grew up on the streets had much of a choice; for most, it was selling or starving.

Still, this took it a step beyond, robbed them of what little power they might have imagined they had. Most he'd known had also pretended to be older, while here it was their inexperience that was the draw. The brief glance into the girls' dormitory turned his stomach. They were dressed in pinafores that gave them the appearance of being even younger than they were, except that the fabric was diaphanous.

In the boys' dormitory, a slender youth who seemed somewhat older than the others looked up from his bunk when Vasily entered. Dark hair and pale eyes suggested a blend of the elements of water and earth—though the earth must surely have come from the aetherial Order of Virtues.

Vasily's escort addressed the youth. "Silk, this is Ruby. See that he's presentable, and explain the rules to him. And make sure he understands them. Seems he's not too bright."

Vasily seethed at the role Belphagor had cast him in. "It's Rubiel."

The escort placed his hand on Vasily's head. "That's what your old master called you. Your name is Ruby now. Do you understand?"

It was an effort not to clench his teeth and growl. "Yes, sir."

"Listen to Silk." He patted Vasily and went to the door. "And Silk, find out if he has any special skills. He's been trained as a submissive, but I don't think he's had much discipline."

Vasily disguised a snort by coughing into his hand.

Silk hopped down from his bunk. "Lovely hair." He took hold of the smooth hank draping Vasily's shoulder and stroked his fingers through it. "It'll be nice when it's clean."

Vasily bristled. He was perfectly clean to begin with, but the glamour had given him the straight, shiny hair he'd always had when he was younger. No one had ever complained about it.

When Silk began to undo Vasily's belt, Vasily slapped him away. "What do you think you're doing?"

"We need to get you bathed." Silk smiled patiently. "Our patrons are very particular. Come on, Ruby. Don't be shy."

He reached for the belt once more, but Vasily stepped back. "I can undress myself."

"Commendable, though not really a skill you need here." Silk gave him a wry smile. "But that's all right. You go ahead for now." He stepped aside and waited while Vasily reluctantly peeled out of his clothes and boots, trying to ignore Silk's appraising eye and the curious glances of the other boys from their bunks. And making a special effort not to meet Khai's amused gaze when he spotted him.

"You can drop them in the bin over there." Silk pointed at what was clearly a trash bin, and Vasily hesitated. "Don't worry. We have clothes in your size."

Vasily swallowed a sigh. He'd agreed to play the role. He might as well do it. When he'd complied, Silk gave him a broad smile, as if his dimwitted charge had managed to use the chamber pot properly, and led him into a curtained-off room in the back. An empty wooden tub sat in the center with a large metal bucket of water beside it.

Silk swept his long fall of hair into a knot and rolled up his sleeves. "Step in." He nodded toward the tub. "Kneel."

Vasily obeyed, with a wary eye on the bucket. When Silk ladled a scoop of water and poured it over his head, he let out a yelp of surprise. He'd expected it to be hot, but it was ice-cold. Instinctively, he increased his body temperature, heating the water as it dripped over him, and Silk watched wide-eyed as it steamed.

"I'm a firespirit," Vasily growled at him. "And you might have warned me."

"Never seen a firespirit do that before." Silk filled the ladle again, but Vasily stopped him.

"Wait." He rose onto his knees and put his hand inside the bucket, heating the water to a decent temperature for a bath.

"Now *that* is a useful skill. Can you concentrate that heat in a particular area?"

Vasily gave him a knowing look. "Yes."

Silk frowned. "Don't answer like that if anyone else asks you. Your slow-witted act will serve you better. You had me going, and you obviously fooled Raum. But they don't appreciate savvy at the Fletchery." He commenced ladling the steamy water over Vasily, adding a few drops of sweet-smelling oil to it. "Rub that through your hair, and then I'll give you a bit for your skin." He stepped back and folded his arms while Vasily stroked the oil over himself. "How old are you, Ruby?"

Vasily paused, and then answered honestly, "I don't know." He shrugged. "Old enough."

"Patrons don't pay for 'old enough.' Say fourteen if you're asked."

"Fourteen? That's illegal trade."

"Legal or not, it's why most of them come. The Immacularium's claims about offering 'unspoiled but mature wares' is bollocks. Nobody wants 'em."

"The Immacularium?"

"The name of the establishment. I suppose you heard 'Fletchery.' It's just a crude street name the uninitiated use as a joke."

Vasily observed him. "How old are you?"

"Older than they think." Silk lowered his voice. "I tell them I'm sixteen, but that's still too old for many of the patrons—even if the Immacularium were to try to pass me off as unspoiled. I'm here as a sort of den mother." His expression was a mixture of self-mocking and apologetic. "It's a nice job. I keep the boys in line, and I make sure no one's hurting them. Unless they don't mind a little pain. You really a submissive?"

Vasily gave him a sidelong glance. "Well . . . I don't mind a little pain."

Silk laughed and crossed his arms on the edge of the tub. "I suppose that explains this." He touched the points of the steel bar in Vasily's skin. "But it'll have to come out. Do these twist off?"

Vasily stood abruptly, nearly upending the tub. "No. It stays."

Silk rose with a frown. "If it's your former master's mark, you have to forget about him. He sold you."

"He's not my master, he's—" Vasily clamped his mouth shut. Fine job he was doing playing his part.

Silk held out his hand. "Give it to me, Ruby. You can't keep it. They won't tolerate it. Whoever you think he was to you, he is nothing to you now. Did you think he loved you?" Silk's gray eyes regarded him with pity. "No one who loved you would have sent you here."

Vasily's hand dropped away from the piercing. Silk didn't understand. He couldn't know what Vasily was really doing here. He had to play his part.

"I thought mine loved me too." Silk loosened the spiked cap. "But I was only a possession, and one he soon tired of when another pretty face came along." The spike fell into Silk's hand, and Vasily felt the bar slip from his skin. Silk dropped the pieces into his pocket and gave Vasily his hand to help him out of the tub. "Come on, Ruby. Let's make you so pretty it kills him when he sees you as another demon's toy."

Vasily submitted to Silk's ministrations, kneeling while the older-but-younger boy combed his hair until it gleamed and tied it off near the bottom with a bright, scarlet bow. Silk dressed him in a pair of the loose linen trousers Vasily had seen on the other boys, like pajamas from the world of Man.

"Here in the dormitory, you'll be glad of the lack of a shirt." Silk directed him back through the curtain. "It gets unbearably warm with all the bodies in here." Silk stopped before an empty bed. "This is your bunk. No fraternizing. No self-pleasuring. No getting up to use the chamber pot without being told to go. And you'll receive an enema after the morning meal to make sure everything's fresh as a rose."

Vasily sat on the bunk at Silk's direction. "What's an enema?"

Several of the boys nearby laughed.

"Proof," said Silk, "that what goes up must come down."

Fledglings had passed through the salon in groups of four throughout the afternoon—none of them, as near as Belphagor could tell, even close to the age of consent—but Vasily was nowhere to be seen. Belphagor was on the verge of blowing his cover and demanding the return of his boy when Khai entered and caught his eye.

Like the other boys he'd seen paraded about, Khai wore nothing but a pair of thin pants with a drawstring waist. The pale flaxen color of the fabric accentuated his rich skin tone, and several heads turned to admire him. The protocol was that prior to an actual purchase, a fledgling could be ordered like a drink by anyone who desired closer inspection.

Belphagor nodded to the hovering attendant, dubbed the sommelier. "I'd like to sample that one." He raised his drink toward Khai.

"Excellent choice." The sommelier handed Belphagor a playing card and made a note on the slate he carried as he continued making the rounds of the patrons, filling up the spaces allotted for each fledgling as they wandered through, some shyly, with eyes downcast, others, like Khai, putting on the charm for every demon who looked their way. At the opposite end of the room, each fledgling entered a separate curtained niche once the attendant gave him the nod that his "tasting card" had been filled.

When it came to each patron's turn, the attendant collected the card, and the patron entered the niche marked with the same suit. The rules had been explained in advance: until purchased, a fledgling must remain chaste, but a patron could inspect the merchandise by hand, so long as no penetration occurred and no one reached any measure of completion.

To avoid suspicion, Belphagor had selected a few of the older boys over the course of the afternoon and spent his reserved minutes speaking to them, politely inquiring about how they were treated and how they'd come to the Fletchery. All had been sold by a parent to pay a debt. It was a common enough tale among demon families—too many mouths to feed and not enough trade apprenticeships to sell one's children to in order to make ends meet. So far, there had been no sign of Armen's nephew—or of any youth being brought here by force.

As Belphagor entered Khai's niche, the young demon sat with his legs stretched out and his ankles crossed, casually awaiting his next patron. "I was wondering when you'd get here. I guess you've noticed there's no one fitting Pavel's description."

"I have. I presume Armen invented him to play on my sympathies, knowing he couldn't otherwise lure me into fulfilling his blackmail scheme."

"For what it's worth, if he did invent him, I wasn't in on it."

"Right. Just the scheme to blackmail me and drag Vasily into this."

Khai shrugged. "A demon's gotta make a facet."

He supposed he couldn't argue with that logic. "I haven't seen him yet. How is he?"

"Ruby? He's fine. Being primped and instructed."

"Ruby?"

"That's the name they've given him. He won't be out on the floor until tomorrow, so you may as well purchase an entertainment package—or come back in the morning, if you aren't capable of keeping your shit together until you've seen him. But Armen's expecting you to be gathering information. The sooner you do it, the sooner we can all be done with this, so I hope you haven't been utterly wasting your time."

Despite knowing Khai wasn't a youth, it was unnerving to hear him speak with such confident cynicism through the illusion of the glamour. "I'm not here to purchase entertainment," he snapped, cross because Khai was right.

"But you could purchase the Ingénue: 'An evening of stimulating companionship and fine dining,'" he recited. "'Companions must be returned in original condition.'"

Belphagor folded his arms with a grudging lift of his shoulders. "I suppose I could."

"I imagine it would give you ample opportunity to observe the angelic patrons. The Ingénue is a favorite of theirs. That's one of the reasons Armen needed someone besides me in on the scheme. They like to behave as if they're keeping their dicks clean, merely interested in the novelty of youthful companionship, and tend to use coercive fletching without paying so no one's the wiser." Khai wiggled his toes.

"Plus, the dinner is fabulous. In the meantime, we have a few more minutes." He rubbed his bare foot up the side of Belphagor's leg. "They tend to look the other way at a little oral sampling."

"Good Heavens, no." Belphagor shuddered and took a firm step back. "Sorry," he amended when Khai looked embarrassed. "The realism of the illusion is far too disturbing."

A tug on the curtain announced their time was up, and Belphagor pulled the fabric aside. "I'd like to purchase the Ingénue package with this delicious little treat for the evening. He is of age, isn't he? Some of these little fledglings seem a bit fresher than I expected."

The sommelier's frown said he didn't appreciate being forced to disavow the illegal trade in which the club was so obviously engaging. "Of course, sir. We take pride, however, in acquiring those who have been sheltered from the harshness of both the realm and the elements." He glanced at his board and shook his head. "My apologies, but his evening has already been purchased."

"Just his evening, I hope, and not his feathers?"

"Just his evening. He'll still be on the market tomorrow, virtue intact."

"May I place a reservation on his fletching?" Belphagor turned and smiled indulgently at Khai. "It seems he's rather in demand, and I'd hate to miss that."

"Certainly. For tomorrow?"

"No." Belphagor twirled his finger in one of Khai's curls. "No, I'm a bit of a masochist as well as a sadist. I'd like to enjoy him in his guileless state until he breaks me down and I simply have to have him. I'll reserve the Ingénue package for tomorrow evening if I may and place a hold on his fletching indefinitely, to be consummated at my discretion."

"Very good." The sommelier made a note.

Khai beamed up at him. "Thank you, sir. I hope I please you."

"I'm sure you will." Belphagor gave him a dark smile. "Since, as we've discussed, you're quite amenable to physical discipline, we'll have plenty of time for exploring that in the meantime."

Vasily sat on his bunk, chagrined by the discovery of what the morning ablutions had entailed, while Silk made the rounds, making sure everyone was presentable and prepared, finally approaching Vasily last.

"Ready for your debut, Ruby?"

"Ready as I'll ever be."

Silk fished in the pocket of the robe he was allowed to wear over his slacks since he was no longer on the market. "Listen, I know you're missing your former master. I had one of the girls make you this." He held out a crocheted choker made from scarlet thread. "Your master's mark is stitched into it here." Silk showed him what seemed to be a decorative knot at the front.

Vasily rubbed his thumb across it, too overcome to speak.

"They'll assume it's only fashion, and the collar will also serve to let patrons know you're trained in submission." He took the choker from Vasily's hand and went around the bed to kneel behind him on the mattress, placing the collar over his throat and tying the loose ends in the back. Vasily put his hand to it and couldn't stop the tears that slipped from the corners of his eyes.

Silk tucked Vasily's hair behind his ear. "It's all right. You don't have to forget him. Just remember that you're worth more than his price. He never understood your true value."

Vasily quickly smudged the tears away, glancing up as Silk rose. "Silk— Why do they call you that?"

The young demon gave him a little smile. "Touch me and find out." He winked and walked away.

Taking his turn around the salon, Vasily's heart sank when he didn't see Belphagor. After a quick glance about to confirm it, he kept his head down, figuring it was in keeping with his role.

Once inside his curtained niche, however, he discovered his card had filled promptly, with patrons coming in practically trembling with anticipation. He was free to refuse attentions from anyone, Silk had told him, but it would arouse suspicion if he refused everyone, so

Vasily played coy as Belphagor had bidden him, keeping his hands in his lap and his eyes downcast while patrons tried to woo him.

His last patron for the morning was Kezef, the handsome, ashen-haired demon he'd seen when they'd arrived at the Fletchery. Kezef was as tall as Vasily's true height, with the trim build and well-developed muscles of a man who was used to physical exertion.

He stood inside the curtain observing Vasily. "My, my. What a divine little devil." His amber eyes—enhanced by topaz oil, no doubt, but striking all the same—slowly traveled over Vasily in a way that made him feel as if he were not only bare-chested but had forgotten to wear the thin fabric pants. "I've been told you follow orders. Is that true?"

"Yes, sir."

"Kneel."

He had only ever knelt before Belphagor. He had only ever *wanted* to kneel before Belphagor. And even so, it was never a simple matter of a command given and a command obeyed. It was much more than that. But he was here to play a part.

This internal debate had taken him only an instant, but it had been an instant too long.

Kezef moved so swiftly that Vasily found himself facedown on the floor of the booth, stunned by the force of the blow, without quite knowing how he'd gotten there. Kezef's boot was on his cheek, grinding his face into the wooden planks. "I was told you were well-trained. A common street cur begging scraps would respond with more obedience." Kezef moved the boot to the floor beside his head. "Thank me for the lesson."

Vasily swallowed his pride, too frightened to care about it. "Thank you, sir."

Kezef dropped to one knee and yanked Vasily's head back with a fist wrapped in his hair. "Not with words, you precious simpleton." He shoved Vasily's head down until Vasily's mouth struck the toe of the boot. Blood trickled from his lip. "Thank—me—for—the—lesson."

Cheeks burning, Vasily kissed the leather, and when Kezef gave no indication of whether his guess was right or wrong, he drew his tongue across it, tasting his own blood.

Kezef's hand loosened in his hair. "And there is your second lesson. Your tongue is not for words. It is merely a tool, an object to be employed by your master for whatever purposes please him—cleaning, polishing. Tasting."

Vasily knew he ought to keep his mouth shut, but the words escaped anyway. "You're not my master."

The grip on his hair tightened painfully. "If I purchase you, I am your master. While you are alone with me in this booth, I am your master. And because you have used what belongs to me for these few minutes, a third lesson will be necessary." Kezef released him and straightened. "On your knees."

Wary, Vasily rose to a kneeling position.

Kezef snapped his fingers. "Look to me." When Vasily met his gaze, Kezef crouched down and brought his face so close that Vasily could feel breath on his cheek. "The lesson is this: When you leave this booth, I will still be your master, because you are nothing but an object. You are a commodity—and one with little value because there are countless numbers like you. Trinkets. Toys. Passing amusements to be consumed and discarded. And you can be made to do anything. If I choose to beat you until you cannot stand, you will be grateful. If I choose to piss in your mouth, you will swallow what you are given. If I choose to strip you and parade you with a bit and lead through the streets of Raqia, you will trot at my side like an obedient yearling. And when you have done these things, when you have demonstrated what you are and what you are good for, you will grovel, eager to show me your gratitude and eager to be made to do them again." Kezef straightened and stared down at him emotionlessly. "On your belly. Thank me for the lesson."

Vasily obeyed without hesitation, the memory of his failure the first time—and the ache in his skull from the blow that had resulted—still fresh as he snaked his tongue over the dusty leather of Kezef's boot.

"You see?" Kezef swept aside the curtain, exposing him where he groveled on the floor, and nodded to the sommelier. "Put me down for the Ingénue this evening." He threw a brief, contemptuous glance back into the booth, the golden eyes raking Vasily. "And see that he's bathed. He smells like a sewer."

When Kezef had gone, Vasily picked himself up and fled to the dormitory, his entire body shaking with anger and shame. In those few moments at Kezef's mercy, he had done as Kezef had said he would, obeying his commands as if he were nothing but a trained dog. He curled into a tight ball on his bunk as if he might become small enough to disappear.

"Ruby?" Silk hurried to his side. "What's the matter? What happened?"

"Kezef had him," said one of the boys. *Fantastic.* His humiliation was already common knowledge.

Silk hissed between his teeth. "That *sukin syn.*" He shooed the boys away to their bunks and sat to stroke Vasily's shoulder, but Vasily rebuffed him. "I'm sorry, Ruby. I should have warned you."

"Please, Silk. Leave me alone."

"Ruby, listen to me. Kezef specializes in exploiting a boy's deepest insecurities. He makes you doubt yourself, believing you're what he says you are. You're not. Don't let him get inside your head." Silk persuaded him to uncurl his limbs, wiping gently at the blood on Vasily's lip with a cool, damp cloth.

Vasily stopped him and took the cloth from his hand, frowning as he regarded the sweet boy who thought it was his duty to take care of him. "Silk. I'm not who you think I am. I've deceived you."

"Nonsense. I make it my business to know things, to know my boys. It's the only way to survive in here. How else do you think I've lasted so long?" He shook his head and lowered his voice. "I know exactly who you are. You think I'm an idiot? You belong to the Prince of Tricks." Silk smoothed the hair that Kezef had twisted in his fist. "And he's a fool."

Belphagor was disappointed to find he'd already missed Vasily by the time he arrived at the salon. Khai had apparently also made his appearance, so there was no opportunity to talk to him before dinner.

The affair began with the patrons being seated about a low lounging table with an array of cushions arranged to give each patron room to have his ingénue recline in his lap if he chose, though there was to be no public intimacy. Khai's prediction had proved true. Of the ten patrons at dinner, six were angelic nobility.

A first course of cold soup was served prior to the presentation of the ingénues, who were then paraded in dressed in their customary attire. The girls led the precession. The first two took their places beside the angels who had purchased them, and the third sat by a demon to Belphagor's right, but the last to arrive took him by surprise.

Well trained in her role, Anzhela gave no sign that she recognized Belphagor as she made her way to the angel across from him—one the sommelier had referred to as Prince Maymon. Belphagor couldn't imagine how she'd ended up in bondage to the Fletchery. Her grandmother owned The Cat, and the last he'd heard, Anzhela was being groomed to be her replacement as the brothel's madam. At sixteen, she seemed to be at the upper end of the age spectrum for the Fletchery's clientele.

His attention was quickly diverted from the dilemma of her presence, however, by Vasily's entrance. Tied back in a large red ribbon, his hair gleamed as if alight with flame, and a thin braided cord in the same shade was tied about his neck. Vasily kept his eyes down as the sommelier led him to his patron at the far end of the table. Belphagor felt his entire being go cold.

Kezef grasped Vasily by his collar and made him kneel on the hard wood without a cushion. A haze of fury blinded Belphagor, and he'd nearly risen from his seat when Khai appeared beside him and laid a hand on his shoulder. Khai gave him a nearly imperceptible shake of his head and a subtle look of warning.

Belphagor forced himself to relax as he took Khai's hand and kissed it. "Sit," he ordered, but when Khai started to kneel beside him, Belphagor pulled him onto his lap and stroked his hair like a prized pet in a show of how a dominant ought to treat a submissive in such a setting. He realized his mistake, however, when Kezef murmured something to Vasily, who looked up and met his eyes. The betrayal in the utterly fireless hazel of his boy's gaze hammered him in the gut.

Vasily's fingers played at his collar. The spiked adornment Belphagor had given him was gone. For a moment, Belphagor couldn't breathe.

The second course had arrived. Khai leaned back against Belphagor's chest and turned his head to the side as if relishing his position. "Stop looking at him," he murmured. "It will only get worse."

He knew Khai was right. Kezef enjoyed an audience, and Belphagor was giving him fuel for his sadism by letting on that it mattered to him at all what happened to Vasily. He turned his attention on Khai to avoid arousing further suspicion with anyone at the Fletchery, determined not to look Kezef's way again.

Belphagor engaged Prince Maymon in conversation while absently feeding morsels of cheese croquettes to Khai. He was here to gather information, after all.

Prince Maymon clearly considered himself above the company of demons, responding in clipped tones to Belphagor's observations on the weather and fashion, until Anzhela began to play the game.

"Angels are always better dressed than demons." She curled about the prince's arm and smiled up at him, fingering the fabric of his sleeve. "What's this made of? It's so pretty."

"It's Vilonese silk, my dear." He smiled indulgently. "As you know, sumptuary laws forbid demons from wearing it."

"Doesn't forbid them from weaving it for you, though." Belphagor smiled at Maymon's cool stare before concentrating on his meal. "It's a pity. Your girl would look lovely in that ice-blue Vilonese." He glanced up with a slight shrug, his fork poised before Khai's mouth. "Of course, what happens at the Fletchery contravenes a number of silly celestial laws."

Khai took the mouthful of croquette with a soft moan, diverting all eyes toward him. Belphagor had to suppress a smile. He had to admit, Khai's glamoured youth reminded him a great deal of himself at fifteen, when he'd first fallen to the world of Man. It had been angels who'd contravened the law of the land there as well. A group of earthbound Malakim posing as monks had taken Belphagor in and introduced him to their fashionable circuit in Petrograd on the eve of the fall of the Russian empire.

The prince unbuttoned his coat, goaded, as Belphagor had hoped, into putting the garment on Anzhela to admire her in it. She beamed up at the angel, wrapping herself in the soft fabric and cooing at its beauty as she tucked her bare legs up onto the cushion and pressed against him. Belphagor felt his smile go hard on his lips. What had reduced her to this circumstance? He would have to stop by The Cat and speak with Masha.

"Be careful not to spill anything on it." Maymon petted her arm. "I'm afraid it's worth more than your virtue."

"Clothing is a waste on such charming playthings." Kezef's quiet, seductive voice drew the attention away from the angel. "Ruby." His tone changed swiftly to one of harsh authority. After a moment's hesitation, Vasily rose and took off his pants.

Belphagor couldn't help but protest, though he tried to keep his voice casual. "That's hardly appropriate at the dinner table."

Vasily didn't look at him as he knelt on the floor. He was certainly playing his part well. He'd never been so obedient for Belphagor. But this was what Belphagor had asked of him. He tried to steady his breathing and keep his eyes on his plate.

"What's inappropriate," said Kezef, "is indulging and fawning over them as if they were anything more than goods we've purchased. Once used, after all, they'll be good for nothing."

Everyone at the table was shifting on their cushions. Naked truths were no more comfortable in this fantasy environment than naked sex slaves.

"Wasting expensive food on them is like baking pastries for a dog. It's not as if they can appreciate it. Their palates are unrefined." Kezef scooped a dollop of cream sauce from a chafing dish beside his plate and flung it at Vasily, splattering his chest. Vasily flinched but didn't move as it dripped down his naked flesh.

Belphagor started to rise, but Khai grabbed his hand under the table and dug in his nails. Before Belphagor could fling him off, one of the angels threw down his fork.

"Listen here, demon. We've all paid a pretty facet for an evening of *entertainment* and *conversation*. No one is interested in watching your display of perversion."

Kezef laughed. "My perversion. You come to the Demon District to titillate yourself with the 'shocking' access to underage sex to be had here and then go home to bed your pristine angel cunts while secretly reveling in the sweet demon ass you've just had. Demons like myself, and our infamous friend, the Prince of Tricks, aren't pretending to be something we're not."

Belphagor clenched his teeth, unable to refute the gist of the speech. It was the maddening thing about Kezef. He was a vicious sadist and yet had an unfailing intolerance for hypocrisy and spoke the truth as he saw it. Under the right circumstances, Belphagor could even see himself treating Vasily as Kezef was doing, and he knew without a doubt that if he did, his boy's eventual surrender would be Heaven-shattering.

But there would be no tender moment afterward if Kezef were to break Vasily, no appreciation for the incredible vulnerability of the gift he was giving, no unshakeable bond that made the one exacting the submission as much a slave to the other as the demon who submitted willingly. With Kezef, there was no gift at all, only taking and conquering. And Belphagor wasn't going to sit by while his boy was taken without his consent.

As Belphagor set down his fork and opened his mouth to speak, Kezef slicked his finger through the cream dripping down Vasily's abs and held it out to Vasily, making Belphagor's mouth go dry.

Khai grabbed the spoon from the dish in front of Belphagor and dribbled sauce down his own chest. "Oh dear. I've spilled some too, sir. Perhaps you'd prefer to eat it off me." He batted his eyes at Belphagor, and everyone laughed, the tension of the moment dissolved. The look from Khai as he glanced up at Belphagor seemed to say, *Vasily's playing his part, now play yours.* He dipped Khai back and ran his tongue down the trail of sauce to a round of applause.

Anzhela's prince held a spoonful of sauce to her mouth. "I'd still prefer that you not spill anything on my silk."

She giggled and let him feed her, and the party went back to its inane conversation and flirtation.

Determined now to make as quick a job of this mess as possible, by the end of the evening, Belphagor had filed away at least half a dozen names and titles to report to Armen, which Khai could corroborate.

Kezef made a show of allowing Vasily to dress as they retired to the salon for dessert, running his hand inside the garment as if to tuck him into it while Belphagor and Khai passed. Belphagor had been too easily provoked. Kezef knew Vasily meant something to him. He did his best to ignore them both for the remainder of the evening, even when Kezef kept Vasily on his hands and knees, feeding him custard on the end of his finger. But Vasily's subservient obedience nearly killed Belphagor.

Reluctantly, he retired for the night while Kezef and the demon with one of the female fledglings were the only ones still engaged in conversation—but not before he had a quiet word with the attendant to ensure that Kezef wouldn't be permitted to take any liberties with Vasily under the terms of the evening's contract.

CHAPTER FOUR

K ezef seemed to lose interest in Vasily as soon as Belphagor had gone, dismissing him when he caught him yawning. But as Vasily headed down the corridor toward the dormitory, his ponytail was yanked from behind, sending him spinning to the floor. Kezef looked down at him, the scarlet ribbon in his fist, as Vasily lay dazed from the blow to the back of his head.

Kezef planted his feet firmly on either side of Vasily's head. "Time for the fourth lesson. You played the part of a submissive well this evening, but it was for the benefit of someone else."

Vasily tried to scoot back, but Kezef stood on his hair.

"Now you will learn what you can be made to do when he isn't involved in your performance. What you are when there is just you and I, with no one watching." He widened his stance, his hand on the clasp of his belt as he slowly unfastened it. "There is a quaint tradition in the world of Man involving the submersion of a soul in water, signifying the soul's redemption and acceptance into its new life." His voice had become strangely soothing. "It's called a baptism. Tonight, your baptism is at hand. Let it rain down upon you, admitting you into the secret sanctum of true submission." Kezef smiled darkly and spoke again, this time with a naked sneer. "Now let's see what you'll swallow. Open your mouth, boy, and find out what it's good for."

The echo of Belphagor's words stuck him in the heart, drowning him in despair. As Kezef undid his fly, Vasily almost gave in and obeyed, his lips parting as if he no longer possessed his own volition.

"Get the hell off of him." The gentle but adamant sound of Silk's voice saved him from himself.

Kezef turned, revealing the young demon behind him brandishing a poker from the coal furnace. "Mind your business, boy."

"Ruby is my business. These boys are my business. If you ever want to be admitted to the Fletchery again, I suggest you take heed. And if you don't step away from him this instant, I'll render you incapable of using that pathetic tool of yours for any purpose."

Kezef moved his foot from Vasily's hair and fastened his pants, but before Vasily could scramble away, Kezef crouched and pinned him with a knee to his groin. "We both know what you are. And when I fletch you, you'll prove it to me."

Silk raised the poker with a snarl. "Go fletch *yourself*."

Kezef smiled and straightened, leaving them without a backward glance.

Silk extended his hand, and Vasily took it, avoiding his eyes.

"Don't you listen to a word that vile creature uttered." Silk's voice was low as he led Vasily back into the dormitory, where the other boys were asleep. "Put it out of your mind."

Vasily shook his head. "You heard him. You saw."

"I saw a piece of filth assaulting you. Do you think he hasn't spent years practicing his technique of exploiting a boy's weakness to make him believe he deserves what's being done to him?"

"You don't understand."

"Don't I? Who do you think he practiced on?"

Vasily's chest tightened at the hard note in Silk's voice. "But I *am* a submissive. I—"

"What does that have to do with it? Do you think he cares? Your weakness isn't that you're a submissive, it's that you fear that submitting means you're weak. I dare say your Prince of Tricks would never think of you as weak. Has he ever said so?"

"You said he didn't love me."

"Oh, what the hell do I know?" Silk still held the poker, and he set it on the floor and leaned it against the wall. He studied Vasily silently for a moment, one foot propped beside the poker. "And if he doesn't, he's a bigger fool than he seems." He pushed away from the wall and caught Vasily's hair, draping it forward over one shoulder to tie it with the ribbon he'd rescued from the floor. His voice dropped to a bare whisper. "A demon would have to be blind and mad not to see what you're worth." Silk drew Vasily to him by the ponytail and kissed him, tentative and haunting, as if waiting to be rejected and scorned.

"Silk." He didn't want to hurt this beautiful boy, but he couldn't take advantage of him like this, regardless of whether Belphagor loved him or not. "You don't understand who I am." He pressed his brow against the dark head. "I've taken a glamour to make me look like a boy, but I'm not."

Silk's gray eyes flitted over Vasily's features. "You're a girl?"

Vasily laughed. "No, I mean, I'm older than I look."

Silk nodded. "So am I. No glamour. I just look young."

Vasily studied him, their faces still close. "How old *are* you?"

"Twenty-one."

"Holy shit." He pulled back in surprise.

Silk laughed softly. "Why? How old are you?"

"I'm not really sure, but I think . . . twenty, maybe."

Silk smiled. "I'm your elder, then. So shut up and kiss me." He curled his fingers in Vasily's hair and brought their mouths together again, his touch still soft and fluttery—like silk. Vasily closed his eyes and explored Silk's mouth, fascinated by the soft, yielding touch, the tongue teasing and dancing over his. So unlike Belphagor.

He drew back. "Silk, wait." Vasily shook his head. "I love him. It doesn't matter if he doesn't love me." He sucked in a sharp breath at the agonizing ways in which that wasn't true.

"And yet he left you here." Silk shook his head. "Left you to that swine." He traced Vasily's lips. "He left you with no one but me to take care of you, Ruby. And I will. By all the Heavens, I will." He kissed Vasily on the cheek and retreated to his bunk, leaving Vasily to stumble in the dark to his own, where he lay replaying the kiss, Kezef forgotten, until he drifted off to sleep.

Belphagor endured the jokes with a patient smile when he presented himself at the door of The Cat after returning from the Fletchery. The ladies there were well aware that their services weren't the sort he preferred.

He maintained his dignity, addressing the doorman. "I have business with Masha. Is she in?"

The half-clad ladies giggling at him in the entryway grew quiet.

"Is something wrong?"

"Madam Marina passed away a month ago."

"I'm so sorry." Belphagor slipped off the top hat he'd worn to dinner. "Who handles the household business now?"

"Madam Pharzuphova oversees the house, but it's owned by a private investor." It was code for angelic slumlord. *Damn it.* What had happened that Masha's property hadn't gone to Anzhela—and Anzhela herself had been traded as property?

He remembered the girl telling him the story of her mother's plight—owned first by Anzhela's father and then lost in a game of chance to another demon who'd killed the father in a duel over the right to keep her, prompting Masha to open The Cat for girls who would belong to no one but themselves. "Do you know where I might find Madam Marina's daughter?"

The doorman folded his arms, glancing back at the girls, who dispersed at his frown. "Koshka is employed by The Succubus." He spoke quietly and lowered his voice further. "But you didn't hear that here. The Cat is not in the habit of sending patrons to other brothels."

Belphagor donned his hat and tipped it toward the girls still huddled together in the interior doorway. "Thank you, my friend. You've been a great help."

It was too late to head to the opposite end of the district to inquire after Koshka. The Devil's Doorstep was best visited in company and early in the evening. And certainly not in tails and a top hat.

Instead, he dropped by in the morning before his meeting with Armen.

The Succubus was quiet at such an early hour but by no means empty. When Belphagor entered the parlor and asked for Koshka, he was taken without question to a room in back, dismayed to discover that a thin curtain divided the waiting area of the little room from where Koshka was currently engaged in business. He was privy to every thump of the wooden bed and every grunt and groan of effort and appreciation exchanged.

The demon who'd concluded his transaction opened the curtain still lacing his trousers, giving Belphagor an absent nod as he held the fabric aside. On the bed, Anzhela's mother lounged topless and mostly bottomless in a sort of garter belt and hose, her legs open and one leg in a high-laced ankle boot draped over the side, arms folded behind her head.

The slender strawberry blonde was as lovely as Anzhela, and in a purely abstract manner, Belphagor could appreciate the beauty of her form, but as always, the particulars of feminine attraction escaped him.

"Don't be shy, lover." Koshka rolled onto her side and propped herself on one elbow, patting the bed. "Come in and close the curtain." The little closet of space placed him right beside the bed as he pulled the curtain shut, and he jumped in surprise as she reached through his legs from behind and cupped his balls. "It's all right, sweetie," she said kindly. "I know all sorts of tricks to perk you up."

With a self-conscious cough into his fist, Belphagor extricated himself and stepped back against the curtain. "I'm not here as a client. But I'll pay for your time."

Koshka sat up, eyeing him with mistrust, and drew a chiffon robe around herself from the chair beside the bed, though the wispy fabric barely covered anything. "I don't need reforming, and I don't sell information."

"I'm a friend of Anzhela's."

The demoness shoved him with such unexpected ferocity as she jumped to her feet that Belphagor almost took the curtain down with him when he stumbled through it and grasped at it for balance. "You got what you wanted. You and your filthy fletchers can go to hell!"

Before he could respond, he was accosted by a thick-armed demon whose intention was clearly to hook one such arm around Belphagor's throat. Belphagor, however, had plenty of experience evading unwanted holds by larger demons. He tucked his chin against his chest, jabbed his elbow into the demon's solar plexus, and ducked out of the loosened grasp as the demon let out a hard grunt and stumbled onto one knee.

Whirling, Belphagor scrambled back onto the bed while another bouncer descended on him. "An *actual* friend!" He expelled the words toward Koshka with a kick of his feet to ward off the second assailant.

Koshka climbed over him and pinned his head back by the hair at his nape. "What 'friend'?"

"The Prince of Tricks."

Her grip on his hair loosened, and her expression went from fierce to surprised and a bit sad as she appraised him. "You're the demon who freed Tabris." She turned to face the bouncers, one dainty knee spearing him in the ribs. "It's all right. He's fine."

In the entrance, the two bouncers straightened their clothes and backed out with wary nods, the larger still red in the face and looking like he might vomit.

Koshka closed the curtain and swung her leg off Belphagor's chest. "Sorry. I thought . . . Sorry. You did a very kind thing, giving the reward you earned to Tabris after what she'd suffered."

"It was the least I could do." The young demoness had lost her sister and had been tortured nearly insensate by the Ophanim Guard because Belphagor had dragged the two women into his scheme.

Koshka studied him as he sat up. "Anzhela spoke very highly of you. I don't know my daughter well, but I know she's smarter than all the demons in Raqia and the supernal family put together."

The prefacing remark struck him as rather tragic. "I came to ask you what happened to her. I thought she was a free demoness, but I encountered her— Well, I believe you know where she is."

Koshka's look grew dark, her good opinion of him clearly evaporating. "You're a patron of that place."

"No," he assured her. "That is, in a manner of speaking, I have been of late, but only to gather information on its clientele. I find their practices repugnant."

She gave him a slow, guarded nod and sighed. "My mother intended for Anzhela to take her place when she retired, to own The Cat and take care of her girls."

"So Anzhela told me."

"But something happened to Masha. They tell me she was acting strangely before she took ill. And then she was gone, and they said The Cat didn't belong to her anymore. She'd sold it and Anyushka with it."

Koshka's face crumpled as she spoke her daughter's nickname. "She wouldn't have done that. She would never have done that."

Belphagor laid his hand lightly on hers, wanting to give comfort without giving offense.

Koshka wiped at her eyes. "I think they killed her."

"Killed her? Masha? Who killed her? How?"

She shook her head and turned her hand so their palms were together. "The investors who bought The Cat. Poisoned her, I think. They've forced the girls to pay a weekly fee to work there, and more for room and board." Her hand closed tightly around his with a sudden desperation. "Please. You have to help my Anyushka. I don't want this for her. It isn't right."

Belphagor squeezed her hand. "I'll do what I can."

By the time he arrived at the Demon Market for his appointed meeting with Armen, Belphagor had come to a decision. No amount of facets were worth continuing with this farce. There was clearly no missing nephew. And the information he'd already gathered was enough for Armen to go ahead with his plans for extortion. But Belphagor intended to put the Fletchery permanently out of business.

Although Armen didn't bother to pretend any longer about the imaginary nephew, he didn't take the news of Belphagor's intent well. "What weight will my demands for payment carry if the angels' temptation is gone?"

"They will still pay to keep what we know quiet." While they wandered the aisles of produce and sweets as if they were only there to shop, he handed Armen the paper on which he'd written the names and ranks of the angels he'd mingled with at dinner and afterward.

Armen wrinkled his brow. "What good is this?"

"Surely, you're joking. Two counts, three dukes, and a prince. I'd say they're good for a great deal."

"Yes, but what do you have on them?"

"What do I *have* on them? My testimony and the corroboration of two other witnesses that they engage in the practice of buying the sexual favors of underage demons."

"Did you actually witness them in flagrante, or were they simply enjoying the novelty of some youthful companionship at dinner?"

"I never said anything about dinner." Belphagor glared at him over the melon he was testing for ripeness. "You've already spoken to Mikhail."

Armen tucked the paper into his shirt pocket. "If perching a boy on one's lap and feeding him croquettes is sufficient to ruin a reputation, I dare say yours is as tarnished as anyone's at that table."

"*Poshël na khui.*"

"I've no interest in your *khui*—nor anyone else's—as you're well aware. I am, however, interested in where those counts, dukes, and a prince are putting theirs. Once you can be certain they've put them where they shouldn't, I'll have enough to persuade them to part with some of their celestial bounty to keep the knowledge quiet. After that, if you feel the need to break up the party, by all means. We'll have to assure them that their names will be kept well out of it so long as they continue to provide their insurance premiums, but it must be the act of fletching itself we hold over them. Nothing less."

Belphagor nearly squashed the fruit in his hand. "The only way I can be certain is to watch them do it. I will not be a party to that. You can keep your damned facets."

"It's not the only way." Armen paused to make a purchase before he continued. "If we know *whose* feathers they've fluffed, we will have the ammunition we need."

"You expect Vasily and Khai to take it that far."

"As far as they possibly can. I thought that was what they specialized in, after all."

Belphagor ground his teeth. "I won't ask Vasily to do that."

"Then I take it you don't care if Khai shares the significance of your ink with your boy." Armen gave him a dark smile. "Or have you forgotten my promise?"

Belphagor's chest tightened. "You have no knowledge of my past, no proof of what you presume to be true, only speculation based on rumor and innuendo. Whatever claims you care to make about me are just that."

"Ah, but *you* know the truth. You know what you were. Do you really want your boy to hear the stories? Even if you deny them, the images will be in his head. How do you think he'll look at you the next time you raise your strop to discipline him? Do you imagine you'll still have his respect—let alone his fear?"

The stalls in the marketplace had begun to feel small and tight as if they were closing in on him.

Armen, damn him, dared to feign a look of compassion. "It really isn't asking all that much. Your boy is a professional, after all. Let him decide for himself whether to close the deal. Khai has it on good authority that one of the angels you dined with last evening has negotiated for Vasily's fletching. All he has to do is say yes." Armen began to peruse a cart of apples as if the matter were settled. "Khai himself is perfectly willing, but he says you've put an exclusive reservation on him. You'll need to relinquish that so he can finish the seduction he says he's engaged in with not one but two of the dukes. With Vasily's angel, that would give us three of your six."

"*No.*"

Armen shrugged. "Or assist one of the other three with buggering some innocent. It's up to you."

"You son of a bitch."

"Leave it up to your boy, Belphagor." Armen patted him on the cheek, and Belphagor struck him away, barely restraining himself from taking him down right there in the market. "Let him decide. And don't forget to free up Khai's virtue."

In the morning, Silk made no mention of what had happened between them, but after Vasily endured the morning ritual and the first group of boys had been sent on their way, Silk approached him with a sly smile.

"Ruby. Just the boy I wanted to see. I spoke with Raum and told him Kezef was pursuing unwanted contact with you after you'd turned down his advances. He's no longer permitted to purchase any of your services."

Vasily regarded him with surprise and relief. "You did? Thank you, Silk."

"I told you I'd take care of you." Silk turned Vasily about to straighten his bow. "I take care of all my boys." He set his hands on Vasily's shoulders. "You're up next. Don't forget: You come to me if anyone bothers you. You're not obliged to take any offers, not even to grant a patron a sample if you don't feel comfortable. And Ruby?" He leaned closer and spoke at Vasily's ear. "Your prince is in the salon. Ignore him."

Vasily managed to keep from looking at Belphagor when he entered the room, but the bastard was impossible to ignore. And, for a change, Belphagor wasn't ignoring *him*. Vasily slipped inside his niche and had barely sat down before the curtain parted to reveal the Prince of Tricks. Belphagor drew the curtain shut and took a step toward him to pull Vasily into his arms, but Vasily ducked away from him with a fiery glower.

Belphagor frowned and crossed his arms over his chest as if he needed something to do with them. "Vasya. You know my indifference to you last night was only part of the act."

"And I suppose your tongue down Khai's pants was an act too."

"It was not down his pants."

"Oh, sorry. I couldn't exactly see once your head went below the table. I was on my *knees*."

"Vasya, you agreed to do this. You've had the power to stop it at any moment with a word. Do you want to use it?"

Tears prickled behind Vasily's eyes. He'd never felt so powerless in his life. But he *had* agreed, and Belphagor was in some kind of mess that had forced him into this game. That much was clear.

Vasily sighed, echoing Belphagor's physical stance. "No. No, I'll do it." Was it his imagination, or did Belphagor look almost disappointed in that answer?

"You know you're still my *mal'chik*."

Vasily flinched slightly as Belphagor reached to touch the choker around his neck.

The rough fingers brushed beneath it over the place where the spiked bar ought to be. "*Mine*." Belphagor's jaw was tight. "I don't want you to accept any more engagements with that Kezef."

The memory of Kezef humiliating him at the dinner while Belphagor simply watched stung like a straight razor cutting into his flesh. "I thought I was supposed to be playing the part."

"Play it with someone else."

It struck him then that Belphagor was jealous. Belphagor had watched another demon enjoying the pleasure that ought to be his. He knew that wasn't entirely fair. Belphagor derived pleasure out of making Vasily admit he desired what he professed to hate, and there had been nothing in the interaction between him and Kezef that had remotely kindled Vasily's desire. Nor had Kezef wanted his desire. There was something cold and calculating about the pleasure he took, as if he enjoyed it all the more knowing Vasily wanted none of it.

Still, Belphagor was possessive. *Mine.* Someone else had touched and enjoyed what was his, and he couldn't stand it—unless Belphagor gave Vasily to someone else to be used for his own amusement; then Vasily was fair game.

"It's not exactly up to me, is it, Bel?" He could see Belphagor didn't care for the footing Vasily had put them on by using the nickname—not *Beli*, which meant *I love you*, and not *ser*, which meant so much more—just Bel, like any friend or acquaintance might call him.

"I understand one of the angels intends to put in a bid for your virtue." Belphagor spoke sharply, as if this simple fact beyond Vasily's control were Vasily's fault. "If you accept, it gives us the leverage we need to finish this and get out of here."

"What leverage? What are you talking about?"

"I won't ask you to do it. It's your choice."

"My choice? Before we arrived here, you said you didn't want me being fucked by one of them. Now you do, and it's my choice?"

Belphagor uncrossed his arms, his fists clenched. "I *don't*. I want this over with. I want you out of here."

Vasily regarded him stonily. "So you want to put the responsibility on me so you can feel like you didn't pimp me out, is that it?"

Belphagor made a strange sound in his throat as if Vasily had knocked the wind out of him. Because Vasily was right. *Son of a bitch.*

"Well, don't worry about it, Belphagor. It's all on me. I'll get your 'leverage.' I'll be your *whore*."

"Vasya—"

"Time's up, sir." The sommelier was at the curtain. He drew it aside and gave Belphagor an uncompromising jerk of his head toward the salon. They had apparently missed the more subtle cues that they'd gone over the allowance for sampling.

Belphagor stepped through and then turned back, his face twisted with conflict. "Say the word, Vasya." Their disagreement had apparently so flustered him he'd forgotten he shouldn't be using Vasily's name.

The sommelier stepped between them and put his hand out flat in front of Belphagor. "Other patrons are waiting. You're done."

"*Say* it."

Vasily narrowed his eyes, letting the heat of his fire flare visibly. "*Nyet. Ser.*"

As Belphagor had predicted, Count Salmay, one of the angels they'd dined with the previous evening, offered for Vasily that afternoon. Like most angels of the nobility, he was handsome in a somewhat sterile way, like a too-perfect painting or an unsettlingly lifelike sculpture one had to touch to be certain it wasn't animate. It wouldn't be a particular hardship to let him take Vasily's imaginary virginity. Salmay was polite and considerate, asking permission to touch while they sat together in the little booth, kissing Vasily's neck and murmuring endearments in his effort to coax Vasily's consent from him.

If Vasily went through with it, Belphagor had said, they could be done with this misbegotten game. He agreed, and Salmay lifted his chin and kissed him on the lips as if Vasily had granted him a great honor. Such solicitous treatment of a demon whore by an angel of the blood ought to have been a warning that something was amiss.

Silk bathed Vasily and dressed him in a special uniform, a robe somewhat like Silk's own, but with short cap sleeves. Elaborate pearl buttons and clasps decorated the front, and beneath it, the same loose pants the boys customarily wore, except this pair was made of lustrous satin like the robe—all in white, as if the boy were a bride being presented to a victorious groom for the consummation of his wedding night.

"I suppose I don't have to tell you what I usually tell the boys." Silk brushed Vasily's cheeks and lips with a ruby stain to match his name. "But you might want to give the impression that you're a little anxious and unsure of what's about to happen. And when he takes you, don't make it too easy. Let him think it hurts."

"I think I vaguely recall the experience."

Silk smiled and then gave him a wistful sigh.

"What?"

"You'll be leaving after. They always do. The patrons here come for the express purpose of being the first. They don't want seconds."

"Yes, I'm well aware. Don't worry. I won't let on I'm used goods."

"No. Ruby . . . that wasn't what I meant." Silk's expression was wounded. "I just wish you'd held out a little longer." He screwed the lid onto the tin of stain, staring down at it. "I'm going to miss you."

"Oh." Vasily blushed as if he were a virginal bride after all. He tried to think of something to say. It wasn't as if he could tell Silk to look him up at The Brimstone; Silk was virtually a prisoner here.

Leaning close to Vasily with his hands on the crocheted collar as if to adjust it, Silk pressed his lips to Vasily's throat. "Have fun." He smiled as he raised his head, though his eyes were bright. "Maybe you can tell me all about it after. If you want. If you come back late, you can slip over to my bunk and wake me."

Vasily returned the smile warmly. "I'd like that."

An attendant escorted him to the upstairs receiving room, where Count Salmay waited.

The count rose from his seat with an eager smile and took Vasily's hand. "Lovely Ruby. You look sweet enough to eat." He winked and led Vasily through a door in the back of the room into a dimly lit corridor where large curtained alcoves were spaciously arranged for privacy. The sounds of varying degrees of intimacy came from behind the curtains as they passed.

They entered the innermost of these rooms, and Salmay closed the curtain and led Vasily to the bed, directing him gently onto his back. "Just relax." He worked his hands down the buttons of Vasily's robe. Vasily closed his eyes, doing his best to tremble a bit as Salmay undressed him. But as the count's hands stroked his bared skin, another hand—a *third* hand—cupped Vasily's cheek.

His eyes flew open, and he stared up into the laughing amber gaze of Kezef. Before Vasily could scramble away, Kezef's hand closed around his throat and pinned him to the bed.

"Did you really think I wouldn't have you? That a few words from your precious nanny, Silk, would matter?"

Count Salmay stood off to the side watching, his lip curled in contempt, no longer playing the part of the enamored, solicitous patron. "I'll take my facets now, demon. Do what you like with the boy."

Kezef let go of Vasily for a moment to untie the purse at his hip, and Vasily vaulted past him over the bed, bolting for the exit. The speed and viciousness with which Kezef hauled him back was dizzying. The tall demon tossed him against the wall, and Vasily grabbed for the table of oils and implements beside the bed to steady himself, but his momentum took the table down with him. He wasn't used to being so slight and tossable, and he sprawled in the wreckage with a groan. The glamour had taken all his strength and muscle with it.

With a swift, efficient motion, Kezef retrieved a leather strap from a hook on the wall above the bed and belted Vasily in the side of the head with it as he tried to scramble up. It set Vasily's ear ringing, blood dripping from it onto the pristine white costume, as he crawled disoriented toward what he thought was the exit but turned out to be a corner, where he was hopelessly trapped.

"Take your damned facets," he heard Kezef say through the muffled ringing. Kezef tossed the purse to Salmay, who spared Vasily a look of mild concern before leaving with a shrug. Vasily's vision blurred as Kezef walked toward him in no apparent hurry and stood over him.

"I see your training has been utterly neglected. You are to kneel in supplication before your master, eager to take what you have coming. You do not cower and whimper like an ignorant whore's whelp."

The strap sang through the air and struck Vasily's shoulder with the sting of a red-hot iron. "Up on your knees, boy."

Gasping at the pain, Vasily complied.

"Better. But not the proper attitude." He struck again, and Vasily couldn't suppress a cry. "Nose to the floor."

Vasily obeyed, unable to concentrate on anything but the stinging agony of the strap. He stared at Kezef's boots before him.

"I will teach you to grovel and beg to be put in your proper place." Kezef's voice was calm and cold. "Before I'm done with you, you will plead with me to be used and degraded. That is the purpose of a demon like you. To provide pleasure through your debasement. Nothing more." He crouched in front of Vasily and propped his chin up with the edge of the strap. "Is that not how your Belphagor used you?" Kezef smiled. "I could see from the moment he arrived with you that you were no innocent. I could have informed the proprietor, but I held my tongue, because as amusing as it is to corrupt the chaste, I find it eminently more satisfying to hear little whores like you admit what they are, beg for what they deserve, and weep with gratitude when they have been reduced to their true natures. Which is what you will do." Kezef rose. "Tell me."

Vasily cried out again as the strap cut into his shoulder.

"What are you?"

"Fuck you." It wasn't defiance so much as an uncontrollable response to the pain. He braced himself for the strap to fall again.

"Get the hell away from him!" Silk's voice from the doorway nearly made him weep.

Breathing out the tight coil of tension that gripped his entire body, Vasily raised his eyes, trying to focus through the burning sweat of his element. But his relief was short lived. Kezef had whirled on Silk, beating him back with the strap in a stunning succession of rapid-fire back and forehand strokes.

Silk stumbled onto one knee. "Go, Ruby!" He groaned under the blows raining down on him. "Get out!"

CHAPTER FIVE

Vasily scrambled to his feet and hurtled past Kezef through the curtain, tangling himself in it and yanking it free from the rod while he continued to run. Patrons and boys peered out of their alcoves as he shouted for help, but they ducked back inside and closed their curtains when he neared them.

"He'll kill him! He'll kill Silk! Somebody help!" Tears of anger poured down his cheeks, his body shaking with delayed fright. If only he had the reversal spell for the glamour, he'd beat the shit out of Kezef himself. Why the fuck wouldn't anyone help?

At the end of the hall, he ran straight into Khai, who grabbed him as he tried to flee past him.

"Let go of me, damn you!" Vasily struggled with him, but the burning sting of the stripes Kezef had cut into his shoulder made it difficult to exert what strength he had, and Khai was determined.

"Vasily." Khai hissed his name, despite the risk of discovery by the patrons in the waiting room. "I don't have time to argue with you. Come with me. Quickly." He spun about and propelled Vasily toward the staircase with him.

Vasily tried to pull away. "He's beating Silk. Someone has to help him!"

"Shut up and keep moving. You can't help Silk. The other patrons won't interfere, and management will turn a blind eye." Khai clutched his hand and ran with him down the stairs, bypassing the corridor to the dormitories and heading straight for the front of the establishment.

Vasily stumbled with him in bewilderment. "What are you doing?"

"Getting the hell out of here." Khai burst through the salon into the entry hall, while patrons gaped at them but made no move to stop them. Apparently, no one had ever tried to make a break for it. For the young demons with no future sold to the Fletchery, what would have been the point?

In a moment, they were on the street, conspicuous in their satin whites. Vasily had only just noticed Khai was dressed for his fletching as well.

He tugged back on Khai's hand. "I can't leave Silk—"

"You *will* leave him. You've left him. It's over by now. He took the beating to give you time to get out."

"How the hell do you know what he did?" Vasily yanked himself free. "You could have helped me. We could have fought Kezef off!"

Khai turned and kept walking swiftly. "We have the bodies of youths at the moment, you fool. Kezef is built like you when you're not stuck in this glamour. He'd have snapped both our necks. And I promised Belphagor I'd make sure nothing happened to you."

"*You* promised Belphagor?" Vasily hurried after him. "When did you promise Belphagor anything?"

"This morning after he met with you. He had to formally relinquish the reservation on me so I could bed the two dukes. He said you were going to take the offer from Count Salmay, and he wanted me to keep an eye on you and see that you weren't coerced into anything against your will." Khai slowed a bit and glanced over at him. "I was in the next alcove reclining with my satisfied patrons when I heard the trouble. I ran for Silk because I knew no one else was going to help. He said he'd keep Kezef occupied while we got out."

"*Occupied*?" Vasily slashed at a hot tear. "He was beating him half to death."

"Silk knew what he was getting into. He's grown up in the Fletchery. They use him to keep the boys in line. He pretends to be younger than he is, since he's got that angelic face, so the boys will trust him."

"He told me the management thought he was younger."

"Oh, I'm sure they know how old he is. They're the ones who've kept him on all these years after he earned his feathers. His presence calms the boys because they feel safe with him. They think he's one of them."

"How do you know all this?"

Khai shrugged. "I'm observant. And I flirt with the attendants. We were there for information, after all. Or did you think you were there to get your wings?"

Vasily scowled. "Very funny. And for your information, I've already gotten my *actual* wings. I've flown. In the world of Man."

Khai glanced at him, impressed. "You have? There are real wings?"

"Incredibly real." He sighed at the memory of his manifest radiance carrying him over the early morning skies of a Russian village on feathers of flame. But the pleasure of the memory was tainted by his worry for Silk. Even if every word out of Silk's mouth had been a lie, he'd thrown himself on the mercy of Kezef—a demon for whom the concept was clearly meaningless—to save Vasily.

They were getting strange looks from people on the street. Khai turned down an alley. "Come on. We need to get out of these doll clothes."

"We need to get out of these glamours," Vasily growled. "I've had my fill of reliving my youth."

Khai scrambled up onto a wall behind a laundress's cottage and grabbed a set of workmen's clothes for each of them, oversized but far less conspicuous, and they tossed their satin costumes up onto the line as compensation for the laundress. The fine fabric would net her more at the Demon Market than the facets she lost on the missing clothes.

Vasily forgot he was still wearing the scarlet ribbon in his hair until Khai pulled it out as if to toss it away. Vasily grabbed it back and tucked it into his pocket.

They made their way through the Demon District, the dirt and cobblestones rough on their glamoured feet, until they reached The Brimstone. In appearance, they were too young to enter on their own, but Khai managed to persuade the bartender at the back door that Belphagor owed him money, while Vasily hung back out of sight.

"That'll be great for Bel's reputation."

Khai shrugged. "Well, you needn't worry about me making it worse. I have no intention of spreading any stories about his tattoos."

"His tattoos? What about them? What are you talking about?"

"What they mean."

Vasily narrowed his eyes. "*What* do they mean?"

"You really don't know?" Khai grimaced as if he'd betrayed a confidence. A confidence it seemed Belphagor was more than happy to share with a rentboy he barely knew before he'd ever deign to tell Vasily. Or maybe Belphagor knew Khai better than he'd let on.

"Belphagor is a very private person." The words sounded like bullshit as they left Vasily's mouth. His cheeks went warm.

Khai shifted his weight, displaying a sudden interest in his own feet. "It's none of my business, but maybe you should ask him sometime. About the red crown in particular."

Before Vasily could say anything else, the bartender returned with the news that Belphagor wasn't around. Time to come clean.

"Oza, it's me." He stepped out of the shadows. "It's Vasily. I'm glamoured, and I need to get inside and take the reversal. Don't ask," he added as Oza gaped at him.

The bartender shook his head and let them in with a sigh. Belphagor had rigged the door to their room with a magical lock that responded to Vasily's touch as well as to Belphagor's, and luckily, the lock recognized his smaller, smoother hand as his own.

Inside, he collapsed onto the stool at the vanity, glad to be home but numb from the shock of their flight.

Khai dipped a cloth into the water in the basin and dabbed it against Vasily's ear. "Don't dwell on Silk." He rubbed at the dried blood. "He can take care of himself."

"The hell he can." Vasily grabbed the cloth and pulled off his stolen shirt with a hiss of pain. "Do you see this?" He nodded at his shoulder, already violently discolored around the red stripe. "He hit me three times, Khai. I nearly passed out. I can take pain, but I've never felt anything like that." He touched the cloth to it and grimaced. "I heard no less than eight blows before I fled, and they happened in seconds."

"We had to go. You understand that."

The latch lifted on the door, and Belphagor entered, stopping still when he saw them, his gaze flitting only briefly over Khai and landing on Vasily. "*Moi mal'chik.* How did you get here?" He went down on one knee in front of the chair, lifting the cloth from where Vasily was pressing it. "What did they do to you?"

"Kezef," said Khai.

Belphagor's fist closed around the cloth, and his coal eyes seemed to go darker. "Give me the tinder box behind you." When Khai handed him the box, Belphagor popped it open and took out a tiny pill. "Open your mouth, *mal'chik*."

Vasily wasn't sure how he felt about Belphagor giving him orders right now. Or calling him *boy*. Or seeming to give a shit. His head hurt like mad and his shoulder and back were throbbing, and he thought maybe he was going to be sick. He opened his mouth and let Belphagor put the pill on his tongue.

"Swallow. It's the de-glamour." He handed the box back to Khai. "There's one for you."

Vasily swallowed and felt a rush of blood that seemed to flow outward to his extremities—all of them, unfortunately, though he was in no way aroused. He gripped the edge of the chair and watched his hands and arms turn sinewy and hard like they ought to be, the downy blond hairs on his arms becoming reddish and coarse.

"Move," he managed, before lunging forward and vomiting between Belphagor's feet.

Khai, looking like his usual self, stumbled onto the bed with his hand on his stomach but managed to keep his breakfast down.

After calmly wiping up the mess and wringing out the cloth in the chamber pot, Belphagor returned to Vasily's side with a fresh towel to wipe his mouth and beard. His beard. *Thank Heaven*. He had a beard.

"*Mal'chik*."

"Stop calling me that." He was gratified to hear his own deep, gravelly voice. Something was tight around his throat, and he reached up to discover he still wore the crocheted collar. Before he could untie it, Belphagor had taken a knife from his boot and slid it under the threads, slicing outward with an angry jerk. The collar came away in Vasily's hand, and he felt the spiked finials of the jewelry knotted inside it against his thumb. He tucked the collar into his pocket next to the scarlet ribbon.

Belphagor rose, gaze pointed toward the floor as if he weren't seeing it. "Khai, would you mind reporting back to Armen that his little venture has capsized? And let him know that you and he can make public whatever knowledge you like about me. I'm done."

"Don't fret." Khai stood and went to the door. "I'm done too. You won't hear anything more from me on the subject."

Belphagor nodded, still staring at the floor, and Khai took his leave. After a long silence, Belphagor glanced up at Vasily. "Why did you accept an offer from Kezef?"

Vasily blinked at him coolly, no fire left in him. "I didn't. I accepted Count Salmay's offer. Kezef was waiting in the room for me. He'd bribed Salmay."

Belphagor's face twisted with a blend of fury and anguish, and he crouched before the chair. "I'm so sorry. My sweet boy—"

"Don't." Vasily shook his head. "I don't want you to call me that anymore."

"Vasya." Belphagor looked almost helpless as he searched Vasily's eyes. "I realize the connotations—"

"It isn't that. It isn't because of Kezef or how anyone treated me there." His voice was rougher than usual, and he cleared his throat. "I don't think I can be that for you any longer. It requires trust, and . . ."

"You don't trust me?" Belphagor's face was ashen.

"You hurt me, Belphagor." Vasily closed his eyes to stop seeing the expression in Belphagor's. "And you didn't ask me if I wanted to be hurt like that. No more than Kezef did."

"*Vasya.*" There were tears in Belphagor's eyes when Vasily opened his. Now Vasily had hurt him. But it was true. "Are you— Will you leave?" His voice broke on the last word.

Vasily looked away. He couldn't imagine leaving, couldn't imagine being without Belphagor. But things couldn't be the way they'd been. "No." He shook his head. "No, I'm not leaving you, Beli."

Belphagor melted against him, head buried in his arms in Vasily's lap. He could see Belphagor was lost, knowing he'd fucked up and not knowing how to deal with it. Before, Vasily would have taken his punishment for him. A part of him wished he could now. But maybe it was time Belphagor learned to really feel what he'd done and not use their arrangement to behave however he liked, knowing his transgressions were the ultimate foreplay.

After a moment, Belphagor lifted his head with a brusque nod as if he'd come to the same conclusion. "I'll go empty the pot. And then we'll tend to those wounds."

"Belphagor." Vasily spoke the word as Belphagor picked up the chamber pot and headed for the door. "There was a boy at the Fletchery—not a boy, really, but a sort of caretaker for the others; he pretends to be younger than he is. Anyway, he's the reason I escaped Kezef. He and Khai. Khai went to get him when he heard what was happening, and Silk came and put himself in front of Kezef's strap to give me a chance to run." He swallowed. "I left him there. I don't know if he's dead or alive. I feel like I have to try to help him if I can."

"Silk?"

"That's his name."

Belphagor nodded. "I've already begun working on a plan to bring down the Fletchery permanently. We'll get your friend out of there. And Anzhela. And the rest. I promise."

Belphagor had made promises before, but these he was determined to keep. He tried to focus on his plans as Vasily submitted to his ministrations and let him clean the wounds. The marks Kezef had left were part burn, part deep cut, as if Kezef had swung the strap on an angle with a powerful, swift thrust like he was wielding a sword—or a machete.

Bruises were spreading outward on the ruddy flesh, demonstrating how much force the sadistic son of a bitch had used. Belphagor had never felt so angry or powerless. At least, not in many years. And not on another's behalf.

Knowing this was his fault, that he'd put Vasily in that place . . . He didn't know how he was going to cope with that. He felt wretched, and there was no way to remedy it. No way to go back and undo those moments that had cost him his boy's trust. Except Vasily wasn't Belphagor's boy anymore, he reminded himself.

He persuaded Vasily to lie down, propping pillows behind him against the wall so Vasily could lie on the side Kezef hadn't touched, and laid a blanket over him. In minutes, Vasily was asleep. He wasn't sure Vasily would want to sleep with him, but he needed to be near him. It was only eight o'clock in the evening, but he climbed carefully under the blanket and turned on his side as well, facing Vasily.

He watched him, aching, feeling there was a chasm between them he might never be allowed to cross again.

In the morning, he was on his other side, facing the room, Vasily's comforting heat radiating against his back. Belphagor had barely been able to sleep without him the past few nights, and for a moment he forgot about the chasm and felt immensely right to have his boy back with him. Until the word *boy* nagged at his memory and Vasily's words came back to him: *"I don't think I can be that for you any longer. It requires trust."*

He slipped out of bed as quietly as he'd slipped into it. As usual, Vasily had thrown off the blanket in the night. It almost hurt to look at him in his gruff and glorious beauty. Belphagor wanted to taste the full lips and feel the rough patch of beard against his cheeks. To run his tongue over the exposed flesh from the Adam's apple to the trail of burnished hair that disappeared into the pants that hadn't been meant for a demon of his size and barely reached his hips. He wanted to pull the pants down and release Vasily's inevitable morning erection among the red-gold curls to taste his smoky heat.

Or, hell, just curl up in his arms and hold him close. His Vasya. His demon. He was those things still, wasn't he? He'd said he wouldn't leave.

Belphagor busied himself with shaving and getting dressed. If he was going to deal with the Fletchery, he'd have to appear as respectable as possible. He'd never done what he was about to do—turn demons over to angelic authorities. But, of course, he was also turning in angels. Which was the only reason the Elysian gendarmes might bother to look into it. They weren't otherwise likely to care about underage peasant whores.

And, in truth, Belphagor himself had never given it much thought. He'd *been* an underage whore. But no one had sold him. He'd been a free demon who'd chosen to make a business out of something he already found pleasurable. At fifteen, he'd considered himself an entrepreneur—and certainly hadn't considered himself a child.

But the roost at the Fletchery had no choice in the matter. By design, they had never experienced their own sexual awakening even insomuch as to determine what direction their own attractions lay. And by and large, they were too young to do so.

He knew Vasily had begun his career at a similar age, but he didn't like to think of it. Belphagor had already been a hustler at the Demon Market, taking facets from boys and grown demons alike in street games of dice and chance, long before he chose to sell his charms. But Vasily had a kind of eternal naïveté about him that suggested he'd been managed by someone who had profited from keeping him sheltered.

At the time they'd met, when Vasily had been a lanky, angry eighteen-year-old trying to pick Belphagor's pocket, there'd still been a startling sweetness to him, an innocence that made him seem younger than he was. And as he'd matured, swiftly developing into his current imposing physique, that innocent quality had remained, somehow unspoiled by whatever life had handed him.

But regardless of Vasily's history or his own, Belphagor intended to put the Fletchery out of business—one way or another. If the Ophanim chose to look the other way after he turned the place in, he'd buy them out, down to the last child. He didn't like to let on that he had such funds. He lived simply at The Brimstone to avoid attention. But decades of being the best wingcasting player in Raqia had left him with more than a reputation.

Occasionally, he had to put on a show of gambling recklessly while over-imbibing on demon ale or contraband vodka from the world of Man. These spectacular losses not only gave rise to speculation that he'd gambled away everything he'd ever earned, but it gave challengers hope that they might be the one to knock him off his winner's pedestal. Otherwise, who would play him?

"You should wear one of the stiff white collars with that." Vasily spoke behind him as Belphagor buttoned his coat.

He turned his head halfway, still buttoning, not wanting to reveal how the sound of Vasily speaking to him made his pulse quicken. Vasily watched him, propped on one elbow.

"Sorry?"

"Instead of a cravat. That tailored coat looks better with a high collar under the chin." Vasily rose and took one of the collars in question from the top drawer of the wardrobe and tucked it inside the linen shirt while standing behind Belphagor. "Maybe a nice brooch to attach it." His warm breath tickled Belphagor's ear. "Where are you going?"

Belphagor straightened the collar, and his fingers brushed Vasily's before they pulled away. "To get my ass kicked by Ophanim, most likely."

"To what?" Vasily scowled at him in the mirror. "What are you up to now?"

"I'm going to find myself some officers of the Supernal Guard and give them the names of the angels I observed at the Fletchery. After which time, if I'm still capable of demon speech, I intend to lead the Ophanim to its current locale."

"Are you out of your mind?"

"Frequently." Belphagor turned to face him. "How—" He paused, as always somewhat startled at how much he had to look up. "How else do you think I'm going to be able to get the place shut down, *mal*—" He swallowed the word and turned back to the vanity to find an appropriate brooch in the jewelry box.

"It doesn't mean I don't love you."

The quiet growl nearly did him in, and Belphagor gripped the edges of the vanity and took a breath. "Vasya." He exhaled, meeting Vasily's eyes in the mirror, and his gaze traveled over the hard chest to the tight, low-slung pants. "For the love of Heaven. Put on some proper clothes." He hadn't meant to say that. He'd meant to open his mouth and try to express how much he'd needed to hear those words, that he'd thought until Vasily said them that he might be dying.

Vasily whirled about and stripped off the pants, snarling the tangled lines connecting Belphagor's head, heart, and cock even further with the view of his tight ass as he jerked open the drawers behind the curtain and rummaged for something to wear.

Belphagor forced himself to stop looking in the mirror, finishing with his brooch and cuff links without consulting his reflection. What was he supposed to do? How the hell was he going to make this better?

When he turned around and found Vasily tucking a tight black T-shirt into the steel-gray utility pants Belphagor had bought him when they were in Moscow, he realized it didn't matter whether

Vasily was dressed to the nines or stark naked. Every inch of him, maddeningly clothed or temptingly revealed, made Belphagor crazy with desire.

"What?" Vasily's growl was like an aphrodisiac. "You have a problem with this outfit?"

"No." He drove his fingers through his hair between the freshly waxed spikes. "Yes."

"What the fuck does that mean?"

"It means you're making me crazy. And I'm not mad at you or blaming you. I'm not. I know I did this. But I don't know how to *do* this." He tugged at his hair. "I'm tearing my own hair out because I don't know how stop myself from grabbing yours and pulling you down to your knees."

Vasily folded his blasted brutish arms over his infuriatingly hard chest. "I don't know what to tell you, Belphagor."

"Well, that makes two of us, because I don't know what to tell me either. Do you want me to touch you? At all? Are you— Am I— I don't— *Fuck*."

Vasily's arms slowly unfolded, and he stuffed his hands into his pockets. "I just want you to give me some time. Some space."

Time and space. That wasn't so much. But it was everything, wasn't it?

Belphagor nodded and swallowed the madness and heartache. "Okay." He finished buttoning his coat. "Let me go do what I need to do, and then when you want to talk—*if* you want to—we'll talk. Or we won't. Whatever you need."

"I'm coming with you."

"No, you're not." He held up his hand at Vasily's look of outrage. "I'm not giving you orders. It won't work if they see you. I'm going for a certain angle here. It's mental wingcasting. Please, Vasya—trust me a little."

Vasily sat on the bed, his mouth set in a tight line, and nodded.

As Belphagor passed through the gaming room on his way to the front of The Brimstone, a chorus of insults and compliments on his attire greeted him—the determining factor between one or the other being how recently or frequently he'd beaten the demon in question at cards. He bowed at both, tugging on the points of his collar, and mounted the steps that led to the street.

The door opened before he reached it, and Armen stepped in. "Well, if it isn't the *Pidor* of Purgatory."

Belphagor's polite smile died on his face. The word was a Russian slur that equated homosexuality with pederasty. He clenched his fists but considered that bloodying them would mess up his meticulous presentation.

"Get the hell out of my way, Armen."

"We had a deal."

"And you have your names. Khai supplied you with positive identification of three who purchased the virtue of demon boys."

"He provided two. Your little *blyad'* failed to consummate."

Belphagor climbed the final step, putting himself within inches of Armen's face. "Fortunately for you, I don't have time to give you a lesson in respect. But I will be contemplating how to deliver that lesson while I'm directing the Ophanim Guard to the Fletchery to shut their shit down."

Armen gave him a cold smile. "If you fuck up what I've got going, I will fuck up your life in ways you never dreamed."

"What you have going?" Unable to restrain himself, Belphagor shoved Armen back through the door so hard he knocked him on his ass. "What you have going," he snarled, "is profiting at the expense of child sex slaves." Though he'd tried to keep his volume down, several patrons near the door turned and stared.

Armen jumped to his feet, his face blazing. "You dare to impugn me? *You*, who are a known member of the Fletchery?" Armen's voice carried on purpose.

Belphagor realized the extent of his mistake in playing this game on Armen's terms. But it was immaterial. He would do what he'd set out to.

"I suggest, Armen, that you run along and collect what blackmail you can, because the Fletchery will be out of business before the day is out."

"And you will be out of business in Raqia. You may have convinced that sissy Khai to hold his tongue about your past, but I will ruin your present. Mark my words."

There was no point in continuing to engage with him. Belphagor was only wasting valuable time.

He set out on his mission to find a squad of officers in the Supernal Army with whom to negotiate with the Ophan. He wasn't fool enough to think angels of elemental fire would listen to a demon thief. He was taking a gamble that the angels he encountered wouldn't be patrons of the Fletchery themselves, though from what he'd seen, the supernal officers were more likely to solicit the comparatively adult companionship to be found in the Market.

It was the older, more privileged class of archangels who seemed to favor the sort of complete control an inexperienced youth afforded them. The archangelic Malakim Belphagor had known in the world of Man were a prime example. Like this Silk that Vasily spoke of, Belphagor had played younger than his years as a matter of survival when he'd found himself in the Malakim's snare.

There were fewer supernal officers about since the scandal of Duke Elyon's downfall and his exposure as a traitor to the crown. Belphagor found himself crossing the Palace Bridge over the Acheron and heading into the Left Bank before he encountered any. His presence was immediately spotted once he had. Demons were as unwelcome in the bohemian quarter these days as anywhere in Elysium proper.

As Belphagor approached a pair seated outside a sidewalk café, one of the officers rose. "Halt, demon. State your business."

"I came to report a crime."

His words were met with laughter.

"You hear that, Erel?" The officer nudged his companion. "This fine gentleman has come to report a crime." The angel looked him over. "Well? What did you do? Steal those clothes?"

"The crime isn't my own." Belphagor kept his voice calm. "I have information on an establishment trading in the corruption of children."

The smiles disappeared from their faces, and Erel rose and stepped into Belphagor's space. "You listen to me, you filthy incubus. We're not interested in your trade. How dare you present yourself to officers of the Supernal Army with such a proposition?"

Belphagor rolled his eyes. "I'm not offering, you halfwit. I'm requesting that the Supernal Guard be dispatched to shut the place down. I can provide you with the names of its patrons, their recent activities, and the location of the domicile in which the children are being kept." In retrospect, he probably should have avoided the dig on the angel's intelligence, but his patience was wearing thin.

Erel glared at him. "If it's a demon establishment and demon children, it's for demons to deal with."

"Even if it's angelic nobles who patronize it?"

The two officers exchanged glances. "That's a slanderous statement unless you have proof."

"I have witnesses."

"Demon witnesses."

Belphagor inclined his head. He'd been afraid it might come down to this. He held out a folded bit of parchment. "Perhaps you could give the address to the Ophanim patrol. I'm sure they'll find enough Union of Liberation sympathizers among the patrons to warrant a raid."

The officer took it with a grimace, as if afraid he might catch something. These definitely weren't the sort of angels he was used to dealing with. "And the names?"

"Those will cost you." He wasn't fool enough to think the names would be turned over to the Ophanim for arrests to be made. Any noble names he provided would be useful bargaining tools for an angel who hoped to advance his place in society or among the supernal ranks.

"Move along." Erel handed back the parchment. "Elysian soil isn't the place for your skunk peddling."

It had been worth a try.

Back at The Brimstone, he found Vasily curled up on the cot reading Dostoevsky. His boy, who hadn't even known how to read simple angelic two years ago, was devouring nineteenth-century Russian literature in its native language.

No, *not* his boy. The reminder punched him in the gut.

Vasily looked up with his unasked questions.

"The Supernal Army apparently isn't interested in demon matters. Regardless of whether they involve angels." Belphagor took off the white gloves he'd donned for the encounter and tossed them on the vanity. "Not a huge surprise, I suppose. At any rate, that was plan A. Care to join me for plan B?"

"Plan B?" Vasily tucked a red ribbon between the pages and set the book aside.

"The direct-confrontation method. I'll need your muscle for it."

Vasily nodded and rose. "I'm up for that."

"And Vasya—let me do the talking. Showing your fire is fine, but I need you to hold your tongue." Belphagor thought he detected the hint of a prelude to the sort of outrage that inevitably led to a physical confrontation between them, and it stirred his desire in a hopeful way, but Vasily only nodded again after a measured breath. Belphagor gave him a nod in return. "Good. I need you with me in case things go south. But violence is the absolute last resort."

All told, it was a good three hours from the time Belphagor had run into Armen to the time they reached the Fletchery. Long enough, it seemed, for the proprietors to sanitize the place. Armen had tipped them off.

The view of the salon through the open double doors revealed an empty room, and the atmosphere looked much more conservative, as if it were a gentlemen's club that was actually for gentlemen—or as near as one could come to a gentleman in the Demon District. The front entrance was laid out like a reception area, and a young demoness—firmly over the age of consent—sat behind the desk.

She lifted her head from a ledger and gave them a quizzical glance. "May I help you?"

Belphagor gripped the sides of the desk and leaned in, focusing his natural ability at influence. "I'm looking for Raum Tephrosovich."

She was either more adept at deflecting suggestion than she appeared, or they'd kept her in the dark. "I'm afraid there's no one here by that name."

"Let's not waste time." Belphagor pressed both palms flat against the desktop. "I'd like to see whoever is pretending to be in charge of whatever this place is now pretending to be, and I would like to see them now, or I'll release the list of names I have in my pocket to the Ophanim I saw down the street."

While she stared at him, flustered and clearly at a loss for an answer, the curtain behind her opened, and Raum stepped out.

"That's all right, Kalee. I'll handle this. Why don't you take a little break?" Raum gave Belphagor a withering glance as Kalee rose and slipped through the curtained partition to make herself scarce. "Your tricks aren't welcome here."

"I've come with a proposition for a business transaction."

Raum's gaze traveled over Vasily standing with folded arms at Belphagor's side. "We're well aware of the sort of transactions you and your ilk engage in. There is nothing you can hope to achieve here. This is a respectable establishment, and I must ask you to leave before I have to call in my security."

"I want to buy them all."

"I beg your pardon?"

"Your entire inventory. I wish to take it off your hands." He sensed Vasily's incredulity beside him, but he stayed silent, as Belphagor had asked.

Raum laughed in amazement. "You couldn't possibly afford any of our inventory—*if* we were in the business of trading in material goods, which we are not." He shook his head. "And such an appetite you must have to think you could consume so many."

Belphagor grabbed the front of Raum's shirt without warning. "Children are not for consumption, you sniveling worm."

"Children?" Raum made a strangled yelp when Belphagor yanked him closer.

"Drop the act. I'm willing to pay whatever price you hoped to gain for them. I'll see that they're all apprenticed in respectable trades."

"You would waste them!" Raum had obviously decided to stop pretending not to understand him. "And for what? To convince yourself you're morally superior? Well, I have news for you, Belphagor. You're as dirty as the rest of Raqia. You're a fucking demon. And you're also wasting your time, because they're beyond your grasp."

"What the fuck is that supposed to mean?" Vasily had evidently reached the limits of his restraint. Legs planted wide, he unfolded his arms, poised to seize Raum and presumably toss him like kindling.

Raum wrested his shirt from Belphagor's fist and stepped back, casting a dismissive glare at Vasily. "Your bodyguard needs to learn his place. This conversation doesn't concern him."

Vasily made a low growl in his throat that a smarter demon would have taken as a warning. "I'm not his damned bodyguard."

Forced to acknowledge him, Raum turned to face Vasily. "Who the hell are you, then?"

Vasily crossed to him in two swift steps and seized him by the neck with a dangerous snarl. "The name's Ruby."

And there went any chance of keeping their deception under wraps.

Raum gaped at Vasily's obvious physical maturity. "I knew it!" He clutched at Vasily's fingers in a futile attempt to pull them from his throat, throwing Belphagor a look of outrage. "You came here under false pretenses. This is your boy!"

"I am no one's boy." Vasily tightened his grip.

Belphagor spoke with eminent calm. "I suggest you explain to us what you meant by 'beyond my grasp.'" He made no move to stop Vasily or assist Raum in his efforts to fend him off.

Raum was beginning to sweat. "They've been sold."

"Sold to whom?"

"Whoever takes them after they're fletched. It's not my job to check identification. We have an arrangement. The used goods are picked up at the end of the week by a resale broker who finds new buyers that don't mind getting it secondhand. These went for a premium since they were still in pristine condition."

Belphagor tried to control his fury at Raum's cavalier attitude, reducing young demons to nothing more than product to be used and cast off. "You sold them all?"

"Thanks to your little stunt, snitching to the angelic authorities, we had no choice. You seem to spend an undue amount of time in the company of angels these days, Belphagor." Still trying to behave as if everything were normal and that Vasily didn't have his throat in a vise grip, Raum threw a scornful glance at Belphagor's clothing. "Putting on airs. You seem to forget that what you are is a petty air*spirit*." His last word morphed into an alarmed squeak as Vasily's hand tightened around his airway. "Call him off!"

"I can't help what Vasily chooses to do." Belphagor was careful not to meet Vasily's eyes. "I don't own him."

Vasily shook Raum like a sack of grain. "Where's Silk?"

"Silk? The sissy dorm boy?" Raum's words ended in another squeak as skin reddened on his neck and throat. Vasily's ire was raised, and the heat of his element streamed out through his pores, steam rising between Raum's hands as he pried at Vasily's grip. "We sold him!"

Belphagor placed a hand on Vasily's shoulder. "Vasya, I suggest you put him down."

The Supernal Guard might pay no heed to the sale of demon children, but outside a duel or drunken brawl, they weren't likely to ignore a murder if charges were brought. And absent due process or incarceration, the only remedy the Heavens had for gross disregard for the law was hanging.

Blisters had begun to form on Raum's skin by the time Vasily dropped him onto the ground.

Belphagor placed his boot against the blistering flesh as Raum cried out. "The boy. Silk. He was beaten by Kezef. How bad were his injuries?"

"Messed him up." Raum gasped like a floundering fish. "But he was on his feet, more or less, when they took him away."

"Who?" Vasily demanded. "Who took him?"

"I told you, I don't know! I only see the broker when he comes."

The sound of Raum's security pounded toward them down the corridor. Kalee had apparently alerted them.

Belphagor took Vasily by the hand to bring his focus back to him. "Come on. There's nothing more we can learn here. We have to go."

Vasily turned on him as if to rebuke him, but the fire had gone out of his eyes. He stared at Belphagor a moment before acquiescing, and they hurried out the front before Raum's security detail arrived to complicate things.

"They've sold him." Vasily's face was grim as Belphagor turned down a side street to avoid attention. "He's gone."

"And we're going to find him," Belphagor promised. "Silk and Anzhela and as many of the others as we can track down."

Vasily still held his hand. Whether it was because he wasn't aware of it or by design was unclear, but Belphagor took comfort in it all the same. They might draw ridicule if they were spotted, but right now, he didn't care. All that mattered was the warmth of Vasily's touch, the proof of their connection. Things weren't hopelessly fucked up beyond repair. He had to believe that.

Setting his sights on bringing down a highly sophisticated child sex ring might be a means of sublimating his fears about their relationship, but it was something that needed to be done. No one else was going to champion the Fallen, and Fallen children were among the most vulnerable, at the mercy of any opportunistic demon who felt like using his own powerlessness as an excuse to exploit those weaker than himself. And Belphagor knew what it was to be a downcast among the downtrodden. A Petrograd prison in 1916 had taught him that.

CHAPTER SIX

Finding out who the broker was turned out to be the easy part. Armen had been busy spreading the word that Belphagor had patronized the Fletchery. The broker came to him.

Oza stopped them as they passed through the back of the bar on the way to their room, his expression dark, and tossed a calling card on the bar in front of Belphagor. "Demon left this for you."

Belphagor studied the fancy script: *Balam Morouyevich Imov, Procurer of Specialty Goods.*

"I told him we don't welcome his sort of business here. And I have to ask you outright, Belphagor. Is there any truth to what Armen Nekirevich is saying? Because if there is, I may have to reconsider your tenancy. I won't tolerate that sort of trade in The Brimstone."

Belphagor tucked the card into his breast pocket. "What is Armen saying?"

Oza lowered his voice. "That you've been purchasing the intimate services of young boys."

Belphagor leveled an icy stare at him. "Of course it isn't true. I'm offended you'd think so."

Oza relaxed visibly. "Well, I *didn't* think so, but then I remembered Vasily coming in yesterday, magicked to look like a youth, with some other boy—"

"Khai was glamoured too," put in Vasily. "He's as old as I am."

Belphagor sighed. "Armen roped me into a scheme to blackmail the nobles frequenting the Fletchery. Vasily and I infiltrated the establishment, and when things went sideways, Armen promised to ruin my reputation. I see he's off to a good start."

"But that Balam." Oza's expression was sour as he uttered the name. "You know what he is."

"I do. I presume he was given my name by someone who heard Armen's slander—which, by now, could be anyone in Raqia. But the Fletchery appears to have sold him their entire 'inventory' to keep from running afoul of the Ophanim, and I intend to emancipate any still in Balam's custody."

Oza raised his eyebrows but went back to cleaning the bar top. "Said you could find him in the Market."

"Thank you, my friend. And I'd appreciate it if you'd correct any gossip you hear about me if you have the opportunity." If he was going to find this Balam, he'd have to change his clothes. The fop look wasn't going to get him anywhere in the Demon Market.

In their room, Vasily watched him change. Out of habit, Belphagor had kept his back turned away. Vasily nodded toward the tattoo on his chest. "I saw that cross symbol in the world of Man. On those cathedrals. Lev told me they worship a god there that's supposed to live in Heaven. Were you— Did you go to church?"

Belphagor couldn't help but laugh. "No—" He managed to catch himself before saying *mal'chik*. "No, Vasya, I didn't. Our kind isn't exactly welcome there. They think we're evil beings sent to tempt Man." He paused in buttoning his shirt and winked. "Well, some of us are, I suppose."

"Then why do you have that?"

Belphagor tucked the black silk shirt into his leather pants, busying himself with the laces.

"You're not going to tell me." Vasily's voice grated like shifting coals.

"It's not important."

"What's not important? The tattoo or telling me anything?"

Belphagor tied off the laces with a sigh. "*Korol vorov*. It's the king of thieves."

"Thieves?"

"You may have noticed I steal things on occasion. It's a symbol of honor among the Russian criminal underground. The *vory v zakone*. Thieves in law."

"How did you get it?"

And there it was. Belphagor turned away from him to put on his boots. "I earned it. That's all you need to know." He expected Vasily to fume at him, but to Belphagor's surprise, he seemed to accept this answer. "I'm going to the Market to find this Balam, but it's probably best that you stay here. I don't want to scare him off."

"What are you going to do if he has some of the children?"

Belphagor shrugged and went to the door, pulling on his leather duster. "Buy them."

"But you were only bluffing with Raum, right? About buying the lot of them?"

Belphagor concentrated on the door as he opened it, as if the knob were giving him trouble. "Of course. You don't think I have that kind of crystal, do you?" Among the many things Vasily was better off not knowing, one was the degree of wealth Belphagor had accumulated over the years.

The sneers and hostile looks he encountered as he headed through The Brimstone confirmed that Armen's story had spread like wildfire. He supposed seeking out the "Procurer of Specialty Goods" in the Demon Market wasn't going to do much for his reputation in that regard, but it couldn't be helped.

He asked after Balam at a few of the less savory kiosks along the seedier alleyways of the open-air market. There were several where a demon could enter behind a curtain and pay for five minutes' entertainment with a working girl or a rentboy, or even with an unknown participant through a hole between two booths.

It might be interesting to take Vasily to one of these sometime and— Belphagor cut off the thought with a frustrated growl. Was he ever going to get used to Vasily not belonging to him? He didn't want to get used to it. He wanted his boy.

A few of the vendors treated him with contempt for his presumed preference, but one directed him without hesitation to the open tent at the end of the aisle. A demon with graying temples signifying time spent in the world of Man sat jotting notes in an accounting book with a fountain pen.

Belphagor made his way to the tent, where the merchant looked up with a quizzical expression. "You left your card for me." Belphagor held it out.

"So I did." Balam nodded, closing the notebook with manicured fingertips. "I was told you might be in the market for a special piece I've recently acquired."

Belphagor frowned. "Only one?"

"How many were you hoping to procure?"

"I'm just curious how many you have. I understand a certain establishment recently offloaded their entire inventory."

"Yes, unfortunate business, that. But fortunate for my customers. And they're always eager to acquire a piece in pristine condition, so I was lucky enough to be able to deliver all but one to my connection." Balam rose and put an arm around Belphagor's shoulder as if to share a confidence with him. "And let me assure you that this one is quite special." He turned Belphagor toward a flap at the rear of the tent that Belphagor had assumed led outside, but he opened it to reveal a dark interior compartment.

"Before I light the lamp for your inspection"—Balam let the curtain fall behind them, leaving them temporarily in total darkness—"there's one small defect I should warn you about. And only a temporary defect, I assure you. But this piece of merchandise was damaged recently by a careless consumer."

He lit a match and held it to the hanging lamp inside the flap, illuminating a boy curled on a straw mat in the corner. A blanket covered him almost entirely, and Balam bent to move it aside, revealing a length of dark, shining hair beside a bruised and battered face. Given his relative maturity—and the "damage"—this could only be Vasily's Silk.

"Damaging such a lovely piece is not behavior I approve of, but I make no judgment about what a customer chooses to do with the merchandise once purchased. You're welcome to examine the piece more closely."

Belphagor crouched beside the mat to feel Silk's pulse, and the boy hardly stirred.

"A sedative has been administered to ensure compliance," Balam explained. "But you have my word that everything is in working order."

Belphagor had to dig his nails into his thigh to keep from punching the coward. "Can he be moved? I don't want to injure him further."

"All merchandise can be delivered to your domicile or any other designated location." Balam carefully avoided any reference to Silk as a person. "I can have the piece transported discreetly in an enclosed, ventilated container, but that will cost extra."

"And how much is extra?"

"Fifty carats. Firm." Balam was shrewd, specifying the crystal size instead of merely asking for fifty facets. That Balam had managed to move his "merchandise" so quickly at such prices was astonishing. And sickening.

Belphagor straightened. "I don't have it on me. But I can pay on delivery."

Balam replaced the blanket. "I'm afraid a substantial deposit is required. And make no mistake. This is only cosmetic damage. There are any number of customers eager to grab up this opportunity."

It was an effort for Belphagor to keep his anger in check. "And how much is a substantial deposit?"

The merchant crossed his arms. "Half." It was still well more than Belphagor was accustomed to carrying on his person.

"I'll be back with it shortly."

The serious look turned into a friendly smile once more. "Excellent! I'll have the merchandise boxed up for you and ready to go as soon as you return."

When he arrived back at The Brimstone with the news, Belphagor tried to dissuade Vasily from returning with him to the Demon Market, but there was no arguing with him. A few days ago, Belphagor might have snapped his fingers and ordered Vasily down on his knees to wait until he'd bidden him to rise again. And other things would have risen with the command.

But that didn't bear thinking on.

"He's going to be in a container when we get there, Vasya. There's nothing you can really do."

"He's *what*?"

"He's not exactly . . . mobile at the moment. Balam uses some kind of delivery crate for discretion."

"I don't care about any damned discretion! What do you mean, he's not fucking mobile?" Flame practically leapt from Vasily's eyes.

"He's unconscious—sedated. To be perfectly honest, he's a mess. From what I saw of him, and from what you witnessed, I think he's lucky to be alive." Belphagor put a hand on Vasily's arm and gave it a squeeze. "I don't think he has any permanent injuries. But carting him through Raqia in that condition ourselves—it wouldn't look good."

Vasily wrenched his arm away. "I don't fucking care how it looks. We didn't beat him and drug him. And I'll be damned if I'm going to let you put him in a box! I'll carry him myself."

Belphagor's reputation could hardly get worse. "If that's the way you want it." He put a pouch of facets together, careful not to let on how many were going into it, and headed out with Vasily at his side.

As they reached the front of The Brimstone, a low mutter stopped Belphagor short. "Does the firespirit take your seconds?"

He turned slowly and leveled his gaze on the demon drinking ale near the door, with his grinning friends slapping him on the back. When Vasily turned also, the grins faded.

"Care to repeat that, my friend? I'm not sure the firespirit heard you."

"Didn't mean anything by it," the culprit mumbled into his ale. "I'm not the one fletching boys."

Vasily had started to turn away, but this brought him back around, and Belphagor took a knowing step out of his way. Vasily's fist struck so swiftly that the smaller demon didn't have time to brace himself, and he flew backward off the chair into the group seated at the table behind him. No one moved to help him, going back to their games and drinks with their heads down.

Belphagor took Vasily by the arm and tugged him up the stairs. "I think he's learned his lesson, Vasya." He prodded him out into the street. "Perhaps it doesn't speak very highly of my character, but I have to tell you, I don't think I've ever been more attracted to you."

As mad as he was, Vasily apparently couldn't hold back a rough snort of laughter, but a reluctant sigh soon followed. "Maybe you're right. Maybe my carrying Silk unconscious through Raqia isn't the greatest idea."

The point turned out to be moot. When they arrived at the Demon Market, Balam's tent was gone.

Belphagor kicked at the metal framework where the tent had been tethered. "*Yebat*! I should have carried him out myself, then and there."

"Or you should have let me go with you the first time." Vasily stared bitterly at the empty plot.

"I'm sorry, Vasya." Belphagor scrubbed his hand across his mouth. "We'll just have to find out who's been buying and track them down."

"And how the fuck do you propose we do that?"

Belphagor slumped against the tent frame, hating the tone of anger and despair in Vasily's voice, hating that he'd let him down. And let Silk down. And Anzhela— He'd promised Koshka. Not to mention the younger children. He had to win this one.

Anzhela. She'd been sold to the Fletchery by the angelic owner of The Cat. And who would know more about the illicit trafficking of minors than an angel who had recently sold at least one?

It had been one thing to inquire after the welfare of the former proprietress and her family the other night. But he'd be pushing his luck—and violating the Whores' Code—if he simply walked in and started asking questions about the new proprietor's business practices. He needed an insider's perspective.

Belphagor pushed himself away from the pole. "Beatrix."

Vasily stared at him. "Beatrix? You're not going to take that glamour again?"

"No, not the glamour." Belphagor shuddered slightly. He didn't relish the idea of using magic to change the entire genetic makeup of his body, no matter how temporary. "But Beatrix had friends at The Cat."

The ladies at the brothel were always friendly to Belphagor, despite his lack of interest—or perhaps because of it. But with Vasily beside him, he might as well have been invisible. Vasily's first experience with a woman had taken place in this very brothel, and by all accounts, he'd attracted quite an audience.

Belphagor stood back with arms folded and watched bemused as the ladies of the evening surrounded Vasily and cooed over him while he stammered and went a delicate shade of pink.

"This isn't exactly your sort of place." The sultry voice from behind Belphagor was warm with amusement.

He turned and smiled at Natalya, a statuesque, raven-haired beauty he recognized from his brief stay while glamoured as Beatrix. "No, but it was my cousin's kind of place. Beatrix recommended it, and I've been wanting to give the boy a treat." He nodded toward Vasily. Despite being engaged in an awkward attempt to fend off the more aggressive groping, he must have heard the word *boy*, judging by the piercing glare he sent Belphagor's way.

"Your boy's been here before."

"So I gathered. He's been a little tongue-tied about the experience, but I've heard from reliable sources that he quite enjoyed himself."

Natalya nodded, tucking her diaphanous wrap about her arms in a comfortable gesture. "From Sefi and Tabris. I know who you are."

He pondered whether that meant she knew precisely who he was. "I wonder if you wouldn't mind providing me with some company while Vasily is being entertained."

She held out her palm. "Time is money."

"Of course." He handed over his facets with a smile.

Vasily gaped at him as Belphagor gave Natalya his arm. "You're not leaving me alone with them?"

"It's not exactly my cup of tea, Vasya." He winked at the petite blonde and the more buxom redhead who had wriggled under Vasily's arms. "Anything he wants is on me. I'll pay whatever you deem fair."

The simmering glow in Vasily's eyes said there would also be hell to pay.

Natalya found a cozy alcove for them and drew the curtain on it. "So." She pulled him down to the cushions with her so that they were both on their knees. "I gather it's not my physical attributes you're interested in today but my mental ones."

Belphagor inclined his head. "I did want to have a little chat, if you're amenable. Beatrix mentioned she was curious about the new ownership here, but I don't want to overstep."

Natalya shrugged. "It's your crystal. What sort of a chat did you have in mind, my dear B?"

Belphagor studied her expression, trying to determine whether she'd said the letter *B* or the name *Bea*. She gave away nothing, so he figured he'd best do the same.

"I'm wondering if you recall the specifics of when Anzhela was sold."

Natalya pulled her wrap over her shoulders. "Masha wasn't herself."

"So I understand."

"The investor arrived to take possession of The Cat the same day she died, and he showed us the deed, which included Anzhela. Anzhi didn't seem surprised, but she said nothing to us. She went where she was told."

Belphagor nodded. Anzhela had always been very pragmatic. It was a trait the smartest demons had.

"And who took her, do you know? Was it a demon named Balam?"

Natalya shook her head. "No, it was angels. Soldiers in the Supernal Army, it looked like. We all thought maybe she was being arrested."

"Angels?" He hadn't considered that they might be part of the trafficking ring.

"They interrogated her first, saying they knew she'd fallen before. They wanted to know where the portal was."

Belphagor frowned. Angels trying to find out how to get to the world of Man? Or were they trying to seal the portal off? "And did she tell them?"

Natalya shrugged. "I imagine she must have, since she's still alive. I understand her master sold her."

"He did. To the Fletchery. And now she's gone, and I'm trying to figure out where."

"How do you know she was at the Fletchery?"

Belphagor sat back against the wall of the little alcove and drew up his knees, hooking his arms around them. "I pretended to be a patron to help out a fool with a blackmail scheme." Heat rose in his face. "And I sold Vasily to the establishment, glamoured as his younger self. It was the price of entry."

Natalia's eyes darkened. "Are you mad? Do you have any idea what it's like for a boy in a place like that?"

"I think it's well established that he's not *actually* a boy, but yes, I have some idea. I'd hoped he would see it as a game—play everyone like I would—but he's remarkably guileless for a demon who grew up on the streets."

"Well, let me assure you that no one comes out of the Fletchery guileless. Half the brothels are filled with former 'fledglings.' And those that don't end up in the brothels often end up in the Acheron." Natalya sighed. "At least they used to do. Now they simply disappear."

"That's why I'm here. I'm trying to figure out where they're going. I want to find Anzhela as well as the others who've been sold. And I'm going to do my damnedest to see to it that the Fletchery stays closed." He ran his fingers over the stiff points of his hair. "If I could just find someone who knew the buyers and sellers in this damned network."

"Would it help if you could interview a former fledgling?" Natalya's expression was sober. "Because you're already acquainted with one."

Belphagor dropped his hand to his side. "You?"

"No. Tabris."

"Tabris? I thought she came to work at The Cat because her mother had died and Ouestucati was all she had."

"Ouestucati." Natalya observed him. "Sefira told you her real name."

"Tabris did, actually. After her sister died."

Natalya nodded. "Well, you're half right about why she came here, but that's only part of the story. When their mother died, Tabris was sold to the Fletchery to pay her debts. Ouestucati had to wait until she was up for sale—after—and then she bought her and brought her here."

Belphagor shook his head. "She had to buy her own sister?"

"That's why they worked as a team. Ouestucati wouldn't let anyone touch Tabris unless she was there to see they treated her fairly. Anyway, if anybody knows who does the buying and selling, Tabris would."

"But I'm not sure where she is now."

"She's still here."

"Not still working?"

"No. She was never the same after the Ophanim. But she has your money, doesn't she, B? She doesn't have to work. And this is her home."

"It wasn't my money," he said automatically. "It was—"

"Beatrix's." Natalya smiled.

Belphagor's cheeks reddened at the thought of some of the compromising positions Natalya had seen Beatrix in. "So you do know who I am."

"Most of us who were working here at the time know. But don't worry. No one here would ever tarnish the reputation of the Prince of Tricks. A working girl never betrays the true name of another girl. That's why I was surprised you knew Ouesti's name." She took his hand and pulled him to his feet as she stood. "Come on, B. Let's go talk to Tabi."

Natalya led him through the parlor and into the private quarters, receiving a few curious glances along the way. The girls at The Cat generally kept their entertaining to the more public areas, and only very special patrons were admitted into this part of the house.

She knocked on one of the doors, and Tabris's soft voice came from inside, bidding them to enter. Tabris didn't look up from where she knelt on the floor moving beads about in a large silver tray.

"Tabris does beadwork for our specialty garments." Natalya lifted the end of her wrap, displaying the intricate design in glass "crystals" and sequins. "Tabi." She spoke more loudly, as if Tabris were hard of hearing. "You remember Belphagor."

Tabris glanced up, her expression fuzzy. "I don't take patrons."

Natalya crouched in front of her. "Not a patron, Tabi. Belphagor, the demon who brought you home to us."

A slight shudder rippled through Tabris that she didn't seem to notice. "You're the fire demon's master."

"Not his master. But yes, he's mine." At least Belphagor hoped to Heaven he still was.

Natalya tried to help her up, but Tabris shrank from the touch.

"No need to rise." Belphagor sat beside her, crossing his legs. "Those are lovely beads. Especially the pale, watery ones. What are you making with them?"

Tabris relaxed and began separating her treasures again. "One of the girls wants her name spelled out on her thong. It's a long name, though, so I have to use the smallest seed beads."

"What's her name?"

"Pussy Familiar."

Belphagor nearly choked on his spit.

"She says Men believe there are people on the terrestrial plane who keep something called 'familiar spirits,' supposed to be demons in cat form, to do their bidding. Pussy thought it was hilarious, so that's the name she took."

"Indeed. It is a rather amusing tale." Belphagor winked at the pun.

Tabris nodded. "She's got one of those too, tattooed on her nether cheek as if it's coming right out of her bum."

"Tattooed." He politely pretended not to have heard the rest. "She has actually fallen, then."

"Oh yes. Lots of the girls have. Masha's portal."

Natalya put a hand on Tabris's knee. "Not for mention, love, remember?"

Tabris cringed and blinked at Belphagor as if seeing him for the first time. "Sorry. I forget myself."

"It's all right. I already know about it." He'd returned through it with Anzhela after Masha had sent her to the world of Man to find him and let him know Tabris had been arrested. "You can count on my discretion."

Tabris studied him with a sudden look of recognition. "You're Beatrix. How'd you do that? Change your face? And the rest." She nodded to his flat chest.

"It was a one-time performance, courtesy of a potent glamour from the Market."

"He did it for *you*, Tabi. You remember?"

Belphagor shook his head at Natalya, not wanting her to encourage Tabris to think about that time. He certainly didn't need her to feel beholden to him. But it was too late. The cat was already out of the bag. So to speak.

Tabris sat back on her heels. "For me?"

"For you and Ouesti. To catch her murderer. And now he's trying to help Anzhi. To bring her home like he brought you home."

"I'm sorry," Tabris whispered, and a tear trailed down her cheek. "I'm sorry I forgot."

"Don't be sorry, sweetheart." Belphagor wiped the tear with his thumb, forgetting she was shy of touch after the electrified hands of the Ophanim had held her down during her interrogation, but this time she didn't shudder. "Sometimes we need to forget things. But I'm afraid I need to ask you to remember some other things you might not want to."

She nodded, solemn.

"Natalya says you spent some time at the—" He hated to say this to her, and he glanced at Natalya, but she didn't stop him. "At the Fletchery."

"The Fletchery." Tabris looked blank.

"When you were a girl, after your mother died and before you came to The Cat."

Tabris swallowed. "Oh. Yes. The Immacularium. They call it that there, don't they? *Fletching.* As if taking something from you could give you wings."

"I'm sorry about what they took from you, Tabris. It wasn't theirs to take. It was yours to give, when you wanted to. Or even to keep to yourself if you liked. And I want to stop them from doing it to anyone else." Belphagor paused a moment to make sure he hadn't unduly upset her, but she gave him a little nod to go on. "What I need to know is whether you remember how the transactions were handled when—when you were sold there, and when Ouestucati bought you back. Do you remember who handled that part?"

"Transactions?" Tabris looked as if she didn't know this word.

"The facets, Tabi." Natalya nodded encouragement. "Who gave the facets to the demons at the Fletchery?"

Tabris shook her head. "I don't know."

"What about after?" asked Belphagor. "Was there someone, a go-between, who brought you to your sister?"

"You mean the drovers?"

"Drovers?"

"Demons that smuggle other demons. Or sometimes angels—whoever they're not supposed to have."

Belphagor had done his share of smuggling through the portal in his possession but never of anyone he wasn't supposed to have. *The portal.* Could the children from the Fletchery be disappearing because they were being taken out of Heaven itself? It would explain why the angels had asked Anzhela about the portal's whereabouts. If so, this conspiracy went much deeper than he'd realized.

A cold feeling of dread settled in his stomach. If it was true, not only were defenseless young demons available for a price in Raqia, but they were being shipped to the lower sphere to be used for the entertainment of Men. Or perhaps by Malakim.

His jaw tightened. "I need to know how to find one of these drovers."

Tabris shrugged. "Then I suppose you need to have something you want smuggled."

"Or something I want that's *been* smuggled."

Too many people knew him in Raqia, besmirched reputation or not. It was probably why Balam had bolted: someone had tipped him off about the Prince of Tricks. Belphagor could try working glamoured again, but even as his own sex, it was exhausting to be someone else, and he was getting too old to be messing with his genetic material. If he wanted to set a convincing trap, he was going to have to go where he was virtually no one. He was going to have to fall.

Though he might be able to use one last simple glamour to do a little snooping here in Heaven before he did.

"Thank you, Tabris. You've been a great help."

"You can call me Tabi, sweetheart." She'd said it in her working persona, as if she'd already forgotten who Belphagor was. "You ask for Tabi next time you come. I'll take good care of you."

He cupped her cheek and kissed her on the forehead without comment before he rose and went out with Natalya.

"She has good days and bad days." Natalya gave him a sad smile. "Sometimes on the same day."

In the parlor, Vasily appeared to be holding court from the center of a pile of cushions by the fire. He looked flushed and a bit disheveled but no longer flustered by the attentions of the two barely clad women in his arms.

Extricating himself from the tangle of limbs, he thanked them politely, making them giggle, and rose to greet Belphagor. "Learn anything?"

"I may have." Belphagor noted the damp, swollen appearance of Vasily's lips; it seemed they'd been put to good use. The corner of his mouth turned up. "And what exactly did you learn?"

Vasily glared, his already flushed cheeks turning a deeper pink. "If I'd realized you were expecting a blow-by-blow account of my activities, I'd have taken notes."

Belphagor's eyes widened. "First of all, surely you can summarize. Second, please tell me there isn't any actual blowing involved. My idyllic fantasies about how such encounters go with the fairer sex will be shattered."

Vasily's eyes flashed fire. "Tell you what, Belphagor." He crossed his arms over his broad chest. "Why don't you tell me something first."

The sudden calm in his demeanor made Belphagor's skin prickle with misgiving. "Such as?"

"How about you tell me what the red crown on your ass means."

Belphagor swallowed, controlling his outward reaction. The heat in the room was suddenly stifling. "On second thought, keep your exploits to yourself."

The silence between them on the way home crackled with an undertone of firespirit heat, but once they'd arrived at their room, the fire ignited.

"Is there something you want to say to me?" Belphagor's voice was tight as he removed his coat.

Vasily slammed the door shut behind him. "You complete and utter son of a whore. You can't keep acting like you own me, like I'm your boy that you can give away for your own entertainment."

"There has been nothing entertaining about your behavior tonight. On the contrary, it seems it was in fact *your* entertainment I paid for. All I required from you was a distraction, yet you seemed quite happy to throw yourself *deep* into the role."

A ring of flame danced inside Vasily's pupils. Not the heat of desire, but the warning of a wild animal about to attack. "You're going to stand there and tell me you didn't use me just now, didn't manipulate me to your own ends like I'm your little *suka*?"

Belphagor counted to ten. He tried to breathe the anger out, reminding himself that Vasily didn't know what he was saying, but that word was a match to the Molotov cocktail that was the bottled-up frustration and hurt of the past few days. Before he knew what he was doing, he'd crossed the room in three swift strides and, with a fist in Vasily's hair, had taken him down to his knees so hard the walls rattled.

He hated that he'd done it as soon as he had. This wasn't an act meant for spite and vitriol between them. He'd only ever done it in love or passion. Belphagor let go of Vasily's hair and took a step back, and his lovely boy who was not his boy stared up at him wide-eyed, as if Belphagor had knocked the wind from his lungs instead of bringing him down to size.

"I don't know any other way to be, Vasya." He kept his voice rough and hard to hide the deep sorrow behind the words. "But let me make one thing clear to you right now. If you ever refer to yourself or me or anyone else as a *suka*, there will be nothing erotic about the beating I'll give you. And if you *ever* bring attention to my less visible ink in the presence of others, so help me, I will thrash you where you stand. If you can't be with me as the man I am, if you can't respect my boundaries as you ask me to respect yours . . . don't be here when I get back."

He turned and went out—his head horrified at the words his mouth had uttered and his heart shouting at him to turn around and take them back—closing the door between them. His hand clutched the knob convulsively, refusing to let go, all his parts rebelling against him. He stood still and pressed his forehead to the wood, feeling broken beyond repair and knowing he'd done this himself. Vasily would never forgive him. He'd go. Belphagor couldn't step away from the door or it would open and his boy would leave him for good.

Vasily, however, must have thought Belphagor had already gone. From the other side of the door, his gravelly voice, full of despair, was barely audible as he whispered, "Beli." And with that mournful whisper, heat rose through the wood, warming Belphagor's forehead. Vasily must have pressed his hand against the door, still on his knees where Belphagor had left him.

Rather than fall to his own knees, Belphagor backed away from the door and ran.

CHAPTER SEVEN

A rush of desire that had nothing to do with sex had flooded Vasily when Belphagor had dropped him to the ground. It was as though his entire being had responded to a silent command. *Da, ser! Da, ser! I'm yours. This is where I belong.* Vasily leaned against the unyielding wood of the door through which Belphagor had disappeared.

What had he said? What had he done? He'd wounded Belphagor with his fool fiery tongue in some way that had been unthinkable. Belphagor had hurt him, yes, but only out of that clueless ineptitude he seemed to have when it came to reading people's emotions—or considering them, at any rate, when he thought he knew them already. But Vasily had pushed at buttons he knew he wasn't meant to touch. He'd let his temper get the best of him. As always.

The word *suka* held greater significance for Belphagor than Vasily understood—as the tattoos meant more than he could ever hope to understand. It was a place inside Belphagor that Vasily was shut out of. Belphagor had warned him before not to say the word. The angelic equivalent was *bitch*, but that wasn't a word that bothered demons. They tossed it back and forth amongst each other, lobbed it back at the angels who used it to demean them by equating their entire race with animals. *Go ahead and call us animals*, it said. *We all know you're the same breed we are.*

Although it had always bothered Vasily that the word was gendered. As if the worst thing anyone could be were female. Perhaps there was something of that in the Russian term that upset Belphagor so.

It didn't matter. It bothered him. Vasily knew better. Saying it deliberately was like Belphagor calling him stupid, knowing it was the one thing that cut Vasily to the core. And Belphagor had never said it. Not once. Vasily kept waiting for him to, treating him as if it was forever on the tip of Belphagor's tongue.

He really *was* stupid.

Belphagor didn't return until late. Vasily had stayed up reading *Demons* by lamplight, trying not to worry and steeling himself for whatever he had coming. But Belphagor said nothing, just took a pair of extra blankets, set up his bed on the floor and climbed between them fully clothed.

Vasily closed his book. "You're sleeping there?"

"Good night, Vasya." Belphagor turned away.

After snuffing the lantern, Vasily sat in the dark with his head back against the wall, his gut churning with turmoil. He hated this, and he'd started it. How did he end it? Fear that there *was* no way to end it, that he'd screwed things up to the point of no return, kept him from taking action.

He couldn't stand the idea that if he went to Belphagor to try to make things right, Belphagor would stay silent and turn toward the wall. And if he did talk . . . it would be a long talk. Vasily would have to try to express what he was unhappy with, not simply cave and say he was sorry and wanted to be Belphagor's boy again.

But he wanted with all his heart to do just that. He wanted to crawl to Belphagor and beg forgiveness and punishment. To be whipped and caned and held down while Belphagor had his way with him, possessing him utterly. To know he was still loved.

He woke in the morning stiff from having fallen asleep sitting up. Belphagor was packing a bag.

Vasily straightened with alarm. "Where are you going?"

Belphagor started at the sound and turned his head, slinging the bag over his shoulder. "I have to pursue a lead."

"What lead? Where?"

Belphagor's expression was closed. "South."

"South? You don't mean the world of Man?" Vasily rose, heat behind his eyes making it hard for him to see, like a debilitating headache. "Were you going to leave without saying goodbye?"

"Vasya, you asked me for space. I need some too."

Vasily moved toward him, feeling sluggish and feverish, like when he'd fallen to the world of Man with Belphagor for the first time and had caught an earthly virus. Belphagor had his hand on the doorknob, but the world of Man was below them. A portal was hidden right here in Belphagor's room.

Vasily could barely form breath enough to speak. "Please don't leave me."

"I'm not leaving you, my—" Belphagor slumped against the door, pressing the back of his head to it and staring at the ceiling. "You see? I can't even talk to you. I don't know how to talk to you."

"I'm sorry." Vasily abandoned his determination and fell on his knees. "I'm sorry, Beli. Forget it. I'll be what you want."

"I don't want you to be what I want." He looked down at Vasily, and his expression hardened. "Don't do that. Get up."

"Beli—"

"Get up!"

The angry shout stunned him, and Vasily rose, his limbs shaking. Something irrevocable had happened between them. This wasn't how they were. Why the fuck couldn't he have sucked it up and not made trouble? Everything was falling apart.

Belphagor closed his eyes, doing his counting breath. "I don't want you to be what I want. I want to be what *you* want."

"You are what I want."

Belphagor opened his eyes and shook his head. "Not right now. Right now I'm angry with you, and I have no right to be, and that makes me angry with myself. I don't want to fight with you, because this isn't a fight. You've done nothing wrong."

"I was rude to you yesterday, saying that word you hate, hassling you about your tattoos."

Unexpectedly, Belphagor smiled. "*Vasya*. You're always rude to me. And under ordinary circumstances, to be frank, I relish your surly, belligerent, *adorable* tantrums, because . . ." He didn't need to finish the sentence. Under ordinary circumstances, Vasily's hot temper was Belphagor's aphrodisiac. "But I can't be this angry with you right now. I want to give you the space you asked for, and to do that, I need some space of my own." He glanced around, lifting his hands at his sides and dropping them in a gesture of futility. "This is an absurdly tiny room. I think it's best if we aren't in it together for a while."

Vasily tried to bury his despair under the weight of anger. "And what do you expect me to do in here by myself while you're gone for Heaven knows how long? Masturbate and read Dostoevsky?"

He tried to maintain a furious expression, but Belphagor, struggling with his own, couldn't keep a straight face a moment longer. He broke down into a wheeze of silent laughter, unable to get enough breath, and watching him made Vasily lose his own fight.

"Thank Heaven you didn't say them in the reverse order," Belphagor managed and then tilted his head with a lift of his eyebrow that altogether undid Vasily. "Or is that what you've *been* doing?"

The heaviness that had been in Belphagor's eyes lessened as he watched the collapse of Vasily's composure, and he stepped away from the door. But the stroke of Belphagor's palm against his cheek cut the laughter short. Vasily held his breath, thinking Belphagor might kiss him, and everything would be okay, but Belphagor shook his head.

"I have to go, love. I have to follow this lead alone. But I'm coming back. And then we'll work it out. I promise."

Vasily brushed his hand away, the urge to laugh smothered. Belphagor was fond of making promises. "What's this lead, anyway?"

"I've gotten the name of a contact in Leningrad on the Celestial Silk Road."

"The what?"

"It's what they call the smuggling ring."

"The smuggling ring?" Vasily's eyes widened. "They're smuggling them out of Heaven to . . .?"

Belphagor nodded grimly. "To sell them in the world of Man."

"*Sukiny synov'ya*." The words were a guttural snarl in his throat. He only realized after it was out that he'd used the very word Belphagor had threatened to beat him over last night. Vasily took a step back. "Shit. I meant—"

"It's fine, Vasya." Belphagor hoisted his pack again, his hand once more on the door latch. "'Sons of bitches' isn't quite the same as calling someone a *suka*. Even if it does unnecessarily insult the women who bore them."

At least he hadn't made things worse. But the door was open, and Belphagor was leaving him—and still not through the portal.

"If you're going south, why are you using the door?"

"Because demons are most likely watching my every move at the moment. If I don't exit The Brimstone, it will raise suspicion."

"Suspicion? Whose suspicion? What demons?"

"Balam's comrades." Belphagor kissed his fingers and blew the kiss toward Vasily before stepping out and closing the door.

From anyone else, it would have been a sweet but empty gesture, but from the accomplished airspirit that was Belphagor, it was a soft, tactile caress of air that lingered on Vasily's lips and made him ache. It was a deliberate distraction. But it was still a kiss, still Belphagor's touch.

He closed his eyes and pressed his fingers to his mouth. Despite the kiss, he hadn't missed what Belphagor was trying to distract him from. Balam had smuggled Silk himself on the Celestial Silk Road. And Vasily wasn't going to sit at home and wait for Belphagor to do something about it. They might be watching Belphagor's moves, but they weren't watching Vasily's.

The portal beneath Belphagor's threadbare rug was hidden by a glamour, but there were ways to reveal what was hidden. Belphagor wasn't the only one who bought his tricks in the Demon Market.

Getting a ticket on the train to St. Petersburg—Belphagor had called it Leningrad, but that had been its name two years ago—wasn't as easy for Vasily as it must have been for Belphagor. His skill at influence increased exponentially in the world of Man. As Vasily's skills must also, he supposed, though other than his trick of lighting cigars with his tongue, he hadn't had much opportunity to test them.

But influence was not in his repertoire. The best he could manage was intimidation. That and a bribe of the *provodnik*—with rubles he'd acquired at the *lombard* in Slyudyanka where he'd pawned a few facets—got him a *platskart* ticket in the open-bunk car.

The last time he'd traveled in the world of Man, it had been winter, and he'd spent the long hours of darkness in the private compartment being sexually teased and tormented by Belphagor, who'd forbidden him to climax. This time, there was no such restriction, but as hard as the memories of that journey made him, he wasn't about to jerk off in an open berth. There was also little darkness, and the heat was unbearable in his top bunk. It was torment of a different and far less pleasant kind.

He felt as if he were racing over the Siberian steppe and taiga. Yet with every kilometer, though Vasily couldn't have been more than a few hours behind him, Belphagor seemed to be carried farther away. It was like he was chasing the memory of those happy days.

Maybe he was fevering again. The last time he'd fallen, after all, he'd picked up the earthly virus right here on the train. And with the heat rising steadily in the car, it was hard to tell if it was his body or the ambient temperature that was exceeding the comfortable range even for a firespirit.

On the third day of the trip, however, as he disembarked to stretch his legs and get a bite to eat in Yekaterinburg, he stepped straight into the path of none other than Belphagor himself. He'd never been so happy to see the furious scowl of disapproval in the dark eyes.

Belphagor grabbed him by the arm and led him away from the train. "What the hell are you doing here?"

"Pursuing a lead."

"What lead?"

"Same one you're pursuing."

"Damn it, Vasya." Belphagor ran his fingers through the spikes of his hair. "I told you to stay in Raqia. I need to do this alone."

Vasily folded his arms and shrugged. "We no longer have an arrangement where you tell me what to do and I do it."

"You can't do something because I ask it of you?"

"Not really."

Belphagor paused to buy the fresh *pirozhki* a vendor was offering him, handing one automatically to Vasily. "You can't stay with me in Leningrad. You'll blow my cover."

"St. Petersburg," Vasily corrected with a mouthful of *pirog*. "And I don't want to stay with you. You've made it perfectly clear you don't want me around."

Belphagor paused in taking a bite of his meat pie. "Vasya. You know that isn't true."

"Yes, yes, I know. We're giving each other 'space.' And it's my fault." Vasily finished off his pie and eyed the third Belphagor had purchased. "I'm fine with that." He paused. "Are you going to eat the other one?"

Belphagor rolled his eyes and handed over the *pirog*. "And where, pray tell, do you plan to stay?"

Vasily shrugged. "Safe house, I guess."

"I suppose you think the city's littered with them. How do you intend to find one? They're called safe houses for a reason."

Vasily glared and concentrated on his food.

Belphagor sighed. "Why couldn't you have let me handle this?"

Vasily swallowed the last of his pie and focused a bit of fire into his gaze. "Because you're following Silk. And I'll be damned if I'm going to let you deal with whoever's got him on your own."

Belphagor didn't deny it was Silk he was pursuing. "Vasya, we can't be seen together. Here or in Leningrad."

"St. Petersburg."

He could tell Belphagor was grinding his teeth before he continued, his voice controlled. "So I will arrange to have someone meet you when the train arrives at *Moskovsky Vokzal*. The password will be—"

"'Seraphim'?"

Belphagor's jaw twitched. "Oh, *now* you can say it."

Vasily blushed. It wasn't as if he hadn't been capable of saying the safeword. He just hadn't needed to. Had he? Doubt needled him, but he brushed it aside.

"Fine. 'Seraphim.'" The train whistle sounded, and Belphagor turned to board without another word. It was because they weren't supposed to be seen together, of course, but it hurt nonetheless.

Vasily returned to his car and spent the next twenty-six hours between Yekaterinburg and Moscow getting and staying stinking drunk with the help of his bunkmates. By the time he stepped off the connecting train from Moscow nine hours later, he was sincerely regretting both his poor decision and his mode of travel. He saw no sign of Belphagor, but as promised, Belphagor's contact found him. It wasn't as if Vasily were hard to spot.

A slender, silver-haired woman he would have taken for much younger had he not learned that the loss of hair pigmentation was a sign of aging in humans approached him and said the password. Vasily picked up his bag and followed her.

She spoke to him in rough angelic as they walked. "Is not good password. We use to warn if fire *angely* come. But you prince, he say 'Seraphim' is you word."

Vasily grunted. "I suppose he figured I wasn't smart enough to remember anything else."

The woman nodded as if this was what she'd suspected, and Vasily sighed, wishing he could get to his bed and lie down before the entire round world, if Belphagor were to be believed, slid him right off into space. To his disappointment, the short metro ride she took him on led to another train. This one was crowded, and they had to stand.

Vasily held on to the post in the center of the train aisle. "Where are we going now?"

"Tsarskoe Selo."

"Tsars-what?"

"Hush. You bring attention."

He could hardly avoid bringing attention, but his stomach was churning too much at this point to continue the conversation. He clung to his post and tried not to think about vomiting. With all the bodies packed into the car in the heat of summer, he was pretty sure he was about to die anyway.

Half an hour later, they stepped off the train into a quiet, suburban neighborhood. He'd been looking forward to staying in the city he and Belphagor had only glimpsed on their last trip, but this was nice, and if the demons here had a bed for him, he wasn't going to argue at this point. Belphagor had obviously wanted him out of the way. Vasily would deal with him later.

They climbed the steps into an apartment complex a block from the station, and Vasily gripped the railing as they turned about the landings, not paying attention when the door to the apartment at the top opened.

"Well, look who's here."

Vasily raised his head at the familiar voice. "Lev?"

Inside the entrance, Dmitri Ilyich stood behind his partner. They were the demons he and Belphagor had stayed with in Moscow on their last trip. What were they doing in a St. Petersburg suburb?

Vasily's guide held out a coin purse, and Dmitri placed a handful of bills in it, frowning at Vasily. "You're not sick again?"

"No." Vasily stepped inside to take off his shoes. As he bent over to remove them and put on the pair of *tapochki* Lev offered, he swallowed a bit of bile in the back of his throat. "Had a little too much to drink." He turned to thank the woman, but she'd gone.

Dmitri was still frowning at him. "How much is too much?"

"Yekaterinburg to Moscow."

Lev whistled. "I'd say that's about twenty hours too much." Mercifully, he led Vasily to the guest bedroom. "All yours. You can pull the blackout curtains over the window if you like. Sun doesn't go down much at the moment. And if you puke on the guest bed, you're buying a new one."

"Please," Vasily groaned as he fell onto the bed and clutched the covers to keep from sliding off. "Don't say 'puke.'"

When he rejoined the world of the living some hours later, Vasily was relieved to find Dmitri had gone out. He didn't really connect with either demon, but Lev was easier to talk to. And he was a fantastic cook.

Stacks of fresh mini-pancakes were waiting at the table with sour cream and jam, and as always, a samovar of hot tea. The weather didn't seem to matter; tea was served hot, three times a day.

Now that his stomach had settled, Vasily gladly drank the cup Lev poured him. "What are you two doing in— Where are we?"

"Pushkin."

"I thought the woman who brought me said something about tsars."

"Tsarskoe Selo." Lev nodded. "That was its name before the Bolsheviks changed it. Some people are calling it that again now that communism's out of fashion. We moved here in the spring." He gave Vasily a significant look as he poured himself a cup of tea. "Kind of had to, after word got out that we'd been harboring a celestial fugitive." Lev took a seat opposite him at the little kitchen table. "So how much of a bastard is Bel being this time?"

Vasily paused with his fork halfway to his mouth. "Sorry?"

Lev smiled over the edge of his cup. "He's in the city, you're here. Doesn't take a genius to guess he's fucked up again."

Vasily snorted and dug into his *blinchiki*. "We're on a break."

"A break." Lev looked amused. But then, Lev always looked amused. Life seemed to entertain him. "Which you both decided to take in the world of Man."

"He's trying to track slavers trading in celestial demons on the terrestrial plane. Thinks he doesn't need my help." Vasily focused on his plate, not wanting to discuss this with Lev, but the demon had a way of making it easy to talk about things Vasily had no intention of talking about.

"And you disagree."

Vasily shrugged. "Doesn't really matter what I think."

"Ah. Yeah. I hate it when Dmitri does that."

Despite himself, Vasily glanced up. "Dmitri does that to you?"

It was Lev's turn to shrug. "He can be kind of secretive. Grigori stuff."

"I thought *you* were Grigori."

"I am, but I didn't grow up with any knowledge of them. I thought I was just a run-of-the-mill demon. Apparently, there are all kinds of political goings-on—rulings by the Grigori Duma, different clans clashing with one another, Nephil rebellions. Dmitri keeps me out of the loop 'for my own good.'"

"*Ha.*" Vasily stabbed at a blin. "I've heard that one before."

Lev gave him a conspiratorial smile. "Guess it kind of comes with the territory when you're dating a dominant demon."

"You and Dmitri . . . ?"

"Nothing as exciting as what you've got going on with Belphagor. But Dmitri definitely prefers to take charge. Anyway, I'll bet you anything Belphagor's going out of his mind wishing he could patch things up with you."

Vasily shrugged and went back to his breakfast. Whether he was or not remained immaterial so long as the hole that needed patching kept getting wider.

The address Belphagor was directed to by his contact wasn't half as nice as his own hotel—and his wasn't all that nice. Like Balam, the others on the Celestial Silk Road referred to "merchandise" and "product." How delightful that free enterprise had come to Russia at last.

It was a member of the *militsia* who greeted Belphagor outside the rundown Soviet tenement. Belphagor balked at the sight of him, ready to take flight, but the officer gave the tattoos on his hands a cursory glance and nodded to him, unsmiling.

"Thirty thousand rubles."

Belphagor wasn't sure if this was the price for the boy or the bribe, but he handed it over. Sometime in the last year and a half, the ruble had been devalued to a fraction of what it had been worth after the collapse of the Soviet Union. The requested amount would barely buy a night's lodging in a youth hostel. The police officer jerked his head toward a dark corridor inside and a set of crumbling wooden stairs that led to a basement apartment. Belphagor took a step down, and the policeman vanished almost as successfully as an airspirit.

Pros were doing business in what looked to be a condemned building—no doors, no amenities, lots of five-thousand-ruble handjobs from the looks of it, exposed bosoms for a few extra, some oral trade, but no one daring to disrobe or touch the floor of the dilapidated rooms for any amount of money. It was a far cry from The Cat or even The Suck, as The Succubus was affectionately known.

At the end of the corridor, a heavy blanket over the doorway announced the seamier trade within. Belphagor avoided eye contact with the patrons lingering in the hallway waiting their turns elsewhere.

Someone spat at his back as he reached the blanket door, and for once he was glad to be earning a man's disgust. He hated to think that buying young boys was commonplace enough to earn anyone's respect.

Inside the curtain, rough pieces of corrugated metal partitioned the room into three, another ratty blanket across each for privacy. Two of the blankets hung open onto empty cubicles, soiled cardboard flats lining the floors. He rapped on the metal wall of the third.

A rough voice came from within. "*Kto tam?*"

He hoped to Heaven he wasn't interrupting a patron. He hadn't planned on killing anyone today. "Grigor Vadimovich sent me."

The blanket was drawn aside just enough for the pimp to stick his head out. "You have money?"

"Thirty thousand rubles." Belphagor used the same figure the policeman had asked for. It seemed to be sufficient.

His host stepped out and took his money, holding the curtain wide for him to enter. "Ten minutes. You take longer, you pay another ninety thousand."

Belphagor waited for the curtain to drop over the opening before he dared to focus on the boy. This was far worse than he'd expected. His whole body shook with anger. On the cardboard mat, the boy, so changed from the one he'd seen before he could only assume it was Silk, lay drugged and listless, a long, dirty undershirt his only clothing. His hair had been hacked off, and he stank of urine. The fading bruises from Kezef's strap were his only positive ID.

Belphagor crouched beside him and lifted the boy's eyelids. The pupils were dilated, and Silk flinched from the light.

"Can you stand?"

Silk staggered to his feet as if it were a command and braced his palms against the back wall.

"*Nyet, mal'chik.*" Belphagor turned him about with an arm around his shoulder. "Come with me."

When he stepped through the curtain with Silk at his side, the pimp sprang forward with alarm. "*Nyet, nyet!* What are you doing?" He tried to pull Silk away.

As much as Belphagor wanted to beat the shit out of the miserable worm, he couldn't afford to blow his cover this soon. "How much to take him off your hands?"

The grubby little bastard looked startled. "Take him? Take him where? What are you going to do with him?" Nice that he asked.

"That's my business." Belphagor pushed up his sleeve to show the dagger tattoo that marked him as an experienced *vor* well versed in cleaning up evidence. "Don't worry. There will be nothing to tie him to you."

The man—no telltale radiance accompanied his spike in anxiety, so not a demon—scratched at his stubble, sizing Belphagor up to see how much he could take him for. "I'm not in the business of moving merchandise."

"That's a shame. I was hoping to be able to do more business with you in the future. If you have better product than this, of course. Fresher."

"I might know of some." His expression turned calculating. "But you're mistaken about the value of this piece. This one will be quite a loss. It'll cost you."

"*Skol'ko?*"

The worm named his price, and Belphagor halved it, prompting the requisite outrage. "Impossible. Do you know how much I can make in a day?"

Belphagor took an envelope from his jacket pocket. "My final offer, in cash." He took a sizable stack of thousand-ruble notes—a denomination he'd never even seen before this fall—from the thick envelope and held it out.

The cash disappeared into the man's pocket. "You wait and leave in ten minutes. I don't want anyone connecting you two with me."

"Where can I find you again to do further business?"

"I'll come to you."

Belphagor gave him the hotel and room number, and the satisfied pimp ducked out.

Silk didn't seem to have noticed this exchange. Belphagor took off his duster and put it around the boy's shoulders. "Just a few minutes. Then we'll go get you something to eat."

Silk roused a bit at that, his stomach growling. Poor kid looked as if he hadn't eaten since Raqia. And probably hadn't. Belphagor's fist clenched at his side.

Getting Silk up the stairs and onto the metro took every bit of influence Belphagor had. He concentrated his energy on drawing attention to his tattoos to the exclusion of Silk's presence and managed to get on the train to Pushkin with him without trouble. They were noticed more in the suburbs, but Belphagor dragged Silk along, berating him for a thief and shouting that he'd find out what happened when someone tried to steal from the *vory*. The sidewalks cleared as if by magic.

Silk stumbled with him, trembling. Though he was far from fluent in Russian, he seemed to understand the threats. Belphagor felt like a heel as Silk pleaded with him in broken Raqia Russian, swearing he hadn't stolen anything, but they'd reached Dmitri's place, and they'd be off the street in a moment.

Lev opened the door when he buzzed, and the Grigori's eyes went wide. "Oh my God, Bel. Get him inside."

"What's going on?" The familiar coal-fire growl came from the kitchen, and Vasily stormed into the entryway but stopped with a look of dismay. "Silk?" He came forward after a stunned moment to take the boy from Belphagor.

Silk looked up at him, his dilated eyes confused. "Ruby?"

Lev glanced at Belphagor. "Ruby?"

But Silk had collapsed in Vasily's arms.

CHAPTER EIGHT

Belphagor followed as Vasily swept Silk up like a rag doll and carried him down the hall to one of the bedrooms.

"He can have the bed." Vasily's voice was a low rumble as he laid him on it. "I'll sleep on the floor."

Silk, vaguely agitated, murmured something incoherent and fell back against the pillow as if he no longer had the strength to hold up his head.

Leaning against the doorframe, Belphagor echoed the feeling. "I don't think he's eaten in several days."

Beside him in the hallway, Lev gasped and did an about-face, heading for the kitchen.

Vasily took the boy's hand, which seemed to calm him. "Where did you find him?"

"You don't want to know."

While Vasily eyed him, no doubt trying to determine whether Belphagor was keeping things from him to be contrary, Lev appeared with a bowl of cabbage soup.

"Help him sit up, Vasily. We need to get some food into him." Lev sat on the edge of the bed while Vasily propped pillows behind Silk. "A little nourishment, a little fluid." Lev held up a spoon. "Just to start with. Vasily, do you want to find him something clean to wear in my room? The top drawers of the bureau are mine."

Belphagor waited until Vasily had gone. "His handler kept him drugged. I don't know what the bastard gave him, but he may be a bit of a mess for a few days."

"A mess?" Lev looked up with a furious scowl. "He looks like he's been under interrogation by the KGB, not turning tricks. What the hell happened to him?"

"He intervened when a sadistic demon took after Vasily with a strap. Guess that was his reward."

"Why was someone after Vasily? Where were *you*?"

Belphagor sighed. "It's a long story."

"Not that long." Vasily was behind him. He pushed past Belphagor. "He sold me to a whorehouse glamoured as a boy and told me to let perverts fuck me."

"I did *not* tell you to let them fuck you. I expressly told you to avoid that."

"Wow." Lev blinked at them, speechless, before offering another spoonful to Silk, but he'd closed his eyes. "Guess that's enough for now." Lev rose and set the bowl on the nightstand.

"I'll get him cleaned up and dressed." Vasily's growl was a clear invitation for Lev and Belphagor to leave.

Lev was quiet while he poured tea in the kitchen.

"I didn't sell him to a whorehouse." Belphagor avoided Lev's eyes as he took the cup. "I mean, I did, but it was part of a hustle. He knew what we were doing. Mostly."

Lev sat. "You don't have to justify yourself to me." His tone said Belphagor did. "So is this why you're on a break?"

Belphagor occupied himself with stirring extra sugar into his tea. "He said we were on a break?"

"You're not?"

"He asked for some space. I didn't think that was a— Fucking hell." He downed his tea like it was vodka and burned his throat. It reminded him of Vasily.

"For what it's worth, he said the word 'break' like you were punishing him. I didn't get the impression it was something he wanted."

Belphagor poured himself another cup. "Well, to be fair, I was the one who said we should spend some time apart. After he asked for space."

"But you're not punishing him."

"Of course I'm not. I'm punishing myself."

"Doesn't that usually mean punishing him?"

Belphagor glared. "We're not doing that anymore."

"Oh. Wow."

"That's why I wanted some time apart. I don't know how to be around him. I think there's something wrong with me."

Lev reached his hand across the table and closed it over Belphagor's. "There's nothing wrong with you. The two of you have a very intense relationship, so it's natural you'd find it difficult to suddenly shift gears."

Lev's touch on his hand brought to mind the fun the four of them had engaged in at the apartment in Moscow. The best part had been punishing Vasily for his role in all of it and how close they'd become through Vasily's surrender. It was afterward that Belphagor had given him the piercing, the promise that he would be Belphagor's always.

The memory of that sublime moment when Vasily had submitted to the piercing of his flesh—not knowing what Belphagor was doing but trusting him so thoroughly that, despite his fear, he'd let Belphagor draw his blood—was painful to think of now.

Vasily appeared in the doorway, and Belphagor yanked his hand from under Lev's, banging his knee on the underside of the table and upending his tea. "Shit. Sorry." He scrambled to sop it up with a napkin, but Lev grabbed a towel from the counter and took care of the mess efficiently.

"Don't worry about it. I'll clean up in here." Lev gave him a pointed look. "Why don't you two relax in the living room for a bit? Dmitri should be home soon."

Relax. With Vasily. Like that was going to happen.

Lev shooed them out, and they sat on the sofa in the living room with a conspicuous space between them that felt like the depths of Lake Baikal.

Vasily broke the silence. "Thank you for finding him."

"I wish I'd managed it in Raqia."

Vasily said nothing to that, which was damning enough.

"You should take him home. As soon as he's better."

Vasily's eyes sparked. "Why would he want to go home? What is there in Raqia for him?"

"What is there in the world of Man? Do you think he wants to stay here? At least in Raqia, the boy can earn a living on his own terms." Belphagor didn't add that Silk's introduction to the world of Man was too like his own to bear thinking on, that every face in the world of Man would remind Silk of faces he'd long to forget, and every human voice would make him cringe for years to come.

"'His own terms'?" Vasily rumbled. "Silk isn't like you—or me, for that matter. He isn't cut out for the street. He needs someone to take care of him."

"And who's going to do that in the world of Man?" As soon as the words were out, a bolt of understanding struck Belphagor through the heart like an electrified arrow, though Vasily said nothing. His boy— because, damn it, *Vasily was his boy*—was prepared to stay here for good to take care of Silk. His boy was in love with another demon.

He rose, agitated. "Vasya, he's—he's just a kid." But maybe that was it. Maybe Vasily only felt protective of him. Maybe it wasn't love he was seeing.

"He's older than me. He's twenty-one."

"*Twenty-one?*"

Before either of them could say anything else, the front door opened, and Dmitri called out from the entryway, "Is that the Prince of Tricks I smell?"

Belphagor stuffed down his dismay, managing a genuine smile as Dmitri came into the room after changing his shoes. "I didn't realize my smell was that distinctive."

Dmitri grinned. "All right, it was your boots by the door that gave you away." He gave Belphagor a hug and a kiss that was somewhat friendlier than Belphagor would have expected and winked as they parted. "But you smell quite nice anyway."

"Well, that's fine," said Lev from the doorway with his hands on his hips. "Kiss Bel first. What am I?"

"You're my *khozyayka*, of course." Dmitri tried to pull Lev into his arms for a kiss, but Lev feigned outrage and turned his head so that Dmitri's kiss landed on his ear.

"You bastard." Lev pushed at him, but Dmitri wrapped his arms around Lev so he couldn't escape.

Vasily glanced at Belphagor. "What's a *khozyayka*?"

Belphagor grinned. "Housewife."

Lev was still steadfastly avoiding Dmitri's lips. "Guess who's sleeping on the couch tonight?"

Belphagor cleared his throat. "Actually, I was hoping I might sleep on your couch tonight."

Dmitri turned, still holding on to the squirming Lev, his look amused. "Why would you sleep on the couch when there's a full-size bed in the guest room for you? After that tiny daybed you two shared at our last place, I'm sure you'll both manage to fit."

"Silk has the bed." Vasily kindly didn't mention that they wouldn't have shared it anyway.

"Silk?"

"He's one of the boys from Raqia I came to track down." Belphagor glanced at Vasily. "Well, apparently not so much a boy as I thought. He's twenty-one. But the demons who sold him passed him off as a youth. He's been beaten and drugged, so he's going to need to recuperate here for a bit."

Dmitri let go of Lev. "*Khrystos*. I'm sorry, I didn't mean to be . . ." He shrugged helplessly.

"Don't apologize. You didn't know. And we don't all need to tiptoe around him being somber and morose. That's only going to make him uncomfortable. Just be kind and friendly. Your usual selves."

"So." Lev threw a sly glance at Dmitri. "You'll be a bastard, Bel will make inappropriate sexual advances toward me, and Vasily will act like he's mad at all of us when it's really Belphagor he wants to punch."

Dmitri looked mortified, and Vasily folded his arms and glared, but Belphagor grinned. "Pretty much."

There wasn't another opportunity to talk to Vasily alone until after they'd eaten dinner and the four of them had shared a bottle of vodka and some smokes. Lev and Dmitri headed off to bed while the midnight summer sun was still shining, but it was difficult to convince a Raqia-bred demon's body that it was time to sleep. Nevertheless, Vasily rose to turn in, taking one of the blankets and pillows Lev had left for them.

"Vasya." Belphagor rose with him, and Vasily tensed. Belphagor steeled himself. It had to be said. "You know that whatever's happening between us, you have my—" *Permission* wasn't the word. Not anymore. "My blessing to do what makes you happy. If that means intimacy with—"

"*Intimacy?*" Flame nearly shot from Vasily's eyes. "You think I want to be intimate with Silk after what's happened to him?"

"Not right now, no. But you obviously care about him a great deal. What I'm saying is that wherever things are with us, I don't want you to worry that you'll make me angry if you want someone . . . who isn't me."

Vasily stared at him, the fire in his eyes going cold. "You're a fucking piece of work, Bel. You can't even conceive of having feelings for someone that don't involve your dick."

"Vasya—"

"Fuck you, Belphagor."

An outline of furious radiance danced over Vasily's skin like the blue glow of the earth's atmosphere he'd seen in pictures of the planet from space. Only Vasily's glow was a painfully beautiful ruby hue that made Belphagor yearn for him. *Ruby.* Like the name Silk had used for him.

"Just fuck you." Vasily took his ruby beauty away from him and closed the door.

"Ruby?"

Vasily lifted his head from the floor. He'd been lying there for hours but hadn't slept, unable to stop thinking about Belphagor's unbelievable arrogance.

Silk peered over the edge of the bed, propped on his elbow. "Is that really you?"

"Yes, it's me." Vasily scrambled to his feet and came to the side of the bed to take Silk's hand.

"Wow." Silk lay back against the pillows, his skin pale. "You're tall. And hairy."

Vasily chuckled softly, and Silk smiled.

"And you've got a really sexy voice. Even your laugh. This is really weird seeing you all grown up."

Vasily sat on the edge of the mattress, squeezing Silk's hand. "I'm so sorry I left you there. I should have taken the beating. It wasn't meant for you."

"Don't be an ass. That was my job, to protect you. It's not like I've never been hit before. And he had a lot worse in mind for you than a few strokes of the strap." Silk closed his eyes. "There've been boys who didn't survive him. He pays extra when things go too far."

"But I shouldn't have run. I should have tried to fight him, to take you with me."

"Ruby—"

"If I'd known they'd sell you right out of Heaven, I never would have left."

Silk sat up, clutching his head. "Out of Heaven? Where the hell am I?"

"The world of Man. The princedom of Russia. You don't remember the Hell Staircase and the train ride?"

"The Hell Staircase? Are you shitting me, Ruby? This isn't funny."

"I'm not. The portals between the spheres use an illusion that makes it seem you're descending into a long, winding stone stairway. They must have kept you drugged for the trip."

"I thought . . ." Silk pushed his hair back from his forehead, his face a bit green. "I thought something seemed weird. I couldn't understand anyone. The patrons—my new master—they didn't look like Raqians. But nothing was making sense anyway; the drugs, I guess. I thought maybe I was hallucinating the weird stuff." He drew his fingers outward through his shorn tresses and gazed up at his fingertips as they came away. "My hair . . ."

"They probably wanted you to blend in." Vasily tried to smooth the hair down. "I'm sorry."

"You're staring at me . . . Is it that bad? It's bad." He bit his lip as he studied Vasily's face. "I can't get over how different you look. I mean, you were lovely before, but now you're—" Silk's gaze traveled downward to Vasily's chest, and he blushed and covered his eyes with his hand. "Sorry. I'm not usually this . . . Gods, I'm acting like a fledgeling."

Vasily gave him a puzzled smile. "Not so lovely anymore?"

Silk moved his hand from his eyes. "*No.* I mean, *yes*, you're—well, lovely's not really the— I guess 'stunning' would be ... Damn it. You're really hot, Ruby."

Vasily withdrew his hand, thinking Silk meant this literally, and then it was his turn to blush. "*Bozhe moi.* Stop it. I am not."

Silk laughed. "Have you seen you?" He sank back against the pillows as if his strength had suddenly left him. "Sorry, I think I'm a little delirious."

Vasily rose. "You must be starving. We should get you some breakfast."

Silk nodded and then looked puzzled, struggling to sit up again. "Don't I have to work? Or do— You didn't buy me, did you?"

Vasily shook his head. "Belphagor did. But not like that. To get you out of there. You're free."

"Free?" Silk's expression changed to one of alarm. "To do what? What am I supposed to do?"

Vasily came back to the bed and took Silk's hand between both of his. "Silk, it's okay. Don't worry. We're at a friend's flat. We'll figure it all out. Right now, all you have to do is rest and get your strength back." He eased Silk back onto the pillows, and on impulse, kissed his forehead. Color washed over Silk's pale face.

As Vasily went to the door, Silk murmured, "Belphagor." His eyes were half-closed. "That's your prince."

Vasily nodded, and his face felt heavy as stone. "That's him."

What little breakfast Silk managed to get down, he unfortunately soon lost. By midday, shaking and feverish, he was racked with stomach cramps.

"Did he pick up a virus?" Vasily stood by as Belphagor examined him.

Belphagor shook his head. "It's the drugs they gave him. They've probably kept him so high he's hardly been aware of what's been happening, which is both a blessing and a curse. He's going to be a bit sick coming off them."

"He was sitting up and talking to me earlier."

Belphagor's expression was guarded as he glanced at Vasily with a nod. "He'll be in and out, I expect." He ran his hand over the spiked tips of his hair. "I need to find out what he knows about the rest of the boys before I make my next move. I can't go into this blind. I guess I'll have to wait it out."

"So sorry he's inconveniencing you."

The hurt and astonishment on Belphagor's face made Vasily's heat with shame. "Vasya." He shook his head for a moment, looking as though he couldn't find words. "We need to talk. This has gone too far."

Belphagor stepped out of the room, and Vasily followed him to the kitchen, hands stuffed into his pockets. He *had* gone too far, and he didn't know what was the matter with him.

He waited while Belphagor poured them both tea from the samovar Lev had left warming when he and Dmitri had gone out this morning. Vasily wished he could say something that would stop this conversation, a quick apology for being a shit. He was behaving out of proportion with events, but anger was choking him—anger toward Belphagor that was so strong it frightened him.

They both remained standing, and Belphagor spoke at last. "I don't know what to do, Vasya. Please. Tell me what to do."

Vasily looked down at the cup and saucer in his hand.

"Are we over?"

Vasily's head shot up. "Well, that would be the easy way out, wouldn't it, Bel?"

"Do you want it to be easy?"

"No, you fucking—" Vasily was gripping his cup too hard, and he cursed as tea sloshed over the sides. Even a firespirit didn't relish boiling water on his skin. "Damn it, Belphagor. Why the hell did you give me this tea?"

Belphagor sipped his. "I thought it would keep you from strangling me or throwing a punch. But maybe that's what you need to do."

"*Strangle* you?" Vasily had certainly considered it.

"I rather hoped you'd choose punching." Belphagor set his cup in his saucer and placed it on the table. "Maybe you just need to have a physical fight." He took Vasily's cup from his hands and set it next to the other. "So go ahead. Hit me. Let me know exactly how you f—" Belphagor's head snapped back in surprise as Vasily's fist made contact with his chin.

"How I feel?" He landed another blow, this time in Belphagor's gut, eliciting a groan and a huff of air. "Did you ask me how I felt when you sold me to the fucking Fletchery and left me there?" Vasily swung again, connecting with a surprisingly hard six-pack as Belphagor braced for it and tightened his abs.

And then, before he knew what had happened, he was on one knee, with Belphagor behind him in a similar stance pinning Vasily's arm at a painful angle, his other arm hooked tightly around Vasily's throat.

"No, I didn't, *mal'chik*." Belphagor's whisper raised goose bumps on his neck. "And I'm sorry. And I love you. And I don't know how to make things right, but I don't want to lose you." He breathed in deeply against Vasily's skin, sending a tremor down his spine. "*Bozhe moi*, I miss fucking you."

The words sent an unexpected, urgent desire rushing through him. "Then fuck me. But quit calling me 'boy.'"

In one swift movement, Belphagor had him up on his feet and bent over the kitchen table, where he unbuttoned and yanked down Vasily's pants with frantic speed. Vasily moaned in anticipation as Belphagor snatched the decanter of salad oil from the table in front of him, belt jangling violently as he released himself.

While the warm oil trickled between Vasily's cheeks, Belphagor set the decanter back on the table as quickly as he'd swept it away, and then, with a groan from both of them, he was in, filling Vasily. He fucked him without mercy, one fist in Vasily's hair and the other pumping Vasily's cock, slick with oil, while teacups rattled and sloshed on the table until they skittered off and shattered on the floor.

Vasily tried to hold out, knowing Belphagor wouldn't come as long as he didn't—wanting to use Vasily when he was spent and moaning softly beneath him, helpless to stop him and incapable of pretending not to want it. But the past couple of weeks without the touch he craved—and the awful tension between them—had him wound so tight that he came far too soon, clutching the edge of the table and groaning through his teeth as his hips jolted.

Belphagor milked his cock until it was almost unbearable, long past empty, and then dug both hands into Vasily's hair like he was gripping a horse's mane and rode him hard, the slap of his hips against Vasily's ass a loud, rapid tattoo, before he let out a deep, guttural shout and let go, jerking powerfully inside him.

Relaxing against him when he'd finished, Belphagor kissed Vasily's neck where the holes of the piercing were closing over, making Vasily tense with a sudden urge to weep. "I can't live without you." Belphagor's whispered breath tickled his skin. "My sweet, angry firespirit. I'll find a way to make you trust me again, I promise."

Vasily's grip loosened on the edge of the table. "Bel—" The front door slammed before he could finish the word.

Belphagor scrambled off him, and Vasily dove for his pants, hitching them up so fast his shorts bunched under his balls.

"I think they heard it that time." Lev's voice held profound amusement. After loudly removing their shoes and slipping into their *tapochki*, Lev and Dmitri sauntered into the kitchen hand in hand. Lev frowned at the broken teacups.

Belphagor followed his glance. "Sorry. Slippery fingers." He wiped oil on his pants. "I'll pay to replace them."

"You're going to clean that up," said Lev a bit tersely. Breaking teacups, it seemed, was crossing a line with him. He motioned with his eyes toward the floor beneath the table. "And you're going to clean *that* up too."

Heat climbed Vasily's face.

But Belphagor's eyes danced with amusement. "I'll take care of the tea and cups, Vasya. You can get the cream."

CHAPTER NINE

Belphagor knew the sex wasn't a magic salve that would fix everything that was wrong between them, but it had taken the edge off the feelings of hopelessness and despair. Not to mention it had been fucking intense.

After the others had gone to bed, he sat on the couch watching television. Even with the windows open, the air was too stifling for sleep. A few annoying mosquitos took advantage of the situation, whining past him, but demons were lucky in that respect: the pests seemed not to like their blood.

Not really paying attention to the news program that was on, he found himself pleasantly uncomfortable as he pictured Vasily bent over the kitchen table. Belphagor unbuttoned and stroked himself, eyes closed as he took himself through the scene step by step. Bringing Vasily to the ground. Eliciting his gruff, unexpected expression of desire. Swinging him onto the table and stripping him. Oil dripping between his cheeks. Vasily's groan. Fucking his boy.

A soft expletive burst out of him with his ejaculation.

The creak of the floorboards gave away someone standing in the doorway. "I see my timing's off again."

Belphagor opened his eyes, unembarrassed, to meet Lev's smirk from where he leaned against the doorframe.

"Too hot to sleep?"

Belphagor smiled, stroking the sticky fluid over his abs. "Was. So I took care of it."

Lev sat beside him on the sofa, casting a fleeting glance at Belphagor's softening erection. "Still seems pretty warm in here to me." He shifted on the cushions, the outline of his own erection unmistakable within the loose boxers. "Sounded like you and Vasily were making up earlier."

"Not exactly. More like a truce."

"I like the way you truce." Lev grinned. "Almost makes me wish you and I would have a fight."

Belphagor laughed. "Stick around. I'm sure I can do something to make you angry."

"*Stick* around." Lev's eyes twinkled. "Is that an order, Prince of Tricks?" He crossed his feet, legs stretched out in front of him in a way that accentuated the hard-on, letting his toes brush against Belphagor's.

Now here was a landmine Belphagor hadn't expected to have to navigate so soon. Under different circumstances, the four of them would be enjoying getting reacquainted. Belphagor had promised them as much on his last visit. He hated to nip such a nascent bloom in the bud.

"I suppose it's more of a hopeful suggestion. But prove to me that you can be a good boy and control yourself, and perhaps at some future date—"

The slam of the bathroom door derailed the sentiment.

"Shit." Belphagor put his clothes back together as Lev pulled a pillow onto his lap. "Dmitri or Vasily?"

Lev gave him an apologetic wince. "Dmitri's not really a slammer."

"*Shit.*" Belphagor got up and went down the hall to the bathroom and knocked.

"Fuck off." The firespirit growl was muffled. *Shit, shit and shit.*

He leaned his head against the wood. "Vasya—" The door swung open, and he nearly fell inside.

"What the fuck is wrong with you?" Vasily was red with fury, and his element sparked along his skin like static charges in the dark, but the worst thing about his appearance was that his face was streaked with tears.

"*Lyubov.* It was only friendly conversation."

"You gave him orders, Beli." The choked-out endearment cut him like a knife. "I can't be your boy, so you found another. Right in front of me."

"*No.*" Belphagor reached for him. "No, *mal'chik*, that isn't true."

"Don't fucking call me 'boy'!" Vasily slammed the door so fast Belphagor didn't have time to move, and it struck him in the face.

While he stood staring at it in shock with blood running over his lip, Dmitri came out of the bedroom.

"What's all this yelling and slamming?"

Lev spoke from the entrance to the living room. "I fucked up."

Still gripping the outside of the doorframe, Belphagor watched a spot of blood drip onto the parquet between his feet. "You didn't do anything, Lev."

"Except spy on you while you were having a lovely orgasm thinking about Vasily and then flirt shamelessly with you." Lev took a tentative step toward the bedroom. "I'm sorry, Dmitri. I should have thought about how it would look."

Belphagor pushed away from the frame and turned, ready to give his own apology, but Dmitri spoke before he could.

"And why would you want to do that, Lyova, when it's so much easier to get your rocks off with the Prince of Tricks while I sleep? Maybe you should just share the couch with him tonight." Dmitri stepped back into the bedroom, shutting Lev out.

After a stunned pause, Lev glanced over at Belphagor. "You're bleeding."

Belphagor shrugged, brushing the back of his hand against his upper lip.

"I'm so sorry about this." Lev was clearly about to cry. *Fuck.* Then he'd have two crying demons on his hands.

"It's not your fault. I should have been more discreet. I'm an asshole."

"That's for fucking sure!" Vasily's angry growl was encouraging. It was when Vasily was silent that Belphagor really had to worry.

"Go ahead and take the couch, Lev. I'll figure something out."

A loud snort came from the bathroom, and Belphagor couldn't help a little smile. He turned back and took a deep breath once Lev had gone. "Vasya?"

"Fuck you."

"I'm going to open the door." He took the lack of response as an invitation.

Vasily was leaning back against the porcelain sink, red-eyed but not with anger. "I actually thought you meant it when you said you'd make me trust you."

Belphagor sighed and scrubbed his hand over his face. "I admit, I'm not off to a good start."

"*Ha*!"

"I'm not going to pretend the flirting was one-sided, and I know I've hurt you. But I want to say this one thing to you: I did not find another boy. I will never find another boy. You are the only boy I will ever have—"

"Damn it, Belphagor—"

"And if I can't win back your trust, if I simply don't deserve your trust, I'll have to accept that I've lost the one thing I value most. But for the rest of my life, however long that is, there will only ever be you."

Vasily was crying again, firespirit tears that steamed as they dripped down his face.

Belphagor took a step toward him. "Please don't cry, love. I'd rather you hit me again."

"You always want to take the easy way out." Vasily swatted at the tears with the palms of his hands. "Was that true what Lev said? Were you really thinking of me when you came?"

The unexpected question took him aback. "Of course. Reliving those moments with you bent over the table today will sustain me for a long time."

Vasily ducked his head as if he'd almost smiled and wanted to hide it. "Well, they may have to. I'm going to stay here with Silk for a while. Not *here*, I mean, but the world of Man. I need you to give me some facets. I know you have a lot more than you pretend, and I need some. I'll pay you back."

Belphagor tried to still the anxious bird that had taken up residence in his chest since Vasily had come along, wings beating hard enough to break. "Where are you going to go on your own? You don't know anything about the world of Man."

"I know enough. We'll find a safe house first, and then I'll find a place we can afford on your facets until I can build up my clientele."

"Your *clientele*?"

Vasily looked up sharply, his eyes fierce. "Don't tell me what to do with my body. Don't you say a word. It's not yours anymore."

He tried to ignore the pain in his chest. "You could be killed for doing business here. You don't understand."

"I am not *stupid*, Belphagor."

"My first time in prison was for solicitation and sodomy."

This actually gave Vasily pause. "What's sodomy?"

"Basically, any sexual act that isn't directly related to procreation." Belphagor folded his arms across his chest. "Trust me when I say you do not want to go to prison for that."

Vasily was quiet a moment, and then he shrugged. "I'll have to make sure I don't get caught, then."

"And you think there's a big market in the world of Man for six-foot-five rentboys with wild, flame-colored locks who look like they could crush a car."

Vasily glared. "There's a market for everything."

While that was likely true, Vasily would be eaten alive in the world of Man trying to find his.

"I understand that you don't trust me emotionally. But I wish you would trust my judgment." He held up his hand before Vasily could interrupt him. "I've also known you long enough to realize I don't stand a chance of dissuading you. So I'll give you the money. *Money*, not facets. You have to start thinking like a terrestrial or you won't last a day here on your own. But please consider undertaking a less dangerous line of work. Dmitri can find you something."

"Bel—"

"If you want my financial support, you will make the attempt. I'll arrange with Dmitri to keep an account for you."

Vasily's lips were a thin line. "Fine."

Belphagor studied him, as if he could memorize everything—the angry set of Vasily's jaw, the spark of fire in his pupils, the firewood scent of him—if he stared long enough. "But this is temporary. When I've tracked down the missing demons and returned them safely to Heaven, we're going to face this once and for all."

Belphagor slept in a chair in the kitchen, not wanting to add any more fuel to the fire he'd ignited between Lev and Dmitri. In the morning, Silk was lucid enough that Belphagor was able to question him, but he remembered little from the drugged haze the traffickers had kept him in. He hadn't been aware that he'd fallen to the world of Man until Vasily had told him.

The only recourse Belphagor had now was to return to his hotel room in the city and wait for the procurer to make contact. But before heading out, a private conversation with Dmitri was in order.

They smoked and walked through nearby Alexander Park, past the museums that had once been the palaces of tsars.

"I'm not pissed at you, Bel." Dmitri took a drag on his cigarette. "It would be a pointless exercise, like being mad at a thunderstorm for standing in its downpour and getting struck by lightning."

"I'm not sure whether to be relieved or offended."

Dmitri exhaled a puff of smoke. "Don't push your luck."

"I don't want to be a source of tension between you and Lev. It truly was harmless flirting, compounded by my own personal lapse in judgment. I admit, I could have exercised a little more decorum. But it's not as if he meant to do something behind your back. If he'd been planning on cheating on you, he wouldn't have done it in the next room."

"Tread carefully." A sharp flick of glowing ash from Dmitri's cigarette landed on Belphagor's sleeve and singed the fabric before he slapped it out.

"You know what I mean—you know him better than that."

Dmitri sighed as they reached the shore of the little lake at the center of the park, pausing to stare out at the water. "Belphagor, it's obvious that you and Lev click in a way that you and I never have. And that's fine. You and I are far too competitive to ever fully enjoy each other sexually on our own. But Lev and I have something real here."

"I know that."

"As real as what you have with Vasily—which you're going to have to come to terms with and do some heavy self-examination if you ever intend to fix the damage you've done. You think every encounter is a game and that everyone else sees it that way." Dmitri turned and met his eyes. "Vasily isn't playing at submitting to you.

I don't think he's fully aware of the sexual subtext between your charged interactions. He's genuinely angry. And so far, you've managed to channel his anger into the intense physical encounters you both thrive on. But make no mistake. Every time you drive him to that edge, he thinks it's the end."

Belphagor stared down at the cigar he was turning between his fingers. "How did we end up talking about me and Vasily?"

"Lev and I will be all right. He explained things. And I've told him that if the opportunity arises, he can play with you on his own if he likes. As long as it's only play. But that firespirit of yours isn't going to see it that way. So I suggest you make things right with him before you have any more lapses in judgment—with Lev or anyone else. And if you don't intend to take your relationship with him as seriously as he does, you should let him go now before you do some real harm."

This wasn't the conversation Belphagor had expected to have. He swallowed uncomfortably. "I do take it seriously. More than anything in my life. He knows that. It's never been a game with him."

Dmitri lifted his brow. "Well, you'd better find a way to let him know that everything else is. Own who you are, Belphagor. And then own him the way he wants to be owned. Or you're going to lose him."

The goodbye with Vasily before Belphagor headed for the train station felt like an irrevocable parting. Worse than he'd felt when he'd left Vasily in the world of Man after deliberately hurting him to keep him safe while he'd returned to Heaven to clear Vasily's name. At least then, he'd known Vasily needed and wanted him. He'd left his boy hurt and angry, but Vasily had been angry because he loved Belphagor, not because he—maybe—couldn't anymore.

After Belphagor said his very chaste goodbye to Lev, Dmitri and Lev made themselves scarce while he and Vasily stood in the entryway of the apartment. Vasily kept his hands in his pockets and his eyes on his feet.

Belphagor handed him an envelope.

The hazel eyes darted upward and down again. "What's this?"

"Dmitri's going to set up an account for you, as we discussed. But it might take a few days before you can access it. He has to get you an identity."

"An identity?"

"Official papers so you can travel and rent property without arousing suspicion. Which will also make it easier for you to get home. If you intend to return to the portal on your own, you'll need to buy tickets for the train since I won't be there to influence them for you." He held his breath, afraid Vasily would say he wouldn't be going home.

Vasily's eyes widened as he opened the envelope and saw the stack of bills.

"That's to tide you over until the account is ready."

"How much is this in facets?"

"Just a handful. The ruble isn't worth much at the moment, so it looks like more than it is." He didn't mention that a handful of facets would probably keep Vasily and Silk comfortably for a year in Russia. In reality, this was the value of a half-carat crystal, and it hadn't come from his stash. He'd kept accounts in the world of Man for decades, nicely maturing. They'd gotten significantly smaller since the last time he'd fallen, but not all of his accounts were in Russia. He still had enough to support a number of demons indefinitely if the idea took him.

"I'll send word to Dmitri when I find anything out." It took every bit of control he had to keep his voice steady. "And you'll keep Dmitri apprised of your whereabouts."

Vasily nodded, and they stared at one another in silence.

"Well." Belphagor gave him a brusque nod. "I'll see you."

He turned and headed for the stairs, silently willing Vasily to come after him, to say it was all a mistake. But there was no sound of pursuit behind him as he descended. There was nothing at all.

Vasily gripped the envelope in his hand so tightly he crumpled the paper bills. Belphagor had left him without a backward glance. Like last time, it was so easy for Belphagor to leave. And to take Vasily's heart with him, crushed on the bottom of his boot.

He closed the door and crammed the envelope into his pocket, heading back to check on Silk. His color was better, and he'd managed to eat some kasha this morning without it coming back up.

Silk gave him a weak smile. "Hey, Ruby. Guess that's not your name, is it?"

Vasily smiled back. "Doesn't matter. I like hearing you say it." He sat at the edge of the bed. "What about you? Has Silk always been your name?"

The smile faded a bit. "It's the name I chose."

"It suits you."

Silk relaxed, and a self-effacing laugh escaped him. "Not right now." He rubbed one of his arms with a grimace. "I'm a bit rough at the moment. Think you could help me get a bath?"

"They have a shower here. Come on, I'll show you." He helped Silk out of the bed and down the hall to the bathroom, Silk leaning heavily against him. Dmitri and Lev were still hiding out in their bedroom, as if they'd expected Vasily to fly into a rage at Belphagor's departure.

He got the water warm while Silk sat on the edge of the tub watching with fascination. "Do you need help with anything? I can give you your privacy—"

"I bathed *you*, Ruby." Silk winked as he slipped out of the borrowed nightshirt. "The least you could do is reciprocate." Vasily blushed, offering him a hand to help him into the bath, and Silk continued holding it once he stood under the water. "Aren't you going to join me?"

"I've already had a shower."

Silk released Vasily's hand and tilted his head back under the spray, his unkempt hair soaking up the water until it lay flat against his head. Vasily couldn't help staring at the fading bruises and cuts, evidence of what Silk had done for him. More than ever, Vasily wanted to take care of him.

With the plastic curtain still open, Vasily's shirt was getting soaked. He took it off and laid it aside, and Silk's eyes opened as he stepped out of his house shoes and pants.

"I'll get your hair." Vasily climbed in and closed the curtain before taking the shampoo from the side of the tub and pouring some into his hand. The scent reminded him of the oil Belphagor used as a lubricant, and there was no way to hide the effect this thought had on him as he reached out to lather Silk's hair.

Silk turned so Vasily could get the back, his own slim cock perking up beneath the warm water. After a moment, he swayed against Vasily, unsteady on his feet, and Vasily wrapped his arms around him. Silk let out a moan, soft skin curving against Vasily's erection as foamy lather ran down his stomach from Vasily's hands into the dusky curls at the base of his cock.

Shivering in the steaming water, Silk rested his head against Vasily's chest. "Damn, you feel good."

"I shouldn't be doing this."

"Why?" Silk glanced up. "Because of Belphagor? He left you. Again. And he was fooling around on you in the next room last night." Silk's body, smooth and sleek like his namesake, slipped against him. "And this is only a bath."

Vasily's arms tightened around Silk. "You heard everything that happened?"

"I've been sick, not dead." He arched slightly, the movement encouraging Vasily's cock to settle in the hollow at the small of his back. "Soap me up?" Silk handed him the bar of soap from the little rack in front of them.

Vasily closed his hand around it and ran it over Silk's smooth chest, the dark nipples peaking at his touch while Silk let out another moan, and downward over Silk's abs. When Vasily hesitated at his groin, Silk took the bar and lathered himself. His erection stood out prominently, slick and waiting.

Silk tossed the soap back. "Lather yourself."

Vasily shook his head. The bitter truth was that even if it was no more than Belphagor might do with a "friend" given half a chance, it didn't feel right. And Silk had been through too much. Vasily felt funny just touching him, afraid he was taking advantage.

"I can't."

With a sigh and a shrug, Silk braced one palm against the wall of the shower, took hold of his own erection with the other, and worked himself, eyes closing and cheeks turning pink and flushed with arousal.

He was almost brutally efficient, bringing himself over in a matter of seconds and letting out a sharp cry as he shot over his fist.

As the water carried the evidence away, Silk's legs wobbled beneath him, and Vasily caught him, pulling him close—which made trying to ignore his own unresolved state a bit awkward. He focused his element, drawing the heated blood up and away from where it was presently concentrated, and breathed it out over Silk's head. For a moment, the shower filled with steam.

Silk raised his head and shivered as he gazed at him. "Your eyes— Heavens, Ruby. How are you real?"

The shower was getting cold. After Vasily turned off the faucet, he picked Silk up as easily as he might have a child, stepping out of the tub.

Silk's arms slid around Vasily's neck while he grinned at him. "Damn. If you weren't already holding me, I think I'd swoon."

Vasily laughed nervously. "I have to put you down to get dressed."

Silk shrugged. "Well, if you have to, you have to." He was still a bit shaky as his feet hit the ground. Vasily wrapped him in a towel before drying off with another and pulling on his pants.

As he stepped into his *tapochki*, he swept Silk up again to Silk's obvious delight. "I'll have to get you something clean to wear."

Silk shrugged. "Can't say I really mind being naked in your arms."

While Vasily carried him down the hall, Lev came out of the kitchen, and Vasily nearly dropped his burden. Eyebrows raised, Lev backed into the room.

Silk glanced over Vasily's shoulder as they passed the kitchen doorway. "That him? The one your prince was fucking around on you with?"

Vasily said nothing until they were inside the bedroom and he'd closed the door. He set Silk on his feet. "That's Lev, yes. I'd rather not make a big deal out of it, though. Belphagor says he was only flirting." He ignored the rude snort Silk offered in response to this claim. "Anyway, we have to stay here for a few more days before Dmitri can set us up in another safe house."

Silk sat on the bed, arms braced on the mattress behind him as the towel fell away. "Safe house?"

"With the demon underground. When demons fall, the underground helps get us acclimated, keeps us from getting noticed by the authorities—local and celestial."

"Who are we hiding from?"

"Well . . . no one, I guess. Belphagor paid for you. But there are a lot of pitfalls here. We can't strike out on our own without easing into it with a little help. That's what the underground is for. But it's only until we're settled and we can get our own place." He took the envelope from his pocket. "I've got enough money—it's like facets— to keep us for a bit, and there's more where this came from."

Silk's expression was one of misgiving. "Settled? I don't intend to settle here."

Water dripped from Vasily's locks onto the floor in the quiet that followed. "Not all the people here are like the ones who hurt you. There are good people too. And things that will amaze you. But if you'd rather, we can go back. I can find somewhere for us in Raqia where you'll be safe."

"Safe." Silk's expression seemed almost pitying. "Ruby. I know I look young, but I'm not a child. I don't need to be kept safe."

"I'm not saying you're a child—"

"Just that you want to protect me. Which is *so* sweet. Really." He held out his hand, and Vasily took it. "But as much fun as it is being carried in your arms, it's not something I . . . need." Vasily pulled his hand back, and Silk frowned. "Now I've hurt you. I'm sorry."

"What do you think you're going to do in Raqia on your own?" Vasily cringed, realizing he was echoing Belphagor's words. "Work the streets? I've done it, Silk. It isn't for you."

"I'll find someone . . . suitable." Silk hastened on when Vasily flinched. "To exploit, Ruby. A mark. Don't you see? Like the curators of the Fletchery. I pretended to be what they wanted me to be. I played a part and was paid well for it."

Khai had said there was more to Silk's story than Vasily understood, that Silk wasn't a victim. But he couldn't have been helping the victimizers. "What part?"

Silk's pallid cheeks went pink. "You know what part. You were there. I made sure everyone was happy."

"*Happy*? What about the boys?"

"What *about* the boys?"

Heat began to boil beneath the surface of his skin. "Did you even care what happened to them?"

Silk reacted with sudden anger, leaping to his feet, though he was still unsteady. "Do you want to know what it was like for the boys when there wasn't someone like me there to see that they were treated kindly and with respect? I can tell you, because I know firsthand. We were sold by our masters or our parents, and no one told us what was going to happen, though we guessed. Some of us tried to escape. The guards punished us. And then our turns came, and we were dragged into the private rooms where our patrons waited. No courtship, no choice in the matter. No comforts offered. And—if we were unlucky enough to get someone like Kezef—no one to heed our cries. You may have noticed that Kezef wasn't strictly interested in fletching. So long as he didn't spoil the merchandise, he could use the same boy again and again—until he tired of him." Silk dropped back onto the bed, his face pale.

Vasily's fire had gone out. "Silk—"

"I don't want your pity or your judgment. Or your patronage."

"My patronage?"

Silk glanced at the envelope in Vasily's hand. "That's what you're offering. To keep me."

Vasily gaped at him, horrified. "No! I wasn't going to ask anything of you!"

Silk sighed and shook his head. "You already have, Ruby. You want me to play a part I can't. Because I care about you. I can't use you the way I'd use a mark."

Vasily stared at the envelope before placing it on the nightstand. "This is for you to get back home. I'll show you where to buy your ticket to the portal."

"Don't be angry with me."

"I'm not angry. I'm confused. They sold you, Silk. The men you worked for—the minute the heat was on them, they drugged you and sold you, as if you were nothing more than livestock."

"Well, I didn't say I'd go back to them, did I? And you're a fine one to lecture me. You worked the streets of Raqia when you were as young as you looked at the Fletchery, didn't you? How is that different?"

Vasily's cheeks burned. "Because I chose to. It was what I was good at. And I didn't have any other options."

"Well, touché, you lovely fiery thing. And stop doing that glowy thing with your eyes. It's making me think of the shower." Silk's fluttering lashes made Vasily smile despite himself, and Silk laughed, holding out his hand. "Come here. Let's not fight. Sit with me." When Vasily took the offered hand, Silk drew him toward the bed. "It was sweet of you to want to take care of me, Ruby. But I'll land on my feet. Don't you worry about me."

Belphagor wallowed. There was no other word for it. After running a bath with water from questionable pipes, he soaked in it until he'd pruned and the water was tepid.

Dmitri's words circled in his head like the bathwater circling the drain. *Let him know that everything else is a game. Own who you are.* Could he do that? Was it that simple? Explain to Vasily that he was the only one who mattered to Belphagor—that Belphagor's desires for anyone else were mere entertainment? It wasn't entirely true, of course. Phaleg, the angelic officer he'd trained as part of his scheme to thwart the principality's assassination, had meant something to him. And, in truth, Lev meant something too. It was a playful bond, but a bond nonetheless.

As he dried off, he noticed the phone on the nightstand. Maybe over the safe distance of wires, he could say the things that didn't seem to come out right when he and Vasily were face-to-face. He wrapped the towel around his waist and phoned Dmitri's place, lying back on the bed.

Lev answered, a welcome reprieve. They chatted and flirted for a few minutes before Belphagor gathered his nerve. "So how's Vasily taking this? Is he still sulking about last night?"

Lev was too quiet. "No. I wouldn't say that."

Belphagor sat up straight. "What's going on?"

"Nothing's going on. He's, you know . . . keeping occupied."

"*Lev.*"

Lev cleared his throat with obvious discomfort. "I think Silk is feeling better."

"Meaning?"

"Dmitri and I heard them . . . showering."

Belphagor steadied his breathing. "Maybe Silk needed help."

"Well, it sounded like he got plenty."

"I see." Vasily had vehemently refuted Belphagor's assumption that he desired Silk. It should have been a glaring sign of what was coming.

"Maybe you should come back and make up with him before things get any weirder."

"This is what he wants." Belphagor's tone was clipped. "No amount of talk is going to change his mind."

"Bel—"

"Thanks, Lev. I'll be in touch."

He'd been a fool to imagine this was only temporary. Vasily had outgrown him. Had outgrown, plain and simple, being a *boy*. What the hell was wrong with Belphagor? *He* was the one who was acting like a child, remaining stuck in an infinite adolescence. It was embarrassing. His rule had always been to keep his heart out of the game, but he'd allowed himself to become sentimental, imagining there could ever be more to it than that. But the truth of the matter was he was the only one playing. And he'd lost.

CHAPTER TEN

There was soon more, however, to occupy Belphagor's mind than self-pity. The *vory v zakone* had taken an interest in him. The attention of the Russian underworld was something he'd spent much of his life within the terrestrial sphere avoiding. During his stints in prison, of course, it had been impossible. The power of influence in such places was a crucial skill—and far more difficult to pull off among those for whom influence was a tool of the trade.

But it was his time in the *zona* that had made him determined not to draw their attention once he was out of it. He'd earned their respect eventually, but it was hard won and constantly challenged, and in the language written on his body in ink, he was a walking contradiction.

Outside the *zona*, only the tattoos on his hands were generally visible unless he chose to reveal more, but those, on this summer morning in the hotel restaurant, were enough.

"*Eto ne tvoe mesto.*"

Belphagor looked up from his porridge into the face of a very surly, very tattooed *vor* whose hands were in his pockets, which didn't bode well. "I beg your pardon?"

"You don't speak Russian?" The other man spoke the words in English with disdain, despite Belphagor having spoken to him in Russian, apparently taking Belphagor for an American or a Brit with his celestial accent. "You don't belong here, *anglichanin*. You'll beg for something else if you stick your nose in Russian business again."

With a mild lift of his eyebrow, Belphagor went back to his porridge. "You're confused. I'm a Russian national." This wasn't strictly true, but he had forged papers that said he was, which was all that mattered.

The *vor* whipped out a pocketknife before Belphagor could react and slammed it into the wood of the table inches from where Belphagor held his spoon.

He stared straight at Belphagor. "Let me spell it out for you in *angliski*, in case you don't understand: if you show up on our turf again, I'll cut your throat."

Belphagor set down his spoon and moved his hand to his lap as the *vor* yanked the knife out of the tabletop. He had no weapons in his pockets, but it wouldn't hurt to let his challenger think he did.

Misdirection was the foundation of all influence. With his other hand, he picked up his teacup, making sure the crown on his left middle finger over the snake-entwined sword was visible as he lifted the cup to his lips. Misdirection number two. He wasn't left-handed, but the suggestion that he was tended to make Russians suspicious that he might be capable of anything. Leave it to the world of Man to be more superstitious about simple genetics than the Heavens.

As he lowered the cup, he brought his right hand back up to the table. The *vor* snapped his gaze toward the motion, missing the fact that Belphagor was aiming the cup at his face as he flung its contents. With a yelp of pain, the man let down his guard for an instant—long enough for Belphagor to snatch the pocketknife and leap to his feet, pressing the tip of the knife against the underside of the *vor*'s jaw. The few other diners slipped out of their chairs and quietly left the restaurant.

"Let me spell something out for *you*," he said calmly. "I've killed men for less disrespect. You come to my table while I'm eating my breakfast and insult me without provocation. Ordinarily, I'd ignore you, since you've made no attempt to even identify yourself in relation to your claim of 'turf,' but it so happens that I'm in a foul mood this morning. I'm inclined to carve out your tongue from below so that you won't make the mistake of insulting someone so out of your league again."

The man raised his arms, palms out. "I must have mistaken you for someone else."

"The hell you did. No one else looks like me." He pressed the tip of the knife a little harder under the man's jaw. He hadn't broken the skin yet, but the slightest pressure would do it. "Who sent you here?"

"We were told by one of our agents that you were attempting to move in on our business. That you showed up asking questions about our inventory."

"Did this agent happen to mention that I'm not interested in selling, I'm interested in buying?" He lowered the knife and pocketed it, sitting down once more and adjusting his sleeves.

The *vor* tried to recover some dignity now that he wasn't in imminent danger. "We don't sell. We rent."

"Anyone will sell for the right price." Belphagor straightened his teacup in the saucer and poured himself another. "And I'm prepared to offer the right price."

The man laughed. "Like the price you offered for the piece you coerced from our agent? It wasn't for sale, and we want it back."

Belphagor sat back in his chair with the cup in hand. "Would a restaurateur request a fine meal be returned after a patron consumed it?"

The *vor* folded his arms. "We don't deal in fine dining. We deal in more durable entertainment. Like video rental. You pay to enjoy temporarily. The tape can be used again."

Belphagor shrugged. "Not this tape. It broke." He sipped his tea. "I have very specific and eclectic tastes. And a rather insatiable appetite. If you feel your supply can't meet my demand for my price, I have other connections."

"Your price is meaningless. Half a million rubles are worth a new car one day and a cab ride the next. A single-transaction trade is of no use to our enterprise for a product that will bring in multiple clients at current currency value if we do no business with you."

"And what if I traded other commodities instead?"

The *vor* looked dubious. "What other 'commodities'?"

"How would diamonds suit you and your organization?"

The *vor* looked Belphagor up and down with a sneer. "You don't have diamonds."

"I have many investments." Belphagor went back to drinking his tea and eating his *kasha* as if the conversation were over, while the *vor* continued to stand in front of his table and stare at him. "Perhaps you'd like to have a more senior member of your organization negotiate with me. You don't seem up to the task of serious business matters."

He took a notecard and a pen from inside his breast pocket and wrote on the card. "Have your boss meet me here at two o'clock." He left it lying on the table for the man to take and paid him no more attention. Wisely, the *vor* picked up the card and left.

The location he'd written down was as public a place he could think of that would allow for privacy while still ensuring the "boss" didn't show up with an entourage of thugs to beat the hell out of him. He'd chosen the Field of Mars.

Tourists wandered about the manicured lawns, its geometric lines and artfully arranged vegetation leaving the vistas of the park wide open to the bordering streets and palace and the Moyka River beyond. Belphagor waited beside the eternal memorial flame at the center of the park, which afforded him an unobstructed view in all directions. Flanked by a modest entourage of two bodyguards—one whose acquaintance Belphagor had already made—the man he'd arranged to meet was impossible to miss in his impeccable Armani suit and silk tie in the middle of summer.

Belphagor, likewise, was conspicuous in his leather duster and spiked hair. Tourists seemed to magically clear the area. Perhaps Belphagor had overestimated the safety of the public space. He might be able to match wits with these thugs and, if it came down to it, match them in a physical fight with the advantage of his elemental radiance, but radiance would be little help against firearms at close range.

The boss wasted no time. "You're the hooligan who insults my intelligence with claims of your vast wealth."

"You can call me *Knyaz*." Belphagor paused politely. "And you would be?"

The gangster laughed. "The Prince, is it?" He folded his arms, clearly not interested in pleasantries. "Yuri Yegorevich Andropov. You should have heard of me, judging by your ink."

"I've been abroad. Which is why you haven't heard of *me*." He mirrored Andropov's stance. "Otherwise, you'd know that my resources are more than adequate to finance my needs."

"And what are your needs, exactly?"

Belphagor began to stroll about the brazier. "I'm interested in acquiring any unique inventory you may have. Anything you want to move quickly."

Andropov watched him circle the monument. "And what do you mean by 'unique'?"

"I think you know. Like the piece I acquired. Wasn't exactly local, was it?"

"You want imports."

"Precisely." Belphagor stopped and met his eyes across the flame. "Perhaps you've recently received a shipment of similar items you need to unload. Perhaps higher quality. Undamaged. Pristine."

The *vor*'s eyes darkened, and his men moved around the monument at a silent command from him. "If you're *militsia*, I have no qualms about burying you at the bottom of the Neva. I have connections. No one will miss you."

Belphagor laughed. "Do I look like *militsia*?"

"How do you know about my inventory?"

"You know how information travels on the underground. Even deeply underground, it can be had for a price. And I always have the price."

Andropov frowned. "Suppose I do have such a shipment. And let us suppose for the sake of argument that you could actually afford to make a trade I would find acceptable. What guarantee do I have that you won't set up business on my turf with my inventory?"

"As I've already stated, I have no interest in private enterprise. I merely wish to purchase and consume."

The *vor* looked him over, scowling in thought. "But you're not the one who will be consuming."

"Am I not?"

"No one with such tastes would have survived in the *zona*." He spat on the ground for good measure, making a loud, raucous production of it, letting Belphagor know what he thought of pedophiles. And yet he didn't mind the money to be made selling children to them. How enterprising.

"What I do with them is none of your business. What *is*, however, is your price. Name it."

Andropov observed him with an unreadable expression before shaking his head. "I'll be in touch."

Damn. Belphagor had hoped this would remain a simple business transaction. He was going to need backup.

Back at the hotel, he was surprised to find a note waiting at the desk for him when he retrieved his papers from the safe. Lev had called.

He collected his keys from the *matrona* on his floor and took his time before picking up the phone to dial Lev. He wasn't looking forward to the lecture—or to hearing more about what Vasily was up to with his beautiful boy.

"Lev." He hurried on without waiting for Lev to say what he'd intended. "Can you put Dmitri on? I need to talk to him about hiring some muscle. It's kind of urgent, so if you don't mind, we can talk later."

"Belphagor."

His heart dropped into his stomach at the sound of Vasily's voice. Lev had ignored his brush-off and handed Vasily the phone. "I thought you were Lev."

"He phoned you for me. He figured you might not want to talk to me." The tight rumble said he was pissed about something. "After what he told you yesterday." So he was pissed that Belphagor knew he'd been fucking Silk. Charming.

"Why wouldn't I want to talk to you? You've made your plans plain to me. I didn't realize how dedicated you were to them, of course, but I would never stand in your way."

There was a slight pause before the gravelly voice became even rougher, if that were possible. "Heaven forbid you'd stand in my way, Bel. Goddamn it. Hang on." His voice became slightly muffled, but only slightly. He clearly hadn't gotten the hang of using the phone. "You talk to him. I can't talk to him."

Lev's reply was too low to hear.

"I hate this thing." And then he was back. "I don't want to argue with you, Belphagor."

"Good. Then don't." Belphagor slammed down the receiver, his heart pounding in his chest and his face unnaturally warm. *Khrystos,*

Bel. Get a fucking grip. This wasn't like him. He was giving Vasily the upper hand in their breakup.

His heart almost stopped. Because that was what this was, wasn't it? A goddamn breakup. He swept up the phone, ready to hurl it at the wall, but paused before letting it fly. He still had to talk to Dmitri. Fucking hell.

When he'd gotten himself together, he sat on the bed and picked up the receiver once more. No dial tone.

"Hello?" The gruff voice sounded surprised.

"The phone didn't ring," said Belphagor defensively.

"It didn't ring here either. I was about to dial."

Weird. The line must not have disconnected when they'd hung up. He could hear the warm breath on the other end of the line.

Belphagor wound the cord in his hand, stroking his thumb against the rubbery plastic as if it were Vasily's flesh. "Why did you call?"

"I told you, I didn't." He could imagine the heat in Vasily's eyes accompanying the irritated timbre of his voice.

"Before. When you had Lev leave me the message."

"Oh." An awkward pause followed before he spoke again. "I need to get tickets to Slyudyanka. The trains are booked for the next three weeks. I thought maybe you could . . . get them."

A small trickle of hope seeped into his veins. Vasily wasn't staying here after all. And then the plural of Vasily's request registered. He was going back to Raqia to be with Silk.

"Sure." The word came out terse and flat, as if there were no air behind it. "I'll get them to Dmitri. Can you put him on, please?" After a pause, a loud thud sounded in his ear, the receiver dropping onto a wooden table. He was considering whether he ought to hang up when Dmitri came on the line.

"Bel? It's Dima. What's up?"

Belphagor smiled at his casual tone, the words delivered as if nothing out of the ordinary were going on. "Well, my friend, I need a small army."

"To do what?" Again, delivered in that matter-of-fact tone.

"I've raised the ire of a local gangster by messing in his business."

Dmitri sighed. "Only you, Belphagor. And I'm guessing Silk was some of his business."

"You guess correctly. There's another group of kids from Raqia I'm fairly certain he's acquired. I dropped some pretty big hints about their origins, and he didn't seem at all confused or surprised. I also offered him a blank check in facets of the realm, but he wasn't biting. My gut says I'll be getting a visit tonight to invite me to do a disappearing act. I was hoping you might know a few Nephilim I could borrow. Enough to storm wherever he's holding these kids and take out his men."

"A few Nephilim. By tonight."

Belphagor grinned. "That would cover it, yeah."

There was a thoughtful pause. "I believe there may be a Nephil or two in town. I'll put out some feelers. Where should they meet you?"

"You're a lifesaver, my friend. I'm at Gostinitsa Oktiabrskaya. I'm expecting my company to show up around dusk, so I guess that's about midnight? My preference would be to take them alive so we can use them to get to the kids. And I'm guessing they'll be armed. Do Nephilim pack heat?"

"Not like your Vasily. But yes, some do carry firearms."

Despite the smirk in Dmitri's voice, the possessive pronoun jabbed at Belphagor's heart, and he barely heard the rest of the sentence. "He's not my Vasily."

"I thought we talked about this, Bel."

"That was before he started fucking Silk the moment I walked out the door."

"So let me get this straight. You, the Prince of Tricks, are giving up on true love because your boy has a passing infatuation for a pretty young demon."

"He hasn't given me reason to believe it's a passing infatuation. He wanted me to go so he could be with him. And now they're going home together."

"And your reaction doesn't strike you as a bit ironic—after you practically tossed off my boyfriend hours after promising Vasily you'd make him trust you again while you had him pinned to the kitchen table?"

Belphagor fumed silently, knowing there was little he could say in his own defense. "How do you know what I said to him, anyway?"

This prompted a snort from Dmitri. "You're joking. Lev and I were standing in the hallway for a good while waiting for you two to finish. If things hadn't been so strained between you both, we might have joined you—well, if you hadn't broken Lev's teacups. He's still stewing over that."

"I'll buy him new ones."

"But it might interest you to know that nothing else seems to have happened between Vasily and Silk since the shower. Vasily's sleeping on the couch."

That did ease his mind a bit.

"Anyway, I need to run if I'm going to get you that backup tonight. Just . . . stop being a baby."

CHAPTER
ELEVEN

Something was up. Vasily had only caught snatches of what Dmitri was saying on the phone to Belphagor, but it was clear by evening that something was going down in the city, and Vasily didn't intend to be left out of it like some child.

He knew where Belphagor was staying, and he knew someone was meeting him there at midnight for backup—though it didn't seem to be anything Dmitri was directly involved in; by eleven o'clock, Dmitri and Lev had gone to bed. Silk, still recovering, had been asleep for hours.

Vasily slipped out into the soft glowing light of the White Nights with a stack of ruble bills in his pocket. It was too late to take the train, but he caught an unofficial taxicab and gave the man a sizable chunk of his stash to drive him to the hotel. He had no idea how much the bills were worth, and he suspected the driver was well aware of his naivety and had taken him for a ride in more ways than one, but Vasily didn't much care about the value of Belphagor's "money."

Once he'd determined where it was, he had the driver drop him off a few blocks from the Oktiabrskaya and walked the rest of the way, looking over his shoulder—for what, exactly, he wasn't sure. The sun was hugging the horizon when he arrived.

A trio of dark-clad men—or rather, two men and one woman, he realized on closer inspection, though each had the build of a prizefighter—passed him on their way into the lobby. These were either the backup Dmitri had sent or the ones Belphagor needed backup against. They were dressed as if they were in the middle of some military training exercise, except their black combat uniforms had no insignia, and one had an object tucked into the back of his waistband that looked suspiciously like a gun.

Vasily had seen the earthly weapons in a movie the last time he was here, and it had unnerved him how easily a man could kill with one. He couldn't take a chance that the gun was intended for Belphagor.

He followed them in but was swiftly intercepted by the hotel's doorman with a hand to his chest. "What's your business here?"

Vasily glanced down at the hand and back up at the doorman's face. "I'm with them." He nodded toward the trio. The man seemed to blanch at the sound of his voice, which he couldn't help but take a little pleasure in. He still wasn't used to being imposing.

Despite being obviously intimidated, the doorman stood his ground. "If you aren't a guest, you sign in at the desk and wait for your party."

"But *they* didn't sign in."

"If you insist on being belligerent, I'm going to have to call the authorities."

Vasily wasn't sure who the authorities were in the world of Man, but if they were anything like the ones in Heaven, he had no desire to see them called. He glared and turned around.

As he stepped down from the entrance, a long, black sedan pulled up to the side of the road, and an even more questionable-looking group climbed out while the driver kept the engine running. This was definitely bad news. Two of them went in the front. Like the military types, they were virtually ignored by the doorman, Vasily noticed bitterly. But two others headed around the side of the building. He followed this pair at a safe distance, hands in his pockets and head down as if he had no interest in them.

Behind the hotel, they climbed a metal ladder mounted on the brick of the building, and Vasily watched from the shadows of the alleyway to see which window they entered. When they disappeared inside, he scurried up the flimsy ladder and climbed in through the same open window. There was no sign of them once inside the darkened hallway, but a sudden loud pop that could only be gunfire came from the other end, followed by a swift barrage of return fire.

Vasily barreled down the hall with radiance roiling over his skin and burst into the room the sounds were coming from. He struck someone with the door and bowled him over, only to realize he had Belphagor pinned beneath him as he hit the floor.

Vasily scrambled off and looked up to see the dark-clad group had the others subdued at gunpoint. One was bleeding from his upper arm, and another, grazed above the ear, held a handkerchief to his head. A third lay moaning on the ground clutching his leg, while the fourth stood warily behind him. Their weapons had been kicked across the room—as had their asses, from the looks of them—despite the fact that it had only taken seconds.

Belphagor grabbed Vasily and whirled him about. "Vasya, what the hell are you doing here?"

"Making sure you don't get killed."

"I'm an airspirit." Belphagor smirked. "It's actually kind of difficult to shoot me. But you need to get out of here."

Vasily folded his arms. "I'm not going anywhere. These are the bastards who had Silk, aren't they?"

"They work for the same organization, yes. And they're going to take us to where they're keeping the abducted children. I've got this covered."

"*Idi v zhopu,*" countered the thug holding the handkerchief to his head wound.

Belphagor raised a dubious eyebrow. "Frankly, I've kissed much better ass than yours." He nodded at one of the dark-clad men. "Apparently, he needs some more persuasion, Ivan."

Ivan stepped forward with a smooth, efficient motion and landed his fist in the thug's gut, doubling him over with a groan of surprise.

Belphagor glanced at the other dark-clad man. "I suppose we don't really need all of them."

The gunman raised his weapon, pointing it at the thug with the arm wound, and Vasily tensed, but Belphagor put out his hand.

"No need to kill them, Soren. We just need to restrain them." As Belphagor looked around the room, Vasily suspected he was using a practiced eye to see what he could improvise as rope. Crossing to the television set, Belphagor yanked the electrical cord from the wall and pulled a knife from his pocket to sever the cord from the set before using it to tie up the moaning man on the floor. The way he jerked the knots tight gave Vasily a pang of nostalgia.

As Belphagor was about to tear the lamp plug from the wall to utilize the only other electrical cord in the room, the woman in military gear held up a pair of metal cuffs. "Will these work?"

Belphagor grinned. "I think I can make do. Thanks, Izabella." He fixed a cuff onto the right hand of one of the thugs and dragged him over to the washroom, where he shoved him to his knees and threaded the chain behind a thick pipe feeding into the toilet. "Bring the other one."

Izabella pushed the man roughly. "Move it."

The miserable human glared as Belphagor pushed him down and cuffed him on the other side. "This will be the last thing you ever do. You think you can stroll into *Malenkiy Yusupovskiy* and steal from Yuri Yegorevich? He'll cut you into so many pieces, they'll never be able to find them all at the bottom of the Neva."

Belphagor raised the knife toward him, and the man flinched. "Maybe I should cut some pieces off of *you* to show I mean business." For good measure, he stuffed flannels from beside the sink into each of the thugs' mouths and used wet, wound-up hand towels to tie them in place.

In other circumstances, the scene would have been incredibly arousing, and Vasily found himself momentarily distracted.

The thoughts must have been written on his face, as Belphagor gave him a wry look. "Much as I'd love to stay and entertain you further, Vasya, we have business to take care of. And you need to get back to Silk." There was a sudden change in his tone when he added the last sentence. So he was jealous. *Fuck him.*

"Silk is perfectly safe where he is." Vasily folded his arms. "If you're liberating the rest of the boys, I'm going with you."

"The hell you are. This is dangerous."

Izabella sized him up with a glance. "He looks more than capable to me. We can use all the able bodies we can get."

Tight-lipped and stewing over being overruled, Belphagor led them down the back stairs after Vasily warned him about the gangsters' car waiting in front of the hotel. Soren snuck around front to incapacitate the driver of the sedan and then circled the hotel to pick them up. In the seat facing Vasily between Belphagor and Ivan, their hostage was compliant but sullen. His comrade had already given away the location of their operations, so he could do little more than go along for the ride.

A fitting base of operations for a wealthy *vor*, Little Yusupov Palace faced the street, no private drive or courtyard protecting it from the "commoners" passing by. A canal bordered the palace on one side, and a park flanked the other. While Soren and Izabella "borrowed" a boat to find an opening on the canal side, Ivan and Vasily came at the palace from the park. Belphagor insisted on taking their hostage alone to the front entrance.

As Vasily and Ivan scouted the windows on the park side from within the trees, Ivan nodded toward the front of the building. "Second-story window's open. Gets pretty hot in these fancy buildings, same as anywhere else. Tsars didn't plan for electric air-conditioning." He studied Vasily. "You a good climber?"

Vasily shrugged. "Can't say I've ever really tried to climb anything."

Ivan sighed. "And I'm guessing your wings aren't subtle, judging by the flash of pink we saw when you broke the door down."

"Not so much. And it's not *pink*," he muttered. "It's ruby."

"Well, try to keep up." Ivan started forward, moving with a smooth, muscular grace as he darted from the trees to the shadows of the building under the eaves, his dark curly hair as indistinct in the predawn light as his clothing. "You armed?" he asked as Vasily reached the wall and flattened himself against it.

"I was born armed." Vasily let his palms glow with elemental heat.

"Won't do you any good from a distance, but the plan is to keep out of sight of anyone we come across until we're close and put them out of commission before they can defend themselves or sound the alarm. Clear?"

Vasily gave him a curt nod. He wasn't stupid.

His jaw dropped as Ivan shimmied up the wall like he had suction cups for hands and feet and disappeared into the open window. Vasily grabbed hold of the drainpipe on the front corner of the building and hauled himself up, scrabbling for hand- and footholds. He managed to make the first-story window and clung to the ledge to catch his breath, his knuckles and fingers already scraped raw.

"Fuck this." He whipped his shirt off over his head and flung out his wings and leapt to the second story. The sky was already flush with dawn anyway after the fleeting summer dusk. It wasn't as if he was strafing fire across a black sky.

Ivan yanked him inside, forcing him to retract his wings swiftly as he tumbled onto the floor. "What the hell are you doing?"

Vasily pulled his shirt back on as Ivan dragged him to the wall beside the doorway just as the sound of running footsteps heralded the appearance of the gangster Vasily had probably alerted with his unwise choice.

Before the startled man had time to react, Ivan punched him in the throat, grabbed him by the hair, and bashed his head against the doorframe. He slumped to the ground, and Vasily winced as Ivan kicked the man in the skull for good measure. Ivan was out the door in a flash, and Vasily hurried after him. Wherever Dmitri had gotten this "backup," they sure seemed to know what they were doing.

At the end of the hallway, a pair of armed men in business suits came around the corner. Ivan charged the first, and while he disarmed him, Vasily employed brute strength to take down the other. Using a move he'd learned from Belphagor, he wrapped his arm around the man's throat, cutting off blood flow to the brain with pressure to his carotid artery, and rendered him unconscious.

At a noise from the room beside them, Ivan threw open the door, his body in a fighting stance, but stopped abruptly with a look of surprise.

"Not another step!" A young woman's voice came from inside the room. "You'll sell them over my corpse." The Russian words had a distinctly Raqian flavor.

"I'm not selling anyone." Ivan held up his hand as if to calm the girl but jumped back with an exclamation, quite out of character with what Vasily had seen so far.

Vasily dropped the unconscious man he'd forgotten to let go of and came forward. Inside the room, Anzhela stood aiming a long gun at Ivan's chest.

She turned it swiftly toward Vasily, and her eyes widened. "Vasily? Is that you?"

"Anzhela—" He grunted in surprise at Ivan's hand between his shoulder blades shoving him into the room.

"Talk inside." Ivan stepped in and closed the door. "And do it quietly."

Vasily had been so startled by Anzhela's presence that he hadn't yet focused on the room behind her. The large space had the look of a ballroom, and the floor was covered with scattered mattresses. And all the boys from the Fletchery were here.

Anzhela lowered her weapon to her side. "We found ourselves here two days ago. They'd given us something that made us sleep on the journey from Raqia. When I came to, I heard the humans talking about how they were going to 'unload' us. I pretended to be asleep until one of them came close enough, and then I hit him with an iron doorstop and took his weapon, and the others backed off."

Vasily regarded her with new respect. "And you've been defending the rest ever since?"

"They've only come back a few times. I guess the 'sale' isn't final. There are bars on the windows, and all the doors are locked, so it's not like they're worried about us getting out, but I think they're a bit afraid of us. I showed everyone how to use radiance."

"I didn't even know you knew about radiance."

"Masha told me."

Vasily shook his head, imagining the room full of young demons all spreading their wings. It was really kind of adorable—and he'd been in need of adorable ever since this whole business started.

"This is all very heartwarming," said Ivan. "But I think the idea is to get them out of here."

"But Belphagor will be looking for them." If he hadn't been caught. "How do we get word to him that we've found them?"

"I think it's more important to get them out than to worry about whether he knows they're here, don't you?" Ivan sighed at Vasily's glare. "Okay, *you* get them out, and I'll find Belphagor."

"Get them out how?"

"The same way we came in."

Vasily frowned. "You want a bunch of kids to climb out a second-story window and hang on to nothing? They're not spiders."

"No, they're Fallen. They have wings. If they slip, they can catch themselves. You've pretty much eliminated the element of surprise there."

The young demons looked rather excited at the prospect. Vasily pictured a dozen winged youths soaring across the dawn sky. That would be subtle. Displaying radiance to non-celestials wasn't just a bad idea; a blatant display would draw the attention of Seraphim, who had arrangements with terrestrial authorities for dealing with the Fallen. Offending demons might never see Heaven again.

"It's up to you." Ivan shrugged. "Take your chances with the window, or take them straight down the stairs, where the odds of getting out of here without bloodshed will be significantly diminished. But make up your mind fast. I hear movement in the hall."

"We'll go out the window." Anzhela gestured to the boys. "Come on, everyone. Let's move it."

Ivan opened the door, swinging it sharply outward to slam it into the thug who'd gotten to his feet. The one Vasily had knocked out was disoriented still, trying to pull himself up against the wall.

Before Vasily could stop her, Anzhela stepped out and pointed her gun at the man. "Stay where you are, or I'll put a hole in your skull."

Vasily gaped at her. She'd seemed like such a quiet thing.

Anzhela shrugged. "Masha trained me to be ready for whatever a situation calls for." She motioned with the gun toward the vicinity of the room where Vasily and Ivan had entered the building. "Get them out of here."

"You're coming too."

Ivan pulled a handgun from his pocket as Anzhela hesitated. "Go on. I've got these two covered."

Vasily waved the young demons ahead of him down the hall before remembering the gangster Ivan had beaten when they'd first climbed in. He hurried past them to the door and looked in to find the man unconscious on the floor. Possibly dead. Dmitri's backup didn't mess around.

"Through here." He directed the boys into the room, making sure Anzhela joined them, and closed the door. "We're two stories up. Use the brackets on the drainpipe to climb down. Flying is a last resort." He might as well have said, *Flaunt 'em if you've got 'em*, as every last demon climbed through the window and took to the air. "Damn it, we have to get them down. They'll be seen."

Anzhela nodded, grim and determined, and with the weapon slung over her shoulder, she leapt also, wispy waterspirit wings stretched out, and circled the others with a practiced spin he couldn't imagine how she'd managed without experience. His own first flight had been a bit wild. She pointed a wing toward the trees and headed down, and like a little flock of ducklings behind her, the boys banked and followed.

Vasily scrambled down the long way, not wanting to take a chance on flaunting his more visible appendages a second time. He joined the others under the cover of the trees and did a quick count to make sure they hadn't lost any.

Anzhela tugged at the collar of her dress, which had been stretched by the unfurling wings. Her element at least didn't burn holes in the fabric. "Where to now?"

Vasily stuffed his hands into his pockets, feeling stupid that he hadn't asked Ivan this before they'd made their escape. "I'm not sure. I guess we just wait here for Belphagor and the others." He glanced around at the boys. It was odd to see them from his normal, adult perspective after the time they'd spent together at the Fletchery. It seemed best not to try to explain that he knew them. "Where are the girls?"

Anzhela shifted the weapon at her side. "They were sold off before we left Raqia, but I'm a bit old for their trade, so buyers weren't as enthusiastic." She glanced around at the young demons. "I call them my Lost Boys."

"Lost Boys?"

"It's from an earthly story. *Peter Pan*. A girl gets whisked away by a shadow boy to an island called Neverland, where no one ever grows up. She takes care of a group of 'Lost Boys' who are stuck there and haven't ever had a proper mother." This phrase pricked at Vasily's most tender spot. He could relate. "Masha read the book to me when I was little. She had a lot of books from the world of Man. She wanted me to learn the stories and the languages. I speak a few of them. Russian. English. French."

Vasily was envious of her skill. He'd had enough trouble learning proper Russian. Every demon in Raqia knew a smattering. It was their secret "peasant tongue" that eluded the angels so Fallen servants could speak frankly amongst themselves in front of their masters.

But learning it fluently was a must for any demon who wanted to pass in the world of Man.

"I was sorry to hear your grandmother had . . ."

"Died." Anzhela shrugged. "It's okay, you can say it." She glanced off through the trees at the gold line of the sunrise spilling over the glittering Neva and bleeding soft color into the steel of the sky. "Someone poisoned her. When I get back home, I'm going to track them down and—" She paused and looked back at the boys, huddled together and watching her expectantly. "I'm going to make them wish they hadn't." Her eyes darkened. "The whole lot of them."

CHAPTER
TWELVE

Things had gotten much bloodier than Belphagor had planned. The *vory* had been aware of his presence the moment he'd crossed the threshold after dispensing with the lock. He'd triggered some kind of silent alarm. Belphagor held his hostage in front of him with the knife to his throat. He hadn't counted on the fact that the hostage was expendable.

Andropov had entered the foyer, where two of his men stood with their guns trained on Belphagor. "If it isn't the *Knyaz*."

Belphagor gave him a curt nod. "Yuri Yegorevich." He prodded his hostage. "I believe you left something at my hotel."

"This one?" Andropov looked the man over. "You told him where to find me?" He adjusted his cuff with seeming disinterest.

"Sergei told him. I didn't say a word."

Andropov shrugged. "Not one of mine."

Before Belphagor had even processed the words, one of Andropov's henchmen raised his gun and emptied a bullet into the man's skull.

Belphagor nearly shit himself. His reassurance to Vasily that he was almost impossible to shoot had been a bit of an exaggeration. His airspirit moves only worked if he had ample warning.

His grip faltered on his lifeless hostage, and the body dropped to the ground. The *vor* who'd fired took the knife from his hand, and the other grabbed him by the arm.

"I made you a perfectly reasonable offer." Belphagor tried to maintain an illusion of calm. "More than reasonable. Do you think you'd be able to find someone willing to pay even half what I can? Someone willing to take them off your hands completely? Or do you plan to set up business here as a brothel for pedophiles?"

Andropov backhanded him with a half-curled fist, the ring on his middle finger making a literal impression as it tore through Belphagor's cheek. It was an effort to stand his ground.

"You come into my territory and steal from me. Then you come into my home and insult me in front of my family. I've never seen you before. I've never heard of any '*Knyaz.*'" With a fist at the front of Belphagor's T-shirt where the tip of his cross tattoo showed above the collar, Andropov tore the fabric, revealing more of the mark. "And you blaspheme against my family with stolen ink. *King of thieves.*" He spat on the floor. "What are you? OMON? KGB? *Spetsnaz*? You're obviously not what you say."

"Or perhaps I'm *Padshiy.*"

Andropov's eyes narrowed. "'Fallen'? You mean 'downcast'?"

Belphagor lunged at him out of reflex, and the man who held him shoved him back against a table lining the wall and shattered the mirror above it with the back of his head. "Say that again," he snarled, ignoring the pain, "and you'll find out how I earned my mark. I'll make a fucking necktie out of your tongue."

Andropov shrugged but took a step back. "You're the one who used the term 'fallen.'"

"*Zloy dukh*, then. Does that ring a bell?"

"You're a demon." Andropov flicked his hand in the air and turned to walk away. "Get rid of this trash."

"So you've noticed nothing odd about those children."

Andropov paused.

"No flickering fields of energy on their skin. No unusual abilities." When the *vor* turned to look at him, Belphagor let his radiance prickle at the surface, sending up fleeting black sparks that were little more than static charge, but the man holding him let go and jumped back nonetheless. "I suppose you're used to getting them when they're a bit older and better trained to hide it. But the men you deal with— they're not exactly *men*, now, are they?"

Andropov folded his arms, his expression grim and his skin a bit gray. "They said they were angels."

Belphagor couldn't help the loud guffaw that escaped him. "Well, that's rich. You've been laboring under the assumption that you've been pimping out underage angelic whores." He took a step toward the *vor*, and no one stopped him, though both guns were still trained on him. If he didn't time his moves right, he'd prove how eminently shootable he actually was.

"Let me explain something to you. Angels are not celestial spirits of purity and grace created by your *Bog* to give Him eternal glory in paradise. They're nothing more than pureblood demons. And while I suppose whoever's smuggling these unfortunate peasants out of Heaven may have kidnapped a pureblood or two here and there, by and large, your 'product' has been street kids from the demon slums, not a steady shipment of the ultimate in virginity for you to enslave so some sick fuck can get off on raping an angel."

Andropov swiftly crossed himself in the Orthodox fashion and punched Belphagor in the face. Perhaps Belphagor had gone a little too far invoking the man's faith. And then pissing on it. He had to remember that however influential the Malakim had been in perverting the spiritual beliefs of Men in their efforts to promote the burgeoning House of Arkhangel'sk, his world had nothing to do with the heaven Men believed in. On the other hand, how pious could a man be who thought he was selling the angels of his own faith into sexual slavery?

As Belphagor stumbled back from the blow, another pair of goons came down the broad pageant steps behind Andropov, dragging a half-conscious Nephil between them. *Damn it. Ivan.* He'd been with Vasily.

"Found this one sneaking around upstairs." One of the goons glowered. "The inventory's missing."

Andropov turned back to Belphagor. "You son of a bitch."

Belphagor shrugged. "I offered you ample compensation. You should have taken the deal."

Andropov swung at him again, and Belphagor held his breath, dematerializing for an instant, but the *vor* didn't stumble or pull his hand back—almost as if he'd dealt with an airspirit before. As Belphagor breathed out, the meaty fist closed around his throat, and Andropov jammed his thumb hard against Belphagor's jugular and held tight until Belphagor nearly blacked out.

He stumbled to his knees when Andropov released him, gunmen moving in from both sides. With the cold muzzles of two Glocks shoved against his temples and blood dripping over his lip, Belphagor tried to catch his breath, waiting to see which side of his head would explode first.

Neither, it seemed. Andropov drew and pressed his weapon to Belphagor's forehead, and his henchmen stepped away. "Your cheap tricks and tales of demons don't impress me. You're nothing but a con artist and a two-bit hustler. And now you're a dead one."

A commotion on the stairs stayed his execution for the moment. From somewhere above, Izabella and Soren arrived on the scene. Izabella incapacitated the men holding Ivan with a dizzying move that seemed to involve ramming their heads together followed by a double punch to the nads, while Soren vaulted over them and landed with a somersault, firing his gun and taking out the armed guards with a single bullet each.

Belphagor grinned. "*Those* are the *Spetsnaz*."

Andropov hauled Belphagor up and swung him in front of his body, his gun under Belphagor's jaw as he faced the Nephilim. "I will fucking kill him so many times, you won't know which pieces of him to pick up and bury."

Before they could respond, a loud crack sounded from behind, and a blaze of firespirit wings rushed through the broken door and knocked Andropov away from him. Vasily's heat was palpable as he tumbled with the *vor* over the tile, a sweet campfire smell filling Belphagor's lungs, and then a loud pop stilled the roiling forms. Belphagor let out a bellow of disbelief as Andropov scrambled to his feet. On the tile before him, Vasily lay bleeding from the center of his chest.

With a burst of strength fueled by rage, Belphagor charged the *vor* and slammed him twice in the kidney. When Andropov managed to swing about with his gun raised, Soren dispassionately shot him in the throat.

Flinging the dying man away from him, Belphagor dropped to his knees beside Vasily. "Damn you, Vasya." He lifted Vasily's head into his lap. "Don't you dare die."

"Not sure I . . . have a choice." Vasily's words ended in a wet cough. He was choking on his own blood.

Belphagor raised him to a half-sitting position with his hands under his arms. The boy was damned heavy. *His* boy. What the hell was he going to do without his boy?

"I'm sorry." He rocked Vasily in his arms. "I fucked up everything."

Vasily shook his head and tried to speak, but another coughing fit gripped him. He put his hand to his chest, eyes widening as it came away sticky with blood. As he clutched the swiftly soaking shirt, a stuttering burst of vermillion fire seemed to flow from his palm and spread until it engulfed him. Belphagor cried out at the searing heat, but he couldn't let go. He wouldn't let go. If this was how a firespirit died, he'd die with him.

But in the center of the pool of red at Vasily's chest, as if the blood had turned to liquid fire, something dripped from the bullet wound that looked like molten metal bleeding out of him. Vasily took a tremendous, heaving breath, and his fire dissipated as he exhaled, the jagged hole in his chest—visible through the torn fabric—cauterizing itself. Vasily sat up and touched his fingers to what was surely the bullet that had been inside him, now melted onto his shirt.

"*Yebat'.*" He growled the word. "That fucking hurt."

Belphagor leapt to his feet, hauling Vasily up with him, a rush of conflicting emotion spurting through him like a shot of adrenaline in his veins. He stared up into Vasily's sweet hazel eyes and slapped him hard.

"What the *fuck*?" Vasily's hand flew to his cheek, but before he could protest any further, Belphagor swung him about and steered him into a nearby parlor. He shut the door with a slam, shoving Vasily back against it.

"Not a word!" he snapped as Vasily's mouth opened. The red bloom on the ruddy cheek looked absurdly like a flower. "You're going to fucking listen to me. I get it. Things are fucked beyond belief, and I have no one to blame but myself. But when I say I want you to stay out of something, you will damned well stay out of it, or I'll put a hole in you myself."

Vasily's chest rose and fell rapidly, his breath steaming out of him, his eyes blazing, and both cheeks now red with anger, but it was several seconds before he finally responded with a characteristic sneer. "And just what are you going to put a hole in me with?"

"*Bozhe moi, miliyy mal'chik*, don't tempt me." Belphagor had never wanted him more. An intense, painful desire nearly choked him with the need to affirm that Vasily was alive by fucking the devil out of him. He closed his fist around Vasily's hair, wanting to turn him about and take him right here against the door. And then strap him with his own belt until he was weeping and begging to be taken again.

Instead, he yanked on the fistful to bring Vasily to his knees, but Vasily was immovable. Hooking one boot around the back of Vasily's leg, Belphagor pushed him off-balance with his knee and toppled him into the supplicant's position.

"Fuck you, Belphagor." Vasily glared up at him. "I'm not your—"

Belphagor bent and silenced him with a kiss, aching at the taste of him, at the rightness of the heat of the sweet firespirit tongue against his own. Vasily melted and whimpered into him, fully yielding, until Belphagor at last tore himself away.

"I know." He shook his head as Vasily blinked up at him with fire dancing in his eyes. "You're not my boy." He tugged Vasily to his feet and opened the door.

"*You're not my boy.*" The words were a terrible incantation repeated in Vasily's head to mock the kiss that had nearly undone him. He was the one who'd created those words, given them life. He was the one who'd pushed Belphagor away. But to hear it on Belphagor's tongue was more painful than he'd expected.

Heading toward the trees in the park where Anzhela waited with her Lost Boys, he glanced down at his ruined shirt, still a bit dazed at how close he'd come to dying and at how his own radiance had reversed it. He'd tried to use it on Ivan—he'd been shot in the arm back at the hotel room, had taken another bullet in the leg, and was vomiting from the concussion he'd gotten trying to get to Belphagor at Vasily's urging—but nothing had happened. Maybe it only worked on mortal wounds. It was a sobering thought.

They arrived at the park, and Vasily breathed a sigh of relief that Anzhela and the boys were still here. He'd wrestled with his conscience about leaving them, but Belphagor had been inside too long, and Vasily had known he was in trouble.

Soren and Izabella stopped under the trees with Ivan between them, looking ill.

Soren nodded to Belphagor. "So where to now?"

Belphagor combed his fingers through his hair. "I'm afraid I didn't think that far. We obviously can't go back to the hotel. There wouldn't be room for all of them there, anyway." He glanced at Soren. "Think we could get them all into the limo?"

Soren scanned the group. "Maybe. Without us."

"Ivan's injured."

Ivan grunted. "I'll mend."

"We have people." There was an air of mystery to Izabella's words. "Don't worry about us. You take the car."

Belphagor nodded and held out his hand, giving each of theirs an odd sort of ritual clasp. "I'll let Dmitri know what a great help you were to us." He stepped back. "Vasya."

It was the first time he'd addressed him since the kiss, and Vasily jumped.

"You wait here with the kids while I get the car."

It was such an odd sentence that Vasily almost laughed, imagining himself and Belphagor as parents. The laughter died in his throat at the unexpected sense of longing this stirred in him. What if they could have what other people had? What if they could be together, a family, with children of their own? The idea was absurd, and Vasily pushed it away. Demons like them didn't have families and didn't father children. And besides, they weren't together.

When Belphagor arrived with the car, Vasily herded the boys inside the long sedan after Anzhela climbed in to pull Ruslan, the youngest—no more than eleven—onto her lap. They hadn't seemed that young when Vasily had been glamoured. But Ruslan was a child. If he'd been born an angel, he'd still have a nurse—some peasant woman assigned to watch over him and see that he learned his letters and ate his vegetables. He'd still be innocent.

Fuck the whole damned universe.

Vasily climbed into the front seat beside Belphagor after the last of the boys had packed himself in, sitting on the floor. While Belphagor pulled out into the early-morning St. Petersburg traffic, Vasily glanced over his shoulder at Anzhela leaning against the darkened window, her chin on the youngest boy's head.

If Vasily and Belphagor were the fathers, she was the mother of the Lost Boys in this imaginary family. He'd never had a mother, though there was a picture in his head of a strawberry-golden-haired angel bending over him with a tender kiss when he thought of one. It was an embarrassing fantasy, as foolish as the idea of Belphagor and himself being parents.

A green suburban stretch of highway lay before them once Belphagor had wound his way through the city.

Vasily turned toward him. "Where are we going?"

Belphagor's jaw was set. "To Dmitri's. Where I'll never hear the end of it."

"Are you out of your goddamned mind?" If Dmitri had been a firespirit, Belphagor would have been lashed by the heat of his tongue. Vasily supposed *someone's* tongue ought to get some action. "Where am I supposed to put them all?"

"It's just for one day while I take care of the travel arrangements."

Silk, rubbing his eyes, appeared in the guest bedroom doorway. "What time is it? What's going on?" He caught himself mid-yawn and broke into a grin. "My boys!" They gathered around him, and Silk put his arms out to welcome them fondly, a wood nymph surrounded by an adoring circle of sprites.

"What happened to your hair?" asked one of them.

"Do you like it?" Silk smoothed a hand over a shorn side where Vasily and Lev had helped him trim it more neatly. "Ruby did it. It's all the rage in the world of Man."

"Ruby?" asked another. "Where *is* Ruby?"

Vasily shook his head at Silk, but Silk gave him a wide-eyed, innocent stare and ignored the silent request.

"Why, he's standing right there." Silk pointed at him.

The boys turned and looked around in confusion before they focused on Vasily, and one by one, their mouths dropped open.

"*Ruby*?" the first boy breathed. "What happened to you?"

"I grew up," he growled, his cheeks hot with embarrassment.

Silk beamed. "He drank a magic potion. It's all very romantic. Isn't he dreamy? He's going to buy me a house."

Vasily's face got hotter. "That's not exactly what I said." His eyes darted to Belphagor's, and he swallowed at the coldness in them.

Silk gave him an exaggerated pout. "Ah, Ruby, are you trying to back out of your proposal already? You promised to take care of me." There was a wicked gleam in his eyes, and he batted his lashes pointedly at Vasily, making sure Belphagor saw.

"Wow, what'd I miss?" Lev appeared behind them in the hallway. "I don't think we have enough *tapochki*." He smiled amiably and passed around a little laundry basket full of socks. The boys had gone barefoot since arriving at the Fletchery, and it took them a few moments to realize what they were meant to do with them. "But there's plenty of *kasha* and *blinchiki*. Come on, boys. You can help me cook." He paused and tilted his head at Anzhela standing by the door, her weapon still at her side. "We've met before, haven't we?"

"Anzhela." She nodded. "At your place in Moscow."

"Oh, right. You came to see Belphagor. Never a dull moment with that one."

As Lev winked at Belphagor, Vasily took the opportunity to push Silk back into the bedroom and close the door. "What the hell was that all about?"

"All what?" Silk put his arms around Vasily's neck, smelling of some delicious musk. "You did say you wanted to protect me from the big, bad wolves of the world of Man. To get us 'settled.'"

"Yes, and you didn't want me to." Vasily pulled Silk's arms away. The scent was stronger at his wrists. "What is that?" He sniffed one of Silk's arms.

"Isn't it lovely? Something of Lev's, I think." Silk breathed in at his wrist when Vasily let go of him. "I found it in the washroom cabinet when I woke up in the middle of the night and couldn't get back to sleep. It's called '*Pachuli*.' At least that's what I think it said. I'm not so good at peasant letters. Hope it wasn't a slow-acting poison absorbed through the skin."

It *was* lovely, but Vasily didn't want to admit it. He was annoyed with Silk. "They're not peasant letters. It's a very rich language. I'm reading one of their famous writers right now. Dostoevsky."

Silk shrugged. "Okay."

"Why were you saying all that in front of Belphagor? He's pissed enough at me as it is."

Silk's dark, elfin eyebrows knitted together. "He's pissed at *you*? He's the one who fucked another demon in the next room while you were sleeping."

"He didn't fuck him, he . . ." Vasily let the words fizzle out with a low growl, realizing how stupid his protest sounded.

"I thought you wanted to make your prince jealous. Did I make things worse? I'm sorry, Ruby."

Vasily sighed. "No, I don't think they could get any worse. It's okay. I did promise to take care of you. I'm being ridiculous."

"And I told you it was sweet. I'm fine playing it however you want. If you want me to back off, I will. But if it'll get that wounded pout off your face when you look at him, I'd be happy to help make your prince very sorry he left you."

Silk stood on tiptoe and put a hand on Vasily's shoulder for balance, reaching up to kiss him with those incredibly soft lips. It was the polar opposite of Belphagor's kiss.

"I like you, Ruby. Very much. And if my life were different—and you weren't so damned tall—" Silk laughed and dropped back onto his heels "—I'd be the one offering to take care of you." The corner of his mouth turned up in a way that was eerily like Belphagor. "And I could take care of exactly the things you need. Your prince isn't the only one who likes to play rough."

Vasily swallowed. He didn't want to play at anything. But Belphagor was the one who had changed the game.

When they came out into the hall, the kitchen was overflowing with laughing boys making a thorough mess of mixing batter and stirring kasha. And Belphagor had gone.

While Silk joined the joyful chaos, Vasily spotted Dmitri at the end of the hall leaning against the bedroom doorframe, looking a bit bewildered. With a curt nod, Vasily headed in his direction instead of toward the overstuffed kitchen.

"Hey." The greeting was a bit too gruff, and he stuffed his hands in his pockets to cover his embarrassment. It was difficult to gauge how his element might permeate his voice in the world of Man. "It's good of you to put up with this. I know it's not what you were expecting when you said I could stay here."

An unexpected smile lit Dmitri's face. "I like to give Belphagor a hard time. But I admit, it's kind of heartwarming to hear them in there, acting like kids after what they've been through."

Vasily glanced back at the kitchen. "Yeah."

"I guess you're familiar with what they've been through."

"Yeah." Stellar conversationalist he was. "So where's Bel?"

"He said he had work to do on the travel arrangements. Influencing that many tickets must be tricky." Dmitri paused. "You don't think he's trying to deal with any of those thugs on his own?"

"No. I think your friends pretty much took care of them. Where did you find those three, anyway?"

Dmitri gave him a cagey shrug. "They owe me favors." He shifted his weight against the frame. "Listen, about Bel, don't be too hard on him."

Vasily's hands balled into fists in his pockets. "Do you know what he did? I mean, besides almost banging your boyfriend while you were sleeping."

Dmitri's face went hard in the way Belphagor's did when Vasily was about to get a whipping. "You're an extraordinarily difficult person to like, do you know that? I opened my home to you because Belphagor loves you."

"I'm not—"

"And you go straight for the jugular no matter whom you're dealing with. What's between Lev and me is none of your business, yet you throw that vulgar exaggeration in my face as if I'm the one who wronged you."

"*Belphagor* is the one who—"

"And what *did* Bel do to you? Did he involve you in his scheme at the Fletchery without your consent? Did he allow someone to do harm to you with *his* consent?"

"I—" Vasily pulled his fists out of his pockets, taken aback. "Not exactly, but—"

"Then what the hell are you moaning about? I swear to all the Heavens—you've got the most notorious player in all the spheres doing his damnedest to change his spots because he's mad about you, and you're in there carrying on with that *barkhotka* because Bel maybe enjoyed it for a moment when a friend batted his eyelashes at him."

"That's *not* what—"

"And if you're punishing him for some unspoken infraction, and you don't have the *yaytsa* to let him know how he hurt you—I don't even know what to say to that level of self-absorption. Do you have any idea what he's been through in his life?"

"No, I don't!" The words burst out of him when he finally had a chance to get them in edgewise. "Because he won't fucking tell me."

With a glance down the hall at the sudden silence from the kitchen, Dmitri lowered his voice. "Well, he shouldn't have to spell it out. The marks on his body should tell you. Try reading a book once in awhile. There's a rather illuminating volume on the history of Russian prison tattoos on the shelf behind you. But whatever you know about him, know this: He can be hard and sharp as obsidian, but he'll crack as easily. So you . . ." Dmitri shook his head like he was trying to come up with a clever rebuke and couldn't. He jabbed his finger into Vasily's chest. "You just *watch* it."

Lying awake on the floor that night, Vasily stared at the shadows changing and stretching across the room through the crack in the curtain as the sun refused to sleep. Silk had given the bed to Anzhela and had gone to the living room with the boys, where the sounds of whispering and giggling had yet to die down.

Dmitri's words reproached Vasily silently. He hadn't had the balls to tell Belphagor how he'd really felt about the con at the Fletchery. He'd consented, and Belphagor had given him more than one chance to revoke his consent. Vasily had stubbornly refused. But the fact remained that Belphagor had put him in danger, and until that moment when Belphagor had let them take him away, he'd never made Vasily feel anything but safe—he was the *only* thing that had ever made Vasily feel safe.

He didn't know, of course, that Vasily had been sold before.

Vasily hadn't thought about it in years, and before the last few weeks, he wasn't sure he'd even remembered it. By his best guess, he must have been about seven or eight. He'd been running with a pack of street hustlers, kids who distracted the victims for older thieves and pickpockets. He'd admired one of the older boys, who in turn seemed to take a liking to him—giving him special jobs, letting him stand lookout when he turned alley tricks. *Kal*. Vasily's skin broke out in a sweat. He'd forgotten the name.

Kal would tease him and say he looked like a girl, and kissed him a few times as part of his teasing. Vasily hadn't thought of those kisses as sexual. They were affection from an older boy who thought he was worth having around. There hadn't been anything more than that, though in retrospect, Vasily remembered Kal playing with himself in front of him.

While there was nothing particularly unusual about such an occurrence—living on the streets, there was no privacy when you huddled together in a crate at night to get out of the rain or shared a spot under a bridge—Kal had done it after kissing him. And after seeing him take a piss. Sometimes he'd bet Vasily he couldn't hit a particular target, and give him a facet chip—brittle pieces of facets that had been smashed and shared—if he did.

Vasily's skin crawled at the memory he hadn't understood before. Kal had been paying him in order to watch Vasily expose himself. And had gotten off on exposing himself to Vasily.

He rolled onto his side and tried to shove the memories away, but now that they'd come back to him, they were crowding his head. He'd run with Kal for almost a year, sharing his food—and his blanket. He couldn't count the number of times he'd curled up under Kal's arm for comfort, pretending it was for warmth. And all the while, Kal had been— Vasily rolled onto his back once more, but it was no good. The memories followed him.

Kal had sent him to make a delivery one afternoon—some black-market vodka from the world of Man, perhaps—to the basement door of a pub. Kal had waited down the alley and promised Vasily a facet chip.

The pubmaster had waved him inside, down the stairs, but instead of giving him the facets to take back to Kal, he'd closed the door and locked it. Vasily had panicked and tried to run for the inside stairs. He'd heard about perverts and freaks who abducted kids who lived on the street and did terrible things to them.

The pubmaster had caught him, beaten the backs of his thighs with a switch, and said he owned him now, that Vasily would do as he was told. After tossing him into a kind of caged area under the stairs, the pubmaster had opened the door to the alley once more, and there had stood Kal. Vasily had cried out for him, calling for help, but Kal had held out his hand with a smile as the pubmaster counted out the facets for Vasily's price.

As it had turned out, the pubmaster wasn't a pervert or a freak, just a merchant in need of a boy to clean the floors under the bar and empty the night soil. Vasily still had a small, scarred brand under the hair behind his temple that said he was this pubmaster's property, though he'd bought his freedom when he was old enough. Timur, the pubmaster, had pimped Vasily out at Vasily's own suggestion and let him earn his price back, having no use for a gangly teenage boy who got in the way and ate too much food.

In the end, without meaning to, Kal had probably saved his life. Vasily had at least had a roof over his head and regular meals, if meager ones. But it had been weeks before he'd been able to fall asleep under the stairs without crying, hoping Kal would come back and get him. He never saw Kal again.

That was the memory he'd carried with him into the Fletchery. The memory he hadn't been consciously aware he was carrying. On some level, he'd believed Belphagor would forget about him and never come back. How could Vasily trust him again when Belphagor couldn't comprehend what Vasily needed from him or what he'd done? Even something as simple and intrinsically Belphagor as calling Lev a *good boy* stung in a way Belphagor didn't seem to get.

Using that word—that word that had belonged to Vasily, whether he wanted it at the moment or not—wasn't just harmless flirtation. It was proof that there was nothing special enough about Vasily that he couldn't be replaced in an instant. It was a doorway from a pub basement that could open at any moment and close again with Belphagor on the other side.

"You're not my boy." The words jumped back in front of him full force, and Vasily crossed his arms over his face and cried into them as he hadn't done since that long-ago abandonment.

CHAPTER
THIRTEEN

Instead of Belphagor, a messenger arrived the next day with an envelope full of tickets. They'd all been given Russian identities—Silk was down as Pyotr Pankov, and Vasily couldn't help but think of Anzhela's *Peter Pan*. Could Belphagor have meant to allude to that?

Among the papers was a letter addressed to Vasily. His hands shook as he opened it. He'd never received a letter from Belphagor before. He had a fleeting hope it might be a love letter, but it was brusque and businesslike.

Dorogoi Vasily, it read—"Dear Vasily." This was not the usual form of address between them.

> *Enclosed is everything you should require for the return trip, including a bit of spending money for meals on the train. I've gone on ahead to make preparations and put in motion a plan to shut down the Celestial Silk Road. It won't do for us to show up at The Brimstone with a passel of young boys after Armen has undoubtedly spent the last two weeks savaging my reputation, so I will acquire lodging for them. I also think it would be unwise for Silk to be seen in our quarters. He's done a convincing job of playing the youth and isn't likely to be viewed as anything other if he's associated with me at this juncture.*
>
> *Which brings me to a rather unhappy decision. I think it's best that you not return to The Brimstone. We have wounded one another past the point of repair and are liable to be at one another's throats in close company. I would rather retain the good memories of you that I have had there. They have been the happiest of my life.*
>
> *I will have your effects delivered to your new accommodations. A messenger will await your arrival at the portal at Lake Baikal to escort you to an alternate entrance to Raqia and direct you to your abode.*

Except insomuch as we have mutually agreed to it for erotic purposes, please believe that it is not and has never been my intent or my desire to hurt you, Vasya. But I have, and I cannot remedy it.

Be well.

The paper combusted in his hands before he realized how much heat had built in them. Flakes of ash and embers fluttered onto the floor like a cruel metaphor. He wasn't weeping. He wasn't anything. Belphagor had stolen his soul.

"This is utterly fantastic." Silk peered out the window of the train car at the world hurtling past. "I think I'm going to be sick." He turned back toward Vasily. "I guess this is commonplace for you, sphere-hopping traveler that you are." When Vasily didn't respond, Silk leaned on his shoulder, taking Vasily's hand and knitting their fingers together. "I hate seeing you sad."

"Why would I be sad? I left him, remember? He's only made it official."

"He's made it official that he's a complete bastard and never deserved you, Ruby. You and I are going to find ourselves a sweet pair of sugar daddies. Preferably rich, aging merchants who've earned their fortunes in the world of Man and want to spend it on some beautiful young things who'll pretend to adore them. And when we've worn them out with how completely fabulous we are in bed, you and I will play with each other—and with their facets."

Vasily doubted there was a glut of rich elderly demons in Raqia who preferred the company of their own sex, but he wasn't about to burst Silk's bubble. "That sounds nice."

"You could put a bit of fake enthusiasm into it like I did." Silk gave him a wink and a wry smile before sidling out of the seat toward the aisle. "Come on. Let me take your mind off things." He rose and tugged on Vasily's hand. "Your miserable prince was good enough to get us this luxury carriage with the little tin piss-pot in it. We should make use of it."

Vasily hesitated, but Silk's persistence was contagious. After prodding him into the bathroom, Silk drew the door shut and pushed him back against the sink, his slender fingers undoing Vasily's belt.

Vasily put a hand over Silk's before he drew the leather out of the buckle. "Silk, wait. I'm not sure about this."

"Your prick seems very decisive." Silk moved his hand down to stroke the outline of Vasily's burgeoning erection, the touch increasing its certainty. "You're still worrying about your prince, despite the fact that he sent you packing in no uncertain terms. Do you think he's taken up the life of a contemplative, ready to hang up his dick and count the stars in Zevul?"

Vasily couldn't help but laugh at the idea, but Silk moved his hand to Vasily's mouth, soft fingers pressed against his lips.

"Hush, Ruby. We don't want to wake the boys. Though what I have in mind is liable to make you croon."

Vasily growled against the tips of Silk's fingers. "I don't croon."

"My Heavens." Silk shivered. "Well, whatever that noise was, you lovely brute, do it again, and I may come in my pants." His other hand dipped inside Vasily's waistband and closed around the now fully committed cock.

Vasily let out a soft hiss of breath as Silk's hand massaged him, and Silk pushed the waistband down so that his handful breached the top of the fabric.

Silk licked his lips and let out a sigh of his own. "Now *that* is a magnificent thing." He bent and lowered his mouth to the swollen head, and Vasily groaned softly at the feathery flick of tongue before pulling back with a hand on Silk's shoulder.

"I know Bel and I aren't together, but I don't think I can. It feels like I'm cheating on him."

Silk straightened, the gray eyes narrowing. "First of all, never touch me when your dick is in my mouth."

Vasily cringed. "Sorry, I—"

"Second, it is not cheating to let a friend suck your cock after your lover spurns you. It's medicinal."

A nervous laugh escaped him despite the tension.

"But we all have our hang-ups, and if you don't want me to suck you, I won't suck you." Silk licked his lips slowly. "Even if I think you're rather cruel to deny me when my mouth is positively watering over that delicious, juicy plum with the skin stretched so taut I can already taste it exploding against my tongue."

"Fuck." Vasily swallowed and took a step back, bumping into the wall. "You're very good at, uh . . ." He gestured vaguely between the two of them. "All of this."

Silk smiled, but it was a smile that didn't quite convey pleasure in the compliment. "I know."

Vasily cleared his throat, shifting his weight uncomfortably. "But it all seems a tiny bit . . ."

The smile faded. "A tiny bit what?"

Vasily shrugged. "Much?"

"A tiny bit much." The intense eyes narrowed on him again. "So exactly how much is enough, Ruby? What is it you want from me?"

"Want from you? I don't want anything. I just want to be your friend."

Silk's expression was unreadable. "A few days ago, you were going to take care of me forever, like a little lost lamb."

"Silk." Vasily shook his head, bewildered. "I didn't mean to upset you. I feel like I'm saying all the wrong things."

The blank, cool expression remained for a moment before Silk sighed and seemed to deflate against the metal sink. "I'm trying to figure out who I'm supposed to be here, Ruby. I'm a tad out of my element."

"You don't have to be anyone but yourself."

"And exactly who would that be?" Silk smoothed a hand over the back of his shorn hair. "You have to understand that I have never not played a part. It has always been my job to ascertain as quickly as possible what someone expects of me in a given situation and to provide that to the best of my abilities. Not performing the expected role has always proved dangerous."

"Well, you're not in danger anymore."

"Aren't I?" Silk leaned toward him as he spoke, the sly smile stealing over his features once more. "Seems to me I've been pitched right out of the frying pan and into the fire." He slipped his arms around Vasily's neck. "Not that I particularly mind the blaze."

Vasily's cheeks warmed as Silk kissed him, and he was careful to keep his element controlled. "As long as I don't burn you with it," he said pointedly after Silk released him, tucking himself back in.

Silk's eyebrows curved upward as his gaze followed Vasily's downward. "*Can* you burn someone with it?"

Vasily concentrated on fastening his belt buckle. "I have, on occasion, forgotten to temper the elemental content of it."

Silk shook his head. "You're incredible."

While he put himself together, Vasily recalled that the only person he'd ever forgotten with was Belphagor. Perhaps it hadn't entirely been forgetfulness.

But the thought of Belphagor unraveled Silk's efforts at distraction, and Vasily returned to his seat and his melancholy, the rhythmic clickity-clack of the train beating out an inescapable refrain: *"You're not my boy. You're not my boy. You're not my boy."*

Belphagor managed to buy himself an extra day to get things sorted before the others arrived in Raqia by booking them on a slower *passazhirsky* train and taking a *firmenny* himself. He was sick to his stomach at the letter he'd left for Vasily. If it worked too well, he wasn't sure he'd recover.

He had written nothing but the truth, knowing that Vasily, as easily wounded as he was and as literal as he could be, would never notice that he hadn't said goodbye. It was the Moscow parting all over again, and he was a despicable bastard. But his scheme wouldn't work if their falling out wasn't believable, and it was Vasily's fury that would make it so.

He'd left another note with Dmitri for Silk, not to be delivered in Vasily's presence, asking Silk to meet with him once they'd arrived and settled in. He couldn't take the chance that Vasily would do anything rash. He needed someone to watch out for him. And Silk was clearly someone who both cared for Vasily and would appreciate the value of a facet.

Though the thought of Vasily's desire for Silk was like wearing a shirt made of coarse hair in front of a furnace, it was also the only thing that might make what Belphagor was doing forgivable. It hadn't been his imagination that the desire was neither negligible nor one-sided. Silk had made that clear with his charming territorial display.

If Belphagor hadn't needed Silk's complicity in his scheme, he might have decked the pretty little tramp then and there. But Vasily's infatuation with him would smooth over any feelings of abandonment. After all, he'd already been planning to keep house with Silk.

The first order of business, however, was finding an investor to buy out the current owner of The Cat. He couldn't do it himself without arousing suspicion, but putting an end to the Celestial Silk Road depended on flushing out the angel or angels who had corrupted the usual dirty business in Raqia, and that meant flushing out whoever had swindled—and likely murdered—Masha and sold Anzhela to the Fletchery. And to buy out an anonymous angel required another not-so-anonymous angel as the front man.

Phaleg was right on time.

Belphagor smiled at the sight of the dashing blond officer over his cup of tea. He'd chosen a café in the Left Bank for their meeting. The bohemian district that lined the opposite bank of the Acheron from Raqia's Demon Market had lost some of its luster since Elyon's set had abandoned it, but no one thought twice about a couple of angelic officers in the Supernal Army stopping in for lunch.

Phaleg glanced at him as he took in the otherwise empty seating under the sidewalk awning. "Are you Arafiel?"

"At the moment." Belphagor smiled with "Arafiel's" face and let his gaze travel over Phaleg's fit, slender form. "How have you been, my exceptional boy?"

Phaleg paused at the chair opposite him. "I beg your pardon?"

"I always did love the way you begged."

Phaleg's eyes went large. "Belphagor?"

"Who else would call you boy? Or have you taken my advice and found yourself someone who can put you in your place?" He nodded at the chair. "Which at the moment would be with your ass in that seat."

Phaleg sat swiftly, gratifying Belphagor's ego. "*Nyet, ser.* I haven't." The Russian address warmed his heart. And other things. But that wasn't why he was here.

"I am both disappointed and irrationally pleased to hear it." He poured Phaleg a cup of tea. "Thank you for coming to meet me—even if you didn't know it was me you were meeting."

"Your message said you had a business proposal. Was that part true?"

"It was indeed. How would you like to own a whorehouse?"

Phaleg choked on the tea he'd started to drink, and he set the cup on the table. "How would I *what*?"

"We had some lovely times at The Cat, didn't we? I understand it's a very lucrative enterprise."

"Belphagor—"

"Arafiel."

"*Arafiel*, you can't be serious."

"It would be purchased with my facets. What I need is your face—which I could simply borrow, but I'd prefer not to sully your reputation without your consent."

Phaleg searched his eyes, a mixture of fear, hope, and dread in his own. "Are you asking me to do this?"

Belphagor set down his cup, his heart aching a bit at the desperation in those quiet words. "You mean am I asking for your obedience?"

Phaleg swallowed and nodded.

Belphagor wished they were somewhere private so he could comfort Phaleg with a touch. Instead, he steepled his fingers to keep them occupied. "I'm afraid not, dear boy. As much as I would love to crop you, mount you, ride you to exhaustion, and put you away wet—I've done enough harm to my relationship with Vasily."

Phaleg's face went pale and then flushed, and he squirmed in his seat. Those elkskin pants of the Supernal Army were unforgiving.

As gratifying as it was to see that he could still incite such a reaction, Belphagor felt more than a twinge of guilt for putting Phaleg in a state he had no intention of remedying. "I'm sorry. That wasn't fair. I didn't come here to tease you or torment you. I can't seem to help myself. I only wanted to present this business opportunity to you. And it is only that. An opportunity. An offer. You're under no obligation to agree to it because of our history. Pretend it isn't me making the offer."

Phaleg gave him a thin smile. "Right. Because that's so easy to do. If it were anyone else making the offer, I'd have walked away the minute you opened your mouth. Or challenged you to a duel for having the audacity to suggest such a thing. I am an officer of the Supernal Army."

He'd definitely hurt Phaleg's feelings. "I've insulted you, and I apologize. The offer was no reflection upon your character. You're just the first person I thought of, since—"

"Since I'm the only damned angel you know."

"Since you were once a patron of the establishment. It's a perfectly respectable brothel. The finest in Raqia. And yes, you are the only damned angel I know." He pushed back his chair with a sigh and started to rise, but Phaleg clasped his arm.

"Surely you're not leaving so soon, Arafiel? You've made a valid point, and I admit I'm curious to hear more."

Belphagor raised an eyebrow and settled back into the seat. "Indeed? Well, I'm pleased. But don't agree to it to please me."

Phaleg laughed. "Don't be absurd." He held Belphagor's gaze over the rim of his teacup as he took a sip, and then set the cup back in the saucer. "There's no other reason I'd do it."

Phaleg was a done deal. Once they'd worked out the details, Belphagor set about making the rest of his arrangements. And part of those arrangements required the help of the rentboy Khai.

Still in his guise as Arafiel, Belphagor found him in the usual pickup spot outside the Demon Market.

Khai eyed him with a beguiling smile as Belphagor paused. "Need a hand with anything, sir?" He tucked his own into his loose waistband to demonstrate the nature of the offered assistance, in case there was any doubt.

Belphagor considered him. "I think I might need more than a hand. How are you at hammering and screwing things?"

Khai laughed. "I excel at all sorts of odd jobs."

"Just the demon I'm looking for. Have you a regular place of business, or shall I provide the workspace?"

"So it's not outdoor work."

"No, it requires too much equipment."

Khai had been moving closer to him during their banter, and he reached down and cupped Belphagor's crotch discreetly as they stood shoulder to shoulder. When Belphagor didn't step away or object, he gave him a sudden, rough squeeze, drawing a groan from Belphagor despite himself.

"I know of a workspace you can rent by the hour, complete with equipment. If you want me to use the equipment, my fee will also be by the hour." Khai lifted his eyebrows meaningfully. "If *you* want to use the equipment, the fee is according to the tool and the application, but I have a few exceptions: no rope, no iron and no other participants."

"A reasonable policy."

"I take it you'd rather I use the equipment." Khai assumed an appropriately authoritative expression and sharp voice as he released him. "Come on, then. Time is crystal."

Belphagor pretended to be intimidated and followed silently as Khai led him to a row of seedy-looking boarding houses on the edge of the Devil's Doorstep that in reality boarded no one more than an hour. At Khai's barked command, Belphagor provided the required deposit of facets to the tired-looking matron in the parlor and allowed Khai to haul him up the rickety stairs. Inside the room, a narrow cot with a straw tick mattress was the only furnishing.

Khai shoved him toward the bed and went to the closet to pick out his tools, tossing orders over his shoulder. "Bare your ass and get on your hands and knees."

Belphagor slipped off the pendant that controlled the glamour and put it in his pocket, standing with his arms folded when Khai turned around holding a leather gag and a paddle drilled with holes.

"I told you to— *Bozhe moi*. Belphagor, you son of a bitch."

"Very impressive." He smirked. "I had no idea you were so versatile."

"A facet's a facet." Khai tossed the toys onto the mattress. "What are you doing here?"

"I need some information, and depending on your answer, I may have a proposition for you."

"Intriguing." Khai plopped himself down on the bed. "Ask away."

"Are you in any way affiliated with Armen Nekirevich or with any present or future scheme of his?"

Khai scowled. "No, and hell no. Not only did he not pay me for his boneheaded Fletchery scam, but he threatened me for refusing to participate in slandering you afterward and had some of his crew try to rough me up." He lifted his shirt to reveal a band of bruises along his ribs.

Belphagor frowned. "Looks like they did more than try."

"They were trying to do much worse."

Even discounting the violence, Khai's grudge against Armen for the lack of payment ought to be plenty to ensure his loyalty. "How would you feel about me hiring you for a couple of weeks?"

"A couple of weeks? Is this more 'punishment' for Vasily?"

"No. Vasily and I aren't together."

Khai stared up at him. "That's . . . surprising. You two seemed—"

"It doesn't matter what we seemed. I fucked up, and he's with Silk now."

"*Silk*? That conniving boy from the Fletchery?"

"Seems he's a bit older than he pretended to be."

"Well, that was fairly obvious."

Belphagor raised an eyebrow. "Not to us old folks, apparently."

"So what do you need me for? My price is still conditional if you intend to play rough."

Belphagor couldn't suppress a snort at that. "I don't intend to play with you at all. Nothing personal, but it's not what I'm looking for. I need you to pose as my new paramour to make my separation from Vasily convincing."

"It's not convincing all on its own?"

Belphagor sighed. "I'm hoping it isn't. But I need Vasily to believe it right now so the rest of Raqia will believe it."

Khai whistled. "Let me get this straight. You dumped your 'boy' as part of a rook?"

"Not singlehandedly. We were teetering on the brink of a breakup. I just pushed us over it. It didn't take much."

"And you want me to make him jealous."

"No! No, not at all. I need to seem . . ." Belphagor floundered for the right word. "Shallow."

Khai observed him with a look of growing understanding. "So you need me around to give the impression that you're *not* falling apart. Which you are."

Belphagor's gut tightened at the keenness of Khai's insight. "Something like that. But mainly, I need to dispel the rumors Armen has been spreading about me. If Vasily's gone and I'm at the tables alone, there'll be no stopping them. And I can't accomplish what I need to accomplish if I'm being shunned by even the most disreputable of demons for being perceived as a pedophile."

"And what you need to accomplish is?"

Belphagor couldn't help the little lift of a smile at the corner of his mouth. He'd never hatched quite such an ambitious endeavor. "I have a number of things to accomplish. But the first is to reestablish my reputation as a perfectly despicable cad."

Khai crossed one ankle over the other and grinned. "As long as I get to dress well, I'm in."

CHAPTER FOURTEEN

As promised, a messenger awaited Vasily and Silk at Baikal, a young demon Vasily had seen fetching drinks for players at The Brimstone for a facet a table. He led them through the Hell Staircase with Anzhela beside him, the boys two at a time behind him, and Silk and Vasily taking up the rear—to Silk's intense amusement, and inspiring a series of puns Vasily was sure he'd never hear the end of. Which prompted another when he said so.

"You're sure they brought me this way on the trip down?" Silk had finally exhausted his vocabulary of innuendos. "I don't remember a bit of it."

"Belphagor said you were unconscious when he saw you in the Market. They probably kept you that way for the trip."

"The Market?" Silk paused on the landing they'd just reached, reeling from the staircase's infamous disorienting magic. Vasily grabbed his lapels to keep him from falling. "When did Belphagor see me in the Market?"

Vasily wet his lips. He probably shouldn't have mentioned that. "He started there, looking for the others from the Fletchery. Apparently, a broker had you in the back of one of the tents."

Silk's expression darkened. "Unconscious? He was selling me unconscious?"

Vasily swallowed. "I . . . don't think he was selling you like *that*. He was offering you to permanent buyers." The topic made him intensely uncomfortable. "Belphagor was going to redeem you then, but the broker double-crossed him and disappeared before we came back with the crystal."

Silk's eyes were piercing. "*We*."

"When I found out what he needed the facets for, that he'd found you, I went with him to bring you home." Vasily felt his eyes flickering with heat. "If that piece-of-shit broker had been there, I'd have killed him."

"Whoa." Silk put his hand on Vasily's chest. "You just got really scary."

"Sorry."

"No, it's kind of hot."

"We'd better keep up, or the stairs will separate us from the others." Vasily started climbing once more, and Silk took his hand, mounting the steps with him.

"I bet there are all kinds of puns people make about you being hot."

Vasily groaned. "Please don't."

Silk didn't, and he kept his thoughts to himself until they'd reached the portal and stood waiting for the last of the boys to climb through. "Thank you," he said.

"For what?"

"For coming to the Market to get me. For wanting to kill that 'broker.' For not giving up on me."

"Silk . . ." Vasily turned to him, miserable. "This is all because of me. Everything that's happened to you is my fault. Because I was stupid enough to let Kezef trick me. Because I ran and left you to him. Because I was even there in the first place, playing Belphagor's game. Don't thank me."

Silk rolled his eyes and hoisted himself over the edge of the open grate of the storm drain, looking back after crawling through into Heaven. "Shut up, Ruby, and get your ass up here. That 'please punish me, I'm such a naughty boy' act might have worked with your poncy prince, but it'll get you nowhere with me."

The portal emerged in a quiet, suburban area of Raqia that Vasily wasn't familiar with. It was the sort of place where the respectable denizens of the district—the nursemaids and seamstresses to the angels, the hansom cab drivers, the cobblers—lived in narrow row houses. The sort of place where demons like Vasily were suspect.

Following the messenger through the neighborhood, Vasily was afraid Belphagor had rented one of the sensible-looking shacks, but they were past it soon enough and found themselves in a block that was part industrial, part entertainment. Not quite the Devil's Doorstep, but nothing so classy as the Demon Market either.

Their accommodations were on the second floor above a bakery, and the scents of fresh bread and caramelizing sugar filled the stairwell as they climbed. Young Ruslan begged to go down and check out the enticing smells, but the others seemed to have a quiet sense of dread at what might await them at the top.

The messenger unlocked the door when they reached the landing, gave the key to Vasily, and bowed out. To Vasily's surprise, the door opened onto the cozy parlor of a sunny, furnished apartment. There was even a staircase at the end of the back hall to the attic floor of the building, which was apparently all theirs as well. The boys pounded up the stairs to investigate the little nooks under the sloped roof.

Vasily stayed on the main floor, looking around in amazement. This had apparently been the apartment of the baker's family at one time, with bedrooms enough for a large family, a well-appointed kitchen, and a sitting room besides. From the size of it, the baker must have been employed by the supernal family.

While he glanced around the kitchen, Silk appeared beside him and hooked his arm, leaning in playfully. "Look, honey, we're home." He picked up a frilly red chiffon apron from a hook on the wall and held it to his waist. "This would be divine on me. Can you imagine my cock standing up stiff behind this little number while I'm bent over the stove making your breakfast?"

Vasily shushed him, glancing about to make sure none of the boys had heard him. "We're not playing house." He snatched the apron, replacing it on the hook.

"What else do you think we're here for? Your prince has a flair for the domestic I wouldn't have guessed at. Do you think he wants to watch?"

"Stop calling him my prince."

"It's telling that you didn't answer the question."

Vasily didn't want to think about the question. He could perfectly imagine Belphagor sitting in a chair by the window stroking himself while he watched Vasily drive his cock up Silk's ass. And he didn't want to imagine that. And now he had. And god *damn* Belphagor.

Silk flicked his eyebrows upward knowingly. "Well, we'll soon find out what the price is for this delightful home-sweet-home."

When he walked toward the door, Vasily followed and grabbed his arm, turning him about. "What are you talking about? What price?"

"I have an appointment with your—with His Highness to discuss his terms. I'm not supposed to tell you." Silk shrugged. "Fuck him. I just did."

Idly watching the cheap sidewalk wingcasting tables under an awning at the Demon Market while keeping an eye out for Silk, Belphagor relaxed when he saw him arrive alone. He'd been afraid Vasily would find out about their meeting and come with him.

He tried to appear nonchalant as Silk joined him. "I take it you found the apartment. Was everything satisfactory?"

"Marvelous." Silk glanced around. "How good of you to set up this meeting here, where I was last on display naked and unconscious."

Belphagor raised an eyebrow. "How did you know you were naked if you were unconscious?"

"I guessed," Silk snapped. "Apparently, I was the special of the day."

The implication made him cringe. "I'm sorry for what you've been through. I did try to get you out of here before they smuggled you off-sphere."

"So I understand. Tell me, Prince of Tricks. Did you sample the wares before you decided to buy?"

Belphagor folded his arms to keep from slapping the boy. "Don't be vile. You know perfectly well I didn't. I don't deserve that."

Silk shrugged but slid his gaze away, looking a bit abashed.

"I think we should talk somewhere else. The tavern at the west end. Try to act like a grownup, and I'll buy you some ale."

Silk nodded stiffly and followed him as he wove through the crowd to the less-populated end of the market. Unlike The Brimstone, where its regulars—mostly locals—could be found any time of day, the more tourist-oriented gambling and drinking establishments bordering the Demon Market didn't get hopping until after dark when angels weren't quite so cautious about being seen.

He tipped the proprietor for a quiet booth in the back and ordered them each a pint of ale.

Silk sipped his cautiously. It seemed it wasn't his drink. "So what's your game? I suppose I'm to keep Ruby happy to ease your conscience, and you'll pay the bills. And how long does that last?"

"You think I'm hiring you as his companion?" Belphagor glowered over his ale. "I'm not quite sure what I did to give you such a low opinion of me."

"Oh, I don't know. Sold the sweetest boy in Raqia to a whorehouse to make a few facets? Tossed off a sexy demon in the next room from him while you thought he was sleeping? Take your pick."

"I didn't actually toss—" Belphagor sighed. "I see your point." He wished things hadn't gotten so complicated, and he knew damned well he'd complicated them. "The reason I asked you to meet me has nothing to do with Vasily. Or very little. I won't deny that I'm worried about him and hope you'll keep an eye on him, but I'm not going to pay you to pretend to care about him. My assumption is that you already do."

"Go on."

"There are a couple of matters in which I'd like to enlist your aid. The first condition is that you allow me to dress you as I see fit—"

"Excuse me?"

"I'd like you to cultivate a more age-appropriate image if you plan to be seen with Vasily. I have an excellent tailor who can see you today and has a few commissioned garments close to your size, never collected by the customer. I think the style will look very smart with your hair if you apply a bit of pomade and smooth it flat, similar to a look that was popular in the world of Man nearly a century ago. You'll be a trendsetter."

Silk opened his mouth, but Belphagor continued.

"In exchange, I will finance your private enterprise. Feel free to tell me to go to hell if it isn't what you have in mind. I'm making assumptions. But if you intend to continue in your accustomed trade, I would like it to be adult entertainment only. Your clientele is not to be given the impression that you are underage. And I will not permit you to exploit the 'Lost Boys.' They are to be kept out of your business entirely. I have something else in mind for them. But if you're amenable, I think you're well positioned to become the proprietor of Raqia's first male-for-male brothel."

Silk's mouth hung open as if he'd forgotten how his jaw worked.

"The young men who work the Demon Market and the Devil's Doorstep have few options for a permanent roof over their heads and are on their own when it comes to angels who decide to abuse them for their entertainment. In a brothel, they would be free to choose their own clients, and they would have the protection of the house from those who would otherwise prey upon them, as well as permanent room and board. And in return, they would pay you a portion of their earnings." He drank the rest of his ale and gave Silk a questioning look as he continued to gape. "Does any of this appeal to you?"

Silk managed to close his mouth and sat back on the bench, a look of suspicion overtaking his frank surprise. "You want me to be a madam. For man whores."

"Well, not strictly a madam. A procurer, yes, but I imagine your services would be highly sought after as well. Again, stop me if I'm making erroneous assumptions. But I'm thinking of something very high caliber. On the up and up like The Cat, with the refined atmosphere of the Fletchery—had its workers been consenting adults. A gentlemen's club."

"And I suppose you get eighty percent of the take."

Belphagor blinked at him. "What? No, why would I get any of it? I don't intend to work there."

"I'm confused. What would you get out of all this?"

"The satisfaction of knowing demons like the Lost Boys will have somewhere to go instead of the streets—when they're of age. I'm not fool enough to think they have any other options, though I will try to give them some. But I insist that they remain out of the business until such time as they are able to choose that life for themselves."

"That's all you want."

"And rent for the establishment I plan to purchase as a silent investor. But don't worry, it will be a nominal amount. Nothing like a percentage of your earnings."

Silk ran his hand over his hair, looking bemused. "You said there were a couple of things."

"Right." For someone who'd just been gobsmacked by the best player in Raqia, Silk was sharp to have remembered that. "The other thing I'd like you to do is help me destroy every demon and angel who's had anything to do with selling demons into terrestrial slavery. I'm going to shut the whole thing down."

Silk laughed nervously. "Oh, is that all? I thought it would be something difficult."

"So are you in on the first proposal?"

"I . . ." Silk shook his head. "I'm going to have to give it some thought."

"Unfortunately, you'll have to do it quickly. The second enterprise depends on the first. I'd like the Stone Horse to be up and running by the end of the week. Tell you what. Come with me to the tailor's and we'll get you set up. Then sleep on it. Discuss it with Vasily if you wish, only I'd appreciate if you wouldn't tell him I've asked you to look out for him. He's liable to go sleep in an alley in the Devil's Doorstep if he thinks I'm influencing your interest in him." Belphagor fiddled with his cuff where he imagined it had gotten damp in a spilled bit of ale. "And if he wants to work for you, that's obviously his prerogative. But I have one absolute condition. No angels."

Silk folded his arms. "I'm sure he'll be interested to hear you've placed conditions on him given that you threw him out."

"I didn't throw him out."

"Didn't you? That's not what he thinks. There was a sad little bag of clothes and a stack of snooty world-of-Man books waiting for him at the flat when we arrived, which, unless I miss my guess, are the whole of his possessions. Looks like throwing him out to me."

"I've given him what he asked for. Facets and a place for him to get settled with you, to do as he pleases. But make no mistake. Anyone who hurts him in any way is and will always be accountable to me."

"So you're the only one who gets to hurt him, then. Good thing you're so good at it." Silk rose without waiting for Belphagor's reaction to this well-warranted punch in the junk. "Well, let's see this tailor of yours, then. As long as I get to keep the clothes regardless of my decision about your 'enterprise.'"

"Certainly." He left some facets on the table and went ahead of Silk to hold the door for him.

"What is it you have in mind for my boys, anyway?"

"Schooling. And a little bit of thieving."

A cooking class was going on in the kitchen. After taking a few of the older boys with her to the butcher's and the greengrocer's to buy ingredients for a traditional demon meal of vagabond's pie, Anzhela had the boys engaged in an elaborate ritual of boiling and baking.

Vasily stayed out of the way and watched. Kitchens were as foreign to him as angelic polo fields. The room wasn't quite big enough for a dozen youths, so a game had started where one who was "it" dashed into the kitchen and tagged another to race him up the stairs, while the winner of the previous race got to roll dough for the little pies. It left him feeling peculiarly left out.

The resulting din was so loud that Vasily didn't notice when Silk returned. A kiss on the back of his neck alerted him to Silk's presence, and he turned, anxious to learn what Belphagor was up to. The sight that greeted him was jaw dropping.

Silk was almost unrecognizable in an exquisite chocolate pinstripe suit, his hair parted on the side and combed slick against his head with some kind of oil. He was, in fact, insanely handsome and a bit intimidating, like a supernal grand duke or a star of the Russian *kinoteatr*.

"Where did you get those?"

"His Highness took me shopping."

The casual delivery nearly knocked the air out of him. Vasily hadn't expected to feel jealousy from this direction. Silk, he'd thought, was the one person on his side—and now Belphagor was buying him fancy clothes, and Silk clearly wasn't objecting. He had to work to keep his face from crumbling, and to keep his voice from being nothing more than the grinding and shifting of coals in a grate against a hot poker.

"He what?"

"It seems he wants to make me his gigolo."

"He wants . . . what?" Vasily's vocabulary had suddenly dwindled to below simpleton.

"Well, maybe 'his' isn't the right word. I suppose it would be more accurate to say he's offered to be my pimp."

The noise in the kitchen had gotten quiet.

Vasily leapt to his feet. "I'm going upstairs." Without pausing to see if Silk would follow, he headed up to the attic, feeling like he couldn't get a breath. The house itself seemed to be closing in on him. The two boys who'd been racing took one look at him and slunk past down the stairs. His eyes hurt.

He waited with his back to the attic window until Silk appeared at the top of the little staircase. "How could you do that?"

Silk paused. "Do what? What am I doing?"

"Letting him buy you. I mean, I guess he *did* buy you, didn't he? From your last owner."

Silk's cheeks went red. "That isn't fair." He stood still for a minute, and then lunged forward without warning and shoved Vasily in the chest, making him stumble back against the windowsill in surprise. "And fuck you, Ruby! Just fuck you!" Tears spilled over his cheeks, and Vasily grabbed his arm and stopped him as he whirled about to leave.

"I'm sorry." Vasily was horrified at himself. "Please, Silk. I didn't mean it."

Silk put up a halfhearted resistance before letting Vasily enfold him in his arms.

Vasily held him as he shook, a bit dismayed at how the tables had turned. "Please don't cry. You'll wrinkle your gorgeous suit." Never mind that the suit made *him* want to cry.

Silk sniffed and wiped at his eyes. "I told you I wanted to find a mark. He's a perfect mark. One that thinks he's playing me when I'm really playing him. It isn't personal." He glanced up at Vasily, his eyes shining with tears. "I don't want him. You know that. It's business." Vasily let his arms slip away, and Silk stepped back, straightening his slightly crushed lapels.

"So you're going to let him dress you?" He couldn't believe how awful that felt to say. "And sell you? That's business?"

"Wasn't it your business once?" As Vasily's eyes flared once more, Silk put out his hand in negation. "I don't mean with him. I mean the trade. It *is* my trade. And if you have a problem with me making a living this way—"

"No, of course not." He had no right to dictate what Silk chose to do, but he couldn't help a troubling suspicion that Silk wanted him to feel as if he and Belphagor had conspired to stomp on Vasily's heart. He tried Belphagor's breathing technique to get control of his wildly spinning thoughts. "It's going to have to be my trade again too. But I don't see why he has to be involved. Can't you do it without him?"

Silk smoothed his hands over the suit jacket. "Do you think I could buy this? The buttons alone would cost an all-night gangbang. Doing it his way, with his facets, I may not have to work much at all except when I feel like it." Silk's gray eyes crinkled at the corners. "I *may* have been misrepresenting his intentions just a teensy bit because I think he's being a prick to you. But what he wants is for me to run a whorehouse."

Vasily nearly choked on his own fiery spit.

"Male whores," Silk clarified. "He's at the Demon Market recruiting right now. And he's bought the building next door. So it's going to happen with or without me."

Vasily grabbed his head with both hands to make it stop spinning. "He bought a *building*?"

"It opens Friday night. The Stone Horse. He says you're welcome to entertain there as well if you choose. But I'm not supposed to let you engage in business with any angels."

A full-on fiery blaze of fury surged inside him so hard he had to choke it down before he opened his mouth and incinerated the attic. Belphagor thought he could throw him away and still control his every move.

"Oh, really. Well, *fuck him*."

Silk gave him a sly smile and sidled up close to kiss his scruffy cheek despite the heat he was giving off. "That's my succulent ruby plum."

The Stone Horse was such a novelty that word of its inception attracted even those who had no personal interest in its wares—among demons and angels alike. Some came to gawk and others for titillation, resulting in a situation where those who had come with the intent of partaking of the offering ended up feigning membership in one of the former two camps.

For Belphagor's purposes, however, the odd cocktail-party atmosphere was a perfectly successful opening. His aim was to be seen shopping for a new "boy." And Silk, for his part, was superb. No one who saw him would have taken him for the seemingly adolescent dorm monitor of the Fletchery. He looked every bit the sophisticated panderer and seemed to relish his role.

As much as Belphagor ached to see him, he'd hoped Vasily would stay home and sulk. Instead, Vasily appeared early in the evening in a stunning ensemble that Silk or Anzhela must have helped him pull together. His matted locks were wound with spun gold and his eyes done up in dark kohl paint that ended in a spiral flourish dotted with imitation crystal chips. Over a bare chest, he wore a sort of velvet smoking jacket that came to his knees in a deep ruby hue with a black collar and cuffs over a pair of black satin lounging pants gathered at the ankles.

Silk, entertaining a group of girls from The Cat who'd come out of curiosity, turned as if on cue when Vasily entered. "Ah, here's my tasty plum." He held out his hand, and Vasily crossed the room to take it, passing Belphagor as if he didn't see him. The waves of angry heat coming off him, however, said he most certainly had. "Vasily, I believe you already know some of the ladies in our sister trade."

Vasily went pink but managed a grunted greeting. Good thing he wasn't trying to sell his services to them with such lack of finesse. Not that Belphagor wanted him selling his services to anyone. He'd been selfish enough to hope Vasily wouldn't want to. The more fool, he.

Surly or not—or perhaps *because* he seemed surly—Vasily was attracting a great deal of attention from prospective patrons, among them a group of angelic nobles Belphagor had been watching since he'd arrived. They had surfaced when Phaleg made his offer on The Cat a few days earlier, perturbed, it seemed, at the competition, though they hadn't turned out to be The Cat's investors themselves.

Nevertheless, they'd taken an interest in not only The Cat but also the Stone Horse. And they made it plain that they'd heard the rumors Armen had been spreading about Belphagor, sneering at him when they entered and making snide remarks about there being nothing rare enough for him on the menu.

As with The Cat, Belphagor was a silent partner here, and he tried to ignore them while simultaneously keeping an eye on them, using his shameless flirting with the demons he'd recruited for the Stone Horse as cover. He'd already arranged to escort a pair of them back to The Brimstone for a late evening of gaming and drink.

When one of the angels began making coarse comments about Vasily in a voice loud enough for everyone within earshot to hear, Belphagor made a move in his direction, but Silk stole the show before he had a chance to act.

"Why, Duke Balkin." He turned his head in the angel's direction. "I had no idea you'd be vying for my disciplinary services so soon. I have a special room laid out for you downstairs. Why don't you go down, disrobe, and wait for me over the sawhorse? I'll be along in a bit to redden your ass to match your face."

On cue, the angel blushed and then went even redder when the laughter around him made the joke clear. "I don't pay demons to beat me," he snapped.

Silk smiled. "That's all right, sweetheart. I'm sure you can find plenty who'll do it for free."

The angel realized there was no graceful way out and turned to his companions with a stony expression that stopped their laughter. "Let's go. This is precisely the sort of freak show I thought it would be and not half as amusing."

"I thought it was hilarious." One of them winked at Silk as they followed their friend out to the street.

"Well, they were unpleasant." Silk smiled amiably. "How about a round of nepenthe on the house for the rest of our guests?"

This proposal was met with cheering, and the stewards Belphagor had hired proceeded to pour the sparkling libation he'd bought. Silk flashed him a knowing look across the room that said he'd spend Belphagor's money all he liked.

"I do have a sawhorse available downstairs with a nice set of manacles." Silk grinned as the guests drank to his generosity. "If anyone actually does want their ass to blush, I'm happy to oblige."

Belphagor raised his eyebrow as the guests began to flirt with Silk in brash terms about being spanked and tied up. It seemed everyone was suddenly horning in on his business. When had bondage and discipline become the kink du jour? It was a tad annoying. He was certain any of those currently sucking up to Silk about it would scream like angelic schoolboys if actually subjected to a good thrashing.

The idea depressed him, and Vasily's stark beauty in his unusual getup was making him feel as if his heart were slowly bleeding into his lungs. He might as well head back to The Brimstone and keep an eye out for the disgruntled duke. He wrapped his arms around the waists of his two escorts for the evening and pulled them close.

"What do you say we take our party to my place?" He swayed a bit drunkenly and winked. "Between the two of you, I'm sure one of you can keep me up." He glanced at Silk as they headed out. "I'll settle accounts when I bring 'em back in the morning. Mostly intact." He felt Vasily's eyes burning into the back of his skull as he lurched through the door.

It had been painful enough to think of Vasily sharing Silk's bed, but the idea of Silk laying a firm hand on him began to eat at Belphagor as he and his companions caroused through the streets. Would Vasily kneel for someone else?

He couldn't stand the thought, and he almost turned around and went back to challenge Silk, before he caught sight of the duke and his friends heading for The Brimstone. He'd gone to all this trouble for a reason, and he couldn't afford to blow it now because his pride was wounded.

The wingcasting table would at least provide an outlet for his frustration. He hadn't played a good game in weeks, and it was time to reclaim his crown as the Prince of Tricks. And in the process, he had an excellent opportunity to loosen some tongues.

CHAPTER FIFTEEN

In the wake of Belphagor's flamboyant departure, Vasily tried to maintain an unaffected air, but Silk already knew him too well. Drawing him by the hand into one of the private rooms, Silk closed the curtain and slipped his arms around Vasily's neck.

"You don't look like you're having any fun. I can't have my plum looking glum."

Vasily groaned. "I think I should head home. No one's buying tonight anyway."

"Why, because His Highness is cavorting about with a pair of fancy boys? He's playing a part, Ruby. You should play one too."

"What part? He's being an ass. That hardly takes skill."

"He's playing the rake, as if he doesn't care at all about whose heart he might be breaking. Yet he couldn't take his beady little coal-button eyes off you. You are simply stunning this evening. Anzhela is an artiste. Who would have thought anyone could make you look both more intoxicating and more terrifying?"

"I look ridiculous. Those angels were laughing at me."

"No, you absolutely do not. That's one of the most endearing things about you. You have no idea of your own allure. You're like some exotic barbarian from the stormy wilds of Ma'on who ought to be wielding a curved blade as you leap through the crowd severing heads. You look like you could breathe fire."

Vasily glowered with embarrassment. "I *can* breathe fire."

Silk's eyes widened. "Oh my Heavens, Ruby. I think I just came a bit in my pretty new suit."

Vasily laughed nervously, but Silk's expression turned serious.

"You could have your pick of any demon or angel out there this evening, and you could charge for the mere pleasure of your company without ever letting anyone lay a hand on you. And I think you should."

"You think I should what?"

Silk rolled his eyes and tapped Vasily's nose. "I think, my ruby plum, that you should go out there and entice someone to take you out for the evening. That other group of angels, perhaps, who've been drooling over you and practically pissing themselves in fear every time you look in their direction."

"They— Who— What?"

"You're adorable. The ones who keep hanging about the girls from The Cat, pretending they aren't actually trying to get your attention. I can't believe you haven't noticed." Silk kissed him and opened the curtain. "Come on. You're going out."

He led Vasily back to the center of the action. "Who'd like to take this fiery beast out for a night on the town? To The Brimstone, perhaps? I hear he's good luck at the tables."

"*Silk*," Vasily hissed under his breath, but Silk pushed him forward.

"You boys look like you can handle him." Silk propped an arm on the shoulder of one of the angels. "Fancy it warm?"

The angel darted his eyes toward Vasily and back down, his cheeks pink. Was Silk right? Did they want him and find him menacing at the same time?

"We'll join you," piped up one of the ladies. It was the redhead Belphagor had bought for him at The Cat. Vasily jumped slightly as she slipped her arm through his and hooked the angel with the other. "I like it hot." She winked. "You remember." She turned to the angel. "It's okay. He doesn't talk much, but he has a wicked tongue."

Before he knew it, he was being swept toward the door between two of the women, flanked by the pair of dumbstruck angels.

"Have a good time," Silk called. "Don't forget to get paid."

It was obvious he wanted Vasily to be seen by Belphagor in the company of angels. Whether it was simply to show Belphagor that Silk was controlling the game or a genuine desire to help Vasily get back at him, he wasn't sure.

Feeling an unaccustomed sense of power, he began to enjoy his role. In the past, he'd been a novelty for angels who clearly held the power themselves and treated him like an overgrown pup. This was the first time he'd felt in control.

The feeling lasted all of twenty minutes while they made their way to The Brimstone—and indeed continued for a few moments as he came down the stairs and every head turned to stare with a gratifying look of awe. And then it was crushed beneath the boot of whatever game Belphagor was playing.

His back to the door, Belphagor was sitting with his chair tilted on its rear legs, one boot heel hooked under the base of the wingcasting table in a characteristic way that said he wasn't nearly as inebriated as he let on, mouthing an unlit cigar stub. The demons he'd picked up at the Stone Horse were standing on either side of his chair admiring his skill and vying for his attention. But the one who had it was his opponent across from him: none other than the angel Phaleg, whom Belphagor had carried on with while he'd left Vasily in the world of Man.

As if that weren't humiliating enough, curled on an extra chair beside Phaleg, that devil Mikhail was flirting with Belphagor, his shirt open to the navel and his hand moving in a languid motion between his pecs. He was the first at the table to notice Vasily and his entourage, and the warm hue of his skin went a bit pale. Beside him, Phaleg glanced up at a murmured word from Khai, and the angel went significantly paler. *Good.* At least this stupid getup was useful for something. He hoped they'd pissed into their boots.

Belphagor never turned.

"Don't look now." Khai brushed his toe against Belphagor's knee. "But your boy just walked in. At least I think it's him. Either that or some eastern prince who's about to declare war on Elysium and slit all our throats."

It took everything Belphagor had not to react as he perused his cards.

"No, it's him," Khai confirmed. "He's burned off one of my nuts with his eyes."

"Please don't engage him. Phaleg, it's your play."

Khai squirmed in his seat. "I'm not engaging him; he's burning my nuts off."

"Well, it's a good thing I don't need your nuts, then, isn't it? *Toad*," he added as the die left Phaleg's unsteady hand.

"How do you always know?" Phaleg shook his head when the die landed on Toad, surrendering a card to the pile. "Incidentally, this is making me very uncomfortable."

Belphagor picked up the card and glanced at his options. "I'm sure your testicles are quite safe, Phaleg." He laid down a Full Choir. "Your facets, on the other hand, are not."

"Why, if it isn't the Prince of Tricks." The derisive voice behind him was one he'd been expecting to hear for some time. Why couldn't the bastard have shown up before Vasily arrived? "Aren't these boys a bit long in the tooth for your taste?"

Might as well get this over with.

Belphagor let the front legs of his chair drop and pushed away from the table. "Armen Nekirevich." He took his cigar from his mouth as he rose and turned, pushing up his sleeves. "Care to make your meaning plain?"

"My meaning"—Armen raised his voice—"is that you prefer little boys to grown men. Isn't that why you've dumped your incubus bitch?"

Belphagor had meant to make a clever retort that would make Armen look a fool. Instead, he found himself on top of the bastard, pummeling his face into the floor of The Brimstone. It took all four of his companions and two of Armen's to drag him off and shove him into a chair.

Armen staggered to his feet, howling and holding his hand to his gushing nose. "I'll have the Supernal Guard in here! I have witnesses who can place you at the Fletchery. I'll have you pilloried for your perversion!"

Belphagor shook off Phaleg and Khai and got to his feet. "You've impugned my honor for the last time, Armen Nekirevich. I challenge you to defend yourself against me in a duel."

"A duel?" Armen laughed. "Now you fancy yourself an angel, putting on airs."

"I fancy you a coward. Take back your slander against me, or name your weapon and meet me on the field of honor."

"You're out of your mind. And drunk! I'll do nothing of the kind."

"So you're a coward, then. Man enough to invent slander about me after manufacturing the circumstantial evidence of it yourself, but not man enough to defend your own craven words. I demand satisfaction before these witnesses. Will you recant?"

Armen's face was red enough to match the blood Belphagor had drawn. The entire den was watching him. Belphagor had put him between brimstone and a hard place.

"I will not recant."

"Very well. Have your second make the arrangements with mine. Captain Phaleg, will you do me the honor?"

Phaleg rose. "Certainly."

"Well, then." Belphagor turned his back on Armen and signaled to the barmaid. "More ale. Issuing challenges makes me thirsty. And randy." He sat back in his seat with a wink and drew Khai toward him with an arm around his waist while the other two rentboys moved behind him and toyed with his hair.

It wasn't popular to make obvious advances to a member of one's own sex in a Raqia gambling den, despite the common practice of bringing one's hired doxy along for good luck, but he figured he'd earned a bit of slack. His apparent drunkenness would be seen as the reason for his lack of propriety. And demonstrating his interest in Khai was essential in dispelling Armen's accusations.

He didn't bother to look around to see what Armen's response was to his indifference. It seemed best to add insult to injury and act as if he'd already forgotten him. The sound of angry footsteps on the stairs and the banging of the door to the street told him all he needed to know, and the resumption of activity within the den confirmed it.

Only then did he dart a surreptitious look around to see where Vasily's party had ended up. They'd taken over a large open seating area by the fire pit in the front, where Vasily appeared to be holding court. Among his admirers were a trio of girls from The Cat and what appeared to be a pair of scholarly Dominions who must have hired him for the night. *Fucking Silk.* Belphagor's one condition had been no angels.

He began to imagine all sorts of scenarios where the Dominions had their way with Vasily, worse than the thought of him kneeling for Silk. He botched his hand in the latest wingcasting round with the challenger who'd taken Phaleg's place and couldn't concentrate enough to achieve even a fifty-fifty outcome with the cast of the die.

"What's wrong?" Khai murmured at his ear. "Feeling the hot seat? Not so funny when it's your own nuts, is it?"

Belphagor tossed a handful of facets into the pot with an angry flick. "Kneel if you're going to hover. You're distracting me."

"Oh, *I'm* distracting you." Khai slid down beside him and perched his elbow on the edge of the table. "Not the Dominion with his hand down Vasily's pants?"

"Do you mind?" His challenger sniffed with distaste. "I came to play cards, not to be subjected to your vulgarian exploits."

With a sigh, Belphagor folded and held out his hand to Khai as he pushed back his chair and stood. "It seems I'm a bit too inebriated to hold my own here." He glanced at the other two demons he'd hired, who were currently scandalizing the gaming room by making out with one another. "Perhaps one of you would like to help me hold my own in my room."

With one arm around Khai and the other around the nearest of the two demons, he headed for the back of the den, sweeping a bottle of vodka off the bar as he passed it. "Put it on my tab." He waved off the bartender's objection, spilling vodka on Khai's chest in his effort to hold on to both.

Once in his room, he extracted himself from his entourage and set the bottle on the vanity. The narrow cot had seemed horribly large since his return, and he could barely stand looking at it.

From his pocket, he took the small pouches he'd kept for the Stone Horse demons and held them out. "You two are free to go. Just slip out the back way behind the bar, if you wouldn't mind." They took the facets, barely aware of him at this point in their mutual interest in one another. "Be careful on the street," he added as they opened the door.

"They're pros." Khai sat on the cot as the demons took their leave.

Belphagor shrugged, slipping out of his coat. "They could still be jumped by angels who've had too much to drink." He kicked his makeshift bedroll out from under the cot and stripped down to his shorts.

"Sure you don't want to share the bed?" Khai lay on his side, his shirt falling open where the last of the buttons had come free. "You *are* paying for my time. And paying handsomely, I might add."

"Thanks. I'm not really in the mood." He climbed under his blanket and pulled it over his shoulder.

Khai snuffed out the lantern hanging from a hook in the wall above the bed that had on occasion held Vasily's bound wrists instead. "You've got it bad," Khai remarked into the darkness. "Worse than anyone I've ever seen."

"Yeah. I know." He was afraid it might be terminal.

Vasily was scaring the Dominions. He couldn't help it. Watching Belphagor treating Khai—*Khai*, of all demons—the way he'd once treated Vasily . . . Was he trying to punish him for being with Silk? After throwing Vasily into Silk's arms, it hardly seemed fair. None of this seemed fair.

He thought back over everything he'd said and done in the past few weeks, and every single word out of his mouth to Belphagor made him cringe. Why had he told him he didn't want to be his boy? It was the worst lie he'd ever uttered. Why couldn't he have explained to Belphagor how he'd hurt him without twisting everything up into such an unfixable mess?

"Ow!" The angel whose thigh he'd begun to stroke when Belphagor had looked his way jumped under his grip. There was a scorch mark on the angel's pants.

"Sorry." The sound of his embarrassed growl seemed to make it worse. He stood, and the angel cowered. "You don't owe me anything for the evening. I've been poor company. Please don't hold it against the Stone Horse. If you could see these lovely ladies back to their residence, I'd appreciate it." He took the redheaded demoness's hand and kissed it. "And if I need to pay for your time—"

"Don't be absurd!" She snatched her hand away and glowered up at him, offended, but her look softened at his abashed expression. "Sure you don't want to come back to The Cat? Maybe what you need is a nice massage. On the house."

"Thanks, but I'm afraid I'm liable to start a fire." He thanked the other demonesses and took his leave.

Back at the Stone Horse, the party was going strong, and Silk was thriving in his new role. Vasily returned to the apartment, where Anzhela was the only one awake.

"Did you have a good evening?" She glanced up from reading one of his books in the parlor.

He dropped into the chair across from her. "Not really. I kept scaring people."

"Maybe the cosmetics were a bit much. I should have done something a little more playful."

"No, it wasn't that. I'm afraid I was miserable company."

"Missing Belphagor?"

Vasily snorted. "I'd have liked to have missed him, but he was everywhere." He sighed. "I think he hates me."

Anzhela set her book down. "That's the most ridiculous thing I've ever heard."

"You didn't see him. His hands were all over these other demons. Right in front of me. He didn't give a damn that I was there."

"Do you see this house you're sitting in?"

"Of course I see it."

"Do you have any idea how much this must have cost?"

"Facets don't seem to mean much to him. He's been throwing them around like candy. Buying Silk suits. Buying him a *building*."

"Silk could live in the Stone Horse. That's generally where the proprietor lives. Instead, Belphagor has set him up here with you in a place that isn't going to pay for itself like the Horse."

"No, but it's for the boys. Where else were they going to go?"

"Yes, it's for the boys. But he went to some trouble to make sure it wasn't just some dormitory like they're used to. They'd have been thrilled with a boardinghouse room. This is a home, and it has all sorts of little touches that say he adores you."

"What touches? It does not."

"This reading lamp, for instance. It's illuminated by spell. Do you think he put this here for me? Silk doesn't even read." She glanced up at the torchère spreading soft white light over the comfortable, stuffed armchair like an earthly floor lamp. "He had all your books sent over."

"Yes, because he threw me out."

"Did you buy these books?"

"Well, no, but—"

"He knew you liked to read, so he made sure you had the books, and he procured a rather expensive magical lamp for you to read by—it's got to be fueled with ophanic fire. I've never seen anything like it."

"So he's buying me off."

"Oh for Heaven's sake. The pair of you. I swear."

"What are you talking about?"

"You should have seen him moping about when he left you in the world of Man the first time, completely convinced you would never forgive him, pining like a lovesick schoolboy. The two of you are exactly the same. You're like children."

"He *threw me out.*"

"And into the arms of your very handsome—and much younger than him—lover. And bought you a house."

"He's not my—" Vasily swallowed and tried not to blush. His behavior with Silk hadn't exactly been platonic. "And what do you mean, he bought it? How do you know he's not renting it until Silk can take over the payments with the profits from the Horse?"

"No one would rent out a place like this. This is the sort of place one stays in until one dies. Or loses at the wingcasting table to the Prince of Tricks." Anzhela rose and left Dostoevsky's *Demons* on the chair. "And if you think it's not killing him to see you and Silk together, you're thicker than you seem. I saw his face back in the world of Man when Silk announced that you'd practically proposed to him. It's the sort of look a man has when he realizes he's lost everything. I can't imagine how seeing you like this tonight must have affected him, but I can guarantee you he isn't bedding the demons he was flaunting. He's probably going completely mad imagining whom you're bedding."

"I'm not bedding anyone!" he protested as Anzhela flounced off to her room. He'd gotten over his reluctance to engage in intimate play with Silk—Belphagor obviously hadn't wasted any time finding other outlets for his urges, and saying no to Silk had begun to seem like punishing himself for no reason—but he was pretty sure it didn't count as bedding if it was only mouths and hands. And besides, it had only happened a couple of times.

Silk had been preoccupied with the opening of the Stone Horse for the past few days, and Vasily had been mostly relieved. The more Silk's dominant tendencies had come out, the less Vasily was sure he wanted to play the role of a submissive. He *wasn't* submissive. And he and Belphagor hadn't been playing. Belphagor had owned him, body and soul, from the moment he'd first laid a hand on him.

He sank into the chair, holding the book under the soft glow of the lamp. Was Anzhela right? Had it hurt Belphagor to think of him with Silk? Somehow, *hurt* hadn't occurred to him. *Angry* had occurred to him. *Arrogant* and *selfish* had occurred to him. Belphagor himself had given Vasily his blessing to be intimate with Silk, which Vasily had just assumed meant he'd wanted an excuse to play with Lev without feeling guilty. But had Vasily's attraction to Silk been hurtful to him all along?

Damn it, he didn't understand Belphagor at all.

He sat up reading, waiting for Silk, but Silk had apparently found a patron or patrons to keep him busy. He reached the end of his book at last, turning page after page as the action in the story spun out of control, feeling anxious for Dostoevsky's Stavrogin. Despite all his self-destructive behavior and inexplicable cruelty, there seemed something in him that wanted to be noble and kind, but it was as if he didn't think he deserved to be.

As the character met his fate, Vasily found himself weeping. Stavrogin had succumbed to a kind of negative inertia, letting his worst impulses spin tragedy out around him when he could have been a different kind of man had he only taken action. He'd seen himself at last as the worst of which he was capable—perhaps because he'd been told that was all he was. Like a demon in Elysium's slums.

Vasily wished he could talk to Belphagor about the book and how it made him feel. He wasn't quite sure he understood it all. He was anxious and sad. And touched by the beauty of the language. And he missed saying the words to Belphagor in their adopted tongue that bound them together more intimately than any angelic words could ever do. *Da, ser, ya tvoy mal'chik. I'm your boy.*

He fell asleep in the chair with the tears still hot on his face.

The break Belphagor had been looking for finally came. Using Phaleg as his front for the purchase of The Cat had worked like a charm. The angels Phaleg had nettled with his inquiries had alerted the actual investor.

"He's from the Order of Powers." Phaleg gave him the news as they met in the Market over a cup of Raqia coffee at a standing bar. Not Belphagor's favorite beverage but thick and dark enough to wake him at this early hour. Khai had been snoring when he left. It had reminded him painfully of Vasily, only the room was too cold. "Sergeant Veloas of the Embankment Patrol."

"A superior of yours?"

"No." Phaleg gave him a patronizing smile. "Powers are not of the nobility. A sergeant is not a commissioned officer."

Belphagor sipped the bitter liquid. "The intricacies of angelic hierarchy escape me. To put it another way, they bore and annoy me. What's the upshot, then? Will he sell? Is your offer an insult?"

"Not an insult. Your figure enticed him. You may not be conversant in celestial rankings, but you certainly know the value of a facet." He smiled at Belphagor's dramatic flourish as he made a mock bow. "He was surprised, however, to hear the offer came from me. I'm afraid my reputation is going to take a bit of a plummet."

"Sorry about that."

Phaleg shrugged. "I doubt it will do me any harm. Being associated with a whorehouse, after all, ought to dispel any rumors of my perversion."

"I thought sucking cock was fashionable among younger officers."

Phaleg choked on his coffee. Apparently, he still had the sensibilities of an angel after all. Belphagor suppressed a grin.

"Unfortunately, Duke Elyon's treason put a damper on the sort of carefree experimentation that was popular a year or so ago. His parties were infamous. Angels who were looking for an excuse to vilify such behavior leapt upon the opportunity. There's an unofficial policy now that commanding officers won't make any inquiries into a soldier's sexual proclivities so long as the soldier himself doesn't advertise any. The upshot being that if one soldier has a grudge against another soldier, he claims he heard him saying he's been 'pilfering from the home till,' and the accused gets a reprimand. If evidence is found, he gets a dishonorable discharge and may even lose his noble rank."

Belphagor's grin had faded. "I'm sorry to hear it. I hope I haven't put you in harm's way."

"No, it's all right. No one knew of our relationship. You were Beatrix most of the time, after all."

"Is that why you haven't found anyone? The danger of being caught?"

"Mostly, yes." Phaleg's gaze flicked to Belphagor's and away, a light blush in his cheeks. "That, and you're a hard memory for any angel to live up to. But I didn't come here to talk about my sad lack of discipline." He made an attempt at a smile. "Sergeant Veloas has agreed to sell his interest in The Cat. And better still, I made a casual remark to him about how convenient it would be to buy a whore one could dispose of when one was through to avoid messy complications, and he mentioned that he knew of a source for purchasing demons that could be dispensed with afterward because they were owned outright, and all one had to do was sell them out of Heaven to 'where they belong.'"

Belphagor leaned forward against the rail of the coffee bar. "He actually said that? Sell them out of Heaven?"

"His exact words." Phaleg finished his beverage and passed his cup along the bar, turning to lean back against it, facing the market. "And he claims to be making a far better return on his investment trading in 'expendables,' as he calls them, which is why he's happy to relinquish The Cat."

"Has a ready supply, I suppose." Belphagor fumed. "Wherever they've relocated the Fletchery."

"I didn't ask him specifically about underage demons. I didn't want to arouse his suspicion."

"Of course. But underage or not, this is an excellent lead." He glanced at Phaleg's profile. "Anyway, I don't want to drag you too far into this."

"Farther than owning a whorehouse?"

"That is pretty far, I admit." Belphagor studied him. "How would you like to own two?"

Phaleg's eyebrows lifted in disbelief. "Two?"

"Come with me and Khai to the Stone Horse tonight. There's someone I'd like you to meet."

"The Stone Horse? Your male-only brothel?"

"Seal the deal with your sergeant this afternoon, and tell him you're interested in purchasing one of the 'expendables' for your personal use—that you've heard demons can transmit disease from the world of Man, and rather than taking a chance on one of the whores who work in your new brothel, you want one that hasn't been broken in. That way your interest needn't appear to be in underage trade but in 'clean' trade. If they happen to intersect, that's no fault of yours."

"Do they?"

Belphagor wrinkled his brow at the expression of concern on Phaleg's face. Had he not understood that this was about the sale of underage virgins? He tried to buy time to think how to answer the angel truthfully without unnerving him and losing his support. "Do they what?"

"Transmit diseases."

The unexpected reply took Belphagor by surprise. "You're asking if we're actually dirty?"

Phaleg blanched. "No! I— You brought it up. I'd never heard that before, except your little tale about 'bugs'—the one you told Duke Elyon when you were trying to avoid bedding him as Beatrix."

The surprise that had been verging on outrage fizzled out. "Sorry, I forget you don't know anything about the world of Man. Disease is rampant there, but I've never heard of a demon bringing any to the celestial sphere. The aether in our air seems to nullify any terrestrial contagion. The story about bugs was based on truth, though. Sometimes a variety of rather embarrassing lice has been known to make it into Heaven."

"Lice?"

Belphagor resisted the urge to roll his eyes. Angels were unbelievably sheltered. "Like fleas on a dog. Only on a person. It's what happens when you don't have personal servants to launder your clothes daily and fetch you clean water, and when you're forced to live in cramped conditions because you can't afford a bloody palace."

Phaleg's pale skin flushed pink. Angels also seemed to blush more than anyone he'd ever known. Except perhaps Vasily, who was at the mercy of his mercurial temperament and the heat in his blood. The thought made him yearn for the things he knew would bring out the flush in the firespirit's skin, but he pushed the longing away.

"Sorry." Phaleg looked mortified. "I didn't mean to be insensitive."

Belphagor touched his hand fleetingly. "I know you didn't. Anyway, never mind that. See if your sergeant will set up a meeting with one of his suppliers, and then you and I can get together to work out how to set up a trap. We'll head over to the Stone Horse for an evening of it. You could come in glamour if you're worried about being seen."

Phaleg gave him a sly smile. "There's another unspoken rule—about not reporting someone you see ogling male prostitutes if you happen to also be ogling male prostitutes at the time. I think I can chance it. But aren't you forgetting something?"

"What am I forgetting?"

"That I'm acting as your second. Armen Nekirevich is still in need of a thrashing on the field of honor. I spoke with his appointed second after I met with Veloas. He's chosen the dueling method, as well as the time and place."

"Ah, the duel." Belphagor sighed. "I was hoping he'd prove a true a coward and flee Raqia. So what's his weapon?"

"Dueling pistols from the world of Man."

Belphagor couldn't help the outburst of laughter. "Dueling pistols? Doesn't he realize gunpowder is inert in Heaven?"

"He does. These are charmed pistols, apparently. The marvelous things you demons get up to. I'd never even heard of pistols until his second showed them to me. He gave me a brief history of how they operate in the world of Man." Phaleg shook his head. "The emotionless efficiency of the weapon is quite chilling. At any rate, this pair, according to Armen, is from your Russia, an authentic nineteenth-century set, except that its firing mechanism has been altered. Instead of firing with gunpowder, the lead ball is expelled via elemental combustion."

"'Elemental combustion'?" It wasn't a term he was familiar with—unless one considered Vasily's talent.

"The mechanism responds to the element of the demon holding it. At least that's how it was explained to me. I didn't really follow the specifics, and I confess I don't quite get the whole elemental magic thing. Manipulating one's element isn't strictly forbidden among the angelic class, but it's frowned upon. At best, it's regarded as peasant superstition. Nevertheless, I've been assured that you'll be able to examine them before you agree to the choice of weapon."

Belphagor folded his arms and crossed one boot over the other, leaning against the bar as he considered. "So when does he want to do this thing?"

"Tomorrow at dawn. Under the Hell's Gate Bridge on the Raqia side."

"Well, then." He allowed himself a sly grin. "We'd best enjoy ourselves this evening."

CHAPTER SIXTEEN

Vasily hadn't planned to go the Stone Horse a second night in a row, but Silk guilted him into it.

Coming home after sunrise, Silk had stripped out of his suit and fallen into bed right after Vasily had climbed into it. When they woke in the late afternoon, Silk asked him how his night had gone, and when Vasily admitted he'd come home without taking the angels' money, Silk gave him a wounded pout that made him feel he'd robbed Silk outright.

Climbing over Vasily—who was still dressed in the ridiculous getup from the night before—Silk sat in his lap completely naked, rocking subtly against him while he complained about how hard he'd worked at the Horse while Vasily had trotted off to play and come back with nothing to show for it.

"I worked very, *very* hard." He emphasized the words with sensuous thrusts that made both of them manifest the concept.

When Vasily reached up to take hold of Silk's cock, Silk rose onto his knees and pinned Vasily's arms under them so that he couldn't reach, clucking his tongue.

"I have to do everything myself." He stroked himself. "Work my fingers . . . to the bone."

Silk lowered his mouth to Vasily's as if to kiss him, but when Vasily lifted his head to meet him, Silk held his free hand to Vasily's mouth and pressed him down against the pillow, trapping him there while he brought himself to completion. With a shiver and a moan that nearly made Vasily come too, he squeezed his fist tight under the bursting head and let the warm drops spill over onto Vasily's face.

When he'd finished, Silk licked the spunk from Vasily's sideburns before scooting back to untie the drawstring on Vasily's pants. Vasily braced himself for Silk's cool hand, but Silk sat back and crossed his arm. "Not even going to lift a hand to help, my selfish ruby plum?"

Vasily peeled down the fabric to release himself, and Silk simply waited with an expectant look until Vasily jerked himself off. As Vasily came with a growl of relief, Silk dipped his head down quickly enough to catch the ejaculate in his mouth, transforming the sound into a groan of surprised pleasure. Good thing he'd kept it cool.

When Silk had swallowed it all, he lifted his head and licked his lips. "You see what I do for you, Ruby? The least you could do in return is come for me tonight."

Against his better judgment, Vasily allowed Silk and Anzhela to make him up again, but this time he insisted on wearing his own clothes—or almost his own, at any rate. He didn't mind the cosmetics so much; they made him feel like he was wearing a mask and could play at being someone else, as Silk suggested. But the costume had made him feel exposed and had drawn too much attention.

On top of a tight pair of jeans tucked into some knee-high calfskin boots Dmitri had given him—secondhand riding boots from the Soviet military that hadn't fit him—Vasily wore a sleeveless black shirt made from a ribbed mesh fabric, courtesy of Lev. The two Grigori had plied him with "castoffs" when he'd started making plans to strike out on his own with Silk. He'd tried to give them back when that fell through, but they'd been insistent, Dmitri professing to take offense that he would refuse a gift.

When he arrived at the Horse, Silk ran his hands over Vasily's chest through the shirt with a purr of approval. "If this is what they wear in the world of Man, I may have to visit again. It ought to be illegal to be this hot, you mouthwatering plum."

Vasily doubted he was all that alluring in it, but it was a size too small, and he had to admit, it defined his pecs quite nicely. He soon struck up a conversation with a demon merchant who seemed somewhat in awe of him but was far more solicitous than the ogling Dominions had been.

It turned out the merchant only wanted a handjob, but he was so shy about it that after leading him into a booth, Vasily stood behind him and reached around to the front so that his patron wouldn't have to look him in the eye. He hooked his other arm around the merchant's chest and held him gently while he tossed him off, letting him feel the firespirit heat pressing against him.

The demon paid him three times what a handjob was worth, all blushing grins afterward, and thanked him far more than was warranted. Vasily felt a little sad for him, imagining he must be too afraid in his public life to indulge in his true desire. Vasily suspected he'd given the demon the first male pleasure he'd ever experienced.

After cleaning up, Vasily stepped out and looked around to see how Silk was faring. His heart gave a frantic leap in his chest: On the fainting couch in the corner of the parlor, Silk was entertaining Belphagor, unabashedly rubbing a hand over his leather-clad crotch, while Khai lounged at Belphagor's feet, his arms hooked over his knee. And on Silk's other side, the angel Phaleg sat watching the three of them with rapt attention.

Vasily stepped back into the doorway, not wanting them to see him, but Belphagor turned, as if he'd felt Vasily's heat from across the room, and gave him a look Vasily couldn't interpret. It was neither a smile nor a frown, but there was something charged about it.

While Vasily hesitated, not knowing whether to close the door between them or to step out and act as if everything was fine, Silk stood and moved closer to Phaleg, twisting the angel's hair around his finger and then yanking it hard, making Phaleg stumble to his feet.

Vasily's chest rose, and he stepped forward once more, ready to come to Silk's defense if Phaleg had said something offensive to him. But Silk had grabbed hold of Phaleg's cravat and turned about, drawing him away from the couch as though dragging him on a leash. He held out a hand to Khai, who stood to accompany him as he went.

Phaleg's skin was flushed and his eyes wide as he hurried after them to keep from being choked at the end of his scarf. Vasily watched in disbelief as Silk headed down the basement stairs.

Across the room, Belphagor was still watching him with the same intent gaze that gave nothing away—his "wingcasting face." He rose after a moment and made his way through the crowd to the foyer and left.

Vasily stood motionless, trying to will down the anger that wasn't warranted. Silk was here to take facets from angels and demons alike. Vasily had just done the same. But Belphagor had brought that angel here deliberately to mess with Vasily, knowing it would bother him. There was no other explanation. More games, the same as his efforts to push Vasily's buttons by buying Silk fancy clothes.

And if Belphagor was trying to get a reaction out of him, all the more reason to ignore him and not give him the satisfaction. But Vasily couldn't.

With swift, angry strides, he followed Belphagor out into the street, turning about to see which way he'd gone, and spotted him heading into the side entrance of the bakery—the stairs to the apartment. What the hell was he doing? Before Vasily reached the door to follow him up, something came hurtling out of the darkness, struck him above the eye, and smashed onto the cobblestones beside him.

He put his hand to his forehead and found blood dripping from a cut through his eyebrow. The smashed object on the ground was a full bottle of ale, spilling its contents among the shards of glass. Vasily turned in the direction it had come from, his eyes glowing to see better in the dark. Two demons who looked about his age stood in the opening of the alley. Even from here, he could see them start at his fiery gaze.

"Filthy sodomite!" one of them yelled before they ran. Probably, they'd intended worse but thought better of it upon seeing him.

Outrage warred with shock, compounding the tempest of emotion already buffeting him over Belphagor's tricks, as he climbed the stairs to the apartment. Part of him wanted to sit down on the stairs and bawl like a child.

Inside the apartment, Anzhela was making Belphagor a pot of tea. Vasily slammed the door.

Belphagor turned, his brows drawn together in consternation, but the irritation on his face was quickly replaced with concern as he got to his feet. "Vasya? What happened?"

"Nothing." When Belphagor came close, Vasily jerked back with a violent motion before Belphagor could touch him. "What the hell are you doing in my house?"

Belphagor searched his face, staring up at him in a way that accentuated the differences in their heights. "It's mine, if you want to be technical. I came to talk to Anzhela."

"After throwing your angel toy at Silk to fuck with me."

"I didn't—"

"You can't toss me out and then manipulate me endlessly for your own amusement. If that's what accepting this apartment means, then I'm out of here."

"Vasya—"

"Sit down." Anzhela's sudden sharp command startled both of them, and Vasily's mouth snapped shut as he stared at her. "Right now." She pointed at the table. "You're bleeding."

He sat meekly as she approached him with a wet cloth to clean the wound.

"Whatever 'nothing' happened, it missed your eye by a hair's breadth. We might need to sew this up."

"It was a bottle of ale. And I don't need stitches."

Belphagor folded his arms, leaning against the frame of the wall that separated the kitchen from the parlor. "A bottle of ale that just happened to make contact with your eye? Did someone at the Stone Horse get out of hand?"

"No."

A slow sigh of breath escaped Belphagor that said Vasily was pissing him off with his reticence. *Good.*

Vasily winced at Anzhela's ministrations. "You haven't told me what you're doing here. What do you want with Anzhela?"

"I believe that's Anzhela's business, not yours."

"I believe Anzhela is standing right in front of you," she countered, perturbed.

Belphagor glanced at her. "I thought you might prefer if I made my proposal in private. It concerns your future."

"You have proposals for everyone, haven't you?" Vasily couldn't help the bitter retort.

Anzhela spoke over him. "I can't imagine any potential future that I wouldn't want Vasily to hear about."

The teakettle began to whistle, and Belphagor went to get it. "I've purchased The Cat." He delivered the words as if they weren't completely outrageous as he poured the water over the leaves in the pot.

Vasily gaped at him. "How many whorehouses do you intend to own?"

Anzhela pressed the cloth against the cut. "Hold that to your head. If you're going to constantly interrupt him, perhaps it would be better if Belphagor tells me what he has in mind without you here."

Vasily took the cloth, chagrined. "Sorry. Go ahead."

While Anzhela brought the teapot and sugar to the table, Belphagor brought the cups, waiting until she was seated to continue. "I've purchased The Cat, and I'd like you to be the procuress if it's what you still want. It should have been yours."

Anzhela gazed up at him. "Belphagor . . . I don't know what to say. I do, of course I want to. But we'd have to work out an equitable arrangement."

"It should have been yours," he repeated. "I don't intend to interfere in its operation. But I would ask something of you in return."

Anzhela waited as he poured the tea.

"It's my opinion that you're too young to be taking on such responsibility. Though I'm sure you're perfectly capable. But I don't think it's a suitable environment for a girl of your age."

"Belphagor, I grew up in the brothel. There's nothing I haven't seen."

"Nonetheless, I don't want you working there yet. I'd like you to serve as a governess to the boys until they're of age. After which, each of you will be free to choose whatever livelihood for yourself you see fit."

Anzhela stared at her cup. "Are you . . ." She took a sip, looking flustered. "Are you proposing to serve as our legal guardian?"

Belphagor threw a glance at Vasily that said this was the part he hadn't wanted to discuss in front of him. "I don't know about legal. In the eyes of the princedom, I'm quite sure I wouldn't be deemed suitable, though celestial law has no problem viewing you as my property. Which you are *not*. But insofar as the law would see it so, I'm prepared to take responsibility for you and the boys until you come of age, at which time I'll formally release you for legal purposes. I hope that doesn't sound too—"

"No, it doesn't." Anzhela smiled. "I think it's a wonderful idea, and you're very sweet."

Belphagor gave her an awkward smile in return, quickly erased when he caught Vasily's icy stare. "At least someone thinks so." He concentrated on his tea.

Being "sweet" wasn't going to cut it with Vasily. "Seems like you're buying people and property up left and right. Like you bought Silk tonight for your fancy angel. Or is it the angel you own? Did he go with Silk to please his master?"

Belphagor set down his cup, but before he could speak, Anzhela rose and took the damp cloth from where Vasily still held it to his brow.

"The bleeding's stopped, but that cut's too deep for my taste. I'll fetch a needle and thread."

"I don't need it."

But Anzhela had slipped out of the room, and he had no doubt it would take her a while to find her sewing box.

Belphagor spun the cup in the saucer. "I don't own Phaleg. And I have no interest in him." Vasily couldn't help the snort of derision that escaped with a puff of steam. The cup clattered against the saucer as Belphagor dropped it. "For Heaven's sake. *All right.* I have an interest in just about anyone with a cock, as you damned well know, but I am not interested in pursuing any kind of relationship with Phaleg. Ever."

"What the hell makes you think I care?"

Belphagor held his gaze. "Have you stopped loving me?"

Infuriatingly, tears prickled behind his eyes. "How can you ask me that?"

"Because I haven't stopped loving you. I haven't stopped wanting you." The dark eyes took in Vasily's mesh-hugged pecs. "And look at you. *Bozhe moi*, you're killing me."

"You threw me away. Because I wouldn't play your game and kneel for you like your new boy, Khai."

"Is that what you think?" Belphagor shook his head and ran both hands through the stiff, dark spikes of his hair, the tattoos disappearing into its camouflage. "I've been trying to play this one close to the vest. It's crucial to the influence I'm attempting to work that I project a very specific, believable persona. But I didn't expect you to accept it so easily." His hand dropped back to the table, where he played with the cup once more. "I've purchased Khai's time to play a part for me. Nothing more. I want you to understand that, if you understand nothing else. He is *not* my boy."

Neither was Vasily. *"You're not my boy."*

"And while I knew what you'd assume when I sent that letter, I'd hoped you might pick up on the subtler nuances eventually. Perhaps you should read it again."

"I can't read it." Vasily growled the words into his teacup. "I burned it."

"I see. Well, I presume you remember the gist of it well enough. But its significance was in what it did *not* say."

Vasily held his breath, trying to suss out what Belphagor was getting at, trying to recall the words he'd been working hard *not* to think of for days. Belphagor's hand inched toward him over the table.

And Anzhela returned at the worst possible moment.

Glancing from one to the other, she set the open sewing box on the table between them, the pincushion perched on top holding a needle and heavy, waxed thread. Anzhela swiped a bottle of spirits from the counter and set it firmly beside the box. "Alcohol makes a good antiseptic." With a pointed look at Belphagor, she left the room.

Belphagor stared at the pincushion.

"I don't need stitches." Vasily's voice rattled in his throat so unconvincingly that Belphagor's head darted up. The dark eyes had a characteristic gleam that was more than a little unnerving.

"I trust Anzhela's judgment." Belphagor proceeded to uncork the bottle and hold the needle and thread under the stream as he tilted it over his teacup. "Sit still." It verged on a command, but Vasily held his tongue. And his position. Belphagor pinched the flesh together over Vasily's brow and poked the needle through, the alcohol stinging like fire. Vasily couldn't help but think of the place on his neck where the flesh had healed over. He let out a slight hiss through his teeth—against the discomfort as much as the feelings the memory stirred.

"What the letter did not say"—Belphagor drew the thread through Vasily's eyebrow and pulled it tight—"was anything suggesting you should stay away permanently." He drove the needle through again. "You told me you wanted to be with Silk, so I've accommodated that." Another pass of the needle served as punctuation, words and stitches forming an alternating rhythm. "I've tried to leave you alone, to give you the time and space you asked for. I've given you an ample allowance to be sure you're comfortable here. Khai sleeps in your bed. I sleep on the floor. In *our* room."

"You got rid of all my things." Vasily winced as the needle made another pass.

"I thought you'd want them here. Should I leave you with no comforts?" Belphagor tied the thread off with a tight jerk, leaning in to cut the end with his teeth. Vasily screwed his eyes shut, trying not to react. "And you clearly didn't check your delivery thoroughly if you thought I'd sent you all your things. Or didn't you want that fancy coat of yours any longer?"

Vasily gazed up at Belphagor standing over him. "You kept my coat . . . for me?"

"Well, you didn't think I could wear it, did you? I look ridiculous in it, as you've pointed out in no uncertain terms. It's far better on you—with your arms stretched over your head, bound and hooked to my wall, and nothing beneath that soft, smooth velvet except a magnificent erection."

Vasily tried to still the one stirring inside his tight jeans, and his breath caught at Belphagor's touch on his cheek.

"I can't make you come back to me. But I imagine it every night. Trussed and gagged and at my mercy while I use you for my pleasure. And this new look of yours, the wild, painted eyes . . . It makes you seem feral, like a creature who needs to be chained and caged. Or a barbarian to be broken with cruelty, raging against the humiliation I choose to inflict, helpless against the pain I mete out." Belphagor let his hand fall away and began cleaning up the table. "But you do what you will."

Vasily made an incoherent choking sound, cleared his throat, and tried again. "Why did you give Phaleg to Silk?" It wasn't what he'd meant to say. His brain was deprived of oxygen from the blood that had drained to his cock.

Belphagor paused and glanced at him, the wingcasting face back. "I didn't give Phaleg to anyone. He's a free angel. I merely introduced them. I thought they'd enjoy one another's company."

"You mean you thought you'd enjoy taking something from me."

Belphagor went back to cleaning the table. "So that's what's bothering you. That Silk should be 'yours.' I suppose I've underestimated your feelings for him. Well, thank you. That douses the idiotic fantasy I shared with you quite nicely."

Vasily cursed himself. "No, that isn't what I meant—"

"How did you get the cut?" Belphagor interrupted as if he were no longer interested in the topic.

Vasily fidgeted, confused by the rush of arousal Belphagor had stirred up and by his own feelings. And by his stupid mouth.

"Not going to tell me. Got it. Perhaps you'll feel more comfortable telling Silk about it in bed tonight."

Vasily rose, anxious, and blurted it out as Belphagor went to the door. "Someone threw a bottle at me when I came out of the Stone Horse."

Belphagor stopped. "You were attacked?"

"It was just a couple of young malcontents. Obviously drunk. They kept their distance. Called me a name and ran away like cowards."

"What name?"

"Sodomite."

Belphagor frowned. "That's an earthly insult. If they're young and yet they've fallen often enough to learn that kind of nonsense, I'd say they must be doing some kind of regular business between Heaven and the world of Man."

"You mean smuggling."

He nodded. "Drovers. I guess that means I'm getting close. Striking nerves." Belphagor reached for him suddenly and pulled Vasily into his arms. "I'm sorry. I didn't mean to put you in danger again."

"You're confusing me." Vasily's voice came out in a harsh whisper.

"That's all right." Belphagor gave him a parting squeeze. "You're confusing me too." He stepped back, hooked his fist into the center of the mesh shirt, and pulled Vasily down to take his mouth in a hard, angry kiss that made Vasily tingle with elemental fire. "We'll figure it out."

Vasily was too preoccupied with what had passed between them to go back to the Stone Horse. Belphagor's admission of desire and the revelation that he expected Vasily to come back to him lingered in his head just as the kiss lingered on his lips.

He waited up for Silk, who returned late, though earlier than he had the previous evening. Perhaps he hadn't enjoyed Phaleg's company as much as Belphagor had hoped. But all Silk could talk about was Phaleg.

"He's a remarkable submissive." His gaze was focused inward as he undressed. "Takes orders without question and endures whatever's required of him, despite a significant amount of fear and a rather low tolerance for pain. I suppose he can be toughened up, though."

Vasily pulled the mesh shirt over his head and tossed it aside. "How can you hit someone after the way Kezef treated you?"

Silk's brow lifted. "'Hit someone'? It's not as if I'm beating him up. I thought you'd been trained by Belphagor. Was it mostly bondage?"

"I don't want to talk about Belphagor. I'm just thinking of your history. It seems odd to me that you'd want to—to play that way."

"You do realize that the way Kezef 'plays' is no game. He's a sadist who enjoys causing genuine suffering. That's not remotely what I'm doing." Silk tossed down the pants he'd stepped out of. "Honestly, I'm more than a little offended you'd bring up that vile creature and me in the same sentence."

"Sorry. That was thoughtless. I don't know why I'm having trouble with the idea."

"The idea of me as a dominant? Or anyone?"

"Anyone, I suppose. Which makes no sense after Belphagor. So . . . tell me about the angel." He climbed under the covers and held them for Silk to crawl in.

Silk cuddled against him. "Well, I could tell right away how easily he could be humiliated—and how much he craved it—so I made him strip while Khai and I remained fully clothed. Khai is versatile, so

I gave him orders, though he was loving every minute of it. I made him suck Phaleg until he was hard—he was too afraid at first to be aroused—and then I bent him over the sawhorse and let Khai fuck his mouth while I cropped his ass and called him names. And I'm telling you, I didn't even hit him very hard before he was crying out in pain. Or at least trying to with his mouth full of Khai."

Silk's hand stole between Vasily's legs and curled around his erection as if unsurprised to find he was sporting one. "I decided to stick with humiliation for a bit, not knowing what his tolerance level was." His hand moved slowly up and down Vasily's shaft. "I fucked him with the handle of the crop—also wasn't sure he could take a cock up his ass."

Vasily arched slightly into his hand. "Oh, he can take it. I've fucked him."

"Have you really, my naughty plum? Goodness, I should have ridden him into the ground. I had no idea."

"Belphagor made me." He groaned as Silk thumbed the head of his cock.

"Of course he did." Silk began to stroke him in a steady rhythm. "So Khai came in his mouth, and I forbade Phaleg to swallow and left the crop up his ass and made him get himself off while he dangled there with a mouthful of spunk."

Vasily groaned with pleasure at the image, and Silk stroked harder.

"You like thinking of that poor, sweet angel being tormented, don't you, my plum?"

"Yes," Vasily moaned.

"Is it you or is it getting awfully warm in here?" Silk threw off the covers to expose Vasily while he stroked, revealing his own erection. "Poor Phaleg was so mortified, he couldn't come, though I made him keep at it. But you'll come for me, won't you, Ruby?" Silk's hand bore down on him, and Vasily clutched the sheets, his fiery breath forming hot rings of steam as he tried to keep from making noise.

And then the orgasm burst out of him, and he gasped, "Move your hand! It's too hot!" in time for Silk to pull his hand away and watch him erupt.

"My goodness." Silk let out a little gasp of delight. "You're like the Pyriphlegethon ... my own little river of fire."

Vasily laughed, falling back against the pillow as his cock still pulsed. "Sorry. I got carried away."

"You can make it up to me while I finish the story." Silk straddled him and rose onto his knees. "Suck or stroke?"

Vasily wrapped his hand around Silk's pennant cock, and Silk settled his thighs on either side of Vasily's sticky abs.

"So there he was," Silk continued, "rubbing his dick raw in that awkward position." He rocked forward into Vasily's fist. "So eager to please that he began to weep because he couldn't do it." Silk gyrated his hips to match Vasily's rhythm. "I ordered him to lie on his back and had Khai sit on his sweet, battered prick and ride it while I rode his mouth, with Khai's spunk still on his tongue." He moaned as Vasily stroked faster. "Khai made him come at last, and I—" Silk tensed, grasping for Vasily's other hand, and shot so enthusiastically that it went right over the pillow. "I came just like that." Silk sighed happily and slipped off to cuddle up against him once more.

Vasily strategically repositioned the pillow. "Do you think you'll see him again?"

"Mmm, definitely," Silk murmured against him. "The way he trembled in my arms afterward and knelt and kissed my feet while I cropped his sweet, pink ass for being a dirty little slut, and how he became the stoic supernal soldier once more as soon as he'd put on his clothes ... A demon could get used to that." Silk snuggled into his warmth, not bothering with the blanket. "After the duel's over, I've invited him to stop by to discuss his interest in a regular arrangement."

"Duel?" Vasily opened his eyes and looked down at Silk, who was drifting into unconsciousness. "What duel?"

"His Highness." Silk yawned. "Phaleg's his second."

He remembered Belphagor shouting something at Armen about challenging him the night before at The Brimstone, but he hadn't thought they were serious. A moment ago, a satisfied stupor had been slipping over him. Now he was wide-awake.

CHAPTER
SEVENTEEN

The sky and the river shared a silvery hue in the glow of the coming dawn. The bridge south of the Demon Market was less traveled than other points between Elysium and Raqia, and there was little chance the angelic authorities would catch wind of a duel between two demons.

Belphagor waited on the north side of the bridge for Phaleg to arrive with Armen's second to let him examine the pistols. Statues of winged lions decorating the bridge rails at the four corners, meant to represent the Cherubim in their leonine aspect, reminded him of the Horse Tamers on the Anichkov in the world of Man. The only Cherub he'd ever encountered, a hired thug who had murdered poor Ouestucati, had borne no resemblance to the beautiful lines of these majestic lions. He'd always wondered who'd sculpted them.

Phaleg arrived from the direction of The Brimstone with a demon Belphagor had seen hanging about Armen on occasion. Behind them, a small crowd was flowing from the darkened Raqia houses. Word of the duel had apparently spread.

Armen's second, Temil, nodded to him, holding an ornate wooden box in his arms, which he handed to Phaleg before opening the hinged top. Inside the purple-velvet-lined case lay a pair of ebony-handled pistols with silver inlays, the wood intricately carved. Belphagor picked one up and opened the chamber to see that it was loaded with a perfectly ordinary lead projectile from the world of Man. He examined the other and found it the same. The magical mechanism still escaped him.

"How do I know both of the pistols function with elemental combustion? And how am I to be sure my element will do as I've been told it will?"

"You may fire each of the weapons at a target of your choosing. I'll reload for the duel, and you can check them again to ensure nothing is amiss."

Belphagor aimed one of the pistols at a wooden piling beneath the bridge at the water's edge. He hadn't fired a gun in years. It had never been his weapon of choice—and weapons weren't his preferred method of achieving his aims—but there had been occasions over the years he'd spent in the world of Man when they had come in handy.

He glanced at Temil. "What do I do?"

"Concentrate on your grip and imagine the pistol as an extension of your hand. When you squeeze your finger against the trigger, your element should spark the flint in the chamber, and the resulting explosion will propel the projectile."

It seemed improbably simple. "How was the spell fashioned? This elemental connection happens every time without being replenished?"

Temil shrugged. "Beats me. I only know it works. And I know it wasn't cheap."

Belphagor raised an eyebrow. Using Armen's weapon seemed like a bad idea, but it was the etiquette of the duel, after all, since Belphagor had challenged. He aimed once more and let himself feel the wood and metal on every surface of his palm and fingers where they touched. When he pulled the trigger, nothing seemed to happen for a second. He had almost turned around with the gun still raised in his hand when he felt a sudden heat rush through the barrel. With the loud crack of an ordinary gun, it fired, his shot straying wide.

The bullet skipped across the water of the Acheron and struck the opposite bank.

Returning the pistol to the case, Belphagor took the other and aimed again, this time holding the gun steady after pulling the trigger and giving his element a little boost with a measured breath. His shot struck the piling perfectly centered.

Returning the second pistol to be reloaded, Belphagor nodded. "Seems fair enough. What is Armen's element, out of curiosity?"

"Earth."

Not a common element among demons. Most were waterspirits, like the Fourth Choir angels they resembled. A fair number were airspirits like Belphagor, and he'd known a few firespirits—though none as potent as Vasily.

But among the earthspirits of the Third Choir were the Virtues, whose aethereal physicality was quite distinct, the Dominions, who had a tendency toward the stout and portly, and the Powers, who were bred as warriors. Armen had neither the statuesque grace of the Virtue nor the dumpy gravity of the Dominion, so his ancestral lineage was likely from the Powers. Which meant he was probably an excellent marksman by blood.

After presenting the pistols to Belphagor for his inspection once he'd reloaded them, Temil closed the box and proceeded toward the strip of sand under the bridge where the duel was to take place. Phaleg stayed by his side to ensure the weapons weren't meddled with post-inspection.

Above on the road, Armen appeared, flanked by a group of demons who had been making their opinions about Belphagor known for some time. In other words, those he'd beaten badly at cards.

"Sure you don't want to call this off?" Armen greeted him with a sneer. "Elementally fired bullets will kill you just as dead as conventional ones in the world of Man." As if Armen knew how anything worked in the world of Man. The fact that he'd chosen such a weapon meant someone was coaching him.

"If you've come to apologize and retract your slander, I'll be happy to call it off. Otherwise, it's your funeral."

"We'll see about that." Armen headed for the bank. Clearly, an apology would not be forthcoming.

Phaleg enumerated the rules of dueling, stating that Belphagor and Armen would count off thirty paces before turning to fire their weapons. Each demon would be allowed a single shot, and any injury to Armen, fatal or otherwise, would constitute satisfaction of Belphagor's challenge.

Should Belphagor be injured, while Armen was not, Armen's slander would stand as fact. If neither were injured, Belphagor could choose to declare his challenge satisfied, at which point Armen's claims about Belphagor would be considered false, or he could insist on a second shot.

Temil stepped forward with the open box for Belphagor and Armen to select their weapons. Belphagor had the privilege of choosing first. This was as fair as it was going to get.

As he took his pistol from the box, something made him glance up. In the pale dawn light, Vasily was charging toward him down the bank.

"Vasya—"

His objection was cut off when Vasily reached him and grabbed him by the lapels of his morning coat, driving him backward into the bridge support so roughly it almost winded him. "What the hell do you think you're doing?" Smudges of kohl paint still ringed his eyes.

He tried again. "Vasya—"

"A duel? A fucking *duel*? Who are you, Nikolai Stavrogin? You think you can just march off to your possible death after everything you said to me last night and not even tell me?"

Belphagor gazed up at him, stunned by Vasily's ferocity and passion despite how things had turned for them of late. And finding it incredibly hot that he was making Dostoevsky references. "Damn, you're beautiful."

That shut him up for a second. But only a second. "I want to know what the hell you think you're doing."

"I'm handling Armen. I won't have any peace from his accusations and slander unless I prove him a liar."

"And you're going to prove that by . . ." Pausing to look down at the gun Belphagor held pointed at the ground, Vasily did a double-take. "That won't work here."

"Apparently it will. Via elemental manipulation." He lowered his voice. "And if you'd let me get this over with, I plan to use mine to ensure that I am not in the path of his." Belphagor cleared his throat. "Now stop sullying my coat and step back with the spectators."

Vasily's hands slipped from the fabric. "But this isn't the world of Man. You don't have that kind of control over your element here. What if you miscalculate the moment he fires?"

"If I'm distracted, that's far more likely to happen. So stop worrying and go away."

Vasily stood a moment longer while Belphagor brushed at his lapels, making a show of being more concerned with his clothing than the duel at hand. "I haven't stopped loving you either." Vasily's words were uttered in a lovely, guttural growl.

Belphagor nodded. "I know that. Now go."

Vasily backed toward the crowd just as Khai arrived on the opposite side of the bridge. Stepping forward to the starting point where Armen waited impatiently to begin counting off his paces, Belphagor made a grand bow and blew Khai a kiss, in keeping with the foppish role he'd been cultivating for the past week. He'd pay for it later with Vasily. Hopefully the payment would be in his preferred currency.

Not bothering with a bow, Armen spun on his heel while Phaleg began the count. Belphagor matched his paces in the opposite direction. They weren't to raise their weapons until Phaleg gave the word, but Belphagor had to be prepared for Armen to cheat. He sucked in his breath as he turned, knowing it would prevent him from firing. His hand still gripped the pistol, but it was as if the molecules weren't bound together, only the aether in Heaven's air keeping the object he held from falling to the ground, like a subtle magnetic field.

He heard the crack and felt the bullet rush into him, pulling his matter apart. Vasily hadn't been wrong. This was nothing like directing his element at the wingcasting table to effect subtle alterations in his favor. Nor was it the familiar elemental control his radiance gave him in the world of Man that let him, momentarily, become fully insubstantial.

Armen's aim was exceptional, as he'd feared. If he breathed out now, the bullet would be lodged in his heart. The earthspirit propulsion of the projectile seemed to make it a solid blow, like a tiny fist slamming through him. He felt it tear through the boundary of the space his physical body ought to occupy, so compelling a sensation he nearly gasped and made it real, but he managed to hold on an instant longer until it had passed.

Breathing out with relief, he fired his weapon. He'd aimed high, hoping to graze Armen's ear, but the bullet ricocheted off as though the other demon were a wall of stone, striking some poor bystander. Armen, too, had used the advantage of his element beyond the simple mechanism of the gun.

Unnoticed in the chaos as demons rushed to the aid of the one who'd been hit, Armen advanced on him, his weapon still raised. But the pistol held only one bullet. He'd watched it being loaded. Assuming Armen had found some other magical method of reloading, Belphagor sucked in his breath once more.

His timing was a millisecond slow.

But he had also moved in the same breath, and the bullet caught him in the shoulder, ripping through it rather than lodging within. As he breathed out, he stumbled and fell to one knee, the unexpected pain nearly whiting out thought. Temil had darted forward and grabbed Armen's wrist, and Belphagor gritted his teeth and seized the moment, hoping Armen would be too distracted to do whatever had made him impervious to Belphagor's first bullet. He also had to hope Armen had applied whatever magic allowed him to fire a second bullet to both weapons, not knowing which Belphagor would pick.

His reflexes and his hunch proved solid, and when he pulled the trigger again, another bullet flew home and caught Armen in the cheek. Belphagor's aim had been a little off.

As Armen howled and stumbled backward with his hand to his face, Temil disarmed him before he could disgrace himself further.

When Phaleg hurried to his side, Belphagor handed over his pistol. "I'm fine." He gritted his teeth. "Keep Vasily away from me. He'll queer the deal." He got to his feet as Phaleg stepped in Vasily's way—he'd come running as Belphagor had expected—while Khai dashed in to support him.

"Just grazed," Belphagor lied with an amiable smile and added more loudly, "I believe Armen Nekirevich has shown himself to be an unreliable witness, has he not? Can't even fight fair in a duel he knows he'd lose." Belphagor glanced at Armen, whose left cheek had a hole blown clean through it, though Belphagor didn't seem to have struck anything vital. Deflected at the last minute, probably, but not quickly enough. "Well bloodied, despite your craven behavior. I'd say you've disgraced yourself thoroughly."

He wrapped his arm around Khai's waist and leaned on him to let Khai lead him up the bank, noting Vasily fuming out of the corner of his eye. Poor Phaleg was having a time of it.

"The other demon who was shot," Belphagor managed. "How bad?"

Khai scowled. "Hit him in the wrist. He'll be fine."

Phaleg threatened to have Vasily arrested if he persisted in trying to see Belphagor. It was only the whispered assurance that he would come by the Stone Horse that evening to apprise Vasily of Belphagor's condition that kept Vasily from calling Phaleg's bluff.

"He's very close. Don't let all his effort go to waste because you have to have everything your way."

"*My* way?" Vasily would have laughed if he weren't so worried. "Since when has anything with Belphagor gone my way?"

Phaleg blinked up at him for several seconds in disbelief. "You must be daft. Just stay away from The Brimstone. It was a superficial wound. I'll let you know how he is later."

When Phaleg showed up that evening, Vasily noted, Silk's eyes lit with a familiar gleam. Dressed smartly in the charcoal suit from the collection Belphagor had purchased for him, Silk waved Phaleg over with a cigarillo at the end of a long bone holder that was perched between his fingers.

"Do you know what I think would be marvelous?" Silk addressed the group he was entertaining as Phaleg approached. "If we took this angelic soldier fellow and my Ruby brute downstairs and put them to a cocksucking contest after baring their bottoms and slapping them pink."

Vasily coughed violently as if he'd forgotten how to breathe.

Silk smiled up at him. "Something go down the wrong way?"

Phaleg managed to act as if he hadn't heard Silk's suggestion when he arrived. "I'm afraid I need to borrow Vasily for a bit."

Silk's eyes widened with exaggerated shock. "You're not arresting him?"

"No, no. Nothing like that. I have a message to deliver to him in private."

Silk puffed on the end of his holder. "Well, hurry back. I'd like to deliver something into your 'private' as well."

Laughter from the demons Silk was entertaining followed them out the door, though it wasn't the mocking laughter Vasily would have expected had they been a group of angels.

Vasily waited until the door was closed. "So you actually pay Silk to humiliate you?"

Phaleg gave him a cool stare. "Are you judging me?" There was a slight emphasis on the pronouns that said Phaleg considered himself above Vasily.

"Oh, right. I'm just a filthy demon. Not an upstanding angel debasing himself for filthy demons."

Phaleg reddened. "That wasn't what I was implying at all. I was under the impression you had the same sort of relationship with Belphagor that I did."

The past tense and the implication that what they'd each had with Belphagor was equivalent needled like a burr caught in his clothes against his skin. "And *I* was under the impression you were in love with him because you enjoyed being made to suffer. Whereas I enjoyed being made to suffer because I was in love with him. *Am* in— Was— *Damn it*." Grammar seemed to be getting the best of him this evening.

"You mean you . . ." Phaleg faltered. "I thought you were a submissive."

"I'm not sure I'd call myself submissive, exactly. It's more like . . . surrender." This wasn't a conversation he wanted to have with Phaleg. "Weren't you supposed to be giving me news from Belphagor?"

"Right. Sorry. He wants you to stop by The Brimstone. Enter the back way. Knock and wait for Khai, and—these are his words—don't go barreling in like an angry lummox. This is covert."

Vasily narrowed his eyes, not sure if he should be insulted. "What's a lummox?"

"Damned if I know."

If Belphagor wanted him there, perhaps he'd been hurt worse than it had seemed. The thought nagged at Vasily as he waited around the corner of a building at the end of the block while the back way into

The Brimstone was blocked by a demoness barmaid in a tryst with her lover.

Anxiety thrummed in his chest while the drunken demon struggled to unlace the barmaid and free her from her restricting garments so he could get to business—followed by an even longer wait once they'd finished while he laced and cinched her back up. One of the advantages of sex with men was not requiring a chambermaid pit crew to get on with it.

When they'd finally cleared out, Vasily went to the door and knocked, only to have Khai yank it open and glare at him.

"Where the hell have you been? Decide to finish someone off at the Stone Horse first?"

"No." Vasily followed Khai down the hall, seething with resentment. "I was waiting for an amorous couple to finish each other off in the alley."

"Oh, them." Khai chuckled. "Did you watch?"

"Of course I didn't watch. Any more than was necessary."

Khai held the door open to what had once been Vasily's room. Regardless of Belphagor's assurances, it was hard to believe Khai had been staying here without providing any sexual favors given Belphagor's poor impulse control.

Tonight, however, Belphagor looked pale, propped up on the cot by a multitude of pillows. In the center of the cloth bandage wrapped around his bare left shoulder, a small circle of blood stained the fabric.

"Belphagor." Vasily was at his side in an instant, kneeling beside the cot to get a closer look at the wound. "How bad is it? Did you get the bullet out? Did you use antiseptic?"

"It's nice to see I can still get you on your knees." Belphagor winked, but Vasily didn't smile. "Don't worry. It's nothing. I was half-substantial when I was hit, so the bullet merely tore a sort of displaced matter hole where it passed through. I'm fine."

"It's not nothing. You're still bleeding. It's inches from your heart. And I happen to know how much one of these damned things hurts, if you recall."

That sobered Belphagor up. "Khai, could you give us a minute?" When Khai had stepped out and closed the door, Belphagor sat up, trying to hide a wince. "I recall very well."

Of course he did. That was when he'd said it: *"You're not my boy."*

Belphagor cleared his throat. "I've been thinking about what to do about us."

"Do about us?" That didn't sound ominous at all.

"If you mean for there to be an us. Which I understood from this morning's comment that you did."

"Of course I do." Emotion made his voice deeper and more growly than usual.

Belphagor's hand moved toward his across the blanket, but Vasily wasn't quite ready to take it. Belphagor casually withdrew it. "I've given serious consideration to where things went astray."

"They went astray when you sold me to the fucking Fletchery."

"Did I, Vasya? Did I sell you, or did I ask you to play a foolish game and pretend that I had?"

"You took the facets."

Belphagor's eyes darkened. "You think facets had anything to do with my sending you there? I have plenty of facets. Or hadn't you noticed?"

Vasily looked down at his hand on the blanket. "How was I to notice? You keep it hidden from me. Like everything."

"What I keep from you is merely that which is of no consequence. How many facets I have, how many rubles in the world of Man—it's immaterial. If I cared about them, I wouldn't live at The Brimstone."

Vasily raised his head. "Why the hell *do* you live at The Brimstone?"

"Because demons who throw facets around find themselves with their throats slit in dark alleys. And because no one would play against me at the tables if they knew how much I was really winning. The game gives me too much pleasure to give it up just to live a little more comfortably. I have all I need."

"You could use a bigger damned bed."

Belphagor laughed. "So I could. If only the room were larger, I'd buy one. But as you know, the real reason I keep this room is the portal. No amount of crystal would be worth trading it for."

"There are other portals."

"Not many. And there's about to be one fewer."

Vasily studied Belphagor's up-to-something gaze. "How are you going to manage that?"

"I'm going to glamour it so it's never seen and so that anyone who's ever seen or used it before can no longer remember where it is. My little enterprise over the past couple of weeks has yielded a great deal of information. The northeast portal is the only route the drovers on the Celestial Silk Road have for their terrestrial commerce. The angelic faction tortured Anzhela to learn its location, which has rapidly increased the trade."

Anger and dismay roiled through him. "*Tortured* her? You don't mean Ophanim?"

Belphagor shuddered. "No, thank the Heavens, but I understand a few Powers were involved. She's a very strong girl, as well as a practical one. When they threatened to start cutting things off her, she relented and told them what they wanted to know. She's afraid the girls at The Cat must hate her for it, but I've assured her that they're very worried about her and only want her to be safe. They understand she did what she had to."

Vasily curled his fist into the blanket at the thought of the angels hurting Anzhela. "We need to kill those fucking bastards."

Belphagor gave him a dark smile. "Which brings me to the second part of my plan. The principality isn't likely to intervene in the case of demons enslaving demons, but the fact that angels are involved—and that on occasion, angels have been sold—is deeply troubling to him."

"How do you know what's troubling to the principality?"

Belphagor's eyebrow lifted characteristically. "I have an in with our dear sovereign. Phaleg is his Chief of Security."

"Oh."

Belphagor moved his hand back across the blanket, and this time, he curled it around Vasily's fist without hesitating. "Please don't worry about him. I ended it with him that day in our room, and there has been nothing for you to be concerned about since." He stroked his thumb over the tightly clenched muscles of Vasily's hand. "You remember that day. How he got on his hands and knees, and you fucked him for me with that delectable and ponderous cock until the poor boy nearly fainted of his own pleasure while I fucked his mouth."

Sweat ran down Vasily's temple, and his pulse fluttered. "I remember."

"Which is what I've been thinking about. A great deal. And to my intense frustration, Khai is always about, preventing me from thinking it through to its natural conclusion." Belphagor winked and played his fingers along the bones of Vasily's hand.

"You're really not fucking Khai?"

"I understand that I've given you cause not to trust me, but no. I am not fucking Khai. Nor is he giving me oral pleasure or tossing me off. I'm as chaste as an angel."

Vasily couldn't help a loud laugh, which made Belphagor's eyebrows draw together in annoyance.

"As I was saying, I've given these matters thought, and my conclusion is that you would be more comfortable joining me in meting out punishment to others than taking punishment from me."

"You what?"

"I think we both know you're not really a submissive."

Vasily yanked his hand away and jumped to his feet. He'd said exactly the same thing to Phaleg not an hour ago, but from Belphagor's lips it struck him like a slap in the face. "*Poshël na khui.*"

Belphagor looked baffled. "What have I said?"

"I'm not submissive enough for your taste, is what you mean."

"*No—*"

"I don't grovel and fawn and look up at you with beautiful angel eyes full of unquestioning obedience."

"Now, wait just a damned minute. I love your eyes." Belphagor threw off his blanket and swung his legs over the side of the cot. "I've told you before I don't want unquestioning obedience and servility from you. I want to break you like a wild, magnificent horse. Every. Single. Time. I want to wrestle you to the ground and hold you down and make you insane with fury at your helplessness before I fuck you senseless."

Vasily's heart was pounding with that fury at this very moment—confounded with desire. "Then why the hell would you take that away from me? Are you punishing me for being with Silk after you told me to go be with him?"

"What? No. Vasya . . . I'm confused. You said you didn't want to be my boy anymore, so I thought—"

"Of course I want to be your fucking boy!" Tears were streaming down his cheeks. Humiliating, stupid tears.

Belphagor stood swiftly and then pitched to the side with a gasp, barely missing striking his head on the side table when Vasily caught him. Belphagor's weight rested heavily against him.

"You are *not* fine." Vasily eased him back onto the cot.

"I suppose I've looked better, but you needn't insult me." Belphagor leaned back against the pillows, his brow white. "Maybe the bullet hit a little more solidly than I thought." He closed his eyes and breathed out. "Did I hear right? You want to be my boy?" The quiet words were full of hope and fear.

Vasily wiped his cuff across his eyes, fear for Belphagor instead of fear *of* him making his hand tremble. "Of course I do, you idiot. I was hurt, and that word—it just . . . I wasn't sure what it meant for a while. I wasn't sure what *we* meant. But I do. Of course I do. Always, *ser. Pozhaluista.*"

"*Milyy mal'chik.*" Belphagor exhaled the words with all the love and desire they'd ever held, and Vasily nearly started crying again.

"When you're better." Vasily tucked the covers around him.

Belphagor nodded, eyes still closed. "Yes. When I'm better. When I'm feeling up to putting you over my knee and giving your sweet, bare ass a thrashing you won't forget until you beg to be my boy again. And when I have the energy to spend the whole night reminding you what that means."

Vasily nibbled his lip, every bit of him melting except one crucial part that was doing the opposite.

"I think I'm going to have to rest now." Belphagor's voice revealed the pain he was hiding.

"I should stay until Khai comes back." Vasily knelt beside the bed once more and rested his head lightly on Belphagor's chest, careful not to aggravate the wound.

Belphagor stroked his temple. "Have Khai tell you the rest." His hand slowed, fingers against the trail of crystal chips in the dark paint at the corner of Vasily's eye. "Wear this for me sometime. And nothing else."

CHAPTER EIGHTEEN

Vasily was gone when Belphagor awoke. Khai assured him that he'd filled Vasily in on the plan. All the pieces were in place. With Armen disgraced, Belphagor's standing in Raqia had improved considerably, and no one would suspect his involvement in the sting about to unfold. Phaleg had set the bait. Now all that remained was to drop the trap on the rats. Help in that regard came from an unexpected direction.

Khai returned from getting breakfast for them the next morning with a stony expression. "There's someone asking to see you in the bar. I told him to fuck off."

Belphagor pushed himself up against the pillows. "Who?"

"Kezef."

Though Belphagor had been expecting the visit, a jet of pure rage pulsed through him at the sound of the name. Grabbing the edge of the nightstand as he swung his legs over the side of the bed, Belphagor pushed himself to his feet. "Help me get dressed."

Khai's hands braced his hips. "What for?"

"So I can kill the fucking incubus with my bare hands."

"Your bare hands. You mean including the one at the end of the arm you can hardly move?"

"I can move it." Belphagor gritted his teeth as he demonstrated. "It just hurts like fuck when I do."

"Belphagor—"

"Give me a shirt, damn it."

"You know, I'm only posing as your boy."

"I swear, I'll beat you like you are—except without any of the pleasure—if you don't give me a damned shirt."

With a sigh, Khai picked up the garment draped over the back of Belphagor's chair and helped him into it, buttoning it when Belphagor couldn't manage the fine motor skill to do it himself. "I really don't think this is a good idea."

"Thanks for the input."

"Are you going to challenge him to a duel too?" Khai crouched to tie Belphagor's boots after Belphagor pulled them on one-handed. "Actually, now that I think of it, that's not a bad idea. Except you should insult him publicly so you can get him to challenge you, and then you can set the date. Give yourself a week to recover—"

"He doesn't deserve a duel." Belphagor grabbed his jacket and slung it over his shoulder, not bothering to have Khai help make him any more presentable, and headed out with Khai at his heels.

Kezef stood at the bar, facing away from it, elbows and long forearms braced against it with his hands hanging over the edge in a stance that said he was completely at ease. He turned his head at Belphagor's approach and appraised him with a look that expressed how thoroughly nonthreatening Kezef found him at the moment.

He glanced over Belphagor's shoulder at Khai. "I've seen you before. But you were younger." His eyes went back to Belphagor's. "Same as your fiery boy was."

Kezef would wipe the floor with him if he tried to fight him now. As appealing as the idea was, killing Kezef with his bare hands—or at least severely maiming him—would have to wait. But the implied threat behind his casual statement couldn't be ignored. Not after Belphagor had finally put Armen's rumors to rest. He jerked his head at a nearby booth, and Kezef pushed away from the bar.

Before he followed, Kezef signaled to the barmaid. "A bottle of mead for my friends." He waited for her to bring it before he sauntered to the booth with the bottle and mugs in hand and took his seat. "You needn't worry that I'll spoil your game, Prince of Tricks." He poured the mead. "So long as you include me in it."

Belphagor leaned over the table. "Listen to me carefully. At the moment, as I'm sure you're quite aware, I'm incapable of throttling you right here at the table as I'd like. But I promise you a thrashing the likes of which even you have never dealt once this shoulder has healed."

"I understand your need to posture, Belphagor. I really do." Kezef pushed a mug toward him. "And perhaps at some future date, I'll give you the opportunity to put your strop where your mouth is— That is your specialty, isn't it? The strop? But at the moment, you need me."

Belphagor's lip twitched as he resisted the words he wanted to say. "And what could I possibly need you for?"

Kezef gave him an insufferable smile. "Well, let me lay out for you what I know, and then you tell me. I know you're planning something that will ruin the livelihoods of a certain group of Raqia entrepreneurs who deal in unsullied goods. I know your scheme involves an angel who has the ear of the principality. And I know you've championed a number of . . . shall we say, *alumni* of a certain defunct establishment. Really, quite a coup that was. I have to hand it to you. If the good demons of Raqia had any idea it was you who had singlehandedly shuttered that establishment after being a patron of it yourself—and yet managed to get Armen Nekirevich, of all demons, to eat his words after he'd blabbed them to half of Heaven—and that you now *owned* those same alumni . . . Well, things in Raqia would be very interesting indeed."

"So you're here to blackmail me."

Kezef laughed—a pleasant, genuine laugh—and drank his mead unhurriedly, setting down the mug when he'd finished. "How would that serve me? I was a patron there myself. Things would be awkward to say the least."

"Then just what do you want?"

"You're so unimaginative. It's disappointing. I want to participate in your little endeavor."

Belphagor sat back with a sharp laugh of his own, all the sharper because the sudden motion had twisted the healing flesh around his wound. This wasn't quite what he'd expected.

He glanced out of the booth to make sure no one was in earshot. The bar was nearly empty. "You want to help me shut down the Celestial Silk Road."

"Precisely."

"And why would you want to do that when you've been so clearly enjoying its spoils?"

"As a matter of fact, I find the whole business rather dull and somewhat distasteful. It was something different to do for a while, but I derived very little pleasure out of purchasing innocence. What I prefer to partake of *is* the spoiled. Those who've been used, know what they're good for and can be made to grovel to prove it." Kezef held his gaze unflinchingly. "Like your boy."

Belphagor nearly lunged across the table, wound be damned, but Khai held him back. "I'll make you pay for every stripe you gave him. And every stripe you gave Silk."

"Have a thing for the pretty ones too, do you? Silk is an interesting creature. He'll do anything for the right price."

Pushing Khai's arm away, Belphagor straightened and forced himself to ignore the discomfort as he let his chest rise with a deep breath. "Meaning?"

Kezef folded his long arms on the table and leaned in. "Meaning you don't own him as thoroughly as you think you do."

"I don't own him at all."

"Come now. Word is you bought him for a substantial price in the world of Man, only to set him up here as your procurer, keeping him in comforts in exchange for his unquestioning obedience."

"Clearly, you don't know Silk as well as you think you do if you believe he'd give anyone his unquestioning obedience."

"That's precisely my point. You and I know he will not, and yet you've invested a great deal of crystal in him. I spoke to him last night at your interesting new venture, and having no loyalty to you, only to your crystal, he readily divulged information to me when I augmented the facets with some of my own."

"You expect me to believe that Silk blithely gave you the time of day after what you did to him?"

"Having been properly trained—unlike some—Silk knew the beating he received was well deserved. At any rate, he was more than happy to give my crystal the time of day. How else would I know that you have an angelic soldier poised to expose the ringleaders of this 'silk road' as we speak? Interesting name, by the way. Did you name it after the slippery little demon?"

"I didn't name it at all. Its creators did, after an earthly trade route." Belphagor chewed on the end of his thumb. The message Silk had sent through Phaleg early this morning hadn't mentioned any facets, only that Kezef had cornered him at the Stone Horse and threatened to reveal certain information about him if he didn't tell Kezef what he knew. Belphagor hoped he hadn't made an error in trusting Silk. Enough facets might have loosened his tongue more than Belphagor had bargained for. "Be that as it may, what reason could you possibly have for wanting to help expose the trade?"

"As I said, I prefer defiling and debasing the deserving to tormenting frightened virgins. This trade damages us all, sending our own—who, if they are to be used, ought to be used here—to an inferior plane. Imagine if their owners in the world of Man discovered their unique abilities and chose to breed them to strengthen their own stock?"

"So you'd prefer that trading in the innocence of young demons be limited to the celestial sphere."

Kezef shrugged and leaned back. "They *will* be sold. It's the law of Heaven that demons may sell what offspring they choose. What you or I think about the practice is of little consequence. My objection is to the proliferation of underage slaves being sold as novelties—and particularly to the involvement of angels in that trade. Think what you will about my proclivities—no matter how similar they may be to your own, despite your superior air—but I'm fully behind your endeavor."

Belphagor didn't buy for a minute that Kezef gave a damn about the young demons caught up in the trade, but even a cretin like him could be useful. "And how, might I ask, do you propose to assist my efforts to halt this trade?"

"Your angelic agent is poised to do business with one of the peddlers today, is he not? On the pretext of purchasing a virgin?"

"Maybe."

"If you ask me, it's an extraordinarily bad idea to let the angel handle it."

"I don't believe I did ask you."

"What do you plan to do once he's made the deal? Send him skipping off to the palace with his purchased whore to inform the principality that some very bad men are selling demons in Raqia?"

For all Belphagor knew, Kezef might be one of the brokers himself. He wasn't about to confirm anything further. "Why don't you tell me what you would do? I'd love to hear your plan."

Kezef smiled. "As a matter of fact, I've given it a great deal of thought. If your goal is to use the supernal connection to shut down the trade, I would think ensnaring the drovers and patrons themselves would be more effective. Allow me to accompany your angelic agent as a means of legitimizing his presence in Raqia business. I'll negotiate with the broker to arrange a private salon for my contacts at the Fletchery and engage drovers for the purpose of transporting the goods to their buyers' preferred locations after they've made their selections. The drovers will take the boys, with the patrons expecting to leave sometime afterward so as not to be seen with them. Have the supernal authorities waiting down the road to ambush them, and they can take in the whole lot with no harm to the merchandise." Kezef's expression was smug. "Assuming your agent can provide the venue—and you can provide the merchandise."

Belphagor curled his hand tightly around his mug. "And what proof would we have of the sale of underage demons to the patrons?"

"The proof of the intent to commit the crime will be in the exchange of facets. By celestial law, the crime itself need not occur. Your agent—and any of his employees who happen to be present to entertain the drovers while they wait—will be witnesses to it."

As much as it galled him to agree to any sort of collaboration with Kezef, the success of this venture might now depend on it. "I still don't see why I need you to accomplish any of this. I could simply go along myself to be the 'legitimizing presence.'"

"I suppose you might, despite your injury. But you've gone to a great deal of trouble to present yourself as a player in a rather different game." Kezef glanced at Khai. "You've replaced one truckling demon tart with another."

Khai leapt to his feet. "Fuck you, you pathetic pervert."

"Mikhail." Belphagor put a firm hand on his arm to pull him back down to his seat. Khai sat with a reluctant glare, and Belphagor turned back to Kezef. "Fuck you, you pathetic pervert. If you think I'm going to sit here while you insult my boys, you're quite mistaken. Come on,

Khai." He scooted out of the booth and held out his arm, ignoring the twinge the motion inspired.

"You're absurdly sensitive about your submissives." Kezef held up both hands in surrender. "I'll refrain from unnecessary insults, but I suggest you consider my offer of assistance. I have the trust of the Fletchery contacts, and you do not. And if the whim took me, I could spoil your game with a word."

So there it was. Belphagor had to work to keep from punching the smug look off Kezef's face. "Exactly what do you get out of offering your assistance, besides your alleged interest in putting the trade out of business?"

Kezef's affable smile returned. "Why, some of those facets you've been so free with of late. Again, not everyone is aware of who the real owner of The Cat and the Stone Horse is, and I'm happy to keep that knowledge to myself. As long as we both understand each other."

"I thought you weren't here to blackmail me."

"Call it what you will. I merely said it wouldn't serve me to divulge information about your connection to the Fletchery. If I only wanted to blackmail you, I'd simply demand the facets here and now. Instead, I'm offering my help and telling you the price."

"And that price is?"

"Five hundred facets."

Khai sucked in his breath.

It was an outrageous demand. Extortion, pure and simple. But it would serve Belphagor's ends. His eyebrow twitched. "Fair enough. Khai will take you to the rendezvous and brief Phaleg."

Khai gaped at him. "You're not going to give him that much crystal?"

"That's not your concern."

Khai narrowed his eyes in a resigned glower of disapproval that would have done Vasily proud. "You're the boss."

When Khai returned to The Brimstone later, he stared down at Belphagor with his hands on his hips. "If I'd known you were throwing crystal away, I'd have asked a damned sight more for my part."

"I'm making the best of a bad situation. Everything else go according to plan?"

Khai grinned. "Facets changed hands. Promises were made. The salon has been arranged. Per your instructions, Vasily knows no more than he needs to. Now it's up to Silk and the boys."

CHAPTER NINETEEN

"I'm not sure I like this idea." Vasily leaned against the doorway to the dressing area with his arms folded, watching Silk and Anzhela get ready.

"I'll have my girls to watch out for me." Anzhela calmly braided her hair at the vanity. "And the boys will have Silk."

"That's what I'm worried about. No offense, Silk, but you're not exactly built to fight off a bunch of angry angels and demons if something goes wrong. I should be going."

Silk rolled his eyes, rubbing the pomade Belphagor had bought him through his hair. "You'd scare them off before we got close." He met Vasily's gaze in the mirror and blew him a kiss. "You're scaring me right now, you lovely brute. Look at him, Anzhi. All fired up." He gave a little shiver. "I swear, painting his eyes was pure genius."

Vasily let out a low growl. "I'll give you fired up."

"Oh my. Save it for later, my succulent plum. I'll—"

"*Silk.*" Vasily cut him off before he could complete the thought.

Silk finished off his tie and put on his jacket, turning around with a mock pout. "Fine. Maybe I'll leave you to simmer all night on your own. But for now, it's show time." He stepped up and put his arms around Vasily's neck. "You'll take good care of my Horse for me, won't you? Don't just stand around and glare at patrons. We want them to feel welcome."

"I'm not the only one who's going to be there."

"But you are the star attraction, Ruby. Don't sell yourself short. Demons and angels are falling all over themselves hoping to get close to you. The mystique is good, but we don't want to frighten them off."

Vasily's "mystique" resulted in a lucrative evening as several patrons paid to watch him stroke himself off after hearing from a happy patron who'd gotten a private show. It was a skill he'd never expected to be rewarded for, even in this business, and with a short refractory period thanks to his element, he managed to impress his audience with more than one performance. His warning not to get too close because of the heat of his emissions only seemed to sweeten the pot.

It was during this second performance, while patrons pressed in against each other to get a look, that he saw Kezef. He threw Vasily a disarming smile from across the room and slung a small pouch of facets at Vasily's feet. The blood nearly abandoned Vasily's cock, but he channeled the heat from his anger into his groin.

"Take off your clothes." Kezef's voice carried above the roar of the crowd. "I'm sure we'd all like to get a better look."

An eager chorus took up the chant of "Take it off!" Vasily felt obliged to comply if he didn't want to make a scene. Steeling himself to ignore Kezef, he pulled off his top one-handed and tossed it down without missing a stroke, to great applause. He was less eager to complete the look, but the chanting continued, and Kezef put him on the spot by calling out, "Earn your facets, boy!"

With his cock poised furiously in front of him, Vasily stripped out of the jeans. This pair had wide bottoms that allowed him to yank them over his boots so he wouldn't have to take those off. Oddly enough, keeping them on gave him a sense of power that would have been absent with complete nakedness.

As he brought himself to a crowd-pleasing finish with a feral roar, Kezef appeared at the front, having pushed his way forward. "Very impressive, firespirit. How much to do it again while you service me orally?"

Vasily scowled at him, his hand still dripping with the last of his spunk. "Not if you were the last demon in Heaven."

Kezef gave him another unnerving smile. "Still afraid to find out what you're willing to swallow?"

"Fuck you, Kezef." Vasily gathered his clothes, using his shirt to clean up as the crowd began to dissipate.

Kezef stepped too close to him. "Like your Silk did last night? I don't mean fucked you, of course. I mean swallowed. Me."

"What the hell are you talking about?"

"About your demon, Silk." Kezef smiled patiently. "Obedient and servile, proving what he is, what he's good for, with my prick down his throat. After he told me everything about Belphagor's plan."

Vasily's heart pounded as he yanked up his pants. "What plan? You're full of shit."

"The plan to entrap the agencies involved in demon trafficking. Belphagor paid me handsomely to keep quiet, and so I will. Although . . . I may have mentioned it to one or two demons before I made that arrangement with him."

"You son of a succubus."

"Is that the best you can do?" Kezef grabbed the hair at Vasily's nape before he could react, digging in his fingers. "I'd love to find out what else I can make you say. Before, during, and after I use you. After is always the most illuminating. Once a demon knows what he truly is and can be made to do, having him acknowledge it aloud is tremendously arousing."

Vasily jerked his head to the side and shoved Kezef away. "Keep your fucking hands off me. And mine."

Kezef laughed. "I'll bet you good crystal you'll come to me on your own eventually to find out what a filthy whore you really are. And I'll be waiting to show you."

Vasily walked away from him, refusing to give him the pleasure of any further reaction. He paused on his way out to find one of the rentboys he trusted to let him know the Horse was in his hands for the rest of the evening. He had to be sure Kezef was lying.

After slipping next door for a clean shirt, Vasily hurried to The Cat. Silk and the others had been gone for a little over an hour by his count. Their plan had been to have everything in place well before the patrons arrived. If Kezef spoke the truth, whatever his treachery had yielded, perhaps there was still time to stop it.

The front door of The Cat was locked. He was pretty sure that was a first. Vasily lifted the unused knocker and rapped it against the wood. A long pause followed before the door opened a crack and one of the girls peered out—the tall redhead with the tail tattoo, who called herself Pussy Familiar.

"Most of the girls have the night off. Private party." And then her eyes lit with recognition. "Oh! Vasily. Are you supposed to . . ."

"No, I'm not. But I need to speak with Silk. It's urgent."

The door opened wider, pulled by someone behind her. Pussy moved out of the way, revealing one of the Dominions Vasily had entertained the night of the Stone Horse opening. "What's the meaning of this?" The scowling Dominion turned toward the parlor. "Why is your firespirit here?"

He'd have to act quickly to take suspicion off Silk. Vasily pushed the Dominion aside and barged in, and after taking in the room full of boys paired off in flirtation with angelic patrons, he turned his kindling eyes on Silk where he reclined with another angel. "Damn you, Silk! How could you do this? After everything Belphagor did for you, you sell the boys anyway?"

Silk stared up at him, outrage warring with confusion. He excused himself and came to the entrance of the room, pushing Vasily back despite his own much smaller stature. "Outside." He snapped his fingers. "Everyone, please excuse the interruption. It's merely a dispute that should have been kept at home." He dragged Vasily with him out the door and slammed it. "What the hell are you doing?"

"Kezef."

Silk's cheeks seemed to color in the dim light. "What about him?"

"He showed up at the Horse and said he found out about tonight. From you. And that he's spread the word. Did you— Did you really—"

Silk put his hands on his hips. "Yes, Ruby. I really. It was part of the plan. Belphagor didn't want to worry you. And now you've spooked everyone here."

"I don't understand how you could let him touch you—how you could touch *him* after what he did to you. He almost killed you."

"It was a business transaction. And I don't have time for this. The raid is supposed to happen any minute. We all thought you were it, actually. So either come inside and shut up about the plan, or get out of here."

"But if Kezef knows about the raid—"

"He doesn't. He thinks the plan was for the arrests to happen once they leave The Cat. What they all think is that they'll have their way with the boys here and leave without them—and *with* their facets—and they'll be untouchable, since their participation in the transaction can't be proved. Drovers were supposed to smuggle the 'merchandise' out through the back and take them straight to the portal. That's the deal I claimed to make with Kezef, though it seems he's changed the game midway through, bringing angels into it to do the smuggling."

"Angels? I don't like the sound of this."

Silk shrugged. "It's immaterial to Belphagor's plan. But if I don't get back in there right now, the boys will be in actual danger. So goodbye." Silk turned and rapped on the door, and when Pussy opened it to let him in, Vasily followed. Silk glared at him, silently ordering him to keep quiet.

The count who'd pretended to buy Vasily at the Fletchery rose with his arm around little Ruslan. "I think we've all made our selections." Ruslan's eyes had gone wide with fear.

"Relax, Count Salmay." Silk didn't miss a beat. "The evening's just getting started. That's why Ruby's here. He's going to perform for us."

Vasily swallowed. "I . . . What?"

"Your fire tricks, sweetie." Silk curled up next to his angelic friend once more on the cushions. The large fireplaces on either end of the room were already blazing as usual. It wasn't as if he could light one for them.

Vasily glanced around the room. "Does anyone have a cigar or a smoke?" He was met with blank stares. The room was mostly angels, and angels considered smoking a demon's vice.

Entertaining the group of angels evidently employed to do the smuggling, Belphagor's friend Natalya rose and came forward from the other side of the room. "I have one." She reached into her corseted cleavage and withdrew a single slim cigarette. The demoness had the coloring of an airspirit, and Vasily suspected that, like Belphagor, she was fond of performing little tricks of her own.

"Put it in your mouth." Silk's instruction prompted a few snorts of laughter.

She held it gracefully to her lips and waited. Vasily had never lit such a tiny cigarette. He stuck out his tongue, narrowed to a point, and leaned toward her, concentrating his element into the tip until it glowed red.

Silk gave an exaggerated shiver. "Imagine that up your bum."

Vasily's cheeks went as warm as his tongue at the laughter filling the room, but Natalya ignored it, taking a drag on her lit cigarette and exhaling the smoke. Despite the laughter, several patrons clapped.

When Vasily straightened, he looked into the eyes of Tabris, holding apart the thick beaded curtain that separated the parlor from the corridor leading to the private rooms.

Natalya caught his gaze and turned. "Tabi?"

"They've hurt the pretty angel."

Natalya went to her and tried to take her arm. "Come on, Tabi. Back to bed."

But Tabris shrugged away from her. "He's bleeding! Does no one care?"

"Bleeding?" Natalya dropped her cigarette and crushed it under her slipper. "What are you talking about, Tabi? Who's bleeding?"

"The pretty angel!" Tabris's shrill outburst made the mirrored walls rattle, coinciding with a sudden, forceful banging on the outer door.

"Open in the name of the law of the Princedom of the Firmament of Shehaqim!" Even as the words were delivered, the doorframe splintered and a dozen uniformed Powers burst into The Cat, blocking any egress, while the angelic patrons jumped to their feet and away from their chosen boys.

The angels engaged as drovers were gone, having slipped out the back during Vasily's stupid trick.

While a pair of supernal soldiers shoved Vasily to his knees, Silk rose amid the chaos, staring through the soldiers as if they weren't there and fixing his eyes on Tabris. "Phaleg."

"He's bleeding," she wailed. "And Anzhela's gone."

"On your knees, demon!" One of the Powers backhanded Silk, sending him sprawling across the cushions.

"Not me." He struggled as the soldier grabbed him about the neck to pull him up onto his knees. "I'm with Captain Phaleg! And he needs help."

The officer in command pushed the other angel out of the way. "Leave him be. We were told to check for purses."

One by one, the boys raised their prizes in front of them: the purses they'd expertly lifted while their patrons were unaware. Trained by the master thief. Belphagor had been busy. The patrons grasped at their sides in disbelief to find their purse strings hanging empty. There was no mistaking to whom each purse belonged. Angels were arrogant enough that they had their house emblems emblazoned upon them.

While the angelic patrons were rounded up, protesting loudly about their own importance, the soldiers verified the full purse still tied to Vasily's belt and let him go. How fortunate for him that he had one tonight. Silk was already headed for the back of the house, and Vasily followed. Inside the corridor, Tabris stood with her back to the wall, frozen with fear at the sight of angelic soldiers in The Cat.

Inside the room where he'd evidently gone with Anzhela to give the appearance of being engaged in their transaction, Phaleg sat dazed against the open door, blood running down the side of his head.

Silk ran to him and dropped to his knees, examining his head. "Phaleg, what happened? Are you all right?"

"Damned drovers." He winced at Silk's touch. "Must've gotten wind something was up. Burst in here and grabbed Anzhela. Going to fall."

"You're already sitting down," Silk assured him.

Phaleg shook his head and winced again at the movement. "Not me. Drovers. With Anzhela." He met Silk's eyes, a light blush rising in his cheeks in response to Silk's genuine concern that conveyed more than words. "I'm okay. Really."

The drovers were headed for the portal—where Belphagor was currently working his glamour. And it was Vasily's fault they'd been spooked.

"We have to stop them." He turned to head out, but the way was blocked by one of the soldiers.

"How do we know you're not one of these 'drovers'?"

"These drovers were angels." Phaleg got to his feet. "And he's with us."

Though he appreciated being vouched for, Vasily wasn't quite sure he was with *them*. Phaleg and Silk seemed to be making a rather definite "us" at the moment, of which he was most decidedly not a member. But that was good. That was as it should be. Even if Phaleg was a precious little prig who didn't deserve Silk.

"Follow me." Vasily pushed through the soldiers with a growl. "Or get out of my way."

Natalya stepped away from trying to calm Tabris and matched his stride. "I'm going with you."

Vasily shook his head. "Too dangerous."

"It's my glamour."

Vasily paused. "What's your glamour?" He eyed Natalya with suspicion, looking for some sign of Belphagor within the statuesque curves.

"The glamour B's working. It's mine, and he's going to need help maintaining the fabric of the spell with demons trying to get through it. And Anzhela is one of ours. I can't leave this up to you and B just because you have cocks."

Vasily raised his brow. "I hadn't exactly planned on beating anyone over the head with mine."

Natalya grinned. "Well, if you do, please promise me you'll charge for the show."

Laying the framework of the spell was like knitting with threads of silicone gel, and they were becoming increasingly sticky. This level of magical interference could only mean someone was actively seeking the portal.

Though its entrance didn't move, its intrinsic magic gave the impression that it did, requiring a certain amount of elemental "casting" to keep from being thrown off its trail in the first place. It was this magical property Belphagor was exploiting with the concealment glamour, fortifying it and warping it at the same time to cause permanent confusion. His own portal in The Brimstone he'd done something of the opposite with, sealing it into one "mental" plane of existence to keep from being constantly confounded in his own room. He'd learned that lesson the hard way.

Belphagor glanced up at Khai, who held the lantern for him as he worked. "Keep a weather eye on the horizon."

"You've been at this awhile. You need to rest that arm."

"I can't stop in the middle of the spell."

"Well, how many times do you have to circle the damned thing before it's finished?"

"I'm not circling, I'm spiraling."

"Because that's hugely different."

Belphagor glared at him. "It is to the spell. I have to reinforce it at regular intervals in an increasing outward revolution. I'll feel it when it's done."

Khai focused on something above Belphagor's head. "You know that weather eye you asked me to keep? Storm's coming."

Belphagor turned. A group of angels so shabbily dressed he would have taken them for demons was approaching on horseback like the four horsemen of the apocalypse. Anzhela sat behind one of the riders. These were the "drovers" Kezef had hired—and they had somehow managed to escape the raid at The Cat.

Belphagor straightened, his shoulder aching as he drew his arm close. There was no way he was going to be able to take these assholes in a fight, but he could sense their uncertainty. Despite being nearly upon the thing they were seeking, they seemed barely aware of either the portal or the presence of the demons in front of them. The glamour was almost in place. If he just added enough of his own influence to hold it, they might be deterred.

As the group drew up their mounts in front of him, one of the riders turned to Anzhela. "This the spot?"

"I think so. Maybe." Her uncharacteristic uncertainty might have been subterfuge, but if she was genuinely confused, it was a good sign.

The rider dismounted and pulled her from the back of the horse. "What do you mean, 'maybe'? Either it is or it isn't. You know damned well where it is. I'm tired of your games."

"You knew where it was yourself an hour ago, yet you don't seem to be able to find it on your own."

As the angel poised to strike her, Belphagor stepped forward to grab his arm. "Don't manhandle the young lady. I believe she answered your question."

"Lady?" The angel shook him off, looking startled to find him there. "She's a whore. And she has a date in the world of Man."

Belphagor folded his arms to cover his physical discomfort. It also served as a sort of visual complement to the verbal misdirection he was about to employ. Even a little would help reinforce the multiple layers of influence at work in driving seekers away. "Who are you to say a whore isn't a lady? I, myself, have been both."

"Both what?"

Belphagor lifted his eyebrow provocatively. "A lady and a whore. But at present, I am merely a whoremonger. And I happen to be the guardian of the young lady in your company, who is, incidentally, not a whore."

"Huh?"

"I do have access to quite a variety, however, if you'd like me to procure one for you. Any preference for size, hue, or endowments can be accommodated. Of course, I can't guarantee that any of my whores will be willing to service all four of you together. That's a recipe for disaster, if you ask me."

The other three had dismounted, looking equally confused.

"What the Hell are you prattling on about?"

"*I* might be willing to do four for the right price." Khai held up the lantern, drawing their attention from Belphagor for the moment. "I mean, not the four of *you*, just four in general."

"You *are* very flexible," Belphagor agreed.

"I don't know what the hell you two are talking about." The frustrated angel glared. "But there's a portal around here somewhere, and my friends and I don't have time for this."

"Maybe we could help you look." Khai started walking away before Belphagor could warn him that his energy was intertwined with the web of the glamour until it was complete. It was as if one of the silicone-like threads stretched taut and snapped. The effect was almost audible.

One of the angels instantly focused on Belphagor. "You. You're that demon they call the Prince of Tricks. This whole thing at The Cat was your setup, wasn't it? You're in cahoots with that Kezef to get rid of the competition."

He'd expected Phaleg's name to come up or Silk's. But not Kezef's. "How's that?"

"Don't play stupid. Everyone knows Kezef wants to be the sole procurer of boy whores to the Academies. You throw in with him? Get him to tell us he was double-crossing you when you were both double-crossing us all?"

Something about this didn't fit with his understanding of the game, but there was no time to puzzle over it as the first angel tightened his grip around Anzhela's arm and made a move for the portal.

Belphagor stepped in front of him. "Where do you think you're going?"

"Out of my way. Demons don't own the terrestrial sphere."

"And we were getting along so marvelously."

The angel let go of Anzhela to swing at him, and Belphagor managed to dodge the move with a quick inhalation, but the errant blow struck Khai and knocked the lantern from his hand, throwing them all into shadow. Just as Belphagor exhaled, another angel sprang forward and landed a punch in his wounded shoulder. The pain took the air out of him, rendering him incapable of the usual evasion.

Before he could catch his breath, Anzhela darted in and seemed to punch the angel lightly in his side. "That's for Masha." She pulled back her hand to reveal a knife dripping with the angel's blood. As he stumbled onto one knee in shock, another of his compatriots struck Anzhela and tried to grab the knife, but she slashed at him and held her ground. "I'll take you all."

Belphagor had no doubt that she meant it, but he wasn't going to wait to see if she could. He steeled himself against the pain in his shoulder and tackled the angel before the man could swing again. "Khai! Get Anzhela out of here."

Khai shook himself and grabbed Anzhela's hand against her protest, and Belphagor saw them run before he went down beneath the third angel's fist.

He hit the cobblestone and rolled onto his right side to cushion the blow, but this left the injured shoulder wide open. Belphagor nearly blacked out when a heavy boot struck it dead on. His body blocked the grate, and the glamour was solid enough that he couldn't see it right in front of him. So long as he remained conscious, they'd still have to struggle to find it. But if he didn't finish the last few layers of the spell, they would uncover it eventually—and if he couldn't remain conscious, the entire glamour would unravel and fly apart.

With a concentrated effort, he forced himself to breathe in deeply enough to affect the shift of his element and hold it until the boot heading straight for him struck the stone curb full force. Judging by the yelp of pain, his attacker had at least broken a toe. Belphagor breathed out once more, becoming solid, and another boot hit him in the gut. This, at least, put him in no danger of passing out. He was too busy vomiting.

While he huddled on his knees, watching his dinner run into a storm drain no one could see, someone grabbed him around the waist and swung him off the ground. He struck out at his attacker only to find himself looking straight into Vasily's eyes.

Belphagor blinked. "Are you holding me off the ground, or have my feet gone numb?"

"Off the ground." It was the loveliest growl he'd ever heard.

"I suggest you put me down this instant and pretend this never happened, or neither of us will be able to walk for a week when I'm done meting out punishment."

"I'm confused. Do you want me to put you down or not put you down?"

"*Vasya.*"

Vasily grinned and loosened his grip, letting Belphagor regain a modicum of dignity as he dropped onto his feet—though the dignifying effect was somewhat mitigated by the demoness Natalya steadying him on his other side. A patrol of supernal soldiers had moved in around them to deal with the angelic drovers, and Vasily and Natalya drew Belphagor out of the fray.

"Wait." He pulled backed. "The glamour isn't finished."

Natalya frowned. "I thought it was a little too easy to find you. I don't see the portal, but I can still feel it."

Belphagor turned to limp back toward the last point of his spell-working, but Natalya stopped him.

"Where are you going?"

"I have to finish. It'll be bad enough if drovers can still find it, but we can't have the Supernal Army becoming aware of the location."

"But where are you *going*?"

Belphagor raised an eyebrow. "To finish working the spell."

Natalya gave him a peculiar look. "Were you manually pacing out the turns of the spiral?"

"How else was I to do it?"

"It's magic, you silly demon. Draw it with your elemental energy." Natalya lifted her hand and made a circular motion toward the general direction of the portal, and light seemed to follow her gesture, flowing out from her fingers in a glowing blue spiral through which the knitted web of the arcane tapestry was palely visible as glittering droplets on gossamer. The wrestling angels seemed oblivious to it, though its threads pierced right through them and entangled them.

He exhaled softly, awed by the beauty of it. "How come I can see that?"

"Because you made it. And it isn't finished." The bit where he'd stopped was like a frayed end on a skein of yarn. Natalya completed the pattern he'd begun, and with another spiraling motion, drew the energy around her fingers like a spool, casting out again and spinning before once more spooling it close. "May the rift remain cloaked in darkness to all who seek it." As she uttered the final words of the glamour, the glowing filaments drifted off her fingers and floated toward the ground, dissipating into the aether.

"Well, I feel a bit stupid." Belphagor grinned sheepishly. "Also . . . what are we doing standing out here at the boring end of the Demon District?"

"Watching them get arrested, I think." Vasily jerked his head toward the miserable-looking angels in the custody of the soldiers. From the end of the lane, a pair of Ophanim marched toward the group—if their odd combination of fluid and jolting motions as their cold fire shifted and phased could be called marching—accounting for the pained expressions.

Natalya shuddered. "Let's get out of here."

"I like that plan." Belphagor took a limping step forward and cursed as his ankle wobbled beneath him. One of the damned drovers had stomped it pretty hard. He let out a yelp of surprise as Vasily swept him up into his arms like a child. "Damn you, Vasya, put me down!"

Vasily ignored him, obviously feeling quite smug.

"I mean it, *mal'chik*." Belphagor's voice took on a deep, warning tone. "You'll pay dearly for this."

"I know." Vasily's grin was unstoppable.

CHAPTER TWENTY

To Vasily's relief, Khai and Anzhela were back at The Cat when they arrived. The details of who had been where kept getting fuzzy, but apparently, Khai had been with Belphagor helping him with the glamour when the angelic drovers showed up.

As battered as Belphagor was from his experiences, his obvious concern for Phaleg stung a bit. When the two of them disappeared into a back room for several minutes, Vasily imagined the worst, but Silk's jealousy was surprising.

He and Vasily waited in the kitchen, not quite in the mood for the celebration going on in the parlor. "He thinks he can manipulate whomever he likes," Silk complained. "It's not as if I didn't know Phaleg was carrying a torch for him, but I thought he was happy enough to suffer over its unrequitedness. But if Belphagor's in there . . . *requiting* it, what chance do I have?"

Vasily tried not to think about any "requiting" that might be going on. "You're pretty taken with him."

Silk gaped at him. "*Belphagor?* Why in Heaven would I— Oh." He sighed, playing with the lapel of his jacket while he leaned back against the counter. "He's an angel. How taken could I possibly be? Besides, he doesn't know the real me. If he did, he'd find me repulsive."

Vasily couldn't help but laugh. "No one could possibly find you repulsive."

Silk's demeanor changed swiftly, the dreamy look on his face replaced with a hard, cold expression and a dark look of warning in his eyes. "How would you know? You don't know me either. None of you know me—what I am."

"What do you mean, 'what you are'? Phaleg knows your history. He's not going to hold that against you."

Silk laughed harshly. "Do you think what I've told you is the truth? Poor little Silk, sold to the Fletchery as an innocent?"

Something about the way he said the word *innocent*, as if innocence was a thing he longed for that remained forever out of reach, made Vasily's heart ache. "You were a boy. You're not to blame for what happened to you."

Silk blinked at him, moisture glistening in his eyes for an instant and then gone. "You don't know."

"I do know," Vasily insisted. "Perhaps not the specifics. But you didn't deserve anything that happened to you. Any more than I did, or any of the Lost Boys."

The mention of the boys seemed to soften the sharp, angry lines on Silk's face, and the challenging look receded. "No, of course they didn't. Not you. Not them. Anyway, why are we talking about me? I was talking about what Phaleg wants."

"I thought we were talking about you want." Vasily smiled. "In other words, Phaleg."

Silk grinned, and the dreamy look was back. "It's just that he's . . ." He shrugged and nibbled on his bottom lip. "I don't know. He's so vulnerable when he's surrendering control. So hungry to be owned."

"In other words, not a bit like me."

Silk gave him a little smile under lowered lashes. "Well, you *are* adorable when you're being tormented, but you do lack a certain . . . humility."

Vasily laughed, and Silk's smile became more confident.

"And also, he's an *angel*. There's a certain inherent thrill in making an angel beg to take it up the ass." Silk grinned. "Plus, he's loaded. Remember when we talked about having sugar daddies?"

"I remember *you* talked about it."

Silk didn't seem to notice Vasily had spoken, his eyes focused on the air beyond him, on the fantasy he was building. "I can't imagine anything more perfect than being kept by an angel—that I get to fuck."

A loud throat-clearing from the doorway made them both turn with a guilty start. Belphagor's face was set in a hard expression. "You don't toy with him."

Silk put his hands in his pockets, his pose contrite, though his tone when he replied radiated defiance. "I wasn't going to toy with him. I was going to fuck him. Or didn't you get all that?"

"Fuck him all you like. But if you fuck *with* him, you'll have me to answer to." Belphagor's demeanor softened. "He did admit he rather enjoyed being at the mercy of two demons at once. Seems to have a bit of an abduction fantasy, no doubt owing to the stories upon which angels raise their children. If you and Khai ever decide to fulfill that for him together and need a few extra hands, I'm sure I can negotiate something with my *mal'chik*." The look he threw Vasily made any retort impossible.

It was past midnight when they headed to The Brimstone after escorting Anzhela and the boys back to the apartment, and Belphagor was ready to collapse. It seemed a given that Vasily would return home with him while Khai stayed behind, content to spend some more time at the Stone Horse with Silk. Phaleg, sporting a small bandage on his head but professing to be none the worse for wear, looked terrified and thrilled as he accompanied them.

"That worked out well." Belphagor leaned against Vasily for support after threatening him with particularly unsexy violence if Vasily dared attempt to pick him up again. "I had a talk with Phaleg to make certain Silk was respecting his boundaries. Turns out he has very few." He smiled to himself, recalling the time he'd ordered Phaleg to fuck himself with a large stone dildo while pressed against a thin door, with his comrades right outside it.

"Is he in love with Silk?"

"I don't know." Belphagor concentrated on not putting too much weight on the ankle. "Are you?"

Vasily stopped in his tracks. "In love with Silk? Of course not." He fished in the pack of his belongings he'd gathered at the apartment and held out something made of red string—the collar he'd worn at the Fletchery. "I belong to you, Beli. Always."

His heart swelled at the endearment. "Seems like you haven't called me that in ages." Belphagor fingered the knotted collar. "I don't understand why you kept this. When I sent it with your things, I was kind of being a dick. I figured it was something between you and Silk."

"Feel the knot at the center."

Puzzled, Belphagor smoothed his thumb along the large, central decoration and then drew back in surprise. Something had poked him, almost hard enough to draw blood. He pried at the knot with his thumbnail, and the tip of a steel spike popped out of it. Belphagor worked the jewelry out and held it in his palm.

For a moment, he couldn't speak. "I thought you threw it away."

"Threw it away?" The furious, almost infrasonic growl made his skin tingle. "You're such an asshole."

Belphagor smiled and closed his hand around the steel. "I really am."

Back in their room, Belphagor put the steel bar on the vanity for later. He wanted to savor the moment he re-marked his boy, and right now he was in no condition to give Vasily what he deserved.

"Lie down and let me look at that bandage." Vasily's tone demonstrated precisely how not-in-condition he was.

Belphagor hobbled to the cot, letting Vasily fuss over him. "I'm going to do horrible, horrible things to you," he promised. "Starting with the punishment for picking me up. Twice." He winced as Vasily slid his shirt down his shoulder to inspect the bandage. "I think I'll keep you naked in my bed and fuck you for a week."

"That's not punishment."

"I know. I just really want to fuck you." He hooked his other arm around Vasily's neck and pulled him in for a kiss, savoring the heat and softness of those lips too long denied him. Warm exhalations vibrated against his tongue like a lion's deep purr, the promise of rising firespirit desire.

With a sigh of regret, Belphagor let his hand slip from Vasily's neck. "And I wish I could do that right now, sweet boy, but everything fucking hurts." He grimaced as he eased himself back against the pillows. "I'm sorry, *mal'chik*."

Vasily shrugged and climbed over him, rolling onto his side and hugging the arm Belphagor draped around him to his chest. Despite the narrow cot, they fit together well. "I can wait."

Resting his chin against the muscular shoulder, Belphagor breathed in the firewood scent. "We should probably talk."

"Yeah."

"I know I hurt you."

"Yeah."

"Vasya."

"I know." Vasily sighed and threaded their fingers together. "When we . . . The way we are together—even if sometimes there are others you decide to include—it's because it makes us both hot."

Belphagor's chest felt tight, waiting for what he knew was coming. "Yes."

"Well, that wasn't hot. Sending me there. Not telling me what was going on. You scared me. Made me feel unsafe. I'd do anything for you, Beli. If you needed me to do something like that again . . . I'd do it. If you told me what was happening, why you needed me to do it. But I know you're still keeping something from me about it. Like you kept your plan with Silk from me so that I almost ruined everything at The Cat."

"Vasya—"

"I'm your boy." His deep, raspy voice said he was anything but a boy. "Not your slave or your lackey. You own me. Always. But not like that."

"I'm sorry." Belphagor could barely get the words out. "I know. I will never, ever treat you like that again." He pressed his cheek against Vasily's shoulder. "I didn't think it would go that way. But it doesn't matter. I was wrong. I'm so used to doing everything on my own, my stupid decisions only affecting me. And you're right that I haven't been completely forthcoming about it. There are some things about my past that are simply too painful to discuss—and Armen threatened to tell all of Raqia. I hope you'll respect that I'd rather not say more. As for my keeping you out of the loop about the plan at The Cat: Silk's past with that devil Kezef complicated things. I was afraid Kezef would manipulate you as he attempted to do with Silk, and I wanted to spare you that. But ultimately, I suppose I didn't trust you enough. So it's no wonder you feel you can't trust me."

Vasily clutched Belphagor's fingers tighter, when he'd feared Vasily would push him away. "There's something I didn't trust you with either that made the Fletchery worse."

Belphagor's heartbeat skipped nervously, but he waited.

"When I was on the street, when I was a kid—I ran with this boy for a while. He was older. Took care of me. I thought he was my friend. He asked me to do a job for him one day, a delivery. But it turned out he was selling me. I was the delivery. I waited for him to come back, and he never came."

Belphagor wrapped his other arm around Vasily, ignoring the pain in his shoulder. He knew exactly what that was like—waiting for the only one he believed in and cared for in the world to come save him, to take him away from the darkness of an unending nightmare, only to realize he was well and truly alone. The one he waited for would never come.

"*Milyy mal'chik.*" The words meant so much more than Vasily would ever understand. "I'm so sorry."

"You didn't know."

"All the same, I'm sorry you had to endure that. And regardless, what I did was wrong. I'll do everything I can to earn your trust again, to make you feel safe."

Vasily relaxed his death grip on Belphagor's fingers and stroked his thumb against Belphagor's wrist. "I feel safe in your arms, Beli."

Belphagor closed his eyes, the shattered pieces of his world sliding back together like mending bone. Everything had been so out of focus. Every color muted, every taste and scent slightly off, every sound lacking harmony. But it was going to be okay now. Vasily was his boy.

"I need to say something else, though." Belphagor took a deep breath. After what Vasily had shared with him, he didn't want to get this wrong. "You made me feel a little unsafe too."

Vasily turned his head toward him, his brow wrinkled with something between dismay and outrage, as though he wasn't sure yet which he ought to feel. "I what? How did I make you feel unsafe?"

"I gave you a word. A *safe*word. That wasn't just for you. It's for me to know when you're not okay. For when things go too far. I asked you more than once if you needed to say it, and you refused. I probably should have known anyway—I *definitely* should have— but you did me a disservice. It isn't fair to let me abuse you because you're too proud to tell me I've exceeded your boundaries. Pushing someone beyond his limits into true torment doesn't get me hot. That's for the likes of scum like Kezef."

Vasily flinched.

A feathery white scar from the beating he'd taken from Kezef was still visible on Vasily's shoulder, and Belphagor kissed the spot. "That doesn't excuse what I did. I was wrong from the start. But you compounded my transgression. Now I have to bear the guilt for both of us."

Vasily was quiet for a moment, and Belphagor feared his confession had undone everything, until the whisper came at last. "What will you do to me?" A shiver went through Vasily as he added, "It will have to be severe."

Blood rushed to Belphagor's cock and his heart in a confusing, marvelous competition. He breathed Vasily's skin like a drug and held him tight, relishing the hardness caught between them. "I love you, sweet boy. And it will be terrible. Mark my words."

CHAPTER TWENTY-ONE

Raqia saw an unprecedented level of arrests in the weeks that followed as angels and demons alike named accomplices and comrades in an effort to save their own necks. It seemed the trafficking of minors had been far more extensive than anyone knew. Belphagor had dreaded the spectacle of hangings certain to take place in Elysium, but the principality chose to exile the participants to hard labor in the stormy east of Ma'on on the border of the frozen Empyrean. It was a rare punishment reserved for those the ruling house wished to make an example of.

Nearly everyone Belphagor had encountered on his detour into the seedy underbelly of Raqia's sex trade had been implicated, including Raum and Balam, and even Armen Nekirevich, who had apparently assisted with the sell-off of the Fletchery's girls because, as he put it, there was "nothing unnatural about the commodification of demonesses." But to Belphagor's disgust, Kezef had somehow managed to keep his hands clean.

For his part in exposing the scandal, Phaleg had received a commendation—and promotion—from Principality Helison. As a supernal staff officer, Phaleg's investments in the Demon District's houses of ill repute were overlooked. So long as every demon in its employ was of an age to consent and had done so, his extracurricular activities would be ignored.

This left Silk happily enjoying his new status as the unofficial Supernal Supplier of Ass, as he termed it, and Belphagor comfortably anonymous as Phaleg's silent partner. Anzhela's Lost Boys had settled into what Silk called "Boarding School for Future Rakes," taking lessons from an angelic tutor Belphagor had beaten at the wingcasting table. And Belphagor continued imparting his particular specialty, employing the boys on occasions where an adult's motives might be suspect and a youth ignored, creating his own little guild of thieves.

But there was one more piece of Belphagor's plan he hadn't implemented yet. Though she'd agreed to abide by his terms, happy enough to keep the boys she'd become quite fond of under her wing, he could tell Anzhela was anxious to return to her duties at The Cat. Not that she didn't trust Phaleg to run it, but he could only contribute so much to the daily operations of the brothel, and the longer she stayed away, the more the procuress appointed by Sergeant Veloas had time to stake her claim and win the girls' trust. It was long past time Belphagor called on The Succubus.

As with his first visit, he was ushered into Koshka's den without so much as an inquiry as to whether she wished to take him as a client. It was early in the day, as before, and this time he was her first appointment. He had thought her quite pretty, but this morning, freshly made up for the day's work without having been mussed, she was stunning. She greeted him in a flowing, diaphanous robe of scarlet, ready to put her arms around his neck and ask his pleasure, until she saw who it was.

Her face lit with genuine happiness. "The Prince of Tricks!" Instead of stepping back, she flung her arms around him in a joyous embrace. "All Raqia is abuzz with what you've done." Koshka pulled herself away after a moment, looking embarrassed at her display. "Thank you for bringing Anzhela home. You don't know what it means to me."

"I did what I could. There were other girls I couldn't help, sold before they left Heaven. I was lucky to find her."

Koshka shrugged, the gesture of a woman resigned to the ways of celestial inequity. "Many of us get our start that way. But it's not for Anzhi. Masha didn't want that."

"And what did Masha want for you?"

"For me?" Suspicion clouded her expression. "She was a very good mother. She did the best she could."

"Please don't misunderstand. I'm not casting aspersions. Perhaps I should have asked what you want. The Succubus . . . Are you happy here?"

Her suspicious look deepened. She'd told him before she didn't want to be reformed. He was treading on delicate territory.

"It's just that Anzhela told me the owner of this establishment 'won' you in a duel. If you're happy working here, I'll leave you in peace, but if The Succubus isn't your choice, I'd like you to know that your master owes me a debt and has agreed to let you return to The Cat in exchange for my canceling that debt."

Koshka's eyes widened and welled with tears that she quickly blinked away. "The Cat? I can work at The Cat?"

"You can do more than work there, dear lady. I'd like you to manage it."

It took him some time to convince her his offer was sincere and that there were no strings attached, but once she'd accepted his word, she didn't waste a minute gathering her things and heading for the door. Belphagor had to stop her and gently recommend that she dress for an outing before they departed.

He gave her the day to get settled—Madam Pharzuphova, who'd tipped off Kezef's drovers, he happily dismissed—and brought Anzhela over in the evening, saying he'd hired a new madam and wanted her approval. He hadn't told Koshka he was bringing her either, and the looks on their faces when they saw one another was worth all the trouble. A sort of shy wonder overtook them both, and he slipped out quietly to let them get acquainted.

He'd sent Vasily off to the Stone Horse for the evening, telling him he needed him out of his hair, wanting to get him good and mad before he had his way with him. He took his time walking back to the Horse and found Vasily finishing himself off for a large crowd of admirers, jism erupting from the head of his cock like lava, so hot it almost glowed. Belphagor clearly hadn't allowed his boy enough indulgence in that department, expecting him to keep his heat contained.

Silk appeared at his side. "Doesn't it make you want to spank him until he cries?" He rested a casual arm against Belphagor's shoulder and followed up with an exaggerated sigh. "That spectacular ass. It's a shame I never got a chance to abuse it."

Belphagor raised an eyebrow. "Didn't you?"

"He only has ass for you, dear Prince. He didn't mind a little cock play, but the pleasure of delivering punishing blows—or anything else—to his backside was something I was never fortunate enough to experience."

"Play your cards right, and perhaps you will. But not tonight." Belphagor's lips curved in a dark smile as he watched Vasily collect his tributes. "Tonight I have plans for him. Don't expect to see him for a few days."

Silk let his arm fall away from Belphagor's shoulder with a look of admiration. "Lucky boy."

"I thought you wanted me out of your hair." Vasily followed Belphagor into their room, seething with resentment. Belphagor had clearly been feeling better for days, and instead of spending time with Vasily, he'd— "Ow!"

After the involuntary exclamation at the tight grip of Belphagor's fingers in his locks, Vasily froze.

"Take off your clothes and give them to me. Folded neatly." Belphagor's voice was utterly calm, which unnerved Vasily more than the usual deep command delivered cold and sharp.

Obeying automatically, Vasily gave him his folded shirt and his belt and bent to untie his boots, but Belphagor stopped him with another harsh jerk against the locks at his crown.

"Pants first, then boots."

"But these aren't wide enough. They won't go over the boots."

"Did I tell you to speak?"

Vasily swallowed and shook his head.

"Pants first, then boots."

Bewildered, he unbuttoned the jeans and tugged them down, followed by his underwear, leaving his cock unabashedly proclaiming his arousal. With the garments pushed down to his ankles, he crouched and tried to tug one pant leg over the heel of his boot. It was impossible, and he only managed to get his boot stuck.

"Try the other," Belphagor suggested.

Vasily glanced up at the placid face, unable to fathom what Belphagor was up to. He tugged uselessly on the other pant leg until it, too, was stuck.

"I'm very disappointed in you."

Furious, Vasily opened his mouth and then quickly shut it. Belphagor hadn't told him to speak. He contented himself with a fiery glare.

"Stay." With the curt command, Belphagor went to the vanity and opened the drawer where he kept his equipment, taking out what he needed before returning. Crouching behind him, he pulled back Vasily's arms and bound them at the wrists with rope. In the silence that followed, Belphagor's shirt hit the ground beside him. Then the pants. Belphagor came around to the front, his heavy boots still on, though his pant legs had been as tight at the ankle as Vasily's. He'd cheated and used airspirit magic.

"You see? It was a simple request." For once, Belphagor was naked in front of him, but the firm erection in Belphagor's hand made Vasily forget the tattoos. "Stroke your cock."

Vasily narrowed his eyes, tempted to charge Belphagor like a bull. What kind of game was he playing now? Issuing commands that couldn't be obeyed?

"Do you refuse?"

"*Nyet*," Vasily growled. He deliberately left off the *ser*.

Belphagor's eyebrow twitched. "Then do as I say."

Vasily jerked at his bound wrists. "*Ya ne mogu.*"

"Can't?" Belphagor's fist rose and fell over his shaft. "Or won't?"

Frustration was getting the better of him. "*Ya ne mogu!*"

"I didn't tell you to speak."

"You asked me a question!"

Belphagor stepped toward him and yanked Vasily up onto his knees by the hair. "Open your mouth."

Eyes sharp with angry tears he wasn't about to shed, Vasily obeyed and nearly choked as Belphagor barreled in without ceremony.

"This ought to keep you quiet." Belphagor kept his voice infuriatingly flat as he held Vasily to his crotch without moving. "I don't know what I'm going to do with you. You're incorrigible, refusing every simple request." When Vasily's tongue curled around him reflexively, Belphagor jerked on his fistful of hair. "Did I tell you to suck?" Belphagor jerked again. "Answer me, boy."

He was too full to do more than make a moaning noise around Belphagor's cock, and Belphagor's fist in his hair prevented him from shaking his head.

"I said answer me. Are you daft?"

Despite himself, a hot tear of frustration and humiliation slid over his cheek. Belphagor had never belittled him before.

Unexpectedly, Belphagor pulled out and went down to his level. "Sweet *mal'chik*. That didn't feel very good, did it?"

"*Nyet, ser.*" He couldn't stop the tears now. Belphagor kissed him, and they flowed harder.

"We have an agreement, you and I." Belphagor lifted his chin. "We submit to our base desires because we find it mutually enjoyable. More than enjoyable. We *need* to submit to them. They bind us closer together. Would you not say this is so?"

Vasily nodded.

"Speak, boy." Belphagor's voice was gentle.

"*Da, ser.*"

"I violated that contract just now and treated you with contempt. The same as I did at the Fletchery. I went beyond your consent, beyond your desire. I behaved as dishonorably as Kezef."

"No. *Nyet.*" Vasily shook his head adamantly.

"Yes, *mal'chik*. And you permitted it. You lied to me with your silence. Letting me behave that way with you was a betrayal, as much as my betrayal of your trust. When I asked you a direct question and then told you I hadn't given you leave to speak, I deliberately violated your trust, yet you allowed me to continue. I told you to open up and take my cock, and you obeyed. Knowing it was the last opportunity you would have to utter a safeword, you allowed me to silence you instead so you couldn't. With your complicity, you put me in a position where I had no way of ascertaining your consent or comfort level in the activities we were engaged in. And I, in turn, allowed it, knowing I was taking away your ability to be honest with me. So now we both know where we went wrong."

Vasily's face heated with shame. It was true. He'd felt abused, and yet he'd opened his mouth to take what Belphagor gave him. As if Belphagor were nothing more than a sadistic prick like Kezef.

Belphagor stroked his cheek. "We have both fallen low. So today we will atone. Today we will learn to use your safeword. We will learn to trust one another."

He rose, drawing Vasily up with a hand around his upper arm, and left him standing in the center of the room as he crossed to the wall where his strop hung. "I plan to hurt you." Belphagor took down the strop and folded it in his hand. "I know that you want me to. I also know there will come a stroke when you do not—but that is still something you want, for me to be cruel and torment you without heed to your cries. The moment my cruelty no longer makes you feel safe, no longer feels like love, the moment it begins to seem for the sake of my pleasure without regard for yours—I expect to hear your word." He stroked the leather over his palm. "Do we understand one another?"

Vasily's skin prickled with apprehension, but his cock was as hard as ever. "*Da, ser.*"

Belphagor turned him roughly toward the bureau and put his mouth to Vasily's ear. "Do you love me, boy?"

Vasily closed his eyes. "*Da, ser. Ya lyublyu tebya, ser. Vsegda.*" *Always.*

"*Khorosho.*" Belphagor swept his arm across the clutter on the bureau, sending it crashing to the floor, and shoved Vasily forward. "Place your cheek against the wood."

Trembling, Vasily rested his cheek on the bureau top. The first stroke hissed through the air without warning and struck, raising heat in his ass as though he'd concentrated it there himself. He remained silent and still. Belphagor struck again, on the other side, and then, without pausing between strokes, the leather strop rained down on Vasily in a brutal rhythm, making it hard to stay steady with so little surface to brace against. Especially with his boots caught in his pants.

His vow to himself not to cry out was soon broken, but he couldn't use the word. Not yet. He needed this. They both did. He needed to know he belonged to Belphagor completely, every sharp sting against his flesh promising he would never be abandoned, every impact delivered with the force of Belphagor's love and desire. Vasily was his *mal'chik*, his boy. He belonged. He was safe.

Belphagor paused to reach between Vasily's legs, and Vasily moaned, almost ready to come in an instant at the firm grip around his cock. He'd forgotten already what they were doing. His ass felt like fire. When Belphagor's hand slipped away and he resumed his blows with the strop, Vasily's flesh tingled with the nearly disembodied awareness, the oneness with Belphagor, the place where pain was no longer recognizable and the thudding impact of the leather felt almost like orgasm itself.

And then the strop sliced through the air and struck his back between the shoulder blades like a knife. The force was so violent and sudden, he couldn't move or think. But the word burst out of him in a surprised ejaculation of sound. "Seraphim!"

Behind him, Belphagor went motionless, and in the absence of new sensation, the stripe on Vasily's back sent searing pain across his nerves, drawing a violent shudder from him with a sound that was half-groan, half-cry. Belphagor raised him off the surface of the bureau and turned him about. His face ashen, which frightened Vasily more than anything, he drew them both down to their knees and gathered Vasily in his arms.

"I'm sorry. I'm so sorry. My sweet boy." He rocked Vasily, who wept silently against Belphagor's shoulder, unable to put his arms around him. "Thank you for stopping me. I don't know if I could have borne another like that."

"I love you, Beli."

Belphagor pushed him back onto his heels and held Vasily's face between his hands. "And I love you, *mal'chik. Vsegda i vsegda i vsegda.*"

Vasily's tears were caught between their lips just as an unexpected sensation of exquisite pain drew a startled cry from him, captured in Belphagor's mouth. With practiced sleight of hand, Belphagor had produced a needle as if from the aether, reopening the holes he'd once pierced in Vasily's skin. The steel bar followed it through, capped with the spiked finial as the needle came away. The throbbing sting sent his overheated blood rushing straight to his cock.

Belphagor cupped his hands against the sides of Vasily's throat. "Will you be mine, always?"

"*Vsegda*," Vasily promised, the last syllable drawn out in a sensuous moan as steel once more pricked his skin, this time beneath Belphagor's other hand.

"I know it's late." With a deft motion, Belphagor threaded the second bar through and capped it. "I didn't think to buy another the first time we were in the world of Man. But I have a supply now to mark you for several anniversaries to come." He stroked his thumbs against the sharp points of the steel. "From now on, everyone who sees you will know that you belong to me."

A wicked smile lifted one corner of Belphagor's mouth, eyes sparkling with ideas—black star sapphires glittering in the lamplight. "But for the moment, I have you all to myself."

He stood and pressed Vasily down against the carpet with a boot to his chest, keeping his eyes on him as he yanked the stopper from the almond oil on the vanity and stroked himself with the fragrant liquid until his cock was glistening. He dropped onto all fours and pushed Vasily's thighs farther apart.

"I mean to fuck you without mercy." Lips pressed against Vasily's throat, he nipped at the tender skin until Vasily whimpered. "But don't come." With his almond-sticky hand, he gripped Vasily's erection like a gearshift in a car, using it for leverage as he worked himself in. "Because I intend to have you until we're both quite out of our senses."

Vasily couldn't keep quiet as Belphagor filled him, one hand braced beside him and the other working Vasily in tandem between their abs.

"I wouldn't be surprised, in fact, if we were both crippled in the effort." Belphagor began to give it to him hard. "But I promise you one thing, *moi mal'chik*. You won't want to say 'Seraphim.'"

Explore more of the *Demons of Elysium* series at: riptidepublishing.com/collections/series-demons-of-elysium

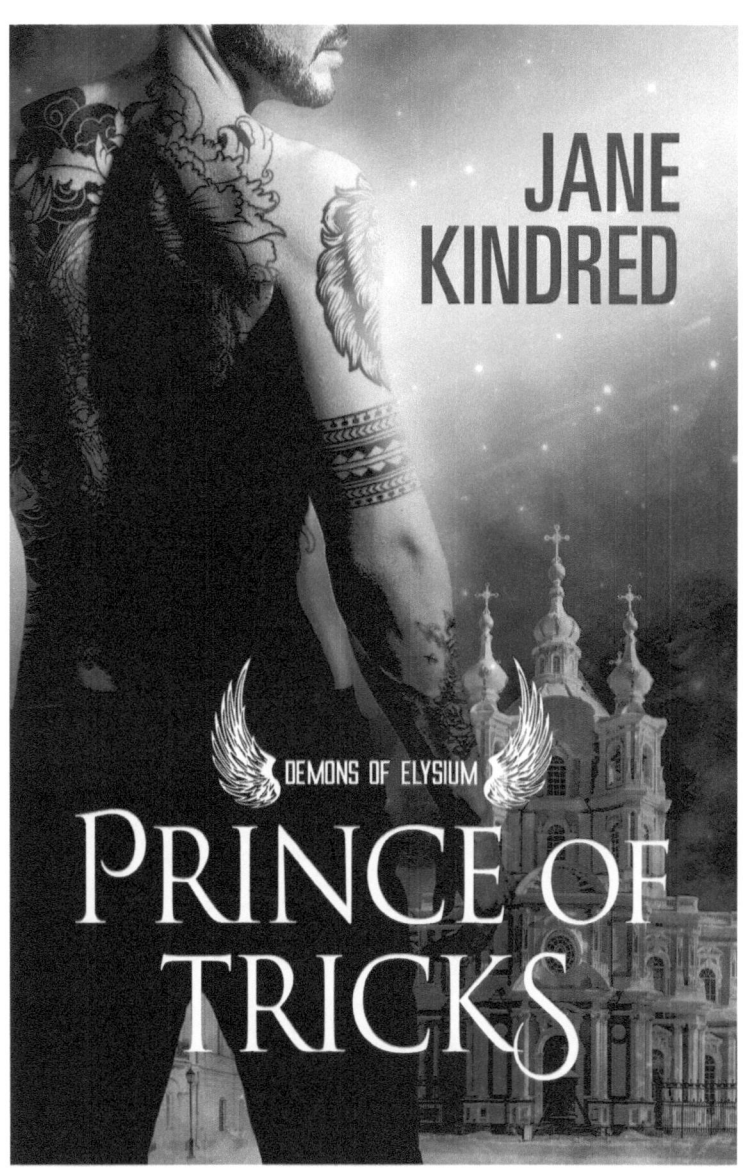

Dear Reader,

Thank you for reading Jane Kindred's *King of Thieves*!

We know your time is precious and you have many, many entertainment options, so it means a lot that you've chosen to spend your time reading. We really hope you enjoyed it.

We'd be honored if you'd consider posting a review—good or bad—on sites like **Amazon, Barnes & Noble, Kobo, Goodreads, Twitter, Facebook, Tumblr,** and your blog or website. We'd also be honored if you told your friends and family about this book. Word of mouth is a book's lifeblood!

For more information on upcoming releases, author interviews, blog tours, contests, giveaways, and more, please sign up for our weekly, spam-free newsletter and visit us around the web:

Newsletter: riptidepublishing.com/newsletter
Twitter: twitter.com/RiptideBooks
Facebook: facebook.com/RiptidePublishing
Goodreads: tinyurl.com/RiptideOnGoodreads
Tumblr: riptidepublishing.tumblr.com

Thank you so much for Reading the Rainbow!

RiptidePublishing.com

ALSO BY
JANE KINDRED

ABOUT THE AUTHOR

Jane Kindred is the author of the Harlequin Nocturne series *Sisters in Sin* and of the epic fantasy series *The House of Arkhangel'sk* and *Looking Glass Gods*. She spent her formative years in the desert Southwest ruining her eyes reading romance novels in the sun and watching *Star Trek* marathons in the dark. She now writes to the sound of San Francisco foghorns while her spoiled cat, Sophie, blinks at her from her fancy bed at the end of the mattress like Baby Yoda having just eaten a Frog Lady's egg.

You can find Jane on Twitter @JaneKindred, on her cleverly named Facebook page, JaneKindred, or via her website, at the unsurprising address of www.janekindred.com.

Enjoy more stories like
King of Thieves
at RiptidePublishing.com!